On Jordan's Stormy Banks is so much more than an inspiring Christian novel. It is a well-written narrative with authentic voices from the Civil War period. Bob Lankford has mastered the dialog and events of those terrible times and presents his moving tale with great understanding and accuracy. The result is a refreshing and uplifting story of forgiveness and redemption set realistically in the most violent era of our nation's history.

—Morris Simon, Ph.D.
Professor of Social Sciences (retired)

ON JORDAN'S STORMY BANKS

F Lankford, Bob
LAN
On Jordan's stormy banks

AZALEA TRACE
Discard 8-14

ON JORDAN'S STORMY BANKS

a man's journey home

BOB LANKFORD

Tate Publishing & *Enterprises*

On Jordan's Stormy Banks
Copyright © 2009 by Bob Lankford. All rights reserved.

No part of this publication may be reproduced, stored in a retrieval system or transmitted in any way by any means, electronic, mechanical, photocopy, recording or otherwise without the prior permission of the author except as provided by USA copyright law.

This novel is a work of fiction. Names, descriptions, entities, and incidents included in the story are products of the author's imagination. Any resemblance to actual persons, events, and entities is entirely coincidental.

The opinions expressed by the author are not necessarily those of Tate Publishing, LLC.

Published by Tate Publishing & Enterprises, LLC
127 E. Trade Center Terrace | Mustang, Oklahoma 73064 USA
1.888.361.9473 | www.tatepublishing.com

Tate Publishing is committed to excellence in the publishing industry. The company reflects the philosophy established by the founders, based on Psalm 68:11,
"The Lord gave the word and great was the company of those who published it."

Book design copyright © 2009 by Tate Publishing, LLC. All rights reserved.
Cover design by Kellie Southerland
Interior design by Jeff Fisher

Published in the United States of America
ISBN: 978-1-61566-017-9
1. Fiction, Historical
2. Fiction, War & Military
09.11.30

Alice, and Sonny, thank you.

DEDICATION

This book is lovingly dedicated to the memory of the author's parents, Maurine Jennings Lankford and Charles Ward Lankford.

It is further dedicated to their grandfathers, who were Southern soldiers:

- Pvt. Phillip Pilgrim (Jessie) Jennings of Co. D, Hardies's Cavalry Btn., Armistead's Brigade
- Cpl. James Marion Lankford, originally of the 5th Alabama Infantry Btn. and later the 18th Ala. and 58th Ala. (Co. A) Infantry Regiments
- Pvt. William Charles White, who served with his father, Sgt. George C. White, in Co. A of the 5th Tennessee Cavalry, under the command of George's brother, Capt. John Fletcher White.

Finally, the book is dedicated to the memory of every soldier and sailor, regardless of race, who served in the defense of the South.

In "The Battle," the two scripture references are from the King James Version.

In "The Reunion," the one scripture reference is from the American Standard Version.

PREFACE

There is a place in Pennsylvania where a shallow, pebbly stream makes its way through a narrow line of trees. Near the little stream rests a large boulder, slightly sloped on one side, which for ages remained untouched by man. But now there are words inscribed on the slope of the rock, gentle words of loss and of hope put there in the cherished memory of a little boy by a grieving, yet joyous, old man. Though set in the North, this is a story out of the South, of how those words came to be there, of the lives lost around that rock, and, over the years, of those that were found.

THE BATTLE

July 1863

*On Jordan's stormy banks I stand,
And cast a wishful eye
To Canaan's fair and happy land,
Where my possessions lie.
American folk hymn*

WEDNESDAY, JULY 1ST

First Light

As he walked eastward on a dusty Pennsylvania road, he looked toward the summer sunrise. Young and wearing Confederate gray, he was not alone. His name was Silas Swann.

The morning was damp and hazy, but before him he could see the darkness giving way to gray as the still unseen sun birthed a new day. It was July 1863, the first day. The South was in the third year of her War for Independence. The air was humid, and a light rain would soon fall, but for now dust still rose from the crushed rock roadbed beneath his feet.

Walking beside Pvt. Swann in the dusky dawn was his friend from infancy, Sonny Simon. They were the Fifth Alabama Infantry Battalion's newest troopers, arriving in Virginia just in time to participate in the invasion of the North.

From the moment they stepped off the train about a month ago, they did not fit in. The Fifth had been at war for two years. Its ranks had been whittled from over three hundred men to fewer than one hundred and fifty. But those who remained were fell fighters all—all save one.

Silas was small and only seventeen years old. He had received a genteel upbringing in Mobile. He was a cherished child of a nurturing, Old South family of prosperous merchants and entrepreneurs. He had never known hunger, hardship, or meanness.

His friend, Sonny, though of almost identical upbringing and background, was obviously a man at eighteen. Tall and well muscled, he had the makings of a real soldier. True to Southern tradition, both were good marksmen. But Silas was just too small and frail for combat. Everyone seemed to know this but Silas himself. He would know it soon enough. As he looked eastward, he would begin to see the light.

The Fifth Alabama Infantry Battalion, which was often confused with the larger Fifth Alabama Regiment of O'Neal's Brigade, had been comprised of four companies: two from Calhoun County, and one each from Sumter and Mobile counties. When Silas, Sonny, and a few other Mobile men left Alabama, they anticipated assignments to the Mobile company, Company D, known as the Daniel Boone Rifles. When they arrived in Virginia, however, they found Company D disbanded and its survivors transferred to the other three companies. Most of the new Mobile men were assigned to either Company A from Sumter County or Company C from Calhoun County. Of all the Mobilians on the train, only Silas and Sonny were assigned to Company B—the Calhoun Sharpshooters, a group of men very different from themselves.

Silas and Sonny were from a multi-cultured, seafaring city. Well-read and highly educated, they had been properly reared in the Episcopalian faith. Their uniforms were as spiffy as a Confederate private's uniform was allowed to be. And to make matters even worse, their uniforms were actually cadet gray. Most of the other enlisted men's uniforms were a color politely called butternut. In truth, it was just a dirty, dusty brown. This was because the fabric had faded to brown over almost two years of arduous service or because gray dye was often in short supply.

Consequently, Silas and Sonny were very conspicuous among the other soldiers.

Few of the men had the hats they had been issued. Many wore what was called a slouch hat, and almost as many wore a wide-brimmed western hat. When it came to shoes, several men in the Fifth had none. Many in the Army of Northern Virginia were barefoot. One such man marched with Silas and Sonny in their squad.

The men of Company B were natives of northeastern Alabama. They had been raised in the Appalachian foothills, and there was nothing genteel about them or their upbringing. They were either deeply religious or brashly irreligious. Most of them were Christian, but Silas's ornate, quiet brand of Christianity was nothing like the no-nonsense fundamentalist sects of the hills. They believed in God the Father, God the Son, and God the Holy Ghost, but the similarities ended there.

In combat, though, religion, or the lack of it, seemed to make little difference for they were all savage fighters. But for those who loved the Lord, the savagery ended when the enemy ceased to resist. No one could be gentler with a dying foe than these grim warriors from the hills and mountains of the South.

A Yankee who was taken prisoner by any man whose hatred for the Northern oppressor was not slaked by a love for God could find himself skewered on a bayonet as soon as he put up his hands. These godless men expected no quarter, and they gave none. There were relatively few of them in the Southern ranks.

In Silas's squad, these men were in a decided minority. There were only two Silas suspected of being capable of killing an unresisting enemy. One was Box, a man about the same size as Silas but whose effectiveness in battle was not questioned. And the other was Moses, quite possibly the biggest lean man Silas had ever seen. There was no fat anywhere on the man. He was simply huge and as strong as an oak. His ferocity was legend. It was generally accepted that he could whip any man in the world. No one who knew him doubted it.

Box was the one man in Silas's squad who had no shoes. He had not found any because his feet were unusually small. Moses, too, had been without shoes until recently because his feet were so big.

Each day, as he observed the men around him, Silas was coming to understand the magnitude of his failings as a soldier. He had heard of "gentleman privates" and thought perhaps he might be one. In order to be a gentleman, however, one first must be a man. He was beginning to doubt his own manhood.

If he lives long enough, there comes a time in the life of every scrawny little fellow when he realizes that that is all he is and all he will ever be. In spite of his mama and daddy telling him he will be big and strong one day, that day never arrives. He finally resigns himself to the fact that he will have to tread lightly through life because he will never be able to whip anyone worth whipping. Silas was approaching that point.

He had never had to deal with the hardscrabble world like the others. The men of the Fifth were just fortunate to have survived their childhoods. With tough bodies and tough spirits, they seldom complained about the discomforts or dangers of military life. To them, deprivation and combat were a part of life.

Silas had not known such people existed, and in Mobile, they didn't. If not for their religion and their respect for and admiration of courage and leadership in mortal combat, they would have been uncontrollable as an army. As it was, however, formed virtually from scratch just a little over two years earlier, man for man, they made up possibly the toughest, most disciplined army in the world. They didn't have enough food, clothes, shoes, medicine, or ammunition. For more than two years, most had scarcely seen the inside of a house. They were rare men. The crux of Silas Swann's problem was that he was a nice high-church boy in a hard shell army. He was miserable.

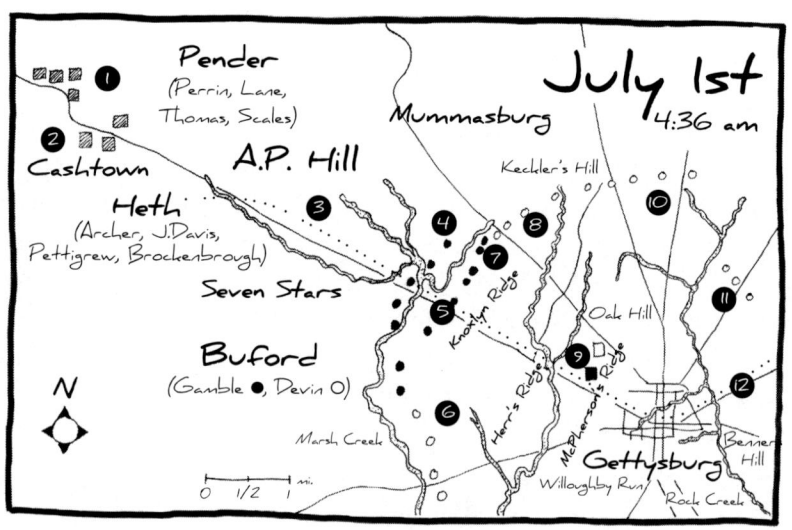

- ① Brigade Camps Pender
- ② Brigade Camps Heth
- ③ Pettigrew Camp
- ④ NC 26th (pickets)
- ⑤ IL 8th Cav. (40 men)
- ⑥ NY 8th Cav. (50 men)
- ⑦ IL 12th Cav.
- ⑧ IN 3rd Cav. (110 men)
- ⑨ Brigade Camps Gamble & Devin
- ⑩ PA 17th Cav.
- ⑪ NY 9th Cav.
- ⑫ NY 9th Cav.

The Fifth Alabama

The Fifth Alabama was commanded by Maj. A. S. Van De Graaff. It was but a tiny part of Gen. Lee's Army of Northern Virginia. The Fifth served in Gen. Archer's Brigade, which was made up of four regiments: the First Tennessee, the Seventh Tennessee, the Fourteenth Tennessee, the Thirteenth Alabama, along with the Fifth Alabama Battalion, which was not large enough to be a regiment. Gen. Archer's Brigade was one of four in Gen. Harry Heth's division. These men served with two other divisions to make up A. P. Hill's Third Corps.

There were two other corps in the Army of Northern Virginia. First Corps was commanded by Gen. Longstreet and Second Corps by Gen. Ewell. They all answered to Gen. Lee, or "Old Bob," as the men affectionately called him.

They totaled about seventy-five thousand men, hardened warriors dedicated to the cause of Southern independence. And in this army was the little Fifth Alabama Battalion, 135 men who felt compelled to fight with the weight of a regiment. Most of the brigades consisted of regiments from top to bottom. Only Archer's and two other brigades had a battalion serving alongside their regiments. The Fifth was by far the smallest of those three battalions. The whole army was committed to the struggle, but the men of the Fifth were perhaps a little more so because they were so very aware of their small numbers in comparison to the regiments with whom they marched. They would soon be facing a Union army of over ninety-three thousand men.

The Southerners were accustomed to being outnumbered, outgunned, and outsupplied. But they were seldom outfought, outmaneuvered, or outgeneraled. They expected to prevail in these areas, and they usually did. However, the Yankees were learning fast.

The Fifth, along with the other twenty-two thousand men of Hill's Third Corps, were the last of the three corps to leave Fredericksburg. They had been marching since early June and had arrived at Chambersburg, Pennsylvania, on June 27. They were camped east of the South Mountains near the village of Cashtown about eight miles west of Gettysburg.

As Silas marched in the faint light, he quietly talked to Sonny beside him. As the sky grew brighter, he could turn and see farther down the seemingly endless line of soldiers behind him. They were four wide, walking at a brisk pace. There was no cadence being called, but they maintained formation anyway. Though not in step, they were moving as one, and they called it a march.

In the growing light, Silas could see the huge form of Moses a few ranks to the front. Beside him was the diminutive, shoeless Box. He had been a source of misery to Silas since they had arrived. Box hated both Silas and Sonny for their nice uniforms, their shoes, and their aristocratic demeanor. But he only tormented Silas. Sonny was much too big for him, no matter how feisty he was. Feistiness can only carry one so far in a fight with a decidedly stronger foe, a painful lesson the South would learn over the next two years.

Silas watched Box for a while. He certainly didn't like the man, but he couldn't help but admire his toughness. He had marched all the way from Virginia to Pennsylvania barefooted. That feat alone amazed the boy. How Box and untold hundreds, or perhaps thousands, of Confederate soldiers could simply walk from state to state without shoes was beyond his comprehension. Silas could scarcely stand barefooted on the ground, much less walk any distance. He had to grudgingly admit to himself that Box was the tougher man.

What made matters even worse was that Silas harbored a dark, shameful secret. He had an extra pair of shoes, a pair that would probably fit Box. No one in the outfit knew about them, not even Sonny. He had managed to hide them through several inspections. His mother had given them to him just before he left Alabama on the train. Not even his father knew. They were hidden in a bag in his kit. His mother had made him promise to keep them for himself. He always tried to be a good boy, an obedient son. But every time he looked at Box or even thought of him, he cringed a little. The more he watched him, the worse he felt. Finally, he simply looked away and made himself think other thoughts. Soon enough, he would have other thoughts forced upon him. As miserable as he was, this day would only see his misery deepen.

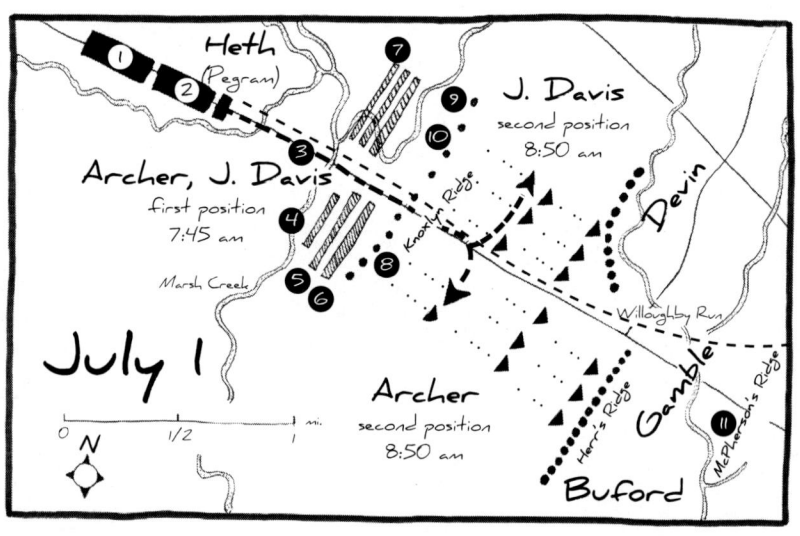

Colors Uncased

In the vanguard of the Confederate column was Pegram's Artillery. They were followed by the Fifth. Behind them was the Thirteenth Alabama followed by the three Tennessee regiments that made up the balance of Archer's Brigade, and behind them the rest of A. P. Hill's Third Corps, over twenty thousand men.

After a two- to three-hour march, Silas saw some commotion toward the front of the column. It was not long before Col. Fry, the commander of the Thirteenth Alabama, rode back to the color bearer and told him to uncase the colors. Silas could tell things were beginning to happen. The men began to glance at each other knowingly.

Sonny said, "I think we're about to see our first action, Silas."

He seemed excited. Silas was feeling queasy and feared he would lose what little breakfast he had eaten. Then Maj. Van De Graaff had his company commanders gather around as he talked to them, moving all the while on horseback.

The men soon were told that the Fifth would be joined by sixty men of the Thirteenth and would form a skirmish line to the right, or south, of the road. Davis's brigade of Mississippians and North Carolinians would do the same thing on the other side of the road.

Shortly after they had gotten the word, orders were bellowed, and the Fifth was sprinting across Marsh Creek Bridge followed by the Thirteenth men. They were ordered to file to the right of an apple orchard and load their weapons at will.

The sun was well up now. Silas could see the skirmish line spread out to each side. He, Sonny, and the rest of their squad were positioned near the right flank of the line. Between them was Cpl. Elder, their squad leader. He seemed to Silas to be a good man, a conscientious soldier. Since Silas and Sonny were new troops, Cpl. Elder deliberately positioned himself between them so he could personally direct them through their first action. They were both grateful for his attention.

Cpl. Elder was more than just their squad leader. He was also Company B's spiritual leader. They didn't have an official chaplain, so he filled that position unofficially in a de facto role. He was a preacher back home in Calhoun County, and most of the men just called him "Preacher" or "the preacher." Silas figured him to be in his forties. He was one of the older men in the Fifth.

The roughly two hundred men on the south side of the road were spread thin over a line several hundred yards long, but each man could see the man on either side of him.

About the time they were in a proper skirmish line, they heard the report of cannon fire from the rear. The artillery unit they had passed and left behind had fired the first Southern shots of the Battle of Gettysburg.

Almost immediately after the cannon blast, Silas heard a distant voice shout, "Forward!" and the preacher said, "Okay, boys. He's talking to us."

The line began to move.

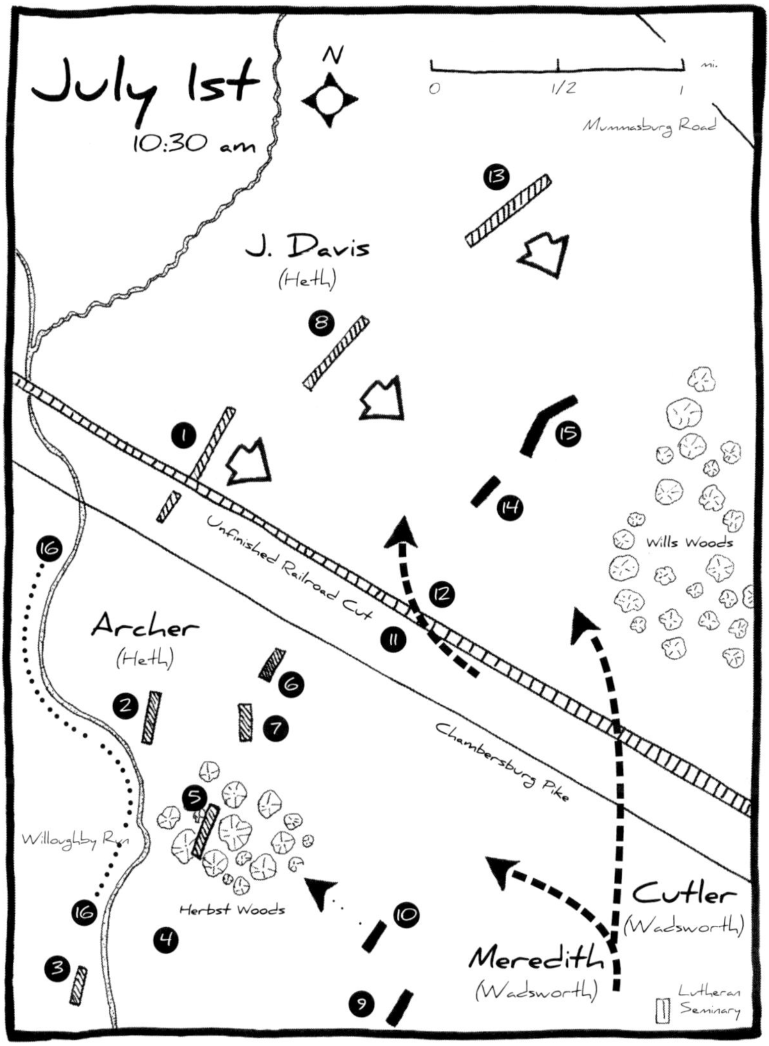

1 MS 42nd
2 TN 7th
3 AL 13th
4 TN 1st
5 TN 14th
6 NY 95th
7 NY 84th (14th Brooklyn)
8 MS 2nd
9 WI 7th
10 WI 2nd
11 ME 2nd
12 NY 147th
13 NC 55th
14 PA 56th
15 NY 76th
16 Skirmishers (AL 5th Bat.)

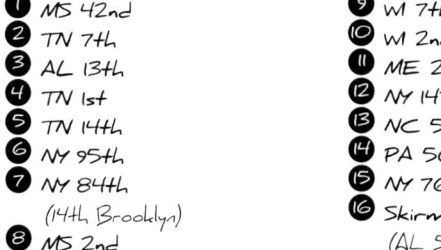

Red Sky at Morning

From the swampy land fringing Marsh Creek, the land angled up gently to a low, long hill called Knoxlyn Ridge, perhaps a quarter mile eastward. A light, misty rain had begun to fall, making it difficult to locate potential targets.

Due to the mist, the sky was red to the east. Being from a seafaring town, Silas mumbled to himself, "Red sky at morning, sailor, take warning."

He heard someone say, "Savor that red dawn, boys. It could be our last."

He heard a second and third round from the Rebel artillery behind him and saw the rounds hit the ridge to the front. He was so busy coping with the swampy underbrush near the creek, trying to keep up, he could locate no targets. Apparently, no one could. Briefly, he heard no rifle shots.

Finally, looking up, he saw tiny puffs of smoke popping out from the ridge. He heard no reports of the distant rifles because of the noise he was making trudging through the underbrush, which would soon give way to crops, mostly wheat and corn. Occasionally, he heard the hiss of a round passing overhead, or the thud of one hitting the ground. Instinctively he crouched a little lower.

The skirmish line seemed to stop momentarily, and Silas raised his head enough to see the preacher, Sonny, and a few other men down the line. The veterans were crouching too, but they were looking toward the ridge. Suddenly, the preacher raised his weapon, aimed carefully, and fired. Many of the men followed with shots of their own. They would then laboriously reload as they slowly advanced. Silas advanced with them, but he didn't fire his weapon, having seen nothing but puffs of smoke.

The skirmish line regained its momentum. The men would locate a target, stop, and fire. Then they would quickly catch up with the others, loading on the move.

Suddenly, the preacher and Sonny both stopped, aimed, and

fired almost in unison. Then they began walking again, loading as they went. Sonny was becoming a soldier. Silas had yet to fire his weapon.

Silas was a good shot, and he knew how to load his Enfield .577 caliber muzzleloader on the move almost as well as the veterans. But he had yet to muster the courage to stick his head up far enough for long enough to pick a target. At this point, his greatest fear was of firing his weapon and, while still reloading, finding a Yankee directly in front of him. He wanted to keep his gun loaded in the event he was forced to defend himself. He knew this was unacceptable, but at this point in his military career, he was motivated more by fear than duty.

The thin Rebel line continued toward Knoxlyn Ridge, firing and maneuvering against the Yankee line. The Rebels would flank them, and the Yankees would move back to new positions and continue to fight. They were not in what one would call a retreat, but they were withdrawing.

The Yankees were slowly pushed off the ridge. All the way, Silas just stayed hunkered down, trying to keep up, never firing his musket. The preacher saw this but said nothing.

Sonny, on the other hand, had seemingly become a veteran in less than an hour. He was quietly and competently following the preacher's instructions, acquiring and firing on targets as they advanced.

As they topped Knoxlyn Ridge, Silas could see another low ridge about a mile away.

"Are we going to take that one too?" he asked the preacher.

"We're sure going to try, son," he said. "I think that one is called Herr's Ridge."

Silas didn't reply but he thought to himself, *Dear Lord, will this ever end?*

Then, as if he could read minds, the preacher said, "Son, it's going to be a long day. You might as well know it and be ready for it. We're just gettin' started. It ain't even nine o'clock yet."

"Yes, sir," he said.

"And you don't have to 'sir' me, son. I've told you before. I'm just a corporal. I just barely outrank you. You can just call me 'Preacher' like the others do," he said.

"Yes, sir. I mean, okay. It's just that I'm accustomed to addressing men your age as 'sir.'"

"I know, son," the preacher said. "I'm not offended. I know I'm probably too old to be here, but here I am. And even though I don't mind you calling me 'sir,' some of the officers might take offense to it."

"I understand, Preacher. I'll try not to let it happen again," Silas said.

"Don't worry about it now, son. We've got other things to worry about now."

All the while, they had been advancing toward their new objective, Herr's Ridge. The procedure was the same. They slowly advanced, firing and loading as they went—all except Silas. He was just advancing and staying low, having yet to fire his weapon.

Silas could hear the others firing up and down the line. He raised his head occasionally to monitor their progress toward the ridge. It seemed to him that there were more puffs of smoke on Herr's Ridge than had been on Knoxlyn. The Yankees seemed to be more numerous now than before.

Suddenly, Silas heard someone bellowing orders in the distance.

Then the preacher shouted, "Halt!"

The line came to a standstill. It was not long before young officers began riding among the Rebel columns with new orders, and the movement resumed. Looking to the rear, Silas could see the Thirteenth Alabama closing in behind them. This comforted him somewhat.

They had not advanced far when Silas heard men shouting. He looked up toward the Union line to see a Yankee cavalryman on a gray horse galloping in their direction. Not five seconds had passed when a single shot rang out and the Union man fell from his horse, disappearing into the wheat. Silas watched as the horse trotted instinctively back to its lines. That was the first Yankee soldier Silas Swann had ever seen. There would be more.

Silas was touched by the dead man's valor and saddened by his demise. He was also impressed by the marksmanship of the soldier who brought him down, whoever he was. A moving target bobbing up and down, and at that distance—that was good shooting. He began to wonder if he could have done it—not that his marksmanship was lacking. He could have done it with a little luck perhaps. That was not so much the question in his mind as whether he could bring himself to raise his weapon, point it at a man's chest, and pull the trigger.

They continued to move toward Herr's Ridge, which was fairly popping with gunfire now. Silas heard shouts to his left, toward the road.

"What happened, Preacher?" he said.

"I don't know yet," the preacher said. After a few seconds of listening to some distant shouts, he added, "One of our boys got hit in the leg. I think it was Worley, a Company A man."

Silas didn't know Worley, but he already felt a twinge of concern for a man he had never met, for a brother-in-arms.

As they moved toward the ridge, Silas became aware of men behind him, hurrying to his right, apparently to flank the Union line. He just continued to move in line with the Fifth, being careful to keep the preacher in easy sight. He was grateful for not having to join the flanking group. They were almost sure to see some hot action soon.

A few minutes later, he heard the rattle of musketry to his right. He knew those men had found the end of the Union line and were pushing it inward and backward. Or at least he hoped they were.

The enemy fire slackened then all but ceased as they neared the ridge. Silas realized they were beginning to walk up the gentle slope of Herr's Ridge. It was almost theirs. He felt the tiniest surge of pride go through him.

Then he mumbled to himself, "You fool. You didn't have anything to do with it. You never even fired a shot."

He was rudely jerked out of his introspection by the barking and snarling of a large dog. He stopped and found himself in front of a small cabin. The dog was standing his ground, protecting his home.

The preacher was quickly at Silas's side. "Let's just walk around him, son," he said. "Give him a wide berth."

Then Moses appeared. "Shoot his ass, you damned piss-ant!" he said to Silas. "Here. I'll do it," he added as he raised his weapon.

"Hold your fire, Jack," the preacher said. "You're sure to need that round before this day is done."

Moses briefly glowered at the preacher and then raised his weapon again at the still-snarling dog.

"I mean it, Jack. That's an order," the preacher said. "If you shoot him, I'll make things hard on you. We didn't come up here to shoot anybody's dog."

"You'll make things hard on me?" Moses said as he lowered his weapon again. "I'd like to see that. I can handle anything you've got. I'm the hardest son of a bitch in this army," he said, raising his weapon again.

"Moses, I'm ordering you not to harm that dog," the preacher said. "I'm tired of your insubordination. Now get back in line, soldier."

The two men stared at each other for a few seconds, long enough for Moses to save some face before he stalked back into position. Then the preacher's demeanor changed completely as he began to gently calm the dog. Soon he, Silas, and Sonny were laughing as they watched the dog trying to decide if they were friend or foe.

The owner soon emerged from the cabin and reassured his mongrel. The man was bareheaded and had his spectacles pushed up on his forehead. He was wearing a leather apron and had a shoe knife in his hand. He had obviously been working in his house. He seemed surprised at the sight of so many armed men in his yard.

"What is this?" he demanded. "What are you here for?"

"This is General Lee's Army of Northern Virginia," one of the men said. "General Hill sent us to drive back the Yankee cavalry. You mean you ain't heard nothin' unusual this morning?"

"I've been busy," the man said. "Tell General Hill to hold up a little. I turned my milk cow out this morning, and I need to get her in before the fighting begins."

There was great laughter among them as the man scurried off looking for his cow. Silas even saw Moses laugh—a rare event.

After a few seconds, the preacher said, "Let's keep it moving, men. We've still got Yankees on the other side of that ridge."

They moved on, leaving the bewildered but unbowed dog in his yard. The Thirteenth was close behind.

Almost immediately, the Yankees opened fire from the top of the ridge.

"Hell, Preacher," Moses carped, "I thought you said they were on the other side."

"I reckon I was wrong. They just fell back to new positions again. Y'all know what to do. Let's get to it."

And so they began firing and advancing again. Their skirmish line was soon overtaken from behind by the Thirteenth and the Tennessee outfits. This strong Rebel force pushed the stubborn Yankees off Herr's Ridge and down its east side.

It wasn't long before Silas, his squad mates, and a lot of other men he didn't know were walking down the moderate eastern slope following the Yankees. He again heard the Rebel artillery open fire behind him and to his left somewhere. He could see the rounds bursting among the trees between him and the next little rise, McPherson's Ridge. And he saw something else.

"Preacher," he said, "is that a creek down there?"

"Sure is, boy. I think that's Willoughby Run," the preacher said.

"Are we going to have to cross it?"

"Probably."

"How deep you reckon it is?" Silas asked.

"Not deep, I think," the preacher said. "Most of these creeks around here are little ol' rocky, shallow things. You might get your butt wet, but you'll be able to keep your powder dry, if that's what you're worried about."

"Maybe we won't have to cross it at all," Silas said.

"I wouldn't count on that," the preacher said. "We better hope we cross it. If we don't, we've got trouble."

They were walking down a slope toward the creek. The Thirteenth Alabama and the three Tennessee regiments had all passed the skirmish line and were to the front of the Fifth. There were Confederate troops in considerable numbers between Silas and the enemy, and that eased his apprehension somewhat. But enemy resistance seemed to be strengthening.

The Rebel artillery stopped firing momentarily. Then the Yankee artillery began its own barrage. They were overshooting their targets, and the shells were bursting behind the Rebel skirmishers. Silas instinctively fell to the ground as the shells began hitting behind him.

The preacher yelled, "Get up, boy. Run forward!"

He didn't have to say it twice. Silas began running and saw everyone else, even Moses, doing the same. They quickly ran out from under the barrage. Silas saw Sonny still moving to the preacher's left. Catching Sonny's eye, they forced a smile and nodded at each other.

The Yankee resistance grew still stronger as they neared the creek. The Fifth was only slightly behind the Thirteenth now. They soon heard the Rebel artillery open up again, with the shot hissing over them en route to the Yankees on McPherson's Ridge. They were still taking fire from the cavalrymen on the other side of the creek, but the men of the Thirteenth, while still on the west side, had driven the Yankees away from the stream.

Both outfits, the Fifth and the Thirteenth, stopped to reload and reform on the west side, preparing to cross the creek and push the Union men off the ridge beyond. The three Tennessee outfits were doing the same between them and the road to their left, northward.

Because of the lay of the land on the other side, they couldn't see much of what awaited them. They received word from Gen. Archer to stay put until further orders. They rested and cooled off, grateful for the respite. There were no friendly forces behind them this side of Herr's Ridge in case they ran into trouble. They couldn't understand why they weren't being closely supported from the rear by the remaining two brigades of Heth's division, Pettigrew and Brockenbrough. That was worrisome.

They didn't get to rest for long, but during that time, Sonny and Silas visited a little.

"How you holding up, trooper?" Sonny asked, smiling.

"Okay, I suppose. How far do you think we've come since we left the road?" Silas asked.

"Oh, a couple or three miles I guess. I don't know," he said.

"I just hope we don't have to go much farther today," Silas said. "This thorny underbrush near the streams is making things pretty hard on me."

"The underbrush!" Sonny laughed. "Not to mention Yankee shells and minié balls flying around. You must be harder than I thought if your main concern is the thorns."

"No, I'm not any harder than you thought. But up till now it's the thorns that are dealing me the most agony," Silas said. "I'm just thankful they're only near the creeks."

They were quiet for a few minutes. Then Silas said, "Have we lost anybody yet that you know of?"

"I'm pretty sure we have, but I don't know how many or who they are," Sonny said.

"What happens to the bodies? Do we go back and bury them later?" Silas wondered out loud.

"Only if we control the field when the fighting is finished," Sonny said. "If we don't control it, they just have to lay there until the Yankees bury them, if they ever get around to it."

"Man!" Silas said. "I don't want to die, but if I do I sure don't want to be left out in some farmer's field just to become so much fertilizer."

"Me neither!" said Sonny. "I tell you what. If you get it, I'll see that you get covered up, even if I have to send some old cat to do it."

They laughed, and Silas hit Sonny on the arm in feigned anger. He couldn't believe they were joking about death with it all around them and so close at hand. He almost told Sonny about not firing his weapon, but thought better of it.

Then they heard the preacher say, "Take your positions, men. We're about to move out."

Sonny ran to his place. To Silas, it seemed like they were taking a little more time and care in getting back into alignment. They moved toward the creek. The Thirteenth's last few men were already climbing out on the other side when the skirmish line and Silas arrived on the western bank of the little stream.

"Well, Swann," the preacher said, "it's about like I thought it would be. We can wade it easy enough. Just be careful not to splash any water on your weapon or powder. And don't lose your footing. The beds of these rocky streams can be tricky. If you fall, you'll get everything wet and you won't to able to fire your weapon for the rest of the day."

Silas thought he sensed a knowing inflection in the preacher's voice as if he knew about him having yet to fire his weapon. There was no time to worry about that now. Some men of the Fifth were already in the water, weapons held chest-high, making their way across the creek. Silas was dreading it and was not quite sure why. But he dutifully stepped into the water and carefully forded the creek without incident. With the help of some others, he climbed out on the other side and turned to help the man behind him, only to discover that there was no one. He was the last.

As he hurried to catch up and take his place in the line, he laughed sardonically at himself, "Yet another heroic moment in my sterling military career."

The water was not quite as deep as he expected. It had just come a little above his knees. None of his gear had gotten wet. But from his knees down, he felt cool, but heavy. Water squished miserably in his shoes.

His father had always told him to savor each and every day as it was a gift from a loving God, no matter how beautifully or poorly it unfolded. He was having trouble savoring this day. But he trudged onward, his respect for his companions growing with each step. They did not complain about discomfort or danger. They showed no fear or hesitancy in closing with the enemy. They were what he wished he could be.

Silas had been reared better, but he had always looked down a little on his country cousins, some of whom couldn't read or write and most of whom used poor grammar. He had always kept these thoughts to himself because he knew his parents would be disappointed if they knew he harbored them. After a month in their company, his disdain for these men from the hills of Alabama and Tennessee was gone forever. He had to painfully admit to himself that he was the least of them. To a man, he regarded each of them as better than he, even Box, and especially Moses.

He thought poorly of himself. He would willingly confess his worthlessness to the world if he could just go home and enroll in the University of Alabama as he had once planned and as his parents had wished. He would immerse himself in academics, become a quaint history professor, and quietly abandon all hope of being a man.

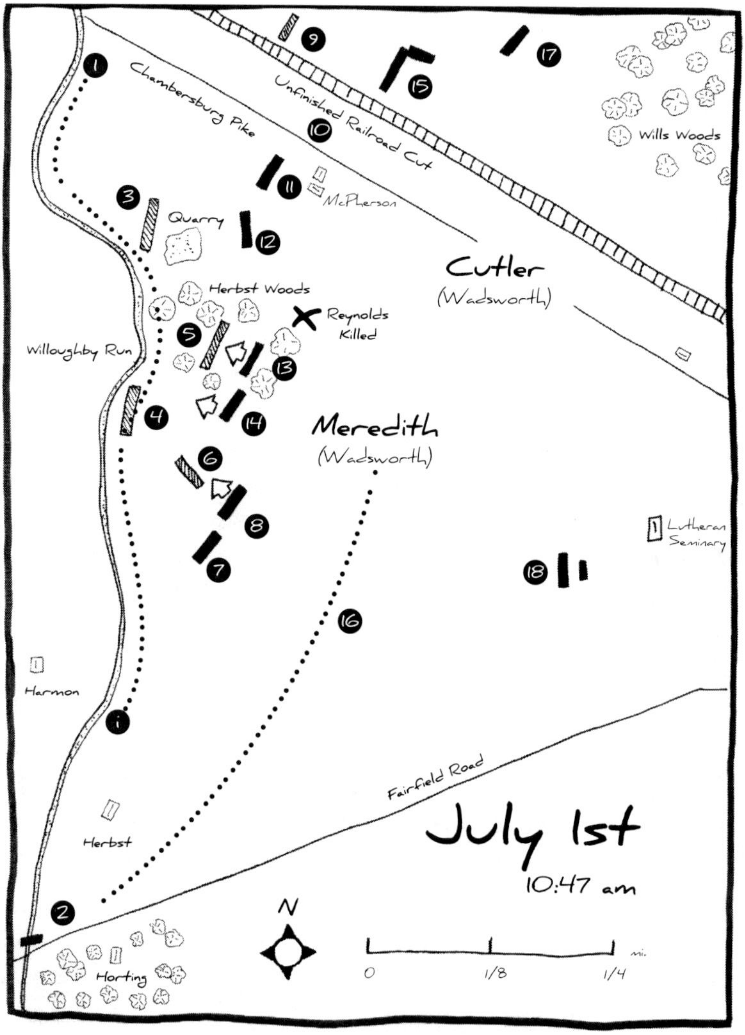

July 1st
10:47 am

- ① Skirmishers (AL 5th)
- ② NY 8th Cav.
- ③ TN 7th
- ④ TN 1st
- ⑤ TN 14th
- ⑥ AL 13th
- ⑦ MI 24th
- ⑧ IN 19th
- ⑨ MS 42nd
- ⑩ ME 2nd Bat.
- ⑪ NY 95th
- ⑫ NY 84th (14th Brooklyn)
- ⑬ WI 2nd
- ⑭ WI 7th
- ⑮ NY 147th
- ⑯ Skirmishers (NY 8th Cav.)
- ⑰ PA 56th
- ⑱ WI 6th Brigade & Guard

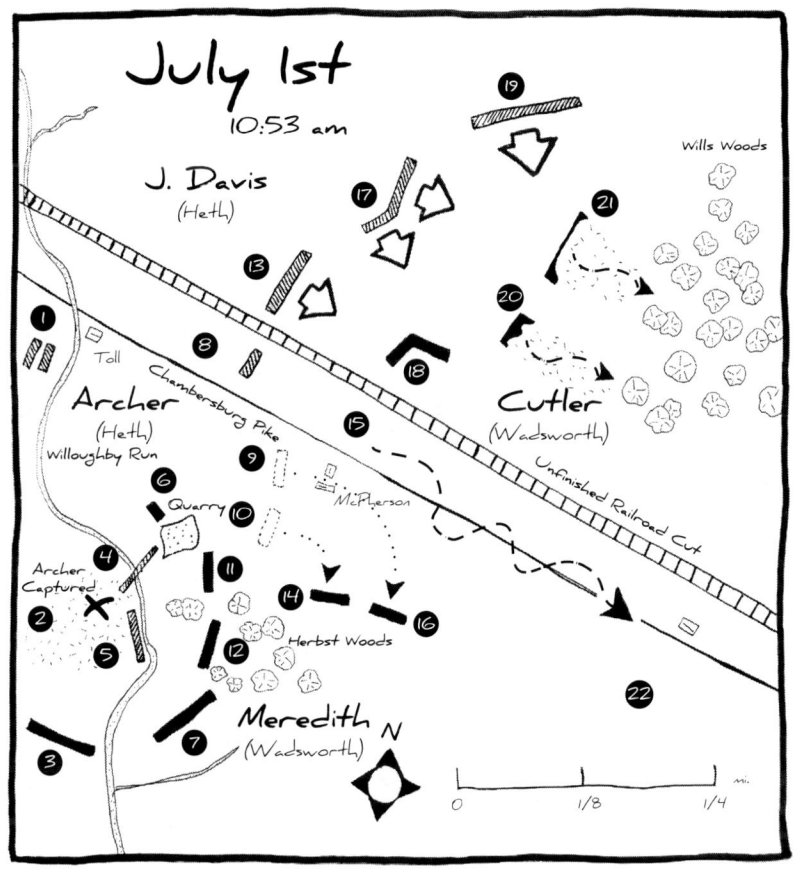

- ① VA 22nd Bat.
- ② Archer (Fry)
- ③ VA 47th
- ④ VA 40th
- ⑤ NC 26th
- ⑥ NC 11th
- ⑦ IL 8th Cav. & NY 80th Company K
- ⑧ WI 7th
- ⑨ WI 2nd
- ⑩ MI 24th
- ⑪ IN 19th
- ⑫ NC 11th
- ⑬ NC 47th
- ⑭ NC 52nd
- ⑮ PA 142nd
- ⑯ NY Light 1st
- ⑰ NY 80th
- ⑱ PA 121st
- ⑲ 4th US Bat.
- ⑳ PA 151st
- ㉑ VA 55th
- ㉒ PA 150th
- ㉓ PA 149th
- ㉔ PA 143rd
- ㉕ NY Light 1st

Retreat

To their front, the sound of musketry was growing. He heard the preacher talking loudly.

"It's getting pretty hot up there, boys. It looks like the Thirteenth is wheeling north to flank them. Just keep moving, and keep your eyes peeled."

After advancing another minute or so, they heard a large volley, and the preacher said, "That's the Thirteenth firing north into their flank."

They were craning their necks to see the action through the smoke when they heard another huge volley and saw a large bank of smoke erupt beyond and to the east of the northerly facing Thirteenth.

Someone down the line shouted, "Shit, Preacher, the sons of bitches just flanked the Thirteenth!"

They heard gunfire like rolling thunder from the direction of the three Tennessee regiments located to the north of the Thirteenth, nearer the road. Then they heard the order to halt.

"Stay low, men," the preacher said, "but keep your eyes open." Then he shouted toward Silas to those beyond him, "You men on the right, don't you let them flank us. Let me know if you see any movement to your right."

Silas heard someone say, "Damn. Sounds like all hell is breaking loose out there. That Yankee cavalry must have been reinforced by infantry."

They crouched there for a short while when a man from the Thirteenth appeared, heading toward the rear in a hurry.

As he ran through the skirmish line, he shouted, "It's the damn black hats. You better git your asses back across the creek purty damn quick."

"What's the black hats?" Silas hurriedly asked the preacher.

"It's the Iron Brigade, maybe the toughest outfit in the whole Union Army. Ain't no way a two hundred-man skirmish line is going to stop them."

Out of the smoke and noise before them, they saw two more men of the Thirteenth coming toward them on the run.

As they sprinted through the widely-spaced skirmish line, one man shouted, "Run, you damn fools. They're right behind us."

The preacher immediately stood erect and shouted, "Hold, men! Hold!"

They all hunkered down but stayed just high enough to see over the wheat into the smoke of the battle roaring before them. Silas saw the men of the Thirteenth fighting but slowly withdrawing. Beyond them, through gaps in the smoke, he could see great numbers of soldiers in blue coming relentlessly toward him. Suddenly, the men of the Thirteenth seemed very few. Whether they had fallen or were simply hidden by the smoke, he did not know. He heard some orders being screamed up the line, but he could not make out the words.

Then the preacher shouted, "Withdraw to the creek! Withdraw to the creek!"

Almost instantly, Silas was sprinting westward, back toward the stream he had recently forded. The wheat did not impede him. He barely noticed it as it flew by. He was highly motivated, and he discovered the one talent he had in abundance over many of his fellows: fleetness of foot. The weight of his weapon and gear did not slow him down.

The creek was not far, and he soon found himself standing on the other side. So great was his haste that he had no clear recollection of crossing it. The thorny underbrush hadn't deterred him. Slightly bewildered, he was staring at three men from the Thirteenth, with them staring back. It was then he realized that of the Fifth, only he had run. Soon, the others began to arrive. He began helping them climb up out of the water. Most were from the Fifth. A few were Thirteenth men. He helped the preacher and Sonny and some others. He was more than just a little ashamed that he had panicked and fled. He quietly confessed his shame to the preacher, who just smiled and told him not to worry about it, that someone had to be first, and that he would do better next time.

Someone shouted, "They're crossing the creek to the south. Make for Herr's Ridge. That's where Pettigrew and Brockenbrough are."

Silas resumed his withdrawal with a little more dignity and in the company of his fellows this time. The underbrush was pulling at him again until he put a little distance between himself and the creek.

They trotted back to the foot of Herr's Ridge and stopped, the Yankees having ceased their pursuit and gunfire shortly after crossing the creek. At the foot of the ridge, they met a line of skirmishers from Pettigrew's Brigade advancing toward the Union line.

Fresh and full of fight, one of the Pettigrew men said, "Y'all let a few Yankee cavalrymen put you on the run?"

One of Archer's men stared at him a few seconds and said, "You mean like y'all did yesterday. We heard about that courageous shoe hunt y'all went on."

"We had orders not to start a fight," the Pettigrew man said.

"You did the Confederacy mighty proud the way you diligently followed those orders."

"Listen, feller!" the Pettigrew man said angrily. "You better…"

"Where the hell were y'all?" Archer's man interrupted. "That cavalry was supported by the damned Iron Brigade. Where the hell was our support? We could have kicked their ass if y'all had been supporting us like you should'a been. Now you come sashaying down the damn hill like the king of damn France looking down your nose at an outfit that got its butt kicked because you didn't do your damn job."

A few seconds elapsed, and the Pettigrew man quietly said, "We never got no such orders. I reckon we'll deal with them black hats this evening."

With that, the conversation ended, neither man wishing to pursue it further.

As the men of Archer's brigade rested, they began to hear dire reports on the condition of their outfit. Of the four regiments, the Seventh Tennessee had escaped with the least casualties, about thirty. The Fourteenth Tennessee had suffered about sixty. But the First Tennessee and the Thirteenth Alabama had been the hit especially hard, with 109 and 168, respectively. And then there was the Fifth Alabama. They too had suffered. But since they had been in a skirmish line, along with sixty men of the Thirteenth, and had been passed by the main body of Archer's troops, they were to the rear when the Iron Brigade struck. Because of this, the Fifth's casualties were relatively light.

Archer had gone into battle with slightly fewer than 1,200 men. After counting heads, they figured they had lost about 370 men, killed, captured, or wounded. Gen. Archer himself was missing and believed to have been captured. Col. Fry of the Thirteenth Alabama was the new commander of the brigade.

Archer's men did not yet know it, but they had inflicted serious casualties on the vaunted Iron Brigade. Of its 1,400 men, about three hundred were dead or wounded. Before nightfall, Brockenbrough and Pettigrew would essentially destroy what was left of it. In addition to the punishment visited on the black hats, they had also inflicted significant damage on the Union cavalry they had faced until the Iron Brigade arrived.

However, Archer's men only knew they had been forced to retreat. Some were humbled, others angry. Moses and Box were in the latter group. And others, like Silas, were simply pleased to be alive. Sonny, too, had gotten back safely, and the two of them quietly celebrated surviving their first action. But the Fifth had lost four men, killed, captured, or wounded. For a unit with only 135 men, it had been a bad morning. The Fifth was small enough that most of the men knew each other. They had been together through two years of war. Even men who did not much like each other would fight fiercely and proudly side by side—

except for Moses; he was a loner. He did not even like his one so-called friend, Box. But then, nobody liked Box, or for that matter, Moses.

Shame and Resolve

It was about midday. It had been a long, difficult morning. Silas prayed, literally prayed, for a better afternoon. But like his daddy often said, "The fervent prayers of a righteous man are always answered, but sometimes the answer is no, and the Lord has a reason for each answer. Someday we may understand those reasons. Or perhaps we will never understand them in this life. That is where trust and faith come in." Silas had trust and faith in God and in his father. He was, however, losing confidence in himself.

They rested and tried to eat a lunch of sorts, the usual fare: hard tack and beef jerky. They also attended to minor injuries, mostly scratches from the underbrush. A few men had minor combat wounds, but they would soon be ready for more action.

After lunch, their commanding officer, Maj. Van De Graaff, spoke to them. The major was a soft-spoken Sumter County man who had been wounded twice, first at Mechanicsville and again at Fredericksburg. Each time, his wounds forced him to relinquish his command while he recovered. Each time, he returned. Even today he had barely escaped injury when a Yankee shell struck near him, showering him with dirt but leaving him unharmed. He was respected by his men. They gathered close around him, some leaning on their weapons. Silas was disheartened to see how small, how seemingly insignificant 130 men look in an army of seventy thousand. And even worse was how tiny they seem against an army of ninety-three thousand.

The major began, "Men, this has been a difficult morning for the Fifth and Archer's Brigade. It looks like we lost four men. We think at least one of those men, Griffin, was wounded and captured. Worley and Barnes were wounded and are now in our field hospital. We think Redman died in action, but we aren't sure yet. He may have been captured. Our regiments suffered greatly, losing many men, most of whom were captured, we think.

"But Davis's Brigade had it even worse," he said. "They were caught in one of the railroad cuts north of the pike, and much of the Second Mississippi and parts of the Forty-second North Carolina were forced to surrender. Many of our brothers died north of the pike in that railroad cut.

"Men," he continued, "I know things look bleak right now. But one thing I've learned over the last two years is that victory is seldom as glorious or defeat as disastrous as they first appear. We know now that we drove Buford's cavalry about two, maybe three miles before they were relieved by the Iron Brigade. When the Thirteenth got flanked, three or four of their men panicked and ran back through our line. But the rest of them stood and fought like the veterans they are. Several of them died, and about two hundred got captured, including General Archer. As you probably know by now, Colonel Fry is commanding the brigade. But the Thirteenth and the rest of the brigade inflicted heavy casualties on the Yankees. Considering the fact that they were without Lt. Crawford and his men, who were with us, the Thirteenth acquitted themselves well in a very difficult situation."

He paused and then continued. "Men, I'm not disappointed in you or in the men of the Thirteenth who were in the skirmish line with us. No one expects two hundred soldiers arrayed in a skirmish line to hold off a force of 1,400. We had no choice but to withdraw. But there is a proper way to withdraw, and there is the way a very few did it today. You withdrew like soldiers, fighting all the way. I'm proud of you men."

Silas froze in his shame, hoping no one was looking at him.

"This afternoon, we are going back toward Gettysburg," the major said. "We will not be spread out in a skirmish line. We will be together, and the entire division will be with us, over seven thousand men. We will destroy the Iron Brigade and push on through Gettysburg. There will be no retreat, no panic this time.

"Rest up, men, but gird yourselves. We will probably move out between 1400 and 1500 hours. But it might be earlier. Be ready. Let's get it done, men. That is all."

The men were called to attention as the major left them standing in a semicircle, a few staring at the ground in shame.

They were dismissed, and someone quietly said, "Never again, boys. Next time I'll die before I turn tail."

Distant Musketry

They had been listening to the distant rattle of musketry and the thumps of artillery to the northeast. They were told it was Ewell's men arriving north of town, well over 20,000 fresh Rebel troops driving the Yankees like cattle. Silas and Sonny stayed pretty much to themselves. They ate and then let their socks and shoes dry out a little. They also slaked their thirst and refilled their canteens.

The preacher came around and said, "Listen up, men. We need to replenish our ammunition before we go back out this evening. I want y'all to drop what you're doing and follow me over to the supply wagons so you can stock up on whatever you need."

The dozen or so men began to form a double line behind the preacher. Even though Silas needed no ammunition, having yet to fire his weapon, he too joined in.

Box said, "What the hell are you doing here, boy? You don't need nothin'. You ain't fired a shot all day."

"You don't know that," the preacher said.

"Yeah, I do. Moses told me," said Box. Then turning back to Silas, he said, "What the hell did you walk up here for, boy, to show off that fine uniform?"

Then Kirby, one of the toughest men in the squad, said, "And just how many Yanks did you lay low today, Box?"

"Just one I know of for sure," he said. "Who the hell do you think dropped that cocky Yankee horseman when he sallied out to meet us? And I fired my weapon plenty of times into the Yankee lines. I don't know how many I killed, but I killed my share. That son of a bitch," he said, pointing at Silas, "didn't do nothin' but walk out there and run back."

"That's enough, Box," the preacher said. "We all had to learn first. When he's been doing this as long as we have, he'll be just as good as you, and without the smart mouth. The mouth don't make the man. Come on, y'all. Follow me."

As they walked toward the supply wagons, Box fell in next to Silas and quietly said, "When this is over, boy, I'm gonna whup your chicken ass."

Sonny overheard him and said, "Why don't you just whip my chicken ass instead, Box? I only fired my weapon a couple of times today, and I probably didn't hit anything. Why don't you just whip me? Do it right now. Don't wait till all this is over. Come on, Box. A veteran like you shouldn't have any trouble with a new troop like me. What's holding you back? Get it done, trooper!"

Box just glared at Sonny's grinning face and said, "You'll get yours in due time boy, in due time."

Then he found his way to Moses's side and was ignored. Sonny chuckled just loud enough for Box to hear him. Silas was grateful for Sonny's intervention but was not amused.

While they were being re-supplied, they heard a brief round of sporadic rifle fire not very distant. They soon learned that it was some of their pickets warning off Union skirmishers who had gotten too close.

After they had returned, the preacher quietly made his way to Silas and said, "Son, you need to remove that percussion cap from your weapon. It's a whole lot safer that way. You can put it on when we go back out."

"Yes, sir. I know. I just forgot."

"I told you not to call me sir. I'm just a corporal."

"Yes, sir. Oh, I'm sorry. I mean, yes, corporal. I guess I just keep forgetting."

The preacher shook his head, smiled, and said, "Listen, son. When we go back out this evening, you'll probably have several opportunities to fire that weapon. I suggest you take advantage of them. The rest of us would like to think you're with us in this thing."

The preacher gave him a fatherly pat on the back.

"And one more thing. You need to take your ramrod and tamp your load down good and snug. If you let the powder sit in there too long without tamping it down, it might misfire. Be sure to keep it dry too. And don't forget to put that percussion cap on when we go back out," he said, chuckling a little.

"Yes, Corporal Elder."

"Okay. Well, that's all I wanted to say. Go back to what you were doing."

"Thank you," Silas said. "I'll do better. I promise."

"I know, son," the preacher said. "Don't worry about it. We have enough to worry about as it is."

"Yes, sir."

1. VA 22nd Bat.
2. Archer (Fry)
3. VA 47th
4. VA 40th
5. NC 26th
6. NC 11th
7. IL 8th Cav. & NY 80th Company K
8. WI 7th
9. WI 2nd
10. MI 24th
11. IN 19th
12. NC 11th
13. NC 47th
14. NC 52nd
15. PA 142nd
16. NY Light 1st
17. NY 80th
18. PA 121st
19. 4th US Bat.
20. PA 151st
21. VA 55th
22. PA 150th
23. PA 149th
24. PA 143rd
25. NY Light 1st

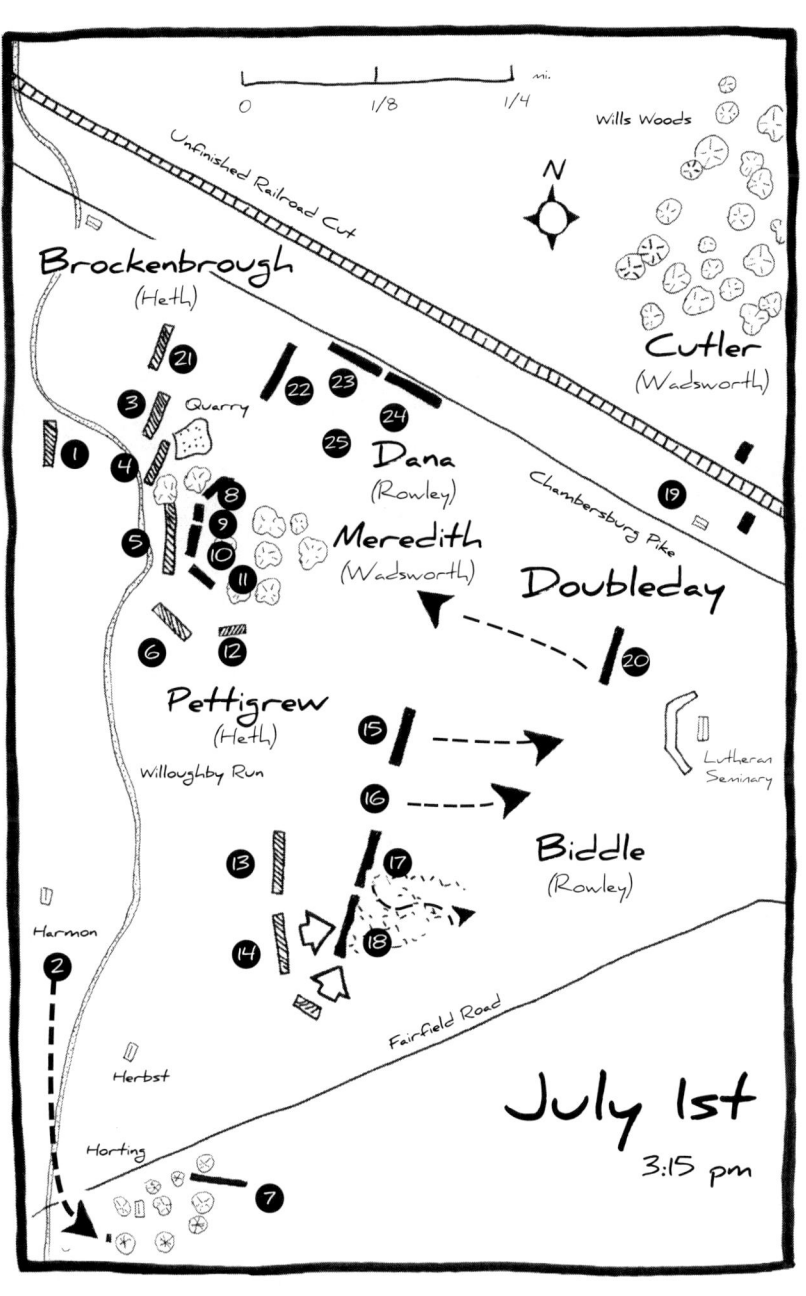

Evening Action

Silas inconspicuously removed the percussion cap from his weapon and tamped the load down. He and Sonny stayed to themselves, talking and trying to find something to smile about. Then they grew quiet.

After a while Sonny said, "What you thinking about? Home?"

"Aren't you?" Silas replied.

"If we were home, you could go over to Molly's house and tell her how pretty she is," Sonny said with a little smile.

"Oh, hush about that!" Silas said. "She doesn't even know I'm alive."

"Oh, I think she does."

"Barely—maybe."

"More than barely."

"She might," Silas said, "but she doesn't know that I think she's just about the prettiest thing in the world and the sweetest."

"You mean she doesn't know you're sweet on her?"

"No."

"You couldn't get up the courage to tell her before we left? Didn't I warn you about leaving home with undeclared love in your heart?"

"I guess I'm a coward in every way."

"Well," Sonny said, trying to comfort his friend, "after all this, when we're home again, you'll be brave enough to tell her. She needs to know she has a sweetheart in the army."

"Yeah. When we're home again."

It was not long before they were told to form up and prepare to move out. When they were in formation, Maj. Van De Graaff addressed them, telling them that they and the rest of Archer's Brigade would be on the extreme right flank of the Confederate advance.

"Men," he said, "our job is to be sure we don't get flanked. We will be facing Gamble's cavalry as far as we know. Pettigrew and Brockenbrough will be to the north of us, on our left. Pender's men will be supporting us."

"Pardon me, sir, but where was our support this morning when we could have used it?" someone asked.

"That's a good question, soldier, but you're asking the wrong man. I'm not high enough in the chain of command to know the answer. That was a costly oversight, but it's done. We intend to make up for it this evening. We're going to push the Iron Brigade off those ridges and back through the town. Be ready to move out on a moment's notice. We'll be getting the word any time now."

Soon, they were moving out of the woods in an easterly direction, toward a farm. Silas could see thousands of his fellows to his left moving eastward. He could hear artillery fire but couldn't tell where it was coming from, only that it was to his left, northward.

Silas didn't understand what was happening, but after a while, they adjusted their alignment to a southeasterly facing position. He soon heard that a detachment of Union cavalry had been spotted to their right, and the brigade was being positioned to protect the advance from being flanked.

They made their way through the fields toward the Fairfield road, called the Hagerstown road by some. The boy could tell the issue was being hotly contested a half mile or so to his left. The rattle of musketry was furious. He knew men were dying by the hundreds. That familiar queasiness returned to his gut. But for the moment, things were quiet before them.

They were nearing the place where the road crossed Willoughby Run.

It was still a few hundred yards distant when Moses said, "Preacher, I saw a glint of metal out there."

Before the preacher could say anything, they heard orders being shouted to halt.

"I reckon somebody else saw it too, Jack," the preacher said.

They maneuvered into position. Silas looked around at the

comforting sight of the thousand men of Archer's Brigade. To his north, he knew there were still thousands more of his countrymen in butternut and gray. Most comforting of all, he could turn and see a few ranks behind him his lifelong friend, Sonny Simon. They exchanged a nod and a smile, and Silas turned to face the foe.

They had advanced another hundred yards or so when, a few hundred yards before them, a single puff of smoke appeared, followed about a second later by the report.

"They done fouled up, Preacher," someone said.

Then several more shots were fired in their direction with no apparent effect. Then the Fifth was ordered forward while the rest of the Brigade stayed back.

Why us? Silas asked himself.

Then he remembered that the Fifth had suffered the fewest casualties of the units in the Brigade that morning and he understood.

They heard, "Front rank only, individual fire. Fire at will!"

Lt. Cox said, "It's their pickets, boys. There's probably a lot more of them hidden in the trees beyond the road and on the other side of the creek. We need to drive them back over the road and across the creek. Pick your targets out with their smoke, and make them pay."

Silas and the other men of the front rank knelt and took aim. When another puff of smoke appeared, a few men would quickly adjust their aim and fire. This happened several times, and Silas could see soldiers in blue sprinting away across the road and toward the creek. There was more fire from the Rebels toward the fleeing Yankees, and a couple more went down. The cavalrymen ran across the road into the trees near the creek. On the near side of the road, Silas could see a few bodies spread at wide intervals in the wheat.

All the men who fired had by now reloaded, and the brigade began to slowly advance toward the road. Of the almost one thousand men of the brigade, fewer than fifty, all from the Fifth, had fired at the union pickets. Even though Silas was in the front rank, he still had not fired his weapon. He had knelt and aimed with the others, and he had even cocked his musket, but he never pulled the trigger. He secretly let the hammer down easy.

They heard the order to fix bayonets, and someone said, "Oh, Lordy."

All the men hated bayonet charges—all save Moses. Even though this would not actually be a charge, they still didn't like having a bayonet fixed to the muzzle of their weapon. It hampered the loading process. Once they had fired their weapon, they were expected to close with the enemy and dispatch him face to face. Most of the men were good at this type of combat, but they disliked it nonetheless. Moses, however, delighted in it.

As they advanced, they saw a large number of men in blue on horseback emerge from the trees beyond the creek hurrying toward the rear, retreating. They reached the position recently held by the Yankees, and Cpl. Elder's squad passed a dead Union trooper. Silas did not gaze long at the body, but he could not help but notice the destruction inflicted on the human form by a lead bullet a little more than a half inch in diameter.

They crossed the road and found a few more dead and some wounded.

Someone shouted, "Watch it, Jack!"

Silas looked up in time to see Moses kick a pistol out of the hand of a wounded cavalryman who was lying on his back. Moses then calmly pinned the man to the ground with his bayonet. The man screamed and thrashed around until Moses pulled the blade out of the man's gut and thrust it into his chest. Transfixed, Silas continued to watch as Moses placed his foot on the still twitching body and jerked back on his rifle, removing the blade. The twitching stopped, and Moses happily stuck the pistol in his belt.

"Dear Lord," Silas secretly prayed, "I don't belong here."

The preacher said, "Jack, that pistol belongs to Lieutenant Cox. He lost his in this morning's action. Hand it over."

"Hell, Preacher, this one ain't his. This one's mine. Tell him to get his own damn pistol. There's probably several laying around here. And tell him not to lose it next time."

"Let's have it, Jack. His pistol is the only firearm he carries. He needs it," the preacher said as he held out his hand.

After a few seconds, Moses slowly pulled the pistol out of his belt and handed it to the preacher.

He quietly swore as the preacher walked away, "Damn officers. Damn corporals. And damn preachers."

Things quieted down. They had killed seven Yankees and taken a couple of wounded prisoners, something Moses had never understood. But most of the Yankees had escaped on foot, wading to the other side of the creek where thick trees and brush concealed them. From there, with the rest of their outfit, they had made their retreat on horseback.

"Preacher," Silas asked, "why wasn't their fire more effective like it was this morning? Not that I'm complaining; I'm just curious."

"Because, son, they are using that breech-loading carbine that shoots fast but doesn't have the reach or accuracy our muzzle loaders have," the preacher said. "One of their men got jumpy and fired before we were in their effective range. Once we knew their position, we could stand back and knock them down, and they couldn't really hit us nearly as hard at that distance. But I heard the brigade still took a couple of casualties."

"If they're cavalry, why didn't they have their horses with them?" Silas wanted to know.

"They had some men holding them across the creek. In fact, most of them were in the rear. They're probably all gone by now. We'll send some scouts to be sure. The men we fired at were pickets, just a small detachment, probably fifty men or so. Except for them, most of the Yankees were already across the creek when we arrived. The heaviest fighting is to the north of us, against the Iron Brigade and some other outfits. That's Pettigrew and Brockenbrough fighting them. From what I've been hearing, to the north, I would say they fought hard against the Yanks, and now Pender's men have begun to relieve them. Hopefully they're about to push the bluebellies back through the town. That's one of the reasons the men facing us withdrew. They knew their friends, including the Iron Brigade, were getting whipped pretty badly."

"And what about us?" Silas asked. "What are we supposed to do now?"

"Our orders are to stay right here near the road and the creek and guard the right flank. I think we've done our do for the day. They'll let those other outfits finish today's action. They're fresh. We're not," the preacher said.

"Man, that sounds good," Silas said. "Hey, Sonny, did you hear that? We're through for the day."

He turned, his eyes searching for Sonny.

"Sonny, where are you, boy?"

Looking for his Friend

He looked in every direction for Sonny. It's easy to lose a face in a crowd of hundreds, but most of the men were accounted for.

"Where is he, Preacher?" Silas asked.

"I don't know, son. We haven't quite finished counting heads," the preacher said.

"I gotta go look for him."

"No, son. You gotta stay right here. We've still got work to do."

"But I thought you said we were finished for the day," Silas said.

"We're through with combat for the day. Leastways, I hope we are. But we still have to stay here until after dark to watch our flank. We're about to fan out some pickets to the front and sides," the preacher said, "and we'll leave some pickets here tonight."

The preacher could see panic growing in the boy, so he said, "Son, we've already got a few details going back over the field of our advance, looking for the wounded. If they find Simon, they'll bring him in, and we'll try to get him to the field surgeon."

"But, but what if he's... what if he is not among the wounded? I mean, what if he's..."

"In that case, there's nothing we can do right now. The man in charge of the detail will make a note of where he is, and we'll go back to bury him as soon as we can," the preacher said.

Bewildered, the boy looked back at the field they had just crossed and could see small groups of men spread out over it, just their upper bodies showing above the wheat.

"Preacher, I gotta go look for him!"

"No, son, you don't."

"Yes, sir, I do. I don't think you understand," Silas said as he began moving in that direction.

"Hold it right there, trooper. You're the one who don't understand. Listen, man. You're not a little boy in Mobile anymore. You're a soldier in the Army of Northern Virginia, and you're deep in enemy territory. We have our orders, and they don't include letting you run off to look for your friend right now. We've got men doing it for you. Now you fall in over there with those other men by the road and watch the creek for enemy activity. That's your job."

"But, Preacher..."

"I don't want to hear anymore about it right now, boy. This war is a whole lot bigger than any of us. You should know that by now, even if you didn't know it when you signed up. Now get on over there," the preacher said none too kindly.

Cpl. Elder had always been very gentle with Silas. He was a gentle man. The people to whom he spoke harshly were soldiers like Box and Moses. Silas knew this, but he hesitated before moving toward the road.

Finally, sounding more like a corporal than a pastor, the preacher said, "Move it, Swann!"

Silas slouched toward the road. He took a place between Waller and Williams. No one spoke. They were watching the creek. Silas stared at the ground a few feet before him, and that is all he did for a while.

Then he whispered, "Dear Lord, please be with him. Send him back to me whole. Do just this one miracle for me, please, Jesus. Please."

He thought about home and his family and Sonny's family. He thought that perhaps Sonny might merely be wounded. But mostly he worried about his friend losing his young life and about himself losing his closest, virtually his only friend.

Eventually, he overheard the leader of one of the details reporting to the preacher.

"Yeah, we found him, Preacher," the man said.

"Did you bring him in?" the preacher asked.

"T'weren't no need. We left all his stuff with him too. We were already carrying too much Yankee stuff to collect his," the man said.

"Are you sure it was him? He's the only man I'm missing."

"Yeah, it was him. He was on his stomach, but I turned his head around enough so as I could see his face. I've seen him before. He's one of those two new troops of yours," the man said.

"Simon," the preacher quietly added.

"Yep, that's him all right. He runs with that little feller, your other new troop. Leastways, he did."

"Yes, that's him," the preacher said softly. "Well, we're obliged to you, John. You can go now. We'll take care of the boy tonight. We'll collect his things then."

"Thanks, Preacher. I hate it about the boy. It was just a lucky shot for the Yankees and an unlucky one for the boy," the man said as he departed.

The preacher turned and said, "Swann, come here."

57

Silas made his way toward him.

"Silas," he said.

Silas held up his hand with his palm toward the preacher, shook his head, and said, "You don't have to say it. I heard."

"I'm sorry, son."

"I just have one request, Preacher."

"What's that, son?"

"I want to be on his burial detail," Silas said looking at the ground.

"I'll see to it."

"Thank you, sir."

He returned to his place, still staring at the ground. Again, no one spoke.

He was resolved not to weep in the presence of the other men, especially Box and Moses, and so he shed no tears.

They could hear the sounds of battle growing more distant in the east, toward the village, and they suspected the South was prevailing.

Waller said, "Somebody's sure raisin' a ruckus over yonder."

"Hope it's us," said Williams.

Regardless of who was prevailing, this day had been hard for the men of Archer's Brigade. Nonetheless, those who had survived felt good about their chances of seeing at least one more sunrise. It was early summer and, in spite of the lateness of the hour, the sun was still far from the horizon. It was not yet time for them to return to their encampment, so they broke out their hard tack, beef jerky, and canteens for supper—all save one.

Standing Alone

Night finally fell, and they marched back to their encampment near Herr Ridge. As they arrived, Silas stared at the ground and slowly made his way back to the spot he and Sonny had occupied earlier in the day. He was almost in shock from the grief and despair of having lost his lifelong friend. As he walked, he became aware of someone standing in his way. He looked up to see Box's grinning countenance.

"Well, well," Box said. "Poor little rich boy don't have his big ass friend to take up for him no more."

As he looked into Box's gloating eyes, he momentarily lost all fear as hate and rage quickly overpowered his grief. He dropped his weapon to the ground, and with no thought or warning, he immediately tackled the unsuspecting Box, throwing him to the ground. Silas was instantly on him, giving him a two-fisted beating that made even Moses smile.

Box's screams brought the preacher and some others running. It had only lasted a few seconds when the preacher pulled Silas off him. Kirby grabbed Box before he could exact any retribution.

"You sorry, bastard!" Silas hissed, "Trash! You aren't fit to lick his boots. Let me go, dammit. I'm gonna kill the son of a bitch."

As the amazed and bloodied Box struggled to get free of Kirby's powerful grip, he said, "Did you see that, Preacher? Did you hear how he talked to me? What you gonna do about it?"

"What happened?" the preacher asked.

"Why, he just jumped my ass for no reason at all!" Box said.

"No reason at all?" Kirby said. "Box was ragging him about Simon getting it today. Swann just lit into him."

"Is that true, Box?" the preacher asked.

"I was just telling him how sorry I was," Box said.

The laughter and shaking heads of the men told the preacher all he needed to know.

"Box," he said, "in this outfit, we don't take pleasure in the death of one of our own. And we sure don't torment his grieving friends. You deserved more than you got. You're lucky he didn't use the butt of his rifle on you. I want you two to avoid each other as much as possible. The next time y'all get into it, there's going to be trouble for both of you."

The preacher released Swann and Kirby let Box go. The two stared at each other until the preacher said, "That's it, boys. It's over. I'm not even going to ask you to shake hands. I don't want to hear anymore about it. Box, you get back where you were and leave Swann alone. Swann, you stay away from Box."

Box stomped away, and the group dispersed, leaving only the fuming Silas with a grinning Moses.

Moses lingered and said, "I declare, boy, you really ain't no better than the rest of us after all, are you?"

He waited a few seconds for a reply. When none came, he turned, still smiling, and walked away.

Silas, with Sonny gone, looked at the backs of a handful of men whom he barely knew but who were now the closest things to friends he had left in his world. He stood alone.

He prayed, "Lord, send me another Sonny."

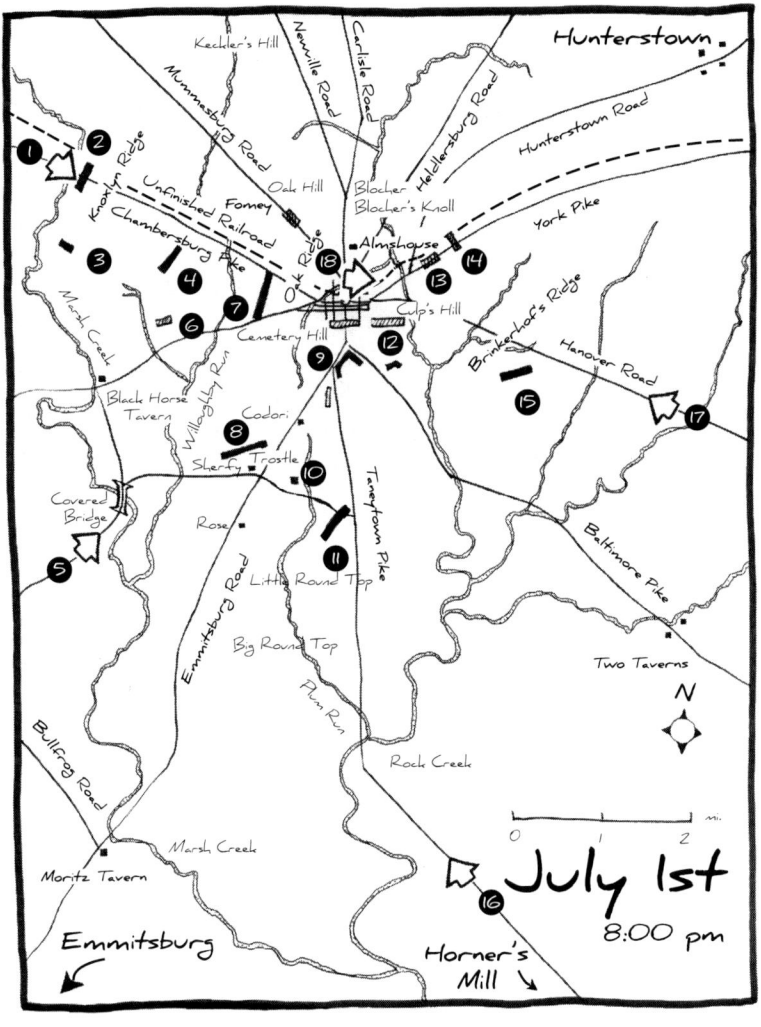

A Cur for a Cur

After a while, the preacher called them together.

He said, "Men, the lieutenant said we have to provide four men to relieve the pickets tonight. It'll be two four-hour shifts, two men on each shift starting at 2100 hours. The rest of us will be on grave-digging duty starting at the same time, 2100 hours. Even though I doubt it, we might still have some wounded out there who need help. But the moon won't come up till eight thirty or nine, and the company only has the one lantern, so this is how we're going to do it. Kirby, Swann, and I will go out early, in just a few minutes. We will take the lantern and try to help any wounded we might find or bury those who need it. The rest of you will wait till nine to come out. The moon should be bright enough by then. We've got enough shovels for everybody in the detail. So y'all need to start getting a little rest as soon as we break up here."

"Waller, you and McClendon, Box, and Moses are on the picket detail. The rest of you are gravediggers. Waller, I'm putting you in charge of the pickets. I don't care how you assign the men as long as you don't put Box and Moses together on the same shift."

"What's wrong with me and Box being on the same shift?" Moses immediately demanded.

"Now, Jack, you know he's a bad influence on you," the preacher said.

There was scattered laughter, with Box laughing loudest until he caught sight of Moses glowering at him.

Just as Moses was about to reply, a man from the Thirteenth walked into the group.

"Hey, y'all," he said. "Y'all having a squad meeting?"

"We're trying to, Mike," the preacher said.

"I'm sorry," he said. "I didn't mean to interrupt, but Colonel Fry just wanted me to spread the word that we're gonna be held in reserve tomorrow. They won't use us unless it gets sho' nuff bad somewhere. We're to spend the day catching up on our rest, cleaning our weapons, and getting our gear in order. 'Course we'll have to provide pickets and the regular details, but we probably won't see any action. And we're supposed to get re-supplied too."

"Good!" said Moses. "I'm gonna clean my weapon and go back out there and shoot that damn dog that snapped at me today."

"You mean that dog at that cabin on the other side of the ridge?" asked Mike.

"Yeah, that's him. The preacher wouldn't let me shoot him this morning. He said I might need that round for something else. But since we're gonna get re-supplied tomorrow that won't be a problem, will it, Preacher?"

The preacher didn't answer, but Mike said, "Well, if you're talking about that dog at the cabin, you can save yourself the trouble. One of our boys done shot him."

Moses laughed and said, "Who was it? I need to shake his hand next time I see him."

"It was Powers. He said he don't take that shit off no Confederate cur and he sure ain't gonna take it off no Union son of a bitch."

The preacher said, "You mean they shot that poor old dog for just guarding his master's home, just for doing his job?"

"Hell yes!" Mike said. "And when the man fussed at him, Powers told him that if the dog had bit him he'd a shot him too. The man's wife cussed us till we were out of sight. Powers wanted to go back and shoot her, but they wouldn't let him. And, Preacher, about that dog—you might not know it, but right here in the Fifth, Company A's little dog got killed first thing this morning. We came across his carcass when we were coming up behind them. We reckoned we sorta owed 'em one."

The preacher said, "No, I didn't know about Company A's dog. That's too bad. He was a cute little fella. But I still say we have better things to do than to spend thirty days marching north to shoot a dog."

Ignoring the preacher, Moses said, "Powers sounds like my kind of man. You gotta introduce me to him sometime tomorrow."

"Well," Mike said, "that'll be sorta hard to do."

"Why's that?"

"Because he got captured with the general and a couple hundred other men."

"Yeah," the preacher said, "we think at least one of our men got captured too."

"Well," Mike said, "I gotta finish my rounds. So y'all just take it easy tonight and tomorrow."

"Take it easy?" Moses said. "We've got picket duty and grave-digging duty."

"I hate it, man, but we're digging latrines. I gotta go. I'll see y'all in the morning."

After he was gone, Waller said, "We must have really taken a lickin' today for them to hold us in reserve."

"Nah," said Moses. "They're just saving us for the really tough stuff, and I'm glad the Thirteenth shot that dog. But you should'a let me do it, Preacher. By all rights, I should have been the one."

"You just love to kill, don't you, Moses?" the preacher said.

"Hell yes! It's my damn job, and it's yours too."

"It's not our job to waste a round on a dog. You shouldn't take any life unnecessarily," the preacher said. "One of these days, Jack, you're going to find yourself standing before an angry God trying to explain why you destroyed so many things He so lovingly created. Someday, the Lord is going to reckon with you. He's going to settle your hash."

Moses's countenance darkened as he took a few steps toward the preacher.

His voice quiet with anger, he said, "Is that the same Lord that let all those men die today? Is that the same Lord that lets

Box go without shoes? Is that the same Lord that let me watch my mama get her brains kicked out when I was just a yard kid? Is that the Lord you're talking about?"

Then he walked to within inches of the preacher, glared down into his eyes, and said, "You can tell that Lord to kiss my bad ass."

He glowered a few seconds more, but the preacher did not flinch.

"I don't have to tell Him," the preacher said. "He heard you loud and clear. You can't hold God responsible for the sins of man. Sooner or later, He's going to show you the light, son."

As Moses broke his gaze and moved away, he grabbed his weapon and his ammunition and said as he stalked out of the camp, "I ain't your goddamn son. I ain't no man's son. Come on, Waller. Let's get our picket duty done."

Night Funerals

In the dark, with the trail illuminated by the company's only lantern, they made their way to the place Sonny had died. Kirby carried the lantern and led as Silas followed, and behind him, the preacher, just the three of them carrying shovels. They could see the lanterns of burial details from other units spread out to the north. They looked like fireflies or what Kirby called lightning bugs in a meadow. The moon soon rose full and bright between the clouds, and more groups ventured into the night searching for their fallen friends—Archer's Brigade, warriors from Alabama and Tennessee burying their own in a far land.

It took a little while to get there, but eventually Kirby said, "Here he is."

He held the lantern over the boy's corpse, which was lying face down with his head turned slightly to one side and with his rifle under him, still in his hands. Kirby and the preacher were silent as they all removed their hats, and Silas wept over his friend.

Finally, Silas got his grief under control, and the preacher asked, "How long had y'all known each other?"

"Always," Silas said. "We've been friends further back than we can remember, since we were babies. Our parents are friends. We grew up in the same neighborhood, in the same school, in the same church. Neither of us had any brothers. We were each other's brother, our only brother."

"What was his faith?"

"He was Christian," Silas said.

"No, I mean what was his … oh well, I reckon that's all that matters," the preacher said.

"He was Episcopalian like me."

"Well," the preacher said, "now he has joined countless thousands of other boys who died as men in a war somewhere in history and before history even began. But that doesn't lessen the loss or the grief."

"It should've been me," Silas said.

"No, son," the preacher said. "Don't say that. It shouldn't have been anybody."

"He was a soldier, Preacher. Me? I'm just a little piss-ant like Moses said, a useless one."

"That's just not true, Silas," the preacher said. "We all had to get used to combat at one time or another. It's still new to you. You'll adjust to it. You did better this afternoon. Come on, y'all. Let's turn him over. We need to collect his things."

The preacher tugged at the body and said, "He's already pretty stiff. Help me, Silas. We need to get his weapon and ammunition. We need his kit and especially his shoes and socks. They're too big for Box, but they'll fit somebody. And we need his trousers too."

"Oh no, Preacher," Silas said. "Don't take his trousers."

"We need them, son. He won't mind."

"He's a Southern boy. He won't mind going home with no shoes, but please don't take his trousers," Silas begged.

"Listen, Silas. We've got men in rags. In rags! He has the best uniform in the company, along with you. We need those pants," the preacher said. "I've got orders to bring back anything of use."

He looked into the boy's pleading eyes and slowly turned toward Kirby, who was looking at the ground.

After a few seconds, and without looking up, Kirby said, "I won't say nothin'."

There was silence for a while as the preacher struggled with himself. But finally he sighed and said, "Okay. He keeps his trousers. Some soldier I am. Come on, Silas. Help me turn him over."

Silas was hesitating.

Kirby said, "Here, Silas. You hold the lantern. I'll help the preacher."

They rolled him over on his back. His eyes were closed. The look on his face was one of almost pleasant surprise. There was a small, nearly bloodless wound in his chest. It was clear that he had died instantly. They took what they needed, and Kirby began making the outline of a grave next to him with his shovel.

Silas said, "Preacher, do you think we could move him out of this field into those trees?"

"We usually bury them where they fall."

"I know, but this field will be plowed each year, and they'll sow their crops and..."

"Sure, Silas," Kirby said. "Come on, Preacher. You grab him under his arms, and I'll get his legs. Silas, you carry the shovels and the lantern. We can leave his weapon and stuff here for now and pick them up when we're through."

With the preacher and Kirby serving as pallbearers, Silas led the sad procession to the trees, where they found a suitable plot among some pines. As they dug the grave, Silas spoke through his tears.

"When we were little, we would make junky little row boats with our friends. They were called bateaus, and they were leaky and dangerous. Our parents—except for Sonny's, who didn't mind for some reason—forbade us to build them. So, of course, we built them. And then we would lie to our folks about it, except for Sonny. I don't think he ever told a real lie, just little white ones. You know, like when you tell some old lady how nice she looks when really she doesn't. That's about the only kind of lie Sonny ever told.

"One day," he continued, "we had been out in one of those bateaus, about five or six of us, and we had left it down by the water, and we were running home. We ran into my backyard and bumped into my mother, who was hanging out clothes. She saw that our pants were wet and said, 'Have y'all been in one of those bateaus, again?' We all lied and denied it. Then Sonny came running up. He was fat and slow back then, but he got lean and hard later on.

"My mother knew Sonny wouldn't tell a lie. She said, 'Sonny Simon, have y'all been building bateaus again?' Sonny didn't say anything for a little while. Then we all looked back at him. He had tears streaming down his face, and very quietly, he said, 'Yes, ma'am.' My mother just told everybody to run on home. She never said anything to anybody about it, and we never built any more bateaus. That was a long time ago, maybe four or five years."

After a few more seconds, Silas added, "He was the best of us."

They reverently placed the barefoot boy in his grave and buried him with his arms crossed over his chest and his Rebel cap over his face. Closing the grave was especially difficult for Silas, but he did it like a man. They hid the grave with pine straw and leaves.

Before they started back, they removed their hats, and the preacher said, "Dear Lord above, thank You for welcoming this good boy into Your kingdom. Comfort us in our grief, and, Lord, be with his family. Forgive us our countless failings. We pray and ask these things in the name of Jesus, our Savior. Amen."

And the others said, "Amen."

As the preacher and Kirby walked away, a quietly sobbing Silas quickly placed a few small stones at the head of Sonny's grave and left him there, his friend from infancy, his only brother, the best of them. His own life yet to live—his death to die—he didn't look back. He shouldered his shovel and followed the others.

The grave of Jean Rameau Simon was lost and never found. He rests there to this day in the lap of Mother Earth, alone amid his pines. Still, his soul is far away, forever found in a fair and happy land.

They were making their way back to the encampment when suddenly a weak voice came out of the dark.

"Johnny! Johnny Reb!"

"Where are you?" the preacher said.

"Over here. Don't shoot, boys. I can't hurt you. I'm dying."

They soon found a Yankee cavalryman in the dark.

"All I want is a drink of water. I'm dying for a swig. I crawled up here from the road. I hid in the underbrush till y'all left this evening. Your pickets don't even know I'm here. Have mercy on me, boys. I don't have no fight left in me," the Yank said.

The preacher knelt beside him with the lantern to look at his wounds. "We can take you to our field surgeon."

"No, no. Please don't move me. I'm done for. I'm all tore up. I've plumb nearly bled out. If you can just give me a drink of water," the man said, his voice dry and raspy.

"Sure, son," the preacher said as he put down the lantern and gently held a canteen to the man's lips.

He drank desperately and stopped only to breathe.

Then the Yank said, as he coughed and strangled a little on the water, "God bless you, brother. That's fine stuff."

Kirby knelt on the other side of the man and said, "Say, Yank, you don't sound like no northern boy. Where are you from?"

"Alabama. Winston County, Alabama."

"Damn!" Kirby said, "A free state man!"

"A what?" Silas asked. "What's a free state man?"

"Don't you remember?" Kirby said, "When Alabama seceded from the Union, Winston County seceded from Alabama. They called themselves the Free State of Winston. Most of the Winston

County men went north to fight for the damn Yankee army. A lot of them ended up in the cavalry, like this man, because they were good horsemen."

Silas looked down into the man's eyes and saw what he thought was a touch of shame.

The cavalryman said, "I hate it, boys. I just did what I thought was right. I hope y'all can forgive me. If you wait around a few minutes, I reckon you can collect my stuff too."

"We can collect your damn stuff whenever we feel like it," Kirby said angrily.

"At ease, Owen," the preacher said. Then, looking back down at the cavalryman, he gently said, "There's nothing to forgive, son. Who knows who needs forgiving? That's Jesus's job. And you don't have to worry about us collecting your stuff. Like you said, you bled out all over it. Nobody would have it, not even your boots. You'll get to go home fully clothed. Now, what can we do to make you comfortable?"

"If you could just put something under my head," he said, and then sounding as if he were requesting a great illicit pleasure he added, "and leave me with a full canteen."

Silas quickly put Sonny's kit under his head as a pillow.

"Here's a canteen full of cold, clear creek water," the preacher said as he placed it in the man's arms. "Now, what else can we do?"

The man hugged the canteen up close to him as if it were gold and said, "Can you pray for me? Any of y'all praying men?"

"Are you a God-fearing man?" the preacher asked.

"Yes, sir, a Christian saved by Jesus's sweet grace. But I'm afraid I ain't much of one. I fell far short of the mark."

"God bless you, son," the preacher said. "Yes, we're praying men."

"All my Winston County friends are dead," the man said. "I'm the last one. Soon, we'll all be gone. Soon, we'll all be together again I reckon."

The preacher took the man's hand in both of his hands and said, "Let's pray, son."

"Thank you, sir," the man said.

Kirby and Silas were both kneeling as the preacher began, "Our Father in heaven, forgive us our grievous sins, and hear my prayer for this sorrowful sinner who is about to enter Your kingdom. Bless him, Lord. Comfort this poor boy from Alabama who is dying so far from home. Ease his pain and clear his path to Your happy land. Let this humble soldier leave in peace. He's seen enough war. We all have. Take him home, Lord. Give him eternal peace and joy." The preacher paused. "Forgive my unworthiness, for I'm asking these things for this man in the sweet name of Jesus, our precious Savior. Amen."

Kirby and Swann said, "Amen."

They opened their eyes and realized the man had passed on during the prayer.

"Bless his poor old heart," the preacher said. "I felt him leave while I was holding his hand. He's home now. He's home."

As the preacher tenderly folded the man's arms across his chest, Kirby said, "Silas, the Bible says the Lord hears the fervent prayers of a righteous man. I reckon we've just seen proof of that. Come on, y'all. We've got strength to dig one more grave for a poor Alabama boy."

Not another word was spoken as they buried the cavalryman with his canteen by his side. When it was done, they removed their hats, and the preacher said, "Be at peace, son."

Their lantern depleted, they silently returned to camp by the light of a mournful moon. Exhausted and weeping, Silas got off to himself and thought, *If ever there is a day in my life worse than this one, it will be the day I die.*

Fatigue overtook him, and he fell asleep. He slept fitfully and dreamt of war. Finally, just before reveille, he had a sweet dream of home: he and Sonny, with their families about them. He awoke and for a few seconds thought he was there. When the hard truth fell in on him, he began the new day as he had ended the old one—in bitter tears.

THURSDAY, JULY 2ND

The Fredericksburg Story

On the second day of battle, Harry Heth's division, which included the Fifth and the rest of Archer's Brigade, was held in reserve west of Herr Ridge while fighting raged in the distance in and around the town. Silas, the preacher, and some others were sitting around talking and working on their gear. A few men were bathing in a tiny creek the name of which no one knew, and others were cleaning their weapons.

Silas did not clean his. He knew, without the preacher telling him, not to clean a loaded weapon. A man from another squad, just relieved from picket duty, was walking past the group. He stopped to relay a rumor that the next day would see a massive frontal assault on Cemetery Ridge. Archer's Brigade and several other units, about twelve to fifteen thousand men in all, would charge up the slopes toward the Yankee middle. After he left, the group was silent for a while, each man pretending to be deeply involved with whatever piece of equipment he was working on.

Finally, someone said, "Y'all remember Fredericksburg."

It was not a question but, rather, a statement. The others were quiet. They had learned over the last two years that rumors, the bad ones at least, were usually accurate. All of them had seen frontal assaults from both sides. They knew more than they wanted to know about them, except for Silas. The only action he had seen was yesterday's. That was bad enough, but at least most of the outfit had survived. With a massive frontal assault up a long, sloping stretch of heavily defended open ground such as Cemetery Ridge, there was the real possibility that the Fifth would no longer exist after tomorrow.

Silas said, "What about Fredericksburg? Tell me about it. I wasn't there."

Still no one spoke. They just worked more diligently on their equipment.

Finally, the preacher said, "The Battle of Fredericksburg, last December."

Silas waited a few seconds for the preacher to continue.

When it was apparent that he had said all he intended to say, Silas added, "Well, I know there was a big battle there and that we won, but that's about all I know. Could one of you tell me about it?"

There was more silence as the men looked at each other as if they were deciding who would relay the story to him.

Finally, the preacher put down what he was doing and said, "Son, it wasn't just a battle, it was also a slaughter." A few seconds later, he added, "Thanks to a lot of brave Yankee soldiers," and after another pause, "and some pretty stupid Yankee commanders."

"Will you tell me about it, Preacher?" Silas quietly asked.

After a few seconds of contemplation, the preacher said, "Do you? Do you really need to know? I don't know if you do or not. I reckon you do have a right to know about what happened then and what's going to happen tomorrow. But I'm not so sure you really need to. Anyway, here it is.

"Even though we won, I'm not exactly filled with pride when I think of Fredericksburg. We lost some good men in mortal combat there, and the Yankees just threw a bunch of theirs away. Let's see. It seems like a long time ago now, don't it, boys?"

1. Davis
2. Brockenbrough
3. Pettigrew
4. Archer
5. Ramseur
6. Iverson
7. Doles
8. Gordon
9. Perrin, Lane
10. Scales, Mahone, Thomas
11. Posey
12. Wright
13. Lang
14. Wilcox
15. Wofford, Barksdale
16. Semmes
17. Kershaw
18. G.T. Anderson
19. Robertson
20. Benning
21. Law
22. Gibbon
23. Eleventh Corps
24. First Corps
25. Twelfth Corps
26. Crawford (Sykes)
27. Ayres (Sykes)
28. Nevin
29. Jenkins
30. Stuart
31. Williams, Smith
32. Steuart
33. Walker
34. Jones
35. Carr
36. Brewster
37. Graham
38. de Trobriand
39. Ward

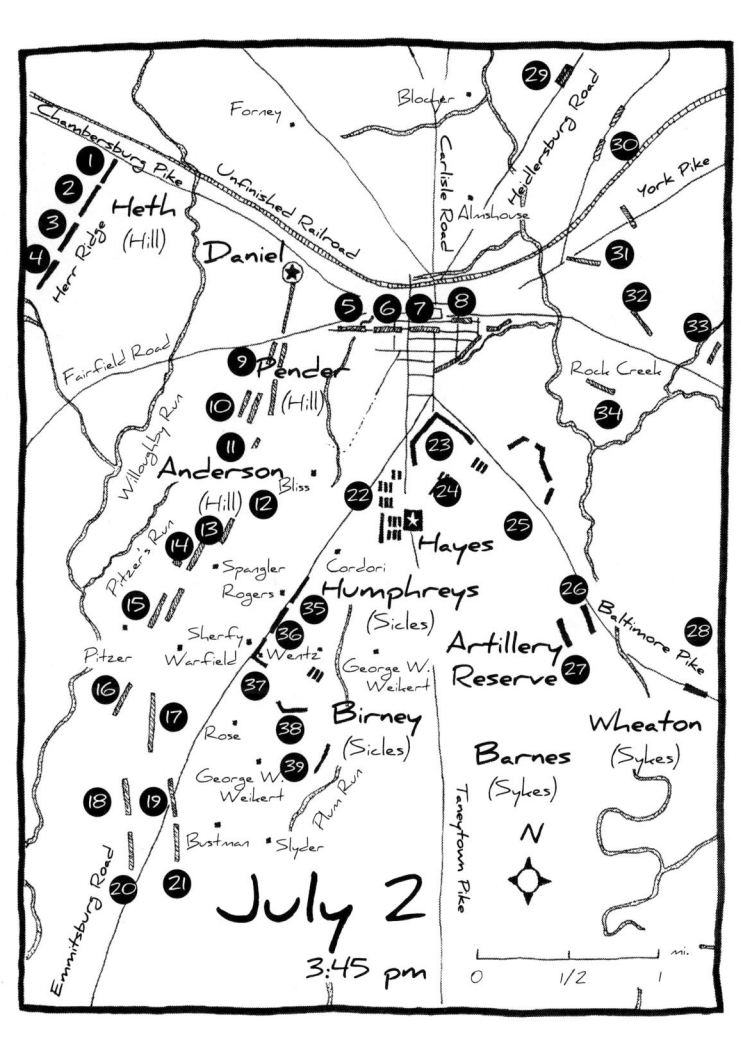

They all nodded.

"But it wasn't quite seven months ago. I remember it was mighty cold at night, freezing. A lot of southern boys got to see snow for the first time. But the thing I remember most is how those Yankees kept coming and how we kept cutting them down. A lot of our barefoot boys had shoes after that battle. Not that I didn't already suspect it, but that was the battle that convinced me for all time that war is a truly great sin. To this day, I still cringe with shame when I think of all the good men I slew that day." He paused and quietly said, "God, forgive me."

The preacher went on to tell Silas how the Confederate infantry was situated at the foot of a hill in a sunken road that provided good cover. Their artillery was behind them at the top of the hill.

He went on. "They came at us six times. They'd line up a few thousand men and make a rush at us, their flags flying. Our artillery would work them over first, and then we would take our turn at them from the road. They could barely touch us, but we killed them by the thousands."

Loathing to continue, he said, "By the time they made their last charge, our artillery was out of ammunition, so they got a lot closer to us than on their first five tries. It didn't make any difference. When they got in range, we knocked them down in the same old way. Some of our men were so sick of killing them that they swore at them and shouted for them to turn around. They kept coming—brave men, those Yanks. After all, they're Americans like us.

"That last charge ended with several hundred more dead or dying men in front of us and a bunch more running back to their lines. But there was this one skinny little flag bearer, just a kid, who kept coming. I don't think he even knew that nobody was behind him, that he was alone. I reckon everybody was just so tired of killing that nobody had enough hate left in them to shoot such a brave little feller who was carrying nothing but a flag. He marched right up to the muzzles of our rifles and stopped. We were cheering, partly because of our victory and also because he had walked unscratched through all that lead.

"Then an officer, a lieutenant from the Thirteenth, walked up and quieted the men. He looked at the little Yank and said, 'Congratulations, private. We surrender.' We all laughed real good. After all that slaughter, it felt good to laugh a little and to let that boy live."

"Then the officer said, 'Turn around, son. Go on back to your lines. We won't bother you. Go on now.'"

The preacher told how the boy did not budge. Tears began flowing down his cheeks as he stood, staring over the heads of the enemy who were standing in the sunken road. The hearts of the officer and most of the men went out to the boy when they saw his tears.

The preacher recalled how the officer gently said, "You did your duty, son. It takes a brave man to carry a stick into a gunfight. You've done yourself proud. You've honored your country and your outfit. Hell, son, you've even honored us. You're a worthy foe. Now turn around and live. Live so you can tell your grandchildren what you did today. Nobody else will believe you. Go on now. You'll be just fine. You'll have other opportunities to die. We all will."

He told Silas how the young trooper saluted and did a slow about face. Tears still flowing, flag still flying, he began his long, lonely march back to his lines, through the scattered bodies of his friends.

Silas sat motionless as the preacher's story continued to unfold.

"'And hold that flag high,' the officer shouted. Then more quietly, he said, 'She's a good one. We loved her once ourselves.'

"About that time," the preacher recalled, "Moses appeared. He had seen the officer talking to the young Yank from his position a couple of hundred feet away. Coming as fast as he could, he loaded his rifle on the way. Arriving shortly after the man told the Yank to hold his flag high, he trotted up next to the officer and took a bead on the boy's back.

"The officer immediately pulled and cocked his navy Colt and put it to Moses's temple saying, 'Let that hammer down real slow, mister, or you'll never see him fall.'

"For a few seconds, nothing happened. Then the officer quietly added, 'I mean it.'

"Moses slowly lowered his rifle, let the hammer down easy, and asked, 'Sir, whose side are you on?'

"'That man was promised safe passage,' the officer replied.

"'He's a blue belly, and our job is to kill as many as we can. I'm pretty clear on that, sir,' Moses said. 'But I ain't too sure about you. Maybe you should ask your commanding officer … '

"'At ease, private,' the officer angrily interrupted. 'What's your name?'

"'Moses.'

"'Oh, yeah. I've heard about you. Now get back in place.'

"'Yes sir. 'Fore I go, I think you should know that the next time you pull that pistol on me, it'll get used on somebody.'

"'Are you trying to get tossed in the stockade, talking to a superior like that?'

"'No sir, but we won't be in the army forever. Someday we'll be equals again. When that day comes, it would serve an officer like you well to watch his back.'

"The officer laughed and said, 'Hell, man, we'll never live that long. We'll both be in the army for the rest of our lives.'

"'That might be true about you, sir, especially considering your confusion about what to do with bluebellies. As for me, I'm going to die an old man, a rich old man.'

"The lieutenant had heard enough. He said, 'Moses, you're a wicked, worthless bastard.'

"'I don't deny being a wicked bastard, sir; kinda proud of it. But I'm worth a sight more as a soldier than any of you because I know my job is to kill Yankees, and I'm damn good at it.'

"Moses smiled wryly, and the officer said, 'I don't care how many Yankees you kill. You're a disgrace to the South.'

"Then someone said, 'He's gone, sir. We can't see him anymore.'

"'Good,' the officer said. 'He made it.'

"'We'll see him again,' Moses said. 'One of these men will probably die because you let him live.'

"'Or perhaps someone will live because we let him live. Now get your surly ass out of my sight.'

"Moses, hoping to intimidate the man, continued to glower at him. His reputation for unbridled evil would have caused many men to blink. The young officer, being a man with a true heart and having some time back given himself up for dead, gazed unwaveringly back at him. Then Moses, smiling again, turned and began the walk back to his position."

The preacher continued and told Silas, "The next night, the sky was all lit up with something they called the northern lights."

"The aurora borealis," Silas said.

"There were red and white streamers flashing through the sky," the preacher said. "It was like nothing we had ever seen before. A lot of the men took it to mean God was celebrating our victory. I never felt that good about it."

The preacher then resumed cleaning his weapon. As Silas went back to working on his gear, he found himself wishing he had not pressed the man on the subject of Fredericksburg. He thought that maybe he would have been better off not knowing so much about frontal assaults.

Even though ignorance isn't really bliss, he mused, *there may be times when it is less daunting than enlightenment.*

Moses

After the preacher's story, Silas could not help wondering about Moses, his background and what made him the way he was. Silas, indeed none of the men, had ever known anyone like Moses. They were convinced he was unique in his callous toughness and his love of things wicked. They knew his reputation, but they knew very little about his early years in the forests around the Ohatchee area of Calhoun County. There was no one close to him to tell them. He had no friends, just enemies.

Wiley Jackson Moses never knew his father and barely remembered his mother, who died in a backwoods barroom brawl when he was five. When he watched her die on the dirt floor of that dark tavern his childhood ended, and his manhood began. He was taken in by an angry, drunken woodsman who had no woman and, in the sturdy little boy, saw someone to work and do chores.

When the boy was old enough, he followed the man into the forest to take up a man's work. He learned to swing an ax and fell trees with formidable skill.

The man gave him room and board and a backwoods education for his labor. That was all he gave him, except for his own dark, malignant spirit. There was no father in the man, no love, no kindness or joy, just anger and hate, and he reared the boy that way.

The beatings did not come very often, but when they did, they were rough. Having no place to go, the boy did not run away. Biding his time, he had a plan. Waiting for his day to come, he would leave when the time was right.

Unsure of his birth date, he figured he was about fourteen years old when the man came at him, once more, full of whiskey and rage. Even though the boy himself did not yet know it, he was already one fell fighter, and he was without doubt or fear. His day had arrived.

The man-sized boy easily deflected the first drunken swing with his left and sent his right fist crashing into the man's face with everything he had, sending him across the dark room. He pounced on the man like a bobcat on a rabbit, and with an animal savagery that came as naturally to him as breathing, he sent pile-driving blows into the man's face as quickly as they could be delivered.

It was over in seconds, and the man was an unconscious, bloody pulp on the floor. The boy casually urinated in his battered face and left, taking the best ax with him. He figured he had earned it.

He went to work for one of the man's competitors but quickly learned he was not suited to taking orders from anyone. So he was his own man at sixteen. Before leaving his employer, he managed to learn enough about reading and math to protect himself from shady sawmill men. No one dared cheat him.

By the time he was twenty, the woods of northeast Alabama were full of grim, hard woodsmen and trappers. He was generally acknowledged by everyone who knew him and most who had only heard of him as the toughest, most relentlessly ruthless beast in the forest.

He didn't drink; he didn't like being impaired. He didn't smoke; there was no profit in it. And as he liked to say, he just cussed a little bit. Truth is he didn't talk much at all back then. He was truly a man of few words. He didn't take any guff off anybody, man or woman. Just an offending glance could earn a man a thrashing quicker than he could explain or apologize. More than once, a man had simply disappeared after having a serious disagreement with him. The law pretty much left the woodsmen to themselves.

Even though he had had several women, he never loved one, and they were all too frightened of him to love him. And besides, none of his women were the loving kind.

Wiley Jack, as he was known, was not brave or courageous, just fearless. He did not fear man, death, or hell—or God. A lean, hard, six-feet-four inches and 250 pounds of cold, heartless steel with a mind as sharp as his ax, and limbs as strong as the trees he felled, he was a giant in his time. Though he thought of himself as the equal of Satan, he was, in truth, owned by the beast and driven by the forces of hell. He was a bad man.

Calm Waters

The rumor of the next day's action had further quieted the spirits of the men. The men of Silas's squad, having recently been reminded of their experience at Fredericksburg, were especially somber. Silas, though he did not see that action firsthand, was also subdued. The previous day's action, his only combat, had been terrifying for him and heartbreaking, the worst day of his young life. He had never seen violent death up close until then. It had put a pall on his spirit.

The men were finishing supper. Distant sounds of battle had subsided. The men in gray had suffered greatly but had performed well, and many considered this a day of victory for the South. The men in blue, however, still held the high ground. Cemetery Ridge glowered down on the Rebels.

Silas had not eaten much. He just did not have an appetite in the face of the morrow. He stared at his mostly uneaten supper and thought about what a fool he was. When he had joined the army against his parents' wishes, he had imagined military life as a great, rollicking adventure, with him and his friends rushing here and there, hooting and hollering as they fired their weapons at a distant, ever-fleeing foe. Until recently, it had not occurred to him that the enemy would not always be fleeing or distant or that he may actually feel a bayonet or bullet enter his body—that he might die. He was, after all, a boy. He was a boy becoming a man the hard way. War was painfully dragging him into manhood.

Silas quietly conceded that he was silly and that his parents were wise. This too was something he had never seriously considered. If only he could go back a few months and undo his enlistment and Sonny's. If only he had listened to his father, to his mother.

From a few campfires away, he heard the sound of a string band gently wafting his way. The instrumentation so common in the hills—guitar, banjo, fiddle, and perhaps a mandolin—

sounded foreign to him. But some of the tunes were familiar: "Amazing Grace," "Jesus Keep Me Near the Cross," and a few others. The music both comforted and haunted him.

Hiding his tears, Silas wept secretly. He wanted his mother, just a kind word from her, or a pat on the back from his father. So homesick and lonesome, and so disappointed in himself, he felt like the prodigal son. But unlike that fortunate lad, he could not get up out of the pig wallow and walk home. Even though many a man in both armies had done that very thing—had gone over the hill, deserted—he could not. His honor wouldn't allow it. He thought it ironic that one could be an honorable coward. Little did he know that most of the men were like him, gripped with fear and bound by honor. His brothers numbered in the tens of thousands and wore both blue and gray. Not knowing this, and with Sonny gone, he felt abandoned. He would feel better if somehow he could talk to Sonny. But he knew a lifetime of consoling conversations was over. He would never hear that voice again. He thought about the shoes hidden in his kit, a gift from his mother. But instead of reminding him of her, they led him only to Box's dirty feet. Silas was approaching the point that most of the men had reached some time back. Having lost faith in life, he was giving himself up for dead. Every way he turned, solace eluded him. Finally, realizing where his last hope lay, he turned toward prayer.

He put down his food and knelt by a tree, one hand on the trunk, the other over his eyes. Tears flowing without shame, he prayed silently.

"Dear Lord, forgive my foolishness. If it is Your will, Lord, please let this cup pass from me. Yet, Your will be done. Help me with my cowardice. Give me the courage to face my fate. Please, send me a Sonny. I need a friend so much. Jesus, comfort me. Strengthen my spirit. Help me conduct myself as You would have me to. Forgive my sins and unworthiness. Dear Lord, please help me. Accept my gratitude for Your countless blessings. In Your precious name, I pray. Amen."

The other men made no comment. The sight of a man praying was not unusual, tears only a little more so. After a moment, he stood and wiped his face on his sleeve. If they thought less of him, it would just have to be. He would never apologize for praying. But no one thought any less of him—no one that mattered. If Box or Moses had seen him, they would have thought poorly of him, but they thought poorly of him anyway. He no longer cared what they thought.

As he stood there wiping his eyes and his nose, he realized that no one had taken much note of him. Perhaps they wouldn't make anything of it. Then he saw another man stepping away from the group to pray alone. Already he felt a little better. Prayer always comforted him. His prayers didn't always receive the answers he liked, but talking to a loving God never failed to ease his worry. Whether he was sailing on a sea of silliness or on one of despair, there was something about humbling himself before the Lord that always calmed the waters and steadied his ship.

Silas had once thought that he was in the army to enjoy a great adventure and defend his country. He was not sure anymore. Perhaps God had a reason for him to be there. Whatever the reason, whether foolhardiness or divine design, he was resolved to live—and if necessary, die—with Christian honor.

Little and frail, Silas was not a physically strong person. He didn't have great physical courage, being fearful of injury and death. Yet he was strong in the Lord. This made him more of a man than he could have ever been otherwise. In spite of his apparent weaknesses, he had strength no one could see, for deep in his heart lived Jesus.

Red-haired Stepchild

After dark, the men not on duty were sitting around talking, but their secret thoughts were on the dreaded morrow. The subject slowly came around to why they were there, so far from home, and why they were fighting.

One of the men said, "I was against secession, but when Lincoln started talking about invading us, I decided I needed to fight. I don't want a bunch of Yankees, or anybody else for that matter, telling me how to live."

Another said, "You know, I ain't all that hot to keep slavery, but the thought of a few million darkies running loose in the land does scare me more than just a little."

Silas listened. He and his family had always been opposed to slavery. They had owned a few slaves, but those were purchased only so they could be freed. Silas's father would occasionally, every few years, buy a slave or a small family of them and allow them to earn their freedom. He would employ them either in his business or in his home. He would pay a salary, part of which would be paid in cash and part of which would be applied to the cost of their purchase. He always provided food and shelter. They would live in a little cottage in the Swanns' backyard and eat from their kitchen.

A free black woman was living with the Swanns now. She had long ago earned her freedom but stayed on as a domestic. Much more than a maid, she was a member of the family and had helped rear Silas and his sister. She had her own room in the house, and everyone, even Mr. and Mrs. Swann, did pretty much as she said. She was the eldest of them. Her name was Mahaley.

Most white Southerners supported slavery, or at the very least did not openly object to it, the Swanns being an exception. Most weren't bad people. When one is born and reared in a society that condones a thing, it is often difficult to see that thing for what it really is. It sometimes takes an outsider, even a hypocritical one, to show one the light.

Most Southerners didn't own a slave, at least in part because they couldn't afford one, and many because they didn't want to be the cause of some poor soul's misery. The average Southerner was hard-pressed to keep his own body and soul together while providing for his family. Buying and supporting another person was simply beyond his means. Only about one white Southerner in twenty actually owned a slave. Perhaps one in four was part of a family in which someone owned a slave.

The expense involved in purchasing and maintaining another human being was why Silas's father required his slaves to earn their freedom. Even though he was prosperous, he was not wealthy enough to make large outlays of money with no prospect of reimbursement. He would have soon been out of business, and his little freedom trail would have dried up.

The Swanns' slaves lived virtually as free men. They could come and go as they pleased as long as they showed up for work, were home by a reasonable hour, stayed out of trouble, and conducted themselves in a circumspect manner in the community. Mr. Swann encouraged them to go to church. He also taught them to manage their finances.

Most people who had large numbers of slaves, people such as plantation owners, were vastly wealthy. Many of them had acquired most of their slaves through inheritance and birth rather than through purchase.

Yet most people tolerated slavery though their own impoverished circumstances were only worsened by its presence in their society and economy. The slaves had been there almost as far back as their societal memory went. Like it or not, they couldn't imagine their world without slavery, and the prospects of holding their society together without it frightened them.

Hatred for the Negro was not significantly more common in the South than in those parts of the North that had a substantial Negro population. There was a noisy minority, such as

Box and Moses, who boasted of their hatred and had nurtured it throughout their lives. However, average Southerners took the teachings of Jesus seriously. They believed in treating others as they would like to be treated. They believed that anger was a natural thing bound to happen from time to time, but to allow it to turn to hate was a great sin. To nurse that hate along so as to keep it seething indefinitely was an even greater one.

Even though the poor, white Southerner was only slightly better off materially than the slave, he would never have traded places with him. He valued his freedom. Sometimes, it seemed his primary freedom was to watch his family starve while slaves always appeared to have enough to eat. But then he was also free to leave, to go where he pleased when it suited him. The love of that one thing—the freedom to wander, the right to roam—is ingrained in the American soul as much as any other. He might never have traveled more than ten miles from his birthplace, but knowing that he could meant everything to him. The choice was his. That is what the white Southerner had and cherished almost above all else, and that is what the Negro longed for.

Slavery never really prospered in the North. Some say it was because the African could not flourish in the cold climate and dark factories there as he did in the sunny fields of the South. Others would say it was because of the moral and religious superiority of the North. The Southerners doubted that. During the war and Reconstruction, they would discover that it was, indeed, a myth. The North turned against slavery when it was discovered not to be as profitable there as in the South. Southern states banned the import of additional Africans, and Congress outlawed it in 1808. This dried up the golden triangle of the slave trade that had made so many Yankees wealthy. No matter; they were now rich and powerful. They would use the very wealth and power gleaned from their miserable trade to turn themselves into gleaming crusaders against the world's most despicable institution. At last, they were at least pretending to see the light. This was the perception in the South.

The Southerner knew he was not solely responsible for slavery. He knew the Northerner was also culpable, not to mention the African still in Africa who sold untold numbers of his brothers and sisters to the Yankee slavers. When the North began to look accusingly southward, the Southerner saw through the hypocrisy. What had been mere tolerance of slavery began to change, in many a Southern mind, to reluctant support as they came together in moral and political self-defense. The North, through the good fortune of a cold climate over a warm one and industry over agriculture, and not through moral superiority, found itself occupying the moral high ground. So the South, due to its gentle weather and agrarian culture, its own character flaws and the character flaws of others, found itself in what appeared to most people outside her borders to be a morally indefensible position. From then on, she would be the world's red-haired stepchild. She would pay dearly for her faults: the destruction of war; the further destruction and plunder of her natural resources during what was ironically called Reconstruction, and her apparent, everlasting economic and political subjugation by the North. Of all those responsible for slavery, only the Southerner would be punished. The African slaver would be benignly neglected, while the Yankee slave trader would be granted virtual sainthood.

It was common knowledge in the South that either New York or Boston was the homeport of every American slave ship. The Southerner was even further convinced of Northern hypocrisy knowing the slaves in the Union were not freed during the war. Then President Lincoln issued the Emancipation Proclamation, which supposedly freed the slaves in the South but kept in chains the slaves in the Union as well as those in the parts of the Confederacy already conquered. The Emancipation Proclamation was, to the Southerner, a transparent political ploy to strengthen the myth of Northern moral superiority and Southern decadence. In the South, it gave the impression, whether true or not, that the North's concern for the Negro was largely false.

Eighty years earlier, the Northerner and Southerner united in their struggle for independence. Whether they supported it or not, both also fought for slavery. The Confederate soldier, when he fought for the independence of the South, its liberty, its honor, its very existence, and when he fought in defense of his home against the invading Northerner, he also fought for slavery. Even though slavery lived for more than eighty years under the American flag and for several months in the Union after it had died in the South, only the Southerner and his revered bonnie blue flag would be remembered as racist.

Eccentrics

Silas had been reared to love and respect his fellow man regardless of color. He took Jesus literally when he said to do to others as you would have them do to you. Silas's family was part of Mobile's genteel upper crust. The Swanns weren't of the old family moneyed set, but Mr. Paul Swann was a very successful merchant and entrepreneur. His unwavering honesty, his noble demeanor, and his Christian kindness earned him the respect of all classes.

Mrs. Swann also was held in high regard. Everyone—white or black, rich or poor—felt at ease in her presence. She was strong willed and universally kind. It didn't hurt that she was also a great natural beauty.

The Swanns counted among their friends the elite of Mobile society, people who thought owning a slave to be almost as natural as owning a horse. They quietly considered the Swanns an eccentric lot for their beliefs regarding slavery, but Southerners love eccentrics. Every little Southern town has at least one or yearns to. The normal citizens roll their eyes and cluck their tongues when discussing them, but they wouldn't give them up for anything. A village without a bizarre citizen or two can be a dull place indeed. The Swanns were more than just eccentrics; they were also respected and loved.

Silas, living in a fairly large town, did not see much of the worst of slavery. Most of the black people he encountered were what they called "house help." They lived relatively comfortable lives compared to the "field hands" who toiled on the farms and plantations. But whether they were worked into an early grave in the Black Belt of south Alabama or doted on in their old age by a family of white folks they helped rear, they were still slaves.

Countless dark-skinned children were born into a world that denied them any hopes or dreams. They would live a life, whether long or short, in which their greatest aspiration was to be well-treated by their master. Many of them would not have known what to do with freedom had it been granted them. Freedom was beyond the realm of possibility and therefore never seriously considered by many. It was a fantasy. For them, life was not something to be savored but rather something to be endured.

Dandy Sprat

Silas had been in the Fifth long enough now to realize that it was just a little piece of Alabama in dirty brown uniforms. With a few exceptions, these were good people, God-fearing, God-loving men. They were fighting for their homes, their mamas and daddies, their wives and children, and for the sovereignty of Alabama. To the delight of some and the despair of many, they were also fighting for slavery.

The conversation began to die, and after listening for a while without comment, Silas put down his work. He found himself rising and saying, "Some of you sound like you don't care one way or another about slavery. And others sound as if you dislike it, but not enough to actually take a stand against it. How can y'all stand here before man and say that you are willing to fight, and possibly die, to keep another man in chains when we all know full well that this time tomorrow we may be standing before God trying to explain ourselves? I'm not dying for slavery tomorrow or any other day. Only a fool would throw away his own life to enslave another. I know I'm not much of a soldier, but I'm no fool. I was until just recently, but not now, not after yesterday. If I die tomorrow, I'm not sure what it'll be for. I hope it'll be for Southern independence and self-determination, for my country. But it sure won't be for damned slavery. To hell with slavery. That's where it belongs."

The words had fairly leaped from his mouth, and now he was standing in the midst of some of the world's hardest soldiers. Alone, he was the center of their silent attention. The looks on their faces ranged from anger to amused respect. Yet no one offered a comment or made a move toward him.

Just as some of the men began to look away, Silas caught sight of a large form approaching from the darkness. It was Moses. He had been just far enough not to be seen, but close enough to hear Silas's little speech.

As he strode into the group, eyes burning at Silas, he said, "I don't aim to die tomorrow for no damned slavery either, but I plan to do a heap of killing for it. But tonight I'm gonna knock a smart-mouth dandy sprat's dumb ass upside the head. Nobody calls me a fool."

Moses began to move toward him. Panic began to run through the boy. Silas would be like a kitten taking on a tiger. He found himself talking again, and he didn't know where the words were coming from.

"That's right. Go ahead and knock me upside the head. You're twice my size, maybe three times. It shouldn't be any trouble. Just go ahead and kill me while you're at it and save me the walk up that hill tomorrow. Do whatever you like, but it'll never change the fact that when it comes to slavery, I'm right, and you and slavery are both wrong."

Moses said, "What you don't understand, boy, is that I like

being in the wrong. It's my stock 'n trade. Now get ready for your whuppin'."

Again, Moses began to move toward him, but suddenly, the preacher, Kirby, and a couple of others were between them. Before Moses could deal with them, someone shouted, "Ten-hut!"

Everyone, Moses a little slower than the others, came to attention.

"Praise God," Silas whispered to himself.

"At ease, men," Lt. Cox said as he walked into the group. "Y'all gather around."

The men of the squad made a semicircle around him. Silas was careful to stand as far from Moses as possible. He quietly said to the preacher, "Thank you. It takes a brave man to come between Moses and his quarry."

The preacher smiled and whispered, "It takes an even braver man to call him a fool."

"Sorry, Preacher. I didn't mean that for you."

"Forget it, son. Don't apologize for speaking God's truth. We'll talk more about it later."

Contrabands

The army had a policy of returning contraband slaves to captivity. Several slaves had been captured on the march north. They had been handed over to the provost guard, who maintained a mobile stockade at the rear of the column. Wherever they went, the provost was right behind with a group of deserters, Yankee prisoners, and captured slaves.

The lieutenant briefly reminded the men of the army's policy and then turned to the preacher and said, "Corporal Elder."

"Yes, sir."

"This afternoon we captured a small family of slaves. They say they were freed by their master in Virginia, but they have no papers as such, and I don't think it would make any difference if they did. They were turned over to me to see that they are delivered to the provost guard. Until recently, of course, we were pulling provost duty ourselves, and someone would be delivering them to us. But now we are the deliverers, so to speak. I don't know which job I find more distasteful, but I am delegating that responsibility to you and your men. You can handle it any way you see fit. But they need to be in the custody of the provost before sunup. I suggest you pick two or three men to accompany you. There are only four slaves in your charge: two men, a woman, and a little girl."

Silas caught sight of a wagon coming toward them out of the night. It was being pulled by two tired-looking mules. An elderly black man was sitting on the bench of the wagon. His hands held the reins, but they were slack. The mules were being led by a soldier. A few more soldiers, all armed, were walking behind. The old man sitting on the bench was the only slave Silas could see. The others, he surmised, were in the canvas-roofed wagon.

Lt. Cox turned and saw the wagon approaching. He turned back to the men, glanced toward Moses, and said, "These people are not to be mistreated in any way. Your job is to deliver them and their rig to the provost." Then, looking at the preacher, he said, "See to it, Corporal."

"Yes, sir," said the preacher, saluting.

As the squad came to attention, the lieutenant returned the salute and left with his men. Silas and the others slowly fixed their gaze on a weary old darkie sitting on a bedraggled wagon.

Eyes Burning in the Dark

"I can't be a part of this, Preacher," Silas said.

"I know, son. I wasn't going to ask you."

"Me and Box will do it," Moses declared.

Not usually one to volunteer, Moses jumped at the opportunity to perpetuate the hated darkies' misery while at the same time increasing Swann's frustration.

"We're your men; we volunteer," he added as Box happily nodded.

"I think not," the preacher said. "I need somebody more levelheaded. You two like it too much."

He called out, "Kirby, White, and Williams. Y'all come with me. We're going to deliver these folks to the provost."

"No thanks, Preacher," said Williams. "I've been thinking about what Swann said. I don't want to be delivering nobody back into slavery the day before I'm probably gonna stand before the Lord. You'll have to use somebody else. Just leave me off this detail, if you don't mind."

"That goes for me too," said Kirby.

"How about you, White?" asked the preacher.

"I feel the same way, Preacher."

The preacher said, "Do I have any volunteers other than Box and Moses?"

There was a long silence. Then Moses quietly said, "Well, well. Looks like you're stuck with us malefactors." With delighted sarcasm, he added, "This man's army has reached a sorry state when you can only find two faithful bigots to carry out your orders. You thought you had a whole squad of them, didn't you? But it's just me and Box. Like I said, we're your men. Now, let's get it done, Johnny Reb."

"I think we should let them go," Silas said. He seemed almost as surprised as the others to hear the words.

"We can't do that, boy, and you know it!" the preacher said.

"On what is most likely the last night of our lives, we can do almost anything we like. What can they do to us?" Silas said. "Besides, the lieutenant will probably die with us tomorrow. It won't bother him if we let them go. And it sure would make us feel better to do something good before tomorrow's action."

"Something good?" Moses said. "You call disobeying orders

good? I thought me and Box were supposed to be the two sorriest troops in the outfit, and here we are trying to talk little Private Starched Ass here into following orders."

"I hate to say it, but I'm with Moses on this one," said Miller. "We can't just go around ignoring orders."

Then Kirby said, "Moses, you never obeyed any orders you didn't like, not unless you just had to. Now all of a sudden you're trying to make us believe you and Box are just a couple of good little troopers trying to please the nice lieutenant. We know you better than that. I'm for letting them go. To those of us with a Christian heart, what Swann said makes sense. The only reason Moses and Box are for following orders is because it gives them a chance to do something bad to some helpless coloreds. Miller, you ought to be ashamed for throwing in with them. You know better."

Miller's gaze dropped to the ground.

Then it was Moses's time to speak. His rage barely contained and his voice menacingly strained, he spoke quietly to Kirby.

"Now, you listen to me. I've been hankering to kick somebody's ass ever since Swann made his little smartass speech, and it was almost him. But y'all stuck your noses in before I could get it done. Swann's got y'all kissin' his ass like he was Old Bob hisself or somebody. But now I don't give much of a damn who it is, Kirby. If you or any of your friends think you're man enough to whip me, I'll not only agree to let them go, I'll even escort them out of here. And I'll never say a word to the lieutenant or anybody else about it. Me and Box will keep it to ourselves. Now, y'all pick some damn fool for me to whip. If he's not standing here before me in thirty minutes, me and Box and the preacher will take the goddamn niggers to the provost. But if you pick a champion and he wins, they go free and nobody says a word, and y'all get to die happy tomorrow."

A grinning Box nodded in agreement.

Kirby was a tough man, and the biggest man in the squad

next to Moses, but he knew of no man who was the equal of him. None of them did. Moses was simply in a class by himself.

Kirby said, "We'll let you know something in thirty minutes. Meanwhile, you and Box stay away from those folks," he said, motioning toward the slaves' wagon. "That goes for you too, Miller."

"You act like you're the damn corporal around here," said Moses, "giving orders to the rest of us."

The preacher said, "Well, I am the corporal, and what he said stands. Y'all stay away from them. You gave us thirty minutes, and we're going to take them."

"So you're a part of this mutiny too. A fine soldier you turned out to be. When did you start disobeying orders?" Moses said.

"About the same time you started obeying them. If I ever have any trouble deciding which side to come down on, I can always look to you. Whatever side you're on is the one I don't need to be on. I can always rely on you to do the wrong thing. Like you said, you're a faithful bigot," the preacher said.

A tolerant man, the preacher seldom spoke harshly to anyone, even Moses. He was, however, growing weary of the big man's venom.

He said, "Moses, the Bible lists seven things the Lord hates—not people; things." "Oh yeah?" Moses said, laughing a little. "You gonna tell me about them? You gonna sermonize my ass?"

The preacher began. "A proud look. A lying tongue. He that sows discord among his brothers." He paused.

"Go on," Moses said. "That's only three. I know you can count to seven. I want to hear them all. And by the way, I ain't your damn brother."

"A heart that devises wicked schemes. Feet that are swift to run into mischief. A false witness and..."

"And?" Moses said. "Go on dammit. You've got one more."

"Hands that shed innocent blood." The preacher paused and asked, "Is there anything there you don't do on a routine basis?"

Avoiding the question, Moses said, "You can add one more thing to that list, Preacher. He hates me, and I hate Him."

"Someday, Jack. Someday…"

"Yeah, I know. Someday He's gonna settle up with me. I've heard all that before. You've got me shaking in my Yankee boots."

"You're right about that, Jack. But it's not because He hates you. It's because He loves you."

Moses threw his head back and laughed, but he quickly steadied his gaze at the preacher and said, "You're the fool if you believe that shit."

"Call me the fool then," the preacher said. "But someday you'll believe it too. It's a sure thing."

He had always thought there was some good in every man, but he had all but given up on Moses.

Moses, angered further by the preacher's rebuke, said, "I'll tell you what, corporal. You and Kirby and Swann or anybody else you want can be the niggers' champion. I'll take on all of you at once. And if y'all whip my ass, you won't hear any whining out of me. I don't think there's a squad of men in either army who can whip me. But if you can, maybe it'll just save me that walk up the hill tomorrow, like Swann said. Time for talking is over, mister. Y'all go pick your damn champion. And whoever you pick better be all prayed up 'cause I'm gonna kill his ass. You've got thirty minutes."

The preacher, Swann, Kirby, and the others left Moses, Box, and Miller and walked toward the slaves' wagon. When they arrived, Silas turned and could see Moses still standing there, glowering at them, Box and Miller beside him. Silhouetted against the faint light and smoke of the dying campfires, he looked to Silas like the beast, eyes burning in the dark.

But Can He Fight?

The slaves had stayed in the wagon, out of sight. Leaving Silas and the others a few feet away, the preacher and Kirby stuck their heads in the back of the wagon and talked briefly to the slaves. Then they returned to the group.

White said, "Y'all know what? He's right. There ain't no squad of men anywhere that can whip him. I don't think we could whip him, even if Box and Miller were with us."

Kirby listened to White and then, smiling at the preacher, said, "That may be true, but there might be one such man."

The preacher walked the few steps to the rear of the wagon and motioned to someone inside. There climbed out of the wagon the largest, most formidable-looking human being any of them had ever seen. Moses was almost a giant in his time, at least six feet four inches tall and about two hundred and fifty pounds. But this man, whose clothes could barely contain him, was a shiny black hulk almost half a head taller than Moses and perhaps thirty to forty pounds heavier. Huge, gleaming muscles bulged everywhere. They all knew he was the most incredible specimen of manhood any of them would ever see, regardless of the length of their lives.

Dumb grins spread across their faces as they anticipated Moses getting his comeuppance. But the black man was not smiling. He did not yet know about Moses, but he knew that a group of Rebel soldiers was unlikely to give him anything to smile about.

Then Silas said, "But can he fight?"

They all looked at each other. Surely anyone built like that could fight.

Kirby said, "What's your name, boy?"

Silas had always been perplexed by the practice of addressing colored males as "boy," no matter how old or how obvious their manhood. It was a practice that would live long after slavery was dead. Kirby did not seem to mean any disrespect.

That was simply the way he addressed colored men. But yet to Silas there seemed to be at least a little disrespect there, whether Kirby intended it or not. He called many a white man "boy" also, but somehow the two things were not quite the same.

"Joseph, sir. Joseph Blount. That's my wife, Ruth, and my daughter, Rose," he said, pointing to the back of the wagon. "And he's my wife's daddy," he said, motioning toward the old man. "His name is Jonah Blount."

"Y'all all have the same last name?" the preacher asked, "even your daddy-in-law?"

"Yes sir. We was all owned by the same man, but I ain't no blood kin to any of them, exceptin' my daughter of course."

"How'd y'all happen to be here up north?"

"It's like we told them others, sir, our master was an old man. His wife up and passed sudden-like, and after he mourned a spell, he just come and told us we could leave; that we was free. He give us this rig and them mules and some food and a little Yankee money, and we left."

"I reckon y'all were glad to get away," said Kirby.

"Well sir, we didn't much want to go, but he wouldn't let us stay. He run us off, made us leave, him crying all the while, and all of us crying too."

"Y'all didn't want to be free?" Kirby asked.

"Oh, yes sir. We wanted to be free; still do. We all lived there on that little farm most all our lives with him and his missus. Ain't nothing wrong with freedom, but we sure did hate leaving our home. We ain't never been away from home before."

"So they treated you well?" Silas asked.

"Well, they was sweet people. We was their only slaves. They didn't have no children of their own. I reckon we was their children in a way," Joseph Blount said.

"Why didn't he give y'all your papers showing you were free?" Silas asked.

"I don't rightly know, sir. I reckon he was so tore up about losing his wife he just didn't think about it," Joseph said.

The old man said, "I don't think he figured we'd need no papers up north. He just hugged us all and told us to head north and get out of Virginia as quick as we could."

Then the big man spoke again. "When we got out of Virginia, my little girl said she was happy to be free. She had big plans for her freedom. She wants to be a nurse. Even though we mighty homesick, we don't really want to go back. But I reckon y'all got to do what ever y'all got to do."

The old man said, "The last thing we expected was to bump into Mr. Lee's army up here in Pennsylvania."

Silas looked over toward the wagon. He could see the big man's wife and daughter. The girl looked to be about eleven or twelve years old. He could see her eyes peering back at him. He looked into them and thought of Moses's eyes. Her eyes also burned. But where Moses's had burned with hate, hers burned with hope, one that was fading.

Looking at her, Silas's heart ached for them. He thought to himself, *I reckon I joined the wrong army.* He looked at his comrades: the preacher, Kirby, White, Williams, McClendon, Ward, Waller, Reagan, and Chandler. "Good men, all," he thought. "But are these good men going to send these poor people back south into bondage?"

Silas could see them struggling with their dilemma. No one spoke for a while.

Silas was about to speak when the preacher said, "Well, men, we have a problem here. I wish to goodness Lieutenant Cox had given this job to another squad."

"Any squad would struggle with it, Preacher," McClendon said.

"I hope you're right, son," said the preacher, "but I'm afraid there's some, like that bunch from Hooten Hollow, that would rough 'em up a little before turning them over to the provost."

"That's why he gave them to us," Silas said.

"Well," the preacher said, "no matter what another squad

would do, we're the squad that has to deal with it, and we have a problem no other squad has. We have Moses."

After a long, pensive pause, the preacher said, "Well, men, what'll it be?"

No one responded for a few seconds.

Then Kirby turned to Joseph Blount and said, "Listen, boy. All of us here in this little bunch want to let y'all go, but there's a man over there," he said, pointing toward Moses and the others who were no longer looking in their direction, "whose ass somebody will have to whip before we can do that. He's a big man, not as big as you, but still plenty big. He's the toughest man any of us have ever known, and we've known some tough men. He's too much for any of us. If you want freedom for you and your family, you'll have to fight him for it. If you whip him, you'll be the first. So what do you want to do? This is your decision."

The big man looked around at his captors and then toward the large, dark silhouette of Moses and said, "I ain't never been in no fight before."

There was dumbfounded silence. Every man there, even Silas, had been in at least one fight prior to his army days. A Southern boy just didn't get through childhood and early manhood without some fights along the way. It was not unusual for grown men to try to kill each other with their hands one day and go fishing together the next. Many a lifelong friendship had begun with a good, bloody fistfight, which would be fondly recounted and embellished many times over the ensuing decades. If the fight was one-sided, friendship did not usually follow—only contempt in the victor and hate in the vanquished. But if it was close, the two combatants often came away with enhanced respect for one another.

Joseph Blount, seeing the disbelief in their faces, added, "We wasn't allowed to fight. And besides, I never got that mad at nobody. I don't reckon I ever had a reason to fight."

"You got one now," Kirby said.

"Listen, son," the preacher gently said to Blount. Silas was a little surprised at hearing him address a slave so tenderly. But the preacher put his hand on the black man's massive shoulder and quietly repeated, "Listen, son. This man you're going to fight is like the devil himself. Let me tell you a story about a fight he had with a fellow almost as big as you."

"Oh," said Kirby, "Jay Bird, and the big Yank."

"Yes, I think he needs to hear this before he decides. We've still got time enough."

Silas wanted to hear it too. The others already knew the story, but they all listened just the same.

Yankee Boots

The incident to which the preacher referred had occurred about two months earlier, just before the Battle of Chancellorsville. The Rebel and Yankee lines were close, and the bluebellies captured one of the Fifth's pickets one night, a sharp-tongued, quick-witted little boy called Jaybird Johnson.

He was captured by an Irish outfit and was being questioned by one of their officers, a lieutenant named O'Rear, when he saw a big Irish sergeant sparring with another trooper. The sergeant was a huge, barrel-chested man with considerable boxing skills and great self-esteem.

As the lieutenant asked questions, Johnson watched the big man prancing and bouncing around, taking jabs at his partner. To Johnson, he looked pretty funny, and the little Reb began to chuckle.

O'Rear became irritated and said, "Just what is it you find so amusing, private?"

Johnson said, "That fat fella prissin' around over there, sir."

The lieutenant said, "That fat fellow can lick any man in the army."

Jaybird replied, "Your army maybe, but we have a man who can lick any man in any army."

"Is he bigger than that man?" the officer asked.

"No, he ain't as big and fat as that man, but he's big enough. We don't have any fat men in our army, not in the enlisted ranks leastways, not anymore."

"And you think your man could take ours," the lieutenant said.

Johnson studied the big Yank a few more seconds and said, "Sir, there is absolutely no doubt in my mind that our man could take yours in a fight. Not boxing; just a plain old fight."

"What makes you so cock sure?"

"Well, sir, I've seen our man in action, and I've seen yours practicing. Our man don't practice, he just does it natural-like."

"How are they different?"

"Your man is a boxer," Johnson said. "Ours is a killer."

"What's this man's name?"

"Moses, sir. Private Jack Moses."

Lt. O'Rear studied the scruffy little Confederate for a while and then offered him a deal. He could have his freedom if he would arrange for Moses to fight the big Yank.

Johnson said, "It's a deal, sir, but don't you think you oughta check with your man first?"

"No. He'll leap at the opportunity."

"Probably the last leap he'll ever make."

Irritated again, the lieutenant said, "How do I know you'll keep your end of the deal? Are you a man of your word?"

Laughing, Johnson said, "Hell no, I ain't. But I wouldn't miss this fight for nothin', and that's the reason you can trust me. You let me go now and have your pickets let me through. This afternoon at 1600 hours, that's four o'clock for you Yankee officers, or maybe I should say when the big hand's on the—"

"At ease, private," O'Rear said. "Anymore disrespect out of you, and I'll just throw your ass in the stockade, and we'll forget about the fight."

"Sir, I sure am sorry, sir. We'll meet you bluebellies—I mean, Yankees—on your side of the creek in that little clearing by that big boulder, sir. You know the place, sir?"

"I know it."

"Sir, it'll be me, Moses, my lieutenant, and one other man—four of us in all. You can bring your man and two more, sir. We'll each have four men. There will be no weapons except your sidearm and our lieutenant's sidearm. We'll arrange for our pickets not to shoot, and you do the same. How's that … sir?"

"I think that's acceptable," the lieutenant said. "But why four o'clock—I mean, 1600 hours—and why four people?"

"Well, sir, that'll give the three of y'all time to drag your fat ass sergeant back up the hill without missing supper, sir," Jaybird said cheerfully.

The lieutenant looked away to secretly smile. Then he arranged for Johnson to pass through the picket line and began making preparations for the four o'clock meeting.

When Johnson got back to his outfit, he was met with great enthusiasm. His sassy wit made him popular among the men. He made them laugh. When asked how he had escaped, he just said he was so little and sassed them so much they just threw him back. He quickly found Lt. Cox, who did not think much of the plan but agreed to talk to Moses about it.

The first thing Moses, who had no shoes, asked was, "This Yank, you reckon he's got feet as big as mine?"

"I reckon," said Jaybird. "Maybe a little bigger."

Moses immediately demanded that the lieutenant allow him to fight. Cox agreed but only if they kept it to themselves until after it was over. It would be the three of them and one more man: the preacher. The lieutenant made the necessary arrangements with the pickets involved, and the small band left camp a little before four, making their way to the meeting place. They stopped just inside the trees on the Confederate side of the creek.

Lieutenant Cox yelled, "Hey, Yank, y'all over there?"

"We're here," came the reply, and the Yanks stepped out of the trees into the clearing toward the stream.

When the Confederates saw the Yankee sergeant, Lt. Cox said, "Holy shi—Oh, 'scuse me, Preacher."

"You're excused, son," the preacher said. "I nearly said it myself."

But Moses just said, "You done good, Jaybird. I reckon his shoes will fit me just fine."

The Southerners walked out of the trees and waded the creek to the clearing where the Yankees were waiting.

As they approached, the Yankee lieutenant smiled at Lt. Cox and said, "Hello, Reb."

Lt. Cox said, "Howdy, Yank," and the two saluted each other, then shook hands, laughed, and slapped each other on the shoulder as if they were old friends.

"Y'all know each other?" Jaybird asked.

"No, private," Cox said. "We're just members of the worldwide brotherhood of commissioned officers."

Then, ignoring the still-perplexed Jaybird, he directed himself to the Union officer and said, "I'm Lieutenant Cox. Private Johnson tells me your sergeant here is quite the fighter."

"I'm Lieutenant O'Rear. Private Johnson tells me that your man, Moses, is the toughest man in any army."

As Moses glowered at him, Jaybird said, "Well, ain't you?"

"I guess we're about to find out," Cox said.

O'Rear said, "Before we do anything, we have to establish the rules."

"Rules?" said Moses. "What kind of fight is this? I ain't never been in no damn fight with rules before. Here's the rules—the winner is the man still breathing when it's over."

"This isn't a killing," said O'Rear. "It's a fight. I don't want anybody to die here today. There will be plenty of time for that later. And you are to address me as 'sir,' just as you do your own officers. I expect the same respect you show them."

"He ain't kiddin', Jack," Jaybird added helpfully. "He means it."

"Here are the rules," O'Rear said quickly to keep from laughing.

But before he could continue, Lt. Cox politely interrupted. "Pardon me, Lieutenant O'Rear, but you don't really want the same respect he shows us. You can trust me on that."

"Oh, very well," said O'Rear. "Thank you, Lieutenant Cox." Then he began again. "Here are the rules, men, and if you don't like them, there will be no fight. Rule one: you can't kill each other. Rule two: the only weapons you can use are the ones you were born with—your hands, your feet, or any other part of your body—and what you're wearing. You can't throw dirt, use rocks, sticks, or anything else that isn't a part of your body or on your body. You two understand?"

"Yes, sir," said the big Yank.

They all stared at Moses, who finally mumbled, "Yeah ... sir."

Then Moses added, "And here's rule three: if I win, I get his boots."

"The hell you do," the Irishman said. "You got no boots. You got nothing to lose."

"That's what makes poverty so wonderful," Moses said sarcastically.

The Yankees quietly discussed it among themselves for a moment and then agreed to the boots rule. But they had a catch of their own.

"Okay. We agree to the boots," O'Rear said, "but if our man wins, Johnson becomes our prisoner again."

"Like hell!" Jaybird instantly retorted.

"Done!" said Moses.

"Like hell, Jack!" repeated Jaybird.

Derisively, Moses said, "What the hell you worried about, you little piss-ant. I'm the toughest man in any army, remember?"

After a few seconds of staring into Moses's fearless eyes,

Jaybird said, "Okay. If your man wins, I'm your prisoner. But if Moses wins, me and Lieutenant O'Rear swap boots."

"Who the hell do you think you are, private?" O'Rear said angrily.

"I'm the man who could lose his damn freedom in a few minutes. I'm the man that could rot his ass off in one your rotten Yankee prison camps. That's who the hell I am ... sir. All I'm asking you to put up is a pair of damn Yankee boots."

After studying Johnson for a few seconds, O'Rear's heart softened, and he relented, saying, "Agreed."

With the rules settled, each group quietly met to discuss any last-minute concerns. The Southerners could see the Yankees talking and occasionally glancing in their direction. Lt. Cox asked Moses what his plan of attack was.

Greatly disappointed, Moses said, "Well, since y'all won't let me kill him, I reckon I'll just knock his ass upside the head."

A complex man, Moses liked to keep things simple. The others nodded their approval.

The two groups turned back to each other. "Any other conditions?" asked Cox.

No one spoke.

"In that case, you two shake hands."

"You're joshing me!" Moses said.

"Nope. Shake hands with the man, Jack," Cox said.

The big Yank had been dancing around, punching the air and occasionally winking at his friends. Moses stuck his hand out and allowed the man to shake it, and then they stepped back a few feet from each other.

Lt. Cox stepped between them and said, "All right, men. You both understand the rules. You can't use any weapons other than your own body or what's on it and," stepping toward Moses and looking him in the eye, he added, "no killing."

He then backed out from between them and quietly said, "Let the fight begin."

Each man peered into the other's eyes. They had both

learned long ago that the eyes can tell much about an opponent. When the big Yank looked into Moses's eyes, what he saw frightened him. He saw a total absence of doubt and fear, and a deep, abiding malice. And Moses—vile, perceptive Moses—saw the man's apprehension.

The big Yank began to dance and bob and weave and duck. Moses just studied him for about twenty seconds with his hands hanging at his side. Then, as if by agreement, they closed, and the Yank delivered a quick, powerful right that caught them all by surprise, except for Moses. He deftly parried it aside and simultaneously sent a big fist smashing into the Yank's nose and instantly followed up with a kick to the groin. The man doubled over in agony, and Moses immediately went to work with his knees, fists, and feet. The preacher said it sounded like someone dumping a sack of potatoes onto a wooden floor; the blows were landing so fast. In seconds, the Yank was on his knees and Moses planted his own knee in the man's face, putting him on his back. He was on him instantly, sending his big, heavy fist crashing into the Yank's face as quickly as he could cock his arm and deliver it again.

Moses heard a pistol cock and once again felt cold steel on his temple as Lt. Cox gently admonished, "Remember the rules, Jack."

Moses glowered at Cox but relented and immediately began removing the Yank's boots. Johnson laughed and began taking off his own worn-out boots while he grinned at O'Rear.

"Damn!" O'Rear said.

But good to his word, he began removing his footgear.

Then Jaybird said, "Jack, you need a shirt real bad. Why don't you take his?" he said gesturing toward the big Yank. "You earned it."

The three standing Yankees began moving toward Moses, who instantly stood and stared them back.

Then, still looking at the Yankees but talking to Jaybird, he said, "I don't want the damn thing. Wouldn't be seen in it. I'll just keep my Rebel rags."

On the way back to camp, with Moses and Johnson each wearing their fine Yankee boots, Jaybird said, "That wasn't much of a fight, Jack. You should'a let him hang around a little longer, just to make it a little more interesting."

"I tell you what, Jaybird. Next time we'll let you whip his ass. That ought to make it a little more interesting for you."

"No thanks, man. I got what I want," Jaybird said, admiring his boots.

A Prayer for the Big Man

After the preacher finished the story, he said, "That was just a couple of months ago. Moses still has those boots, and he's going to try to kick you to death with them. He hates just about everybody, but he especially hates coloreds. If you fight him, he's going to try to kick you in the cods, poke your eyes out, knock your teeth out, bust your eardrums, and a bunch of other stuff you never even thought of. He has been brawling since he was a boy, and as far as anybody knows, he's never been whipped."

"That's right, boy," Kirby said. "You listen to the preacher. Everything he's telling you is true. Moses will probably try to kill you, but we'll stop it before it gets that far if we can. But we can't promise anything."

Then the preacher said, "We're on your side, son, but this is something you'll have to do for yourself. You're the only man I know of who might be able to best him."

"But you'll have to protect yourself," Kirby jumped in. "Are you right or left-handed?"

"Right," he said.

"Then keep your left up like this," Kirby demonstrated. "Use it like a shield to protect yourself from his blows. Watch his hands and feet. If he tries to kick you, just turn away a little so as to make him hit you on the thigh or butt. If you get a chance to put your fist in his face or his gut, do it, but do it quick. He won't give you time to land any haymakers. He knows how to handle hisself."

Then the preacher said, "Your best chance is to get your arms around him and turn it into a wrestling match. If you can hold his arms to his body and throw him on his head or just kick or butt him into submission—that might work. I would feel a lot better about this if you had had just one fight in your life. But you're about to get a lesson from the master. That is if you decide to fight him. What's it going to be, son?"

Joseph Blount was clearly worried. He said, "I don't have no choice, sir. There's too much riding on this. I got to fight him. If he kills me, then so be it. Leastways I'll know I tried. And my family will know I died trying to earn their freedom for them. Maybe the Lord will be with me."

"You a Christian?" the preacher asked.

"Yes, sir. All of us are, even my little girl."

"God bless you, son," the preacher said.

Turning to Kirby, he said, "Owen, y'all go and tell Moses we have our champion, but don't tell him who it is. Just tell him we'll meet him in the little clearing in the middle of that thicket over yonder. That way nobody will see what's happening. Meanwhile, Brother Blount and I will be praying together."

Kirby, Swann, and the others left to find Moses. The two black men and the preacher knelt to pray.

The preacher said, "Dear Lord above, please forgive us if what we're about to do is wrong. But sometimes, Lord, it just seems like a fellow has to fight for his people and what he knows is right. Be with this brave young man in his quest to free his family. Bless him, Lord, and protect him. Intercede, Lord, and intervene in this combat in a way that only You can, in a way that we would never even think of. Let him be victorious, Lord. Please let him win." He paused and then said, "I ask these things in the sweet name of Jesus, our Savior. Amen."

The preacher looked up and saw the two black men still on their knees, looking at him with newfound respect.

"Thank you, sir," Joseph said. "Thank you for your prayer."

"Son, just get in there and let it fly," the preacher said as they rose to their feet. "Don't hold back. And don't worry about fighting fair or being nice. There aren't any rules. Just fight like a bobcat. Use your teeth, fingernails, elbows, anything you can. Choke him. Break his neck. Kill him if you can, because if you don't he will almost surely kill you."

As the three of them made their way to the thicket, they didn't notice the woman and the little girl secretly following them.

The old man shook his head and said, "Moses. A Bible name for such a man as you described."

The preacher said, "Moses is a biblical name for sure, but as you will soon see, he is hell in a man."

One Fell Fighter

Kirby, Swann, and the others found Moses and his two attendants not far from where they had left them.

"Well, which one of you polecats is it going to be?" Moses queried.

"None of us polecats," Kirby answered. "We have a special critter lined up for you. We're supposed to escort you to the clearing in that thicket over yonder."

"And that's where the whole bunch of you are gonna jump my ass. But that's okay; I can handle all of you."

"No, nothing like that. Just come on," Kirby said as they started toward the thicket.

Then Box said, "Don't worry, Jack. Me and Miller are with you."

Moses, not one to laugh without ample reason, looked down

at Box and chuckled a little at the thought of being rescued by the feisty little boy.

Box persisted. "Well, we are, Jack."

Miller just looked away as Moses said, "Don't worry about me, Box. You just save yourself for the walk up that hill tomorrow. Old Bob's probably counting on you to pull his bacon out of the fire. I'm sure he's heard of you and how you whipped up on Swann last night."

Miller giggled, and Box fumed in silence.

They reached the thicket before the preacher and his group.

"Well, Kirby?" Moses said.

"They're coming," Kirby replied.

A few seconds later, they saw the preacher approaching out of the darkness, and then Moses caught sight of the two men behind him. All eyes were on Moses as he realized who his opponent was to be. He was not a man to be shaken.

Box swore when he saw the big black man, but Moses quietly said, "Shut up, Box! You talk too damn much. I've been wanting to kick Kirby's ass or Swann's." Then he looked at Joseph Blount and said, "But I reckon a big-ass nigger will do."

"Yeah, but he looks like three or four big-ass niggers," Box whispered.

"I've seen bigger," Moses said.

"Who?" Box asked. "That big Yank?"

"None of your damn business."

Yet even Moses had to admit, if only to himself, that he had never before seen a more monstrous human form in the flesh—only in his nightmares. He studied the man closely, looked into his eyes. He saw courage and resolve. He also saw concern, but he saw no cowardice. Another thing he did not see was what the other man saw in him: a hate-filled heart. Moses had the cold, calm, lifeless heart of a killer, but his spirit was tormented. Joseph Blount lacked these qualities. Where Moses was fighting only for himself, Blount was fighting for his people.

Moses sized up the man and decided this would be the fight

of, and possibly for, his life. He was careful not to let anyone see it in him, but he too was a little concerned. But his lack of regard for life—any life, even his own—kept at bay any real doubt or fear.

"So," Moses asked the preacher, "who's it gonna be, you or Swann?"

Everyone laughed, except the two black men—and Moses. Moses didn't laugh.

"No, Jack. Me and Swann are sitting this one out. This is our champion," the preacher said, looking toward Joseph Blount. "I hope that's okay with you."

"Hell, Preacher, I don't care one way or the other," Moses replied. "I ain't fighting him. Box here is our man."

There was more laughter, louder than before, the terror-stricken look on Box's face adding considerably to the merriment. Even the black men smiled a little. But Moses still did not laugh or smile.

After the laughter had subsided the preacher said, "Look, Jack. There's no need for you, or this man, or Box, or anyone else to get hurt tonight. Me and Kirby and Swann can lead these folks outside our lines. The rest of you can just stay here and get a good night's sleep. What do you say, Jack?"

Miller said, "That sounds pretty good to me, Jack. Why don't we just let this thing pass?"

Ignoring Miller, Moses said, "You know me better than that, Preacher. I wouldn't miss this for nothin'. I walked a long way to see it. No, he's gonna have to pay the price for his freedom. He's gonna have to earn it, suffer for it—like us."

Indeed, Cpl. Elder knew Moses better than that. Yet he felt he had to at least try to defuse the situation. After a pause of disappointment and resignation, he turned to Joseph as if to say, "I tried."

But before he could speak, Blount quietly said, "That's all right, sir. I'm ready."

The old man turned to Joseph and said, "I want you to know

that no matter how this ends, no matter what happens to us, I'm proud of my son-in-law."

The two men briefly embraced.

Moses had already walked to the center of the clearing. The preacher led the slave to meet him. As the big men stood there, silently facing each other, Silas could not help but notice the contrast in the two. The slave was obviously well fed. He was wearing relatively good work clothes and they were fairly clean, as was he. Moses, on the other hand, looked gaunt in comparison from the long march north and from the meager diet of a Confederate soldier on the move. In spite of the bath of sorts he had taken in the creek that morning, he was dusty. His uniform was little more than a collection of dirt-encrusted rags. It hadn't been washed in months for fear, he said, that if the dirt went away, the uniform might go with it. He was, however, better shod than his opponent. Those Yankee boots were still mighty fine.

The preacher turned to the spectators, only about thirteen men in all, and quietly warned them to remain silent during the fight, no matter what. If their little group attracted any attention from outside the thicket, it could be bad for everyone involved.

He then turned back toward the combatants and said, "Gentlemen, are you ready?"

Without taking their eyes off each other, they nodded. The preacher knew better than to ask Moses to shake hands. This was not that kind of fight. Nor was he that kind of man.

"Very well then." the preacher said. "Let the fight begin. Have at it, men. And may God forgive us all."

A Lesson from the Master

For a few seconds, no one moved. Then Moses assumed a rather loose fighting position. He, like Blount, was right-handed. Blount followed his lead, and the two began a slow, clockwise orbit opposite each other, illuminated only by the full moon.

When fighting a large man, Moses generally waited for his opponent to make the first move. After about a minute of making circles, he decided this man would not be the first to move. If there was going to be a fight, Moses would have to initiate it himself. He knew instinctively that he would have to avoid the other man's grasp. If ever enfolded in those massive arms, he would probably be finished.

Moses made a few feints toward the man to judge his reflexes and skill. He was impressed with the quickness for one so large. He couldn't tell much about the skill, but he decided to discontinue the feints because the man seemed to be learning from them. His reactions improved with each one, and he began to make some feints of his own.

It was a little scary for everyone watching to see such a gigantic man move with such quickness and athleticism. Hope began to swell in Silas's heart.

Moses, while impressed, was not frightened. Not since he was a little boy watching his mother get beat to death in that dark little tavern had he been frightened. Since that night, he had been incapable of real fear. When he watched her die, all love, all kindness, and all things good in him died with her. And when the loveless old man reared him, it just nurtured the boy's already-dark spirit.

Moses was a rational man. He knew he was in danger of losing his life. But no life—his own, or any other—meant much to him. His animal ferocity was what had always delivered him in the past, not his love of life.

Like a mantis, Moses patiently stalked his prey and made a lucky guess as to when the next feint would come. He caught Blount in a vulnerable instant with one of his famous, face-crushing rights and sent him staggering backward. But the man did not go down. It was almost unheard of for anyone to take one of Moses's blows full in the face and remain standing. There were gasps all around. Moses, too, was impressed when the man steadied himself and came back at him.

It was as if Blount had received a wake-up call. His nose pouring blood, he began pursuing Moses around the little clearing, deflecting some of the white man's blows, absorbing the others. Lacking the skill to punch his way through Moses's defenses, he took the preacher's advice and simply pushed his way through the blows enough to get his arms around him. He threw him down. His left hand pinned Moses's throat to the ground. Over and over a black fist the size of a whiskey keg crashed down into his tormentor's face.

Moses was fighting back, landing blows on Blount's face and head. He was, after all, Moses. But his blows, while powerful, did not land with the same force as those coming down.

Quietly, the preacher said, "Oh, dear Lord. He's going to kill him just like I told him to."

Only a man like Moses could have taken the thrashing he was now enduring. Most fights between really powerful men don't last long. If one gets the upper hand, even briefly, such destruction can be delivered as to make further resistance impossible. Moses had already received enough punishment to kill some men. But he was still landing blows. It looked like he was weakening when he managed to bring his knee up with great force between Blount's legs.

The black man collapsed in agony on top of him. Moses quickly threw him off and stood up. He took just a few seconds to catch his breath and steady himself before going back to work on his opponent, who had barely managed to get up to all fours but could not yet stand. Moses kicked him in the ribs with everything he had, almost falling down himself.

Damn those Yankee boots, Silas thought.

With quiet desperation in his voice, the preacher said, "Get up, son. Get up!"

Moses was beginning to enjoy himself. He was strutting around, glowering at his enemies around him. Blount was struggling upward again when Moses happily delivered another powerful kick into his ribs.

Silas said, "We've got to stop this, Preacher. He's going to kill him."

The preacher did not respond. The agony Silas saw on his face indicated that he was almost feeling the blows himself. All he could do was bow his head, put one hand over his eyes and say, "Dear Lord, help him."

While Blount was coughing, retching, and trying to regain his feet, Moses swaggered. He had everything completely under control now and, in spite of his battered face, was enjoying himself. This was the moment he had lived for. It was the realization of his darkest, most cherished fantasy. He was flying high.

"Y'all ever wonder what nigger brains look like?" he chortled.

No one responded, not even Box.

Then Kirby said, "Don't, Jack. It's over. You've won."

"Like hell it's over," Moses answered. "I ain't won yet. I ain't through. He's still breathing. I'm gonna knock this nigger boy's ass upside the head." Then, looking around defiantly, he added, "And I'll kill anybody who comes between us."

Blount had managed to rise to a kneeling position with one hand on the ground and the other on his knee. His head was perfectly positioned to receive the deathblow.

Moses was maneuvering into position, and most of the men, Swann included, began turning away, not wanting to watch his end game. The preacher had not been watching for some time. He was staring at the ground. Only three men were still looking on: Kirby, Box, and the old man.

Moses was through strutting and posturing. He began making his way toward the man, building up momentum as he went. He was within a few feet of delivering the final kick when suddenly a small, dark form appeared, standing between him and his prey, her eyes flooded and her face streaming and dripping with tears; it was Rose, Joseph Blount's daughter.

She stood, hands at her side, almost as if at attention. Terror and courage in her face, she did not budge or even twitch when Moses barely checked his kick just inches from her body.

Her father, still struggling to rise, did not know she was there. As those who had turned away looked on again, what they saw astounded them: a skinny little girl, sobbing and terrified, staring down the world's wickedest man. She did not speak. There was no need. She stood, steadfastly looking into the bad man's eyes. He glowered, but she did not waver.

As he glared, he began to see her heart breaking for her father as his own was broken when, in horrified silence, he watched his mother die after he desperately tried to rescue her from her murderer. Reflected in the girl's eyes, he saw himself as he was: a little man, an owned man, owned more surely than she. It was then he knew she was free and that he was the slave.

After a few seconds of staring into her eyes and hearing nothing but her soft sobs, his cocky, hate-filled deportment was replaced by one of confusion and fear. His eyes fixed on hers, he began backing up. He tripped and fell backward, his eyes never leaving hers. He got up and, with panic and terror in his face, began to look around for an escape route. He bolted between two men, knocking one down as he went through a small opening in the thicket. Moses fled into his darkness.

Silas was the first to speak. "What happened?"

Very matter-of-factly, the old man said, "The Lord done got a holt of him."

"He's right," the preacher said. "Come on, Silas. We've got to follow him. He's going to need us."

"Moses is going to need us?" Silas asked. "Since when has Moses ever needed anybody?"

"He's always needed somebody, just like the rest of us. He just never knew it, but he's about to find out. Come on, son," the preacher said.

On the way out of the thicket, Silas saw Joseph Blount's family attending to him. Kirby and some others were trying to help.

Silas said to the preacher, "He almost did it, didn't he, Preacher? He almost bested the world's toughest man."

"Yeah," the preacher said, "he probably came as close as any man ever has or ever will. But Moses was bested by the righteous, shaming gaze of a brave little girl, with the blessings of the Master. No mere man could have ever done it."

They could barely see Moses ahead of them in moon-dappled darkness. He had run into a wooded area where no one was camped. They could hear him crashing through the underbrush, almost like prey fleeing a predator.

He finally stopped, exhausted. He was on his knees, leaning against a tree. They quietly walked around in front of him. He did not look up or acknowledge them. He was weeping softly.

The preacher waited a short while and spoke very gently, "Son."

"I ain't your goddamn son," was the instant reply. Then more softly, he said, "I ain't nobody's son."

"Jack," the preacher continued, "God's trying to show you a new way."

"Oh, shut up, Preacher. Don't you ever think of nothin' else? You beat all, you know that?" Moses had just barely finished the sentence when he threw his head back in agony and wailed like an animal.

"Oh, damn. Leave me alone!" he screamed.

Silas recoiled in fear, but the preacher steadied him and said, "Don't worry, son. He's not talking to us."

Moses struggled to his feet and said, "Preacher, I'm warning you. Get the hell away from me. And take that with you," he said, motioning toward Silas.

"Okay, Jack. We're going to leave you alone," the preacher said. "But we're going to pray for you."

"I don't want your damn prayers. You keep them."

"You're going to get them whether you want them or not," the preacher said.

"You know where you can stick 'em."

Swann and the preacher started toward camp, and as they

walked, they could hear Moses behind them, railing against his tormentor.

"Dear Heaven above, Preacher," Silas asked, "what's happening to him?"

"The Good Lord is convicting him of his sins," the preacher said.

Silas said, "He convicted me when I was a kid, but I don't remember anything like that."

The preacher smiled and said, "Son, you're just an ordinary sinner. You have a good heart, but we all sin at least a little. That's why we all need Jesus, because it just takes one sin to keep us out of heaven. But Moses has a black, sin-filled heart. I was beginning to wonder if he even has a soul. I reckon he does. Where you're just a little sinner, he's a great one, maybe the greatest. It can be a painful experience when the Lord gets a hold of someone that evil and turns them to good. But don't worry about Moses. God loves him just like He loves us; else He wouldn't be putting him through all that discomfort right now. And don't you worry about the Lord either." The preacher laughed. "He can handle Mr. Moses."

"Man, that little girl sure handled him, didn't she?" Silas said.

"That she did. You know, Silas, the Bible says that God shall use the weak things of the world to shame the mighty. That's what we saw tonight, that and answered prayer. The longer I live the more I am in awe of my Creator."

They paused long enough to say a brief prayer for Moses, asking only that God turn him to good and give him peace. Then the preacher said, "Come on. Let's go see how our little family is doing."

Their Own Country

As they walked, the preacher said, "Silas, you don't really believe we're fighting for slavery, do you, son? I only know of a few men in the Fifth who even own a slave. Some of the men never even saw one till they were almost grown. I don't know what in the world makes you think we're fighting for slavery, but you're just plain mistaken."

Silas could see that the preacher was a little worked up. He said, "Well, why did some of the men sound like they want to preserve it?"

The look on the preacher's face was one of exasperation. But he smiled and said, "You folks down on the coast really are just a little different from us. Why are we fighting? Only each man knows in his own heart why he is fighting. Only you know why you are. At least I hope you do."

Silas didn't respond because he was not really sure anymore. But the preacher didn't wait for an answer.

"Let me tell you why I am fighting, Silas. I just hope I can explain it. Here goes. You know, son, my granddaddy fought in our first war for independence at Kings Mountain. He was just a boy, and he fought beside his daddy. He felt like we had the right to throw off an oppressive government and make our own. This is our second war for independence. And we wouldn't even be here now if Mr. Lincoln had let us go in peace. But no, he had to raise an army and invade us. Surely we have a right to defend ourselves."

"Yes, that sounds reasonable," said Silas.

"And then," the preacher continued, "when he passed that so-called Emancipation Proclamation, it didn't even apply to the Union states that have slaves. If we lose the war, the only slaves in the country will be in the North. Most of us aren't fighting to preserve slavery any more than most of the Yankees are fighting to end it. We're fighting to gain our independence, and they are fighting to preserve the Union. But in doing so, they are also fighting to deny us our independence when we have just as much right to it as they do. And by the same token, when we fight for our independence, we are also fighting to deny the coloreds their freedom when, by God's mercy, they have just as much right to it as we do. I don't like it, but that's the way it is. But while some of our people are fighting to keep slavery, most aren't. And while some of the Yankees are fighting to end it, most aren't. I'm convinced that they have just as many bigots up North as we do down South. That proclamation is just a political trick to make the Yankee soldiers think they're doing a noble thing by invading us, so they can feel all good about their aggression against us. It's just another way for them to look down their noses at us even more than they usually do, if that's possible.

"And, son, when we fought for our independence from England, all the rebels—Southerners and Northerners—were fighting for slavery whether they wanted to or not. It was just one more part of the whole deal, just like it is now.

"Son," the preacher said, "the Constitution says we have a right to our own government, our own country, without a bunch of snooty outsiders shoving stuff down our throats just as much now as we did back in the seventies and eighties. When this thing is over and we've won, we'll have to deal with slavery somehow. It'll be painful and difficult, but it's wrong. Deep down, most of us know that. The South is like a poor, old drunk. She's addicted to slavery. She has to have it to get through the day, but it's killing her. I know there are some who want it preserved. Mostly they're the ones who own slaves, or fellows like Box and Moses who just plain hate them. Those people are in the minority, a loud and powerful one. Most of us just want to win this war so the Yankees will leave us alone. You won't find very much of what you could call love of slavery in this army. What we love is freedom. After we win our own, maybe we can find a way to give the coloreds their freedom too. And who knows. Maybe those hypocrites up North can be persuaded to free their slaves as well. That'll take some doing though. Those Yankees don't like to be told what to do any more than we do.

"And don't forget," the preacher added with his finger in the air, "it was those New England traders who made their fortunes bringing the coloreds over here and selling them into slavery. Now they want everyone to forget about that so the world will blame us, and only us, for all of it. They are trying to arrange it so only the Southern race is held accountable when it is actually the fault of the whole human race. We're all guilty, not just the Southerner. That's why I'm fighting.

"And there's something else you might not remember," the preacher continued, still fired up, "since you were just a kid when it happened."

"What's that, Preacher?"

"When Fort Sumter was fired on, there were just seven states in the Confederacy. There were eight slave states still in the Union. But when Mr. Lincoln mobilized his army to invade us, Virginia, Tennessee, North Carolina, and Arkansas all seceded and joined the Confederacy to protect the South. You're serving in the Army of Northern Virginia alongside a lot of boys from Virginia, Tennessee, and North Carolina. And there are a lot of Arkansas boys serving out west. I can see how you might think most of us Alabama boys are fighting for slavery, but you'd be wrong. But I don't see any way you can believe those men from those other four states are. We're defending our homes, boy. We're doing what any honorable man would do when someone invades his home. It's mighty unfortunate that slavery got thrown into pot with all the other stuff. Slavery might be the cause of this war, but I ain't even sure about that. Some people say it's just economics. But I do know this. Slavery ain't the reason we're fighting. I think this war has woken a lot of our people up. Slavery is bad for everybody. But of course, the poor, colored folks are suffering most of all. I think more and more people are beginning to see it for the terrible sin it is. Leastways, I hope so. I've never been comfortable with it."

Silas could tell the preacher had said his say. He said, "I'm sorry for what I said, Preacher. But I've studied enough history to know that if we lose this war, we'll go down as a bunch of sniveling bigots and hatemongers no matter how well we argue our points. The Yankees will all be crusading angels, and we'll all be denigrated to mean-spirited cowards because the North will get to write the history books."

"In that case, son," the preacher said, "I reckon we just have to win."

"I reckon so."

Much of a Man

When they got back to the campsite, they found Joseph Blount in the wagon being attended by his wife and daughter.

They removed their hats, and the preacher peeked into the back of the wagon.

"How's our man doing?"

The woman said, "It's kinda hard to tell how bad he's hurt in this light, but he says he's gonna be all right. Thank you for asking, sir."

"Is he awake?" the preacher asked.

"Yes, sir, I'm awake."

The preacher saw a large head rise from the floor of the wagon. Even in the low light, he could tell the man had taken a beating. His eyes were almost shut, his mouth and nose were swollen, and there were cuts on his face.

"How you feeling, son? How bad do you think you're hurt?"

"Well, sir, I think my nose is broke, and I probably have some broke ribs, but I reckon I'll live."

"Well, Joseph Blount," the preacher said, "if it's any comfort to you, you came as close to whipping him as anyone ever has. Next time you'll take him."

"Naw, sir!" Blount said. "I don't want no next time. He's much of a man not to be no bigger than he is."

"No bigger than he is?" the preacher laughed. "Next to you, he's the biggest man I know."

Silas and the preacher looked at each other in amused disbelief.

"No bigger than he is," the preacher mumbled.

The preacher looked back into the wagon and said, "Well, no matter how big he is or isn't, you did a good job. We're all proud of you. You just lay back down there and rest."

"Yes, sir. And thank you, sir," came the words from the wagon. "Thank you for that prayer."

Two chairs had been removed from the wagon, and sitting in them were the little girl and her grandfather.

"And how 'bout you, tiger?" the preacher quietly asked the girl. "How are you doing?"

"Fine, sir. Thank you," she said, not quite sure how to take his question.

The preacher and Silas smiled, put on their hats, tipped them to the ladies, and walked away. They had only taken a few steps when they were confronted by Box.

The Faithful Bigot

"Well, Preacher, did you tell them to start loading their stuff for the trip to the provost?"

"No, but directly I'll tell them to load their stuff for the trip out of our lines."

"Like hell you will," Box answered. "Moses beat that boy like a damn borrowed mule. They're going to the provost."

"Box," the preacher said, clearly fed up with the little troublemaker, "Moses took off. He ran. You can't win unless you stick around for the finish. Now get some sleep. Me and Swann will handle this."

"Preacher, I know you're a great big ol' corporal and I'm just a little ol' private, but if you let them go, I'm going to the lieutenant."

"Listen, Box. You and Moses and the rest of us all agreed to keep this to ourselves and to abide by the outcome of the fight. Moses ran away, son, so he loses. If you cause any trouble over this, I'll see to it that you never get any shoes. Now climb in your bedroll and get some sleep. We'll handle this."

"I think we ought to wait till Moses gets back and ask him," Box said.

"Moses don't have a say in it anymore. It's over, and he lost. And besides, there's no telling when or if he's ever coming back. He's probably on his way to Ohatchee by now."

"I'm telling you, Preacher, if you don't ask Jack first, I'm going to make trouble. You can let them load their stuff, but you better not take them anywhere except the provost unless you ask him first."

"Box, you don't have to make trouble," the preacher said. "You are trouble. I wish you were on the other side. I wish some poor old Yankee corporal had to deal with you all day and all night."

"Sometimes I think you're on the other side, Preacher, you and Swann."

"Well, Box," the preacher said, "we're both fighting against the same foe, but in a way, we are on different sides. I'm on God's side—leastways I try to be. I'm going to let you figure out whose side you're on."

"There he is now," Box said. "Here comes Moses."

They looked around, expecting him to approach, but he avoided them and everyone else.

Box said, "I'm gonna ask him about this."

"I think I'd leave him be for a while," the preacher said. "I don't think he wants to talk to you just now."

The Edge of Light

Moses quietly sulked back into camp and found a log to sit on, barely out of the light of the fires, on the edge of darkness. Trying to settle himself down, he stayed there, separate from the others. They were some distance away and pretended not to notice him. None dared approach.

He was exhausted. It had taken a lot out of him to administer a severe beating to such a stalwart man. He had endured a fairly severe beating himself. He had also been battered by his flight through the dark wilderness. But more than that, his soul had been pummeled and was still in agony. He had never before known shame. But now the indelible image before his mind's eye of a heartbroken little face with deep brown eyes shining with tears was burning hot holes in his heart and soul. Inside, he was writhing in agonizing shame, and he had no idea how to ease his pain.

Tormented, he again lashed out. "Damn you, God. Damn you. I hate you," he said under his breath through clenched teeth. "I hate you. I hate you," he repeated over and over.

He began to sob quietly, "I hate you. I hate you. I hate you. I hate… I hate… I hate… I hate… myself. I hate myself. Oh God, damn me! I hate myself. I hate myself."

He stood and tore at his sad Rebel shirt and threw his head back and quietly swore, "God, damn me! I hate myself!"

So great was his torment that he briefly fell to his hands and knees, with his forehead on the ground. He managed to get back on the log and put his head between his knees and retched. "God, damn me."

Then, like a baby crying himself to sleep, he quietly repeated, "God, damn me." Then, more quietly still, "God, damn me, please."

Over and over, he said those words while they became quieter and quieter, each utterance more pathetic than the last, until finally no words left him.

He wept. He cried softly until he had cried himself out. He had reached bottom. For the first time ever, he had no plan, no scheme, no will to extricate himself from his predicament. The rebel had been utterly routed by the all-conquering love of the Father, his rebellion forever crushed. He resisted no more. His strength had left him. Only his misery remained.

He reckoned only time would help. He thought his only hope was to wait it out. He would stay there alone, in the dark, until sunrise. Surely by then he would be himself again.

So there, on a log at the edge of light, he sat, the world's toughest man, his head in his hands, staring at the ground between his feet, beyond consolation, barren of hope, his broken spirit whimpering in abject defeat.

It was over.

A Child Shall Lead

Some time had passed when he sensed someone approaching from the light. He looked up to see the little girl a few feet away, carefully moving in his direction. He quickly diverted his eyes from hers. He could not bear looking into them again just now.

"You all right, mister?" she cautiously asked.

"Hell yes! Now leave me the hell alone. Git! Go back to your mama."

"I was just worried about you. I saw you over here crying, and I was worried about you."

"I don't need no little girl worrying about me. I'm all growed up. Now clear out. I don't want to see your ugly face again."

As with all little girls, regardless of how fair or plain, it hurts deeply when someone, anyone, tells them they're ugly. The hurt was immediately visible in her face as tears began to flow.

She was walking away when, from Moses's changing heart, came the words, "Wait, little girl. Come on back. I'm… I'm sorry."

The healing had barely begun, and hope was approaching from a direction he had never before considered.

She turned and studied him briefly.

He said, "Come on and sit down right here beside me." Then, in begrudging tones, he added, "I'll try to be nice. I promise."

She studied him a little more and looked into his eyes. He was different. She cautiously sat down on the log beside him, and he tenderly tried to wipe her tears away with his huge, dirty hand.

He began trying to explain his behavior to his reserved acquaintance. "You see, little girl, what I said about you being ugly, well, that was just a lie. I'm a bad man. I've always been a bad man. And I'm a liar."

"You ain't no bad man," she said. "Not now, leastways."

"Yes, ma'am. I'm almost the devil himself—have been as long as I can remember."

The little girl looked at him askance. "Go on now. You ain't no devil. The devil don't cry."

"Well, I always thought of myself as the devil, or his equal, or leastways one of his top hands. But I don't know now. I reckon I'm beginning to wonder."

"You ain't got no horns, no tail. Besides, if you was the devil, you would of killed my daddy back there, but you didn't."

"Well, I wanted to. I sure tried to. But he just takes a heap more killing than anybody I ever come up against. The reason he's alive is … he is alive, ain't he?"

"Oh yes, sir. He's gonna be okay," she said. "He's stout."

"Good. But the reason he's alive is because of you, not me."

"No, sir. It wasn't me that stopped you. It was Jesus."

"Jesus!" he said. "What the hell does—I mean, what does Jesus have to do with it?"

"It was Jesus that got a holt of you."

He studied her momentarily and said, "Whoever it was has some kind of a holt. What makes you think it was Jesus?"

"Who do you think it was?"

He had no answer.

"He convicted you of your sins," she continued. "All that time you was running and trying to hide in the dark, Jesus was convicting you of your sins in your own heart. And now that you've been showed the light, it's time for Him to save your soul."

"Now I don't know much about Jesus," Moses admitted, "but I do know that he's only for good folks, nice folks like you, not bad folks like me."

"We all bad. The Bible says none of us are good enough to get into heaven without Jesus—not me, not you, not anybody."

"You must take me for one of them fools I serve with."

"No, sir."

"You've got to be joshing me. Not anybody? Not even you?"

"Not me or anybody. Have you ever knowed anybody who never did anything wrong, not one single sin?" she queried.

"Well, no. I never ran with people like that. But there must be one somewhere."

"Nope. The Bible says there's not even one, 'ceptin' Jesus, of course."

Moses stared at the child incredulously. "You mean to tell me that the whole damned world is going to hell? How are all you good folks gonna get to heaven?"

"Same way you are."

"Me? I told you, I'm a bad man. There ain't no way in hell they'd have me in heaven. Listen to me, girl. You don't know what 'bad' is. To you, it's sneaking off to the creek for a swim without telling your mama. When I tell you I'm bad, it means… well, I can't tell you what it means, but when it comes to 'bad,' we're in two different worlds."

"No, we ain't. We're all in the same world, this world. And we're all sinners. Jesus took the punishment for all the bad things all of us ever did. Jesus paid the price for all of us sinners, the little ones like me and the big ones like you. He didn't cull nobody. He was punished for all of us so we wouldn't have to be punished ourselves. All we have to do is ask for His forgiveness, and He gives it to us. It's called getting saved."

He stared intently at her and then said, "So, are you saved?"

"Yes, sir!" she said, slightly flabbergasted that he had not yet figured that out. "About three years ago, when I was eight."

"Do you have to be a child like you, or can a grown-up get saved?"

"To Jesus, we're all children."

Neither of them spoke for a little while. Then Moses said, "Do you reckon Jesus could, I mean, do you think He would … save me?"

"He will if you ask Him to. He loves you."

There was another pause, and with disbelief in his voice he asked, "Jesus loves me?"

"Yes."

"How can that be? There's nothing about me to love. And besides, I always hated Him."

"But you don't hate Him now, do you?"

After a few seconds of introspection, and surprised by what he discovered, he said, "No … I reckon not."

She watched him while he stared at the ground, not believing what he had just lost. With his hate gone, it was as if he had wakened from a long nightmare.

"No. I don't hate Him," he said, sounding bewildered. "I don't reckon I hate anybody, 'ceptin' maybe … me."

"He didn't have to die on the cross, you know," she said.

"He didn't? I thought He did. I thought it was his duty or something."

"No. He volunteered. Like I said, He did it because He loves you. And all you have to do to get forgiveness is ask Him for it and mean it. Confess your sins to Him. He already knows all about them anyway. Tell Him you're sorry, and ask Him to forgive you, and then do your very best to live the way He wants you to. You'll still sin, but you won't sin as much, and you'll do a little better each day than you did the day before. He'll always be there to forgive you. But once you're saved, if you're really saved, you're saved forever. My daddy says there ain't no force on earth or in hell strong enough to pry a saved soul out of the all-powerful hands of Jesus."

"I ain't believing this."

"What ain't you believing?"

"I ain't believing Jesus loves me enough to volunteer to die for me and forgive me just so I can stink up heaven for Him."

"Well, you better believe it because my daddy says without Jesus, what hope would we have? Besides, you won't stink up heaven. Jesus will clean you up. We all have sin in our lives, and they don't allow any sin in heaven. None of us can be good enough to get there on our own because no matter how good we are, we still have at least some sin with us. We can't work our way into heaven. The good works come after we're saved. You can't pay your way in. Poor folks like us wouldn't stand a chance. They don't pit our good deeds against our bad ones and then take us, bad deeds and all. No, the only way to get into heaven is to get rid of your sins, and only Jesus can do that for you. My daddy says there's more rejoicing in heaven when a great sinner like you gets saved than any other time."

"I reckon they'd have a parade down those streets of gold if I got saved," he said with a touch of sarcasm. "So, you say Jesus will save me just like I am if I ask Him to and mean it? I don't have to undo all the evil I've done? I don't have to straighten myself out, clean my life up first?"

"No, sir. He'll help you do that after you're saved. It'll be your job to pray every day and read your Bible and try hard to live right. Jesus does the cleaning. Besides, if you tried to do it yourself, you'd never get saved. It just can't be done without Jesus. Nope, the saving comes first, along with the cleaning, and then the works."

Shaking his head and moving backward in disbelief, he said, "You know, I just don't deserve this. The things I've done, the things I've said and meant, I deserve hell."

"I know," she said.

He turned from her to hide his moist eyes.

"That's okay," she said. "I won't tell nobody you cried. A lot of people cry when they get saved. I did."

"You mean I'm saved?"

"No, not yet. You gotta pray. You gotta ask Jesus to forgive you, to come into your heart so you can start all over again with a clean slate, like being born again."

"Well... say, just what is your name anyway?"

"It's Rose, sir. Rose Blount."

"Well, Miss Rose, my name is Jack Moses. In the last couple of hours, I've gone from hating you and God and the whole world to hating myself. Now I'm all the way back to where I reckon I was when I was born, to not hating anyone at all, maybe not even me. I can't remember ever being here before. I did the devil's work every chance I got. Now, after talking to you, I think I might understand getting saved. Even though I deserve to go to hell, Jesus, who never sinned, let Himself be punished for my sins so He could forgive me. What I'm still having the most trouble with is how Jesus could love me that much. Nobody ever loved me but my mama, and she died when I was little. I'm having a little trouble understanding that part of it. I just can't quite get a grip on it."

"You don't have to understand His love, just believe it. Trust Him. My daddy says that the longer you're a Christian the more you'll understand. It'll make more sense to you as time goes by," she said.

She could tell he was still struggling.

He said, "Miss Rose, in all my life, I've never said anything nice to God. I've done nothing but cuss Him. After all I've done, I'm too ashamed to beg Him to forgive me now. I wouldn't know how to pray anyway. Maybe I just oughta let Him out of this one and save Him the trouble. I'm probably more trouble to Him than I'm worth. Hell's never scared me all that much. I just don't know. What do you think I should do?"

"You don't have to worry about putting Him to any trouble. He's already gone to the trouble for you a long time ago. My daddy says Jesus is always eager to forgive and that He wants us to come to Him so that He won't have suffered for nothin'. He's waiting on you right now," she said and paused as she watched for a reaction from him. "I'll pray with you," she said. "It ain't hard. All you have to do is talk to Him and be respectful and honest. Here. Let's get on our knees."

She knelt, and he followed without question.

"Now," she said, "I'll start praying, and then I'll tell you when it's your turn."

She looked up at the big man and saw the fear in his face. Along with the apprehension, there was also the beginning of childlike hope and trust.

"Now, Mr. Jack," she said, "put your hands together like this, and close your eyes."

After he had followed her instructions, she began, "Dear heavenly Father, this is Rose. I want to thank you for my new friend, Mr. Jack, right here next to me. He's lost, and he wants to get saved. But he thinks he's too bad to get saved, but You've probably seen worse. I told him what to do the best I could. So if he don't do it just right, please don't hold it against him. This will be his first prayer, so please, Lord, cut him a little slack if You can see Your way clear. Help him through this, Lord. In Jesus's sweet, wonderful name, I pray. Amen."

She gently touched his arm and said, "Now, Mr. Jack, it's your time."

There was a rather long pause. She peeked to check on him. His eyes were closed tightly. He was having great difficulty getting the first word out.

She was about to speak for him when he finally said, "Well, Lord, it's like Miss Rose said. I need forgiving. You probably already know about that. Trouble is, I ain't no ordinary sinner. I'm Wiley Jack Moses. You probably heard lots about me—all true. I'm so bad there might not be enough forgiveness up there for me and the rest of the world too. I don't want You to use it all up on me. You can probably save a million ordinary sinners with what it'll take to deliver my worthless soul. So if you can't see Your way clear… I'll understand. I always expected to go to hell anyway. But if You can somehow find a way—I mean, if little Rose is right about You being willing to forgive anybody, even me, I promise to spend the rest of my life trying to make up for all the bad things I've done. But hell, Lord, to be honest with You, I probably ain't gonna live past tomorrow no way. So I might not be around long enough to make up for everything. It'd take a long time, because I've done an awful lot of stuff. I just want you to know that before you decide on what to do. But ever how long my life is, I'll try to live it right. And, Jesus, I want You to know that I'm obliged to You for taking my lickin' for me, and I truly am sorry for all the things I did to bring it down on You like that. And even if You don't save me, I ain't gonna carp about it; I ain't gonna hold it against You. If anybody ever deserved hell, I reckon it's me. But I'm gonna try to do better from here on out, even if You don't save me. I'm just tired." He was weeping again now. "I'm just so tired of… I'm so weary of my hate."

Little Rose, on her knees beside him, looked up when she heard him sobbing.

With his voice shaking, he said, "Help me, Jesus. I'm so rotten I can't stand myself. I'm so sorry. Please accept my prayer. Forgive me. Change me."

A few more seconds passed, and he regained his composure, saying, "And, Jesus, I want to thank You for little Miss Rose beside me. She's the first friend I've ever had. She is more than I deserve, her *and* You. Thank You, Jesus."

A few more seconds passed in silence.

"Now say, 'Amen,'" the child gently instructed.

And the man said, "Amen."

He opened his eyes, and the first thing he saw was Rose's little face smiling up at him. His was overcome with joyous love. Still on his knees, he put his powerful arms around her, pulled her up next to him, and held on like a little boy crying on his mama's shoulder. Then he kissed her on the forehead. She wrapped her skinny little arms around his neck and kissed him on the cheek. No words were spoken as they held on to each other for a while.

Finally, he composed himself and said, "I'm not for absolute sure, child. I don't know how I'm supposed to feel, but I think He saved me. I'm different. I'm ashamed and humbled. But I've got happiness in me. I don't think I'm mad at nobody now."

The child just smiled in sweet awe of her Creator and said, "Yes, He saved you. He never says no."

Then he said, "I'm finally a real man, a whole man. I'm gonna try to be God's man, like the preacher, like your daddy. I have Jesus. I ain't never going back. I'm free, and I'm gonna stay that way."

Rose looked at him and, with just a touch of envy in her voice, said, "Maybe someday I'll be free too."

Perplexed, Moses said, "You mean you ain't free? I took off. Didn't that make your daddy the winner?"

"No, Mr. Jack. Some of them said you beat him."

"No, ma'am. I ran away. He won."

"Some of them said you won and that we have to go back."

Jack rose to his feet and took her by the hand and said, "Now you listen to me, Miss Rose. Your daddy won that fight. You show me the way. I've got work to do."

So she put her hand in his and led him to the wagon as, together, they walked toward the light. As they approached, Moses could see all her family there except her father, who was resting inside. The preacher and Swann were there talking to the old man, Rose's grandfather, who was sitting in a chair behind the wagon.

The Rise and Fall of Box

"What's this shi—I mean, what's this mess about them not being free?" Moses demanded of the preacher as he strode into the group, hand in hand with Rose.

"According to Box and Miller, you won the fight," the preacher said. "And Box threatened to go to Lt. Cox if we let them go."

"That's right," Box said as he walked toward them with Miller behind him. "You whupped him just about every way he can be whupped. It was plain for everybody to see that you won. So they go to the provost. And they stay slaves."

"But I didn't win, Box; I ran. He won," said Moses. "What do you say, Miller?"

"Well, it never mattered much to me one way or the other, Jack," Miller said.

"But he never even knocked you down," said Box. "He just wrassled you down. And even then he couldn't keep you there. You got up and whupped his ass, but good. If it hadn't been for the little girl, you would of killed him. The fight was over before you took off."

Ignoring Box, Moses turned toward Rose's family and said, "Y'all put your chairs in the wagon. You're going free."

"Like hell," Box said. "They ain't going nowhere 'cept to the provost. It ain't even legal to let 'em go. Our orders are to take 'em to the provost."

"We all agreed—you too—" Moses said, "to let 'em go if their man won. And he won, so they go. It's that simple, boy."

"Okay then," said Box, "he goes. Just him. The one you say whupped you, even though he can't even stand up. He goes, but the others stay."

"They all go," said Moses.

Everyone was watching this exchange with fascination. They couldn't believe that Box was standing up to Moses. Even more unbelievable, Moses was standing up for the slaves.

"Only he goes," Box insisted. "Only he beat you, so only he goes."

Everyone sensed that Moses had had enough of this when he grabbed the front of Box's shirt and lifted him to his tiptoes.

Their noses almost touching, Moses snarled down at him, "You listen to me, boy. I'm gonna knock your sorry ass—"

Then he caught sight of Rose staring at him. He released the shaken boy and let him down easy, took a deep breath, and quietly said, "Listen, son. They all go. Not just him; all of 'em."

"But why all of 'em, Jack?" Box asked, his voice quivering just a little.

Then, with a gentleness of which they had never thought the man capable, Moses said, "Because, son, he paid the price. He paid the price for all of 'em."

Box looked at Moses for a few seconds, and they could see the fight leaving him. His shoulders slumped, and he very quietly conceded. "They're free."

The reaction was immediate, quiet but exultant celebration among the slaves and soldiers alike, except for Box. Miller, always one to follow the path of least resistance, joined in the celebration as well. They quickly loaded the two chairs back into the wagon as the preacher, Swann, and Moses devised a plan for getting the family out of the Confederate lines.

Fervent Prayers

The family was soon in the wagon and ready to go, with the old man at the reins. Even the mules, looking back at the wagon with their ears perked up, seemed excited.

The Lord had provided a full moon to show the way. The preacher and Swann would lead the mules down the little road, with Moses walking behind the wagon. All three would be armed. They figured it would look better to the guards that way. However, only Silas's weapon was actually loaded.

The tiny detail quietly moved down the narrow, moonlit lane. They passed between camps of soldiers and through the first guard post without stopping. The preacher just explained, as they walked past, that they were delivering contrabands to the provost's holding area in the rear. The sentinels nodded and waved them through, northward, toward the Chambersburg Pike, where they turned westward.

So it went through the next few checkpoints. Except when passing through a guard post, Rose sat on the lowered tailgate of the wagon and talked to Moses. Her hope overflowing, she told him how she wanted to be a nurse when she grew up. It had never occurred to him that a colored child might have dreams and aspirations. As she talked, he slowly began to realize how grievous a sin slavery is. To deny a person his own humanity, his own life, to make a person live, but at the same time not let him live was a crime worse than murder. To rob him of a future and any dreams was to take away all hope in this life. He began to understand why so many slaves were believers, Christians. Jesus was their only hope, all of it. And that hope lay in the next life, the life which no man could deny them.

He looked back on his own life and saw nothing but meanness and evil. Even though he felt secure in his salvation, he was not confident in his ability to live a godly life. His hope, he thought, lay not in life, but in death. And so he yearned for the morrow's action. It would be virtual suicide. He could get on with heaven and be shed of this rotten world he had so horribly befouled. That was his hope.

"I hope you get to be a nurse, Miss Rose," he heard himself say. "You'll be a good one."

"I pray every day for the Lord to let me be a nurse," she said.

Her hope was visible in her eyes and audible in her voice. He began to worry about the dreams of a precious child being dashed on life's jagged rocks.

"Miss Rose, if there was anything I could do to make it happen for you, I'd do it."

"You could pray for me."

"Huh?"

"I said, you could pray to the Lord to let me be a nurse."

"Miss Rose, you know how hard it is for me to pray," he said. "If you hadn't helped me back there, I never could have got through that prayer tonight. I'd still be lost."

"You don't need no help to pray now," she said. "The Lord expects to hear from you every day; He's looking forward to it. You're His child, and He loves you. You should never forget that. So when you pray, just add a little prayer for me. Ask Him to let me be a nurse."

It was so obvious to her, so simple. Just pray.

Again, he saw the hope in her eyes and the excitement of being free and having a future, a life of her own.

He said, "I probably won't live past tomorrow. I'm not gonna get to pray for you very much. But I promise that I'll pray every day for the rest of my life for the Lord to let you be a nurse, a good nurse."

She smiled and said, "And I'm going to pray for God to spare you tomorrow and give you a long, happy life."

Moses could see her unwavering faith, and a tiny seed was planted in his heart.

Then Rose's father reared up from the floor of the wagon and said, "The Lord hears the fervent prayers of a child, and that child prays the most fervent prayers I ever heard. So you better be ready to live."

Moses said, "I don't think y'all understand what's gonna happen tomorrow. The word is that we're just gonna march straight up an open hill into all those guns. They say our outfit will be on the front. I doubt if any of us will come back."

Joseph Blount said, "With all respect, sir, I don't mean to argue, but I think you the one who don't understand. The Bible says that with God all things are possible. If it's the Lord's plan for you to live, you'll live. And if it's His will for my Rose to be a nurse, she'll be a nurse."

Moses looked at the man and then at Rose's smiling face and said, "You'll be a good nurse, Miss Rose."

And she smiled all the more.

Rose's father added, "And remember, sir, you said every day for the rest of your life you'd be saying a prayer for my Rose. God also hears the fervent prayers of a righteous man. The Bible says that."

Moses laughed. "A righteous man? Well, that culls me."

"I wouldn't be too sure about that, sir," Joseph Blount said. "The Lord is changing you. Everybody can see it. He done laid his hand on you in a big way. He has a plan for you. I 'spect you to keep your promise. I covet your prayers for my child."

Moses could see that the big man was serious, and he saw Rose beaming with hope and promise.

He walked up closer to the wagon and took the man's hand and said, "I give you my word, sir, for whatever it's worth, that Rose will be in my prayers every day for the rest of my life."

Rose watched the two men shake hands. She could see the earnest determination in Moses's face, and she could hear it in his voice. She saw tears of joy and hope in her father's eyes as, for the first time ever, he was being addressed by a white man as an equal. She was so proud of them both, her brave father and her faithful friend. But she was proud, most of all, of her Jesus.

They eased past a road that went to the right. A little ways down it, they could see campfires, tents, and wagons.

Moses said, "That's the provost guard, Miss Rose. Not long ago, our outfit was assigned to the provost. I liked that duty then. I'm glad I'm not part of it now."

"Are they gonna come after us?" she asked.

"No. They're not gonna bother us. I think we've only got one more guard post to go through. Then we'll be in the clear."

The last guard post would be the most difficult because the officer would know that beyond them there was no holding area and no provost.

Answered Prayer

As they neared the post, Silas asked the preacher, "How are we going to handle this?"

"I'm not sure," the preacher said. "I can't see him too well yet, but I think I know the officer in charge here. Pray it's who I think it is."

They got a little closer, and the preacher whispered, "It is, praise the Lord! It's a man I baptized when he was just a boy. Let me do the talking."

They got closer still. The guards halted them and one said, "Who's there?"

The preacher replied, "Corporal Elder of the Fifth Alabama Battalion."

The officer looked over at the preacher and said, "Brother Elder, how are you doing?"

The preacher said, "Why, Phillip, I mean, Captain Jennings, what a nice surprise." He saluted the captain, but Jennings ignored it and strode up to the preacher and hugged him, slapping him on the back.

The captain turned to his men with one arm still around the preacher and said, "Gentlemen, this is the man who led me to the Lord when I was just a yard kid." He gently squeezed the preacher one more time and said, "It's so good to see you, Preacher. I heard Archer lost a lot of men yesterday. I was worried about you."

"You can stop worrying about me, Phillip. I'm still in this man's army."

"Yes, sir. That's good to know. I don't know what good all my worrying does anyway. I reckon what's going to happen is going to happen."

"That's right, son," the preacher said. "You know, the Bible says not to worry about anything but to pray about everything."

"Yes, sir. I've heard that sermon before. I don't have any trouble praying. Seems like I do it almost all the time lately.

But I've been having an awful time not worrying," he said with a smile.

"I know, son."

"So, what kind of detail is this you're on, Reverend?" the captain said as he turned toward the wagon.

"Well," the preacher quietly said, "I need to talk to you in private about that, sir."

The captain invited him into his tent, where the preacher, in hushed tones, told him everything. He told him about Lt. Cox, the fight, about Rose, and about Moses's conversion. He left nothing out and told no lies.

"Moses got saved?" the captain asked in disbelief. "Wiley Jack? That Moses? The one who lives in the woods around Ohatchee?"

"Yes, son. That one. Not much more than an hour ago."

He knew the preacher wouldn't lie to him, but he was having trouble believing until he peeked between the flaps of the tent. There stood the unmistakable figure of Wiley Jackson Moses peacefully talking to the people in the wagon.

The captain stared a while and then, very quietly said, "Dear Jesus, forgive my doubt."

"What?" asked the preacher.

"Oh, nothing. I was just thinking out loud. I suppose some day I'll finally learn not to underestimate the Lord. Wiley Jack coming to Jesus—that's just one step short of the devil himself getting saved. If I die tomorrow—and there's a fair chance I will—I can at least say I lived long enough to see a true miracle."

"Well," the preacher said, "We need another one right now, son. We need you to help us free those poor folks out there. They've suffered enough."

Jennings said, "When you were telling your story I sort of figured you were going to ask me to do something like that. Of course, you know you're asking me to disobey standing orders."

"That's right, son. I'm asking you to make the same decision we all made, me and Moses, young Swann, and all the other men in the squad. When we decided to do this, I asked God to make a way for us and to show us that way. He put you here tonight for a reason, Phillip. I know I'm asking a lot, but you're a man the Lord can count on to do the right thing, even if it is against orders. We need another miracle tonight, son, from you."

The captain said nothing for a while. Then he looked over at Moses holding Rose's hand and said, "What kind of soldiers do you reckon this makes us, Preacher?"

"Godly ones, I hope."

"Well," he said, after a pause, "I doubt if I'll even live past tomorrow. They can't execute a dead man, can they?"

"We're all pretty much counting on that, Phillip."

"I can't involve my men in this," Jennings said. "They're all good men, and I don't think any of them would make a fuss. But I can't make them accountable in this thing. I have to bear this alone."

"I understand, son."

"I'm going to lie to my men. Is there such a thing as a good lie?"

"I've never been quite sure. But I do know this: Jesus will happily forgive you."

"Let's go, Preacher. Let's get it done."

As they slowly walked back to the guard post, the captain quietly explained that he was going to tell his men the preacher's detail was delivering the slaves to a special unit far to the rear for immediate transport back to Virginia. The guards had no reason to doubt him.

Jennings then told the preacher, loudly enough for the old man to hear, that when they reached the next fork in the road, about a mile away, bearing left would take them south to the proper area. A right turn, he warned as he glanced at the old man, would take them north, deeper into Yankee territory, toward Harrisburg. Then he quietly told the preacher to return by a different route.

The preacher and the captain then shook hands, saluted, and said their good-byes. The tiny band was allowed to pass.

From inside the wagon, Rose looked over the now-closed tailgate and watched the young officer as she moved past him. She wondered why he looked at her, almost enviously, with a wan smile as he raised his hand in a brief, casual salute in her direction. Her eyes fixed on his, she watched him, with his men, slowly fade into the night.

Where Freedom Begins

They traveled in the peaceful moonlight for a while with no one speaking, until they stopped at the fork in the road. They helped Joseph climb out, and they all gathered at the back of the wagon, the seven of them standing there together.

The preacher said, "Well, folks, this is where your freedom begins. From here on, you're responsible for yourselves. We can't help you anymore, except to pray for you."

"God bless you, sir. God bless you all," the old man said.

"Amen," Joseph added.

Then the old man asked if he could pray. No one objected. The soldiers slung their rifles over their shoulders, and the seven of them held hands, forming a circle. Rose was holding Moses's hand on one side and her father's on the other. Beneath the glow of a smiling moon, she could not help but marvel at the sight of three Confederate soldiers joining hands with her family in their little prayer circle. To her, it was one of the most beautiful, inspiring sights God would ever show her, one she would never forget.

Then her grandfather said, "Let us pray."

Seven heads bowed, and he began.

"Dear Lord, here we stand at the beginning of our new lives. We humbly ask for your guidance and blessings all the way through. Lord, we mightily praise your mercy for delivering us here tonight, for sending these godly men to do your work. Be with them in times of peril. May you bless them all for the rest of their days. In Jesus's merciful name, I pray. Amen."

It took a little while, but both parties shook hands with and hugged each member of the other. The soldiers were especially careful not to inflict any further discomfort on Joseph Blount when they said their farewells to him.

When it was Moses's time, Blount tried to hug him. Moses refused to allow it, saying, "No thanks, mister. I done been hugged by those arms all I care to be. Let's just shake and let it go at that."

The two men smiled and shook hands while the others laughed.

The Blounts climbed back into their wagon, with Jack, Rose, and her mother carefully helping her father in.

Then Jack, looking down at Rose still standing beside him, said, "These are the arms I want to feel around my neck once more before I die."

He got on his knees like before, and she put her little arms around his neck and allowed him to enfold her once more as she kissed his cheek.

She said, "Thank you, Mr. Jack. Remember, I'm gonna pray for you tonight and especially tomorrow. Just like you promised to pray for me, I'll pray for you for the rest of my life."

"Oh, sweet girl, you'll be praying for a dead man."

"No, I won't. You'll live. I've got faith. You'll be like Job in the Bible, old and full of years."

Moses remained clearly skeptical, but he relented, smiled, and hugged her so gently. After a few seconds of what he was convinced was his final embrace in this life, he kissed her on the forehead and carefully placed her in the wagon. The other two soldiers looked on enviously, for they coveted her prayers.

The wagon began to move, slowly leaving Swann and the preacher behind. But Moses, still holding Rose's hand, walked on a few feet.

"Good-bye, Miss Rose. I hope you have a happy life. And you be a good nurse, you hear? You be a good nurse."

"I will, Mr. Jack. I promise. And we will see each other again someday. You'll see."

"Sweetheart, It's a big world and—"

"We will," she said. "We'll see each other again. I know it just like I know you're gonna live."

Moses stopped walking, and the wagon continued down the road into the hope-filled night. Rose's hand pulled out of his, and she began to wave slowly at him.

She quietly said, "Good-bye, Mr. Jack. I love you, and I'll never forget you. Good-bye."

He removed his slouch hat and held it high as her shiny, tear-streaked face receded into the shadows of the forested lane.

Soon, he could make out the distant shape of the wagon but nothing else. He lowered his arm.

Just as he could see her no more, he heard, from the darkness, her faint voice: "Good-bye, Mr. Jack. I'll see you later."

He gazed into the night long after she was gone.

They walked back to camp by a different way, as Captain Jennings had told them. The preacher and Silas talked a little on the way, but Moses was silent. He followed a few feet behind, staring at the ground like a bewildered child.

When they arrived at the campsite, it was late, and everyone who was not on duty was already asleep. Each of them quietly went to his own place for the night.

From birth, Moses had been different, aloof, and usually pitched his camp away from the others. Tonight, again, he would sleep off to himself as he remained aloof, if only for the present. Yet, he would always be unlike other men. Though unchanged in some ways, the man was not the same. He would never be the same again.

FRIDAY, JULY 3RD

But Now Are Ye Light

Moses awoke a little later than usual. The sky showed faint light in the east. A new day was being born. For Moses, it was the first day of his new life. Some early risers already had breakfast sizzling in their pans. Though hungry, he was not quite sure who to eat with, if anyone. Those who had passed for his friends yesterday—Box and Miller—were now possibly his enemies. The men he had scorned the day before—Swann, the preacher, and most of the others—hopefully were his friends. For once, he was unsure and a little apprehensive. He decided to eat alone.

The night before, after climbing into his bedroll, he had lain awake for a while. He gazed through the trees above into the heavens and found himself praying alone, unassisted.

"Dear God in heaven, help me. I don't know who I am anymore. I know who I was. I was a man who knew how to handle himself. I was a man who could take care of himself. I knew my world inside and out. But Lord, I was lost, and now I'm saved. Thank You, dear Jesus, for that, but I don't know how to act or what to do. Please help me. Send me some friends who'll show me how to act like a saved man, how to live like a Christian. And, Lord, most of all, don't ever let go of me. I beg You, Lord, keep me close. Be with Rose and her family. Please bless that child and let her life be a happy one. Let her be a nurse, a good nurse. And, if it's Your will, Lord, let me live long enough to find her and thank her proper-like for all she did for me. But if I should die before that day arrives, just love her for me. And please don't let me neglect her in my prayers no matter how long I live. Keep me faithful. I'm asking all these things in the name of Jesus, my Savior. Amen." Soon, he fell into a deep, restful sleep.

Shortly after he woke the next morning, he was digging through his kit, looking for something to eat when he was tapped on the shoulder.

He looked up, and the preacher said, "Come with me, son. Your friends are fixing your breakfast for you."

Moses grabbed his mess kit and silently followed him to a small group of men cooking on two fires. They had a pot of Confederate coffee going on one and two frying pans of eggs and meat on the other. To a hungry man, the smell of coffee and the sound of food sizzling is almost heaven on earth.

He was admiring the food when he noticed Swann's smiling face and heard him say, "Sit down, Jack. We've been waiting for you."

He found his place on a log among them, and the preacher said, "Men, let's return thanks."

He wasn't exactly sure what returning thanks meant, but he looked around and saw the others bowing their heads. He followed them. The preacher prayed. He thanked God for the food, the fellowship, and for the newly reborn brother in Christ.

Then he concluded with, "And thank You, Lord, for this band of believers. Keep our souls safe in the cleft of Your rock. Amen."

And they all said, "Amen."

Looking up from their prayer, they saw the sun peeking over the low ridge. As was their custom in perilous times, they each paused to admire the new day. Their faces to sun, someone said, "Let's savor it, y'all."

The preacher said, "Savor them all. Each and every one is a gift from a merciful God. Whether the day turns out to be a blessing or a trial, it is a precious gift."

They all gazed a few seconds more. Then they began to pour the coffee and deal out the food. The empty frying pans were refilled with a new round of eggs and meat, and the sizzling began anew.

Moses, in delighted awe, asked, "Where did y'all get all this?"

The preacher just smiled and said, "God shall supply all our needs. He is sufficient in all things. This is a special morning, you know. I'm going to baptize a new believer."

Moses looked around to see everyone smiling at him. Then he realized whom the preacher planned to baptize and said, "Well, Preacher, you reckon they got a river around here big enough to wash away my sins?"

They all laughed and the preacher said, "Son, your sins have already been washed away by the innocent blood of Jesus. The saving isn't in the baptizing. It's in the heart of the believer. That's where the miracle is."

Moses nodded his understanding. He knew his heart was different. Where he had once taken great joy in the misfortunes of others, particularly if he himself had taken a part in bringing them on, he now winced in pain at the thought. He had been forgiven by the Creator of the universe. Mankind, too, was forgiving him, and that forgiveness would soon be complete. But it would be years, almost a lifetime, before he would completely forgive himself. Only God and Moses himself knew the true depth and width of his sins. With this full knowledge, only an omnipotent God had the power and enough love for the sinner to truly forgive and forget such transgressions.

Moses, though much of a man, was nevertheless just a man. It would take him years of growing in the nurturing love of

Jesus to finally forgive himself. His once-hard heart was now tender beyond words. He loved everyone but himself. It would take time, but one day that too would turn. He was at peace with God. He was making his peace with man. Someday he would truly be at peace with himself.

The preacher talked about looking forward to dipping a great sinner. Several of the men in the circle protested in jest, saying they had already been baptized. Moses had thought of himself as the only real sinner in the group. Yet here they were confessing to bearing great guilt themselves. This eased his discomfort somewhat.

The preacher smiled and said, "Yes, we all have sinned and fallen short of the mark. But we've all been baptized—all but Moses here," he said as he put a fatherly hand on the big man's shoulder. "Today, we'll baptize our newest brother in Christ."

Moses looked deep into the preacher's eyes. He saw nothing but God's goodness. As the others got up from their breakfast, they each patted him on the back. He had never known a kinsman. But now, at last, he was in the midst of his brothers.

As he sat on the log and watched his tears hit the ground, he felt each man's gentle touch, and he heard the preacher say, "You're with us now, son, and we're with you. Baptizing is nothing to worry about. It represents Jesus's death, burial, and resurrection. It also symbolizes the death and burial of your old, sinful life and your rebirth to a new life with Jesus. And it's a statement to the world that you've accepted Jesus and that He lives in your heart. You just sit here and enjoy your coffee for a while. I'll send Swann for you directly."

He sat there alone, sipping his coffee and staring first at the ground and then into the woods and then back at the ground again as he thought back on the last couple of days. This was Friday. Just two days earlier, on Wednesday, he had almost been killed in combat. The things that had saved him were his own prowess as a fighting man and his animal-like ferocity and instinct for survival rather than a love of life. He preferred life over death, but not by much. He went to sleep that night actually a little disappointed at still being here, in this life. Thinking himself one of Satan's disciples—a demon perhaps—he had always considered hell his eventual home. It was his opinion that he would fit in just fine there. He did not fear death.

And then there was yesterday, Thursday. Archer's Brigade had been held in reserve. They could hear the battle raging in the distance, but they saw no action. It was a day for them to pull themselves together in preparation for imminent combat. It stayed that kind of day till supper when Rose and her family were brought into their midst. Then Moses's world was turned on its head.

Now, today, Friday, Moses would start learning his way around his new world even though he fully expected it all to end by sundown. Old Bob had already tried the right and then the left. Everyone was convinced that today he would make one last desperate charge up the middle. They were right about Old Bob. The Fifth would be in the middle of the middle and on the front.

Moses was still in deep thought when Swann approached and said, "Preacher's ready for you, Jack."

He followed Swann to the creek, a small tributary of Willoughby Run located near the southwestern slope of Herr Ridge, close to their camp. There, he saw the preacher standing waist-deep in the middle of the little stream. He was fully clothed except for his shoes, socks, and hat, all of which were on the creek bank under the watchful eye of a trusted friend. It was summer, and the clothes would dry soon enough, but the precious shoes were to be carefully preserved. Swann and Moses removed their shoes, socks, and hats and put them in the safekeeping of the preacher's friend.

As they were wading toward the preacher, Moses asked, "You getting baptized too?"

"No," Silas said. "I've already been baptized, sprinkled when I was little. I'm just going to help the preacher baptize you."

"You mean I'm a two-man job?"

"No." Silas laughed. "But somebody has to hold the preacher's Bible while he dips you. He can do it by himself, but it will definitely take both hands."

When they got to the preacher, he positioned Moses on one side and Swann to the other. A sizable crowd had gathered on the creek bank to see if what they had heard was true. Moses's infamy was widespread.

The preacher put his hand on the man's shoulder and, with his other hand, held his Bible high in the air, silencing the whispering congregation.

"Brothers," he said loudly enough to be heard over the gently flowing waters, "we have gathered to welcome a newly reborn child into the cleft of the rock. This man has proclaimed his love of and trust in Jesus, our Savior. He has confessed his sins to God and has been forgiven. If any saved man here has an unresolved difference with this man, he must forgive as he was forgiven. Your differences are no more. You are brothers in the Lord. Let us pray."

Most of the hats were already in hands, but those few that remained on heads were discretely removed as they bowed and the Reverend Elder began.

"Merciful Father, thank You for Your saving grace and for this precious soul who has seen the light. And for the little angel You sent to show him the way, thank You. Make this man strong in the Lord and in Your love. Fill his heart with Jesus, and never let him stray. Thank You for Jesus's love, for it is always in His name that I pray. Amen."

And the multitude said, "Amen."

The preacher turned to Moses, who was looking more like a man condemned than one saved, head bowed, hands crossed in front of his body, almost as if they were tied.

"Wiley Jackson Moses," he said strongly. After pausing long enough for the words to bounce off the trees and soak into the ears of all present, he said, "On your profession of faith, and in obedience to His command, I baptize you, my brother, in the name of the Father, the Son, and the Holy Ghost." He handed his Bible to Swann and said, "We are buried with Him by baptism unto death."

The preacher lowered the big man into the water and kept him there until he was totally engulfed. Moses was as compliant as a trusting child. Brother Elder was an old hand at baptizing. As he deftly lifted the man out of the water, there was another strong chorus of amens. The green water around him turned slightly brown as his filth drifted away.

"And just as Christ was raised from the dead, so shall you walk in new life," the preacher said. "For ye were sometimes darkness, but now are ye light in the Lord. Walk as children of light."

He no longer bore the countenance of one condemned. He was unbowed, and he was smiling through the water dripping down. His arms lifted high in victory, his battered, yet handsome face looking toward heaven, it was plain to see that he had been born again.

He lowered his arms and looked at the preacher, saying, "Thank you, Preacher. God bless you."

"He just did, son."

Suddenly, a man on the creek bank shouted, "Jesus, Jesus forgive me! I doubt You no more."

He jumped into the water, boots and all, and began wading toward the preacher, saying, "If he can save Wiley Jack Moses, he can save me. I've asked the Lord to forgive me, and I'm a saved man. Please, baptize me now, brother. I'm next."

As the preacher talked to the man, Moses made his way to the shore and put his shoes on as he sat on the ground. When he stood up, someone shook his hand, and he saw a line of men waiting to do the same. Most of them were just familiar faces, and some he knew not at all, but he was well acquainted with a fair number of them. Most of the men who knew him personally were a little skeptical about his salvation. Many of those who had only heard of him were just as skeptical, considering his reputation. When shaking his hand, these men would hold on a little longer than the others and stare into his eyes, waiting to see who stared back. Without fail, the faces of these men would go from stern, justifiable doubt to a soft smile as they tried to offer some kind words of encouragement.

One Ohatchee man who knew Moses better than most held tight to his hand and said, "Is that really you in there, Jack?"

"It is, Bill. It's really me. I got saved. Can you believe it?"

"I'm trying."

"I know it don't seem possible, but it happened. All my hate is gone."

The man released his grip on his hand but continued to look into his eyes for a few seconds and said, "Then I reckon our little war is over?"

"My part of it is," Moses said. "The rest is up to you."

The man studied him a little longer and finally said, "It's over."

They shook hands again. The man walked on, and the line began to move once more.

Soon, the preacher had baptized all the new converts, and everyone had climbed out of the water onto the bank. There were hugs and handshakes all around. The little string band that had been playing hymns finally stopped and shook hands with the new believers. Here and there, individuals and small groups were kneeling in prayer. Moses looked around at his new friends and realized that they cared for him. They actually considered him their friend. And yes, perhaps, they really did love him.

This thing about love, in any direction, whether coming in or going out, was completely new to him. He watched young Swann and the preacher as they laughed and talked with the others, and he knew that he loved them. Knowing today's action would be lethal, he was deeply concerned for their lives.

As he watched them, he became even more aware that he was standing on the cusp of a new life. Once again, he looked back over the old one, his first thirty-three years. He thought back on the way he had been just twelve hours before: the anger, the hate, the incredible cruelty and savagery, the seemingly unquenchable thirst for vengeance against countless ubiquitous offenders.

What had made him that way? Was it his mother? At some point when he was a teenager, he realized that she must have been a whore. But what little memory he had of her was sweet. Though she was not what anyone would call a nice lady, she was, as far as he could remember, a loving, nurturing mother. He could not and refused to fault her for his vile nature.

Perhaps the blame could be laid on the drunken woodsman who reared him. He was, after all, a seemingly worthless specimen. Looking back on the old man, he saw that he had been haunted by his own ghosts, driven by his own demons. He could not bring himself to lay any blame at the feet of that pathetic soul.

Was it because he never knew his father or even his name? He had decided long ago that even his mother did not know who had fathered him. Perhaps he had just gotten his bad blood from his father, whoever he was.

As he tried to determine where to lay the blame, he watched his new Christian brothers around him. He thought about what he had often heard the preacher say about returning kindness for meanness and love for hate and what a fool he had thought the man for thinking that. He thought about the choices he had made in his own life and what he, himself, had always returned for meanness and hate. He had seen countless opportunities to turn, to show love in hate's place, to offer forgiveness instead of vengeance, to do what is known in the depths of every heart to be noble and good. Yet, he had let them all pass—until the night before. Now he understood that the responsibility for his wicked, wasted life lay within. He, and only he, was to blame. But that was over now and he was resolved not to waste his new life, this precious gift. Whether it lasted five hours or five decades, this one would be different.

Much about Moses had changed. But as his gaze moved from the past to the future, one thing was again the same. He was, as usual, without doubt or fear.

The Blessing

After the baptismal service, Silas thought about the extra pair of shoes his mother had secretly given him. The shoes on his feet were still in pretty good shape. They looked a bit rough from the march north, but in spite of that, the soles and the uppers had a lot of service left in them. They were good shoes, better than the ones the army had been issuing back when they had some to issue. His mother had spent a fair amount on them and the extra pair just like them.

Silas worried almost constantly about the extra pair being discovered, and he felt great guilt each time he looked at Box's filthy feet. Silas was a good-hearted, generous boy, full of God's kindness. Yet he had promised his mother to keep the shoes for himself. Silas going off to war at such a young age had been difficult for her. Giving him the shoes was just one more expression of love from a devoted Christian mother to her precious little boy.

But to Silas, who was at first glad to get them, the shoes had become a great burden. He was torn between the love for his mother, of which the shoes were his only tangible reminder, and his Christian teachings since infancy that compelled him to share with those less fortunate.

With all the stress on him, facing the possibility of death, he needed a blessing. Through prayer and reading his Bible, he decided to give his extra shoes away, and he had to do it before the big charge expected that afternoon. He had thought about giving away the used pair and keeping the new ones for himself.

But he knew that was not acceptable. He had to give away the new ones.

Box was the only possible recipient because only his feet were small enough. He was a hate-filled, foul-mouthed smart-aleck whom Silas hated to see coming. Though he was little, like Silas, the similarity ended there. He was reared in the hardscrabble world of the Appalachian foothills of northeast Alabama. If nothing else commendable could be said about him, he was tough. And he hated Silas.

Silas knew that two nights earlier, Box would have gotten up off the ground and cleaned his clock had the preacher and Kirby not stepped in. He and the thousands like him who were of Anglo-Saxon and Scots-Irish descent were the primary reasons the Confederate Army had performed so well against overwhelming numbers and wealth.

In Silas's mind, all these things made Box the perfect recipient of the gift. He dragged the bag containing the shoes out of his kit. He stuck it under his arm and went looking for the "little demon," as the preacher quietly called him. He soon found him on the creek bank, washing and inspecting his feet.

"Hey, Box," he said.

Box looked up and, just as Silas expected, said, "What the hell do you want?"

Silas had to smile. "This really is going to be a blessing," he said to himself.

"Nothing. I don't want nothing...I mean, anything."

He was trying hard not to adopt the vernacular of the hills, but it was difficult.

"Well then, what you doing down here? The preacher told us to stay away from each other."

"I just came down here to give you something. It's in this bag," he said as he held it out.

Box looked at it suspiciously for a few seconds, remembering the times in his childhood he had given sacks of cow manure as a mean joke. He carefully took the bag and, holding it at a distance, opened it enough to peek inside. His look of suspicion changed to delighted disbelief.

"Shoes!" he breathed. "Shoes!"

He pulled them out of the bag and quietly admired them.

Silas sat down beside him and said, "They're yours. I think they'll fit. We're about the same size."

Box reached in one of the shoes and pulled out a neatly folded pair of new socks. His eyes began to water. He silently slipped on the socks and reverently put on the first shoe. Then he pulled another pair of socks out of the other shoe.

Silas said, "I had forgotten about the socks, but they're yours too, both pair. My mother asked me to keep the shoes for myself, but I couldn't stand the sight of you walking around barefooted anymore. So there they are. My mother will understand."

"I'm sure she will," said Box. "She's probably a real nice lady."

"Like your mother," said Silas.

"Nah!" Box laughed. "My mama's something else. She's probably not like your mama at all. But she sure does love me. You said your mama gave you these shoes. You know what my mama gave me?"

"No, what?"

"A kiss on the cheek. She said that was all she had. And she told me to come back alive and to bring our independence with me."

"That would be nice," Silas said.

"Yeah," Box said. "I sure hope I can give her at least one of those things. Both would be nice."

He very carefully fastened the other shoe to his foot and got up and walked around in them a little and said, "Silas, you better not be joshing me about this 'cause you'll play hell getting them off me now, boy."

Silas had not done much laughing lately, but he laughed a little now and said, "I'm not joshing you. They're yours, a gift from a loving God."

"Who, you?"

"No, man! I'm not talking about me."

"What are you talking about then? What made you do it?"

"Nothing made me do it. Like I said, I just got tired of watching you running around without any shoes. I guess you could say Jesus told me to give them to you."

Box looked at him askance, so Silas added, "Oh, I don't mean He walked up to me and told me to give you those shoes. He just laid it on my heart, and I knew what I had to do."

Box was silent as he admired the shoes. Then he said, "I ain't never had no new shoes. I've had a few pair of used ones, hand-me-downs, but no new ones. These are the first. Even the ones the army gave me were used."

Silas said, "Well, no man has ever been in those but you. They're virgins."

Box laughed and said, "Boy, they sure feel good. And all this time, Silas, I thought you were just a spoiled little mama's boy, a dandy sprat. I couldn't figure out what you were doing in an infantry outfit like the Fifth. I reckon I was wrong about you."

"No, you weren't wrong," Silas quietly confessed. "I am a spoiled little mama's boy. And I don't know what I'm doing here either. I'm just not as tough as you and the others. I'm really worried about this afternoon. I just hope I can hold up my part and not show yellow. I'm just plain scared."

"Hell, boy, you think I ain't scared?" Box said. "I'm mighty scared. After a while I reckon it just don't show as much, but it's still there. But leastways now I got shoes on my feet, thanks to a pretty decent fella from Mobile, and his mama. Silas, I'm obliged to you, and I sure am sorry about all the hard times I've been giving you. Moses was right to call me a little piss-ant."

"Moses called you that?"

Box grinned and said, "Yeah, when there weren't nobody else around."

"Well," Silas said, "that's what he called me the other day when I wouldn't shoot that dog."

"You don't mean it!" Box said. "And all this time I thought I was the only one in the outfit."

"Nope. There's two of us."

"Hey, I reckon that sorta makes us like brothers, don't it, Silas?"

"I reckon, that and a whole lot more. We're brothers in more ways than one."

Laughing, Box quietly said, "If we're a couple of little piss-ants, what do you reckon that makes Moses?"

"I guess that makes him just about the biggest piss-ant we've ever seen. But don't tell him I said so. I wouldn't want to test his salvation so early in his walk."

They laughed together, and Box said, "From here on out, you've got a friend in me. Here. I want you to have these," he added as he handed Silas the extra pair of socks.

"No," Silas said. "Those are yours. You keep them."

"Now listen, boy," Box said, feigning anger. "In all my life, nobody's ever give me nothing till now. And I ain't never give nothing to nobody either—mainly because I ain't never had nothing to give. But right now I have an extra pair of brand-new, virgin socks, and I want to give them to my new friend. Come on, Silas. Please take them. Let me give them to you."

Silas smiled as he hesitated, and then he took them.

"Thanks, Box," he said. "I'm gonna put them on right now."

As the proud benefactor looked on, beaming, Silas took off his shoes and old socks with holes in the toes. He washed his feet in the cool creek and dried them with his old socks. Then, with much more pomp and flourish than such an event could possibly merit, he pulled the new socks onto his feet. Before putting his shoes on, he stuck his feet out and wiggled his toes admiringly. He was hoping his comedic antics would amuse his new friend. But Box was not amused. He was moved, almost to tears. When Silas realized how much it meant to the poor boy to give him the socks, he stretched out the process as much as possible. He could almost hear him smiling next to him.

Then he said, "Box, thanks man. They're mighty fine. They feel so good."

"Don't they though," he said knowingly.

"Yeah, they do. Listen, Box. I wonder if I could ask you to do something for me?"

"Sure, boy. You just name it."

"I'd appreciate it if you wouldn't say anything about where you got the shoes," Silas said.

"Why, Silas?"

"I don't know. I guess I'm just a little ashamed that I didn't give them to you sooner."

"Aw, don't you worry none about that," Box said. "But I won't say nothing. I won't have to. They'll figure it out quick enough. But I'll keep your little secret. It's the least I can do for my friend."

"Thanks. I really do appreciate it."

They talked and laughed a spell, and for a little while, they were what they were meant to be: two little boys sitting on a creek bank enjoying a summer morning.

"Silas, you know what you said while ago about Jesus laying it on your heart to give me these shoes?" Box said.

"Yes."

"Well, I've been thinking. I know it don't show, but I got saved when I was about nine or ten. I went to church for a while, but I drifted away a few years back, fell in with a rough bunch. I pretty much forgot about Jesus. But I reckon He didn't forget about me, did He?"

"No, He didn't forget you. He still loves you just as much now as when He saved you, just as much as when He died for you."

"Well, I reckon I need to get back to Him. This morning when I watched Moses get baptized, it started me to thinking. If Jesus can save him and change him the way He did, I reckon He can do anything."

"You reckon right," Silas said. "He found a way to put a new pair of shoes on your feet in the middle of a war way up here in Yankee land, didn't He? He probably had you in mind when my mama gave me those shoes. I was just the delivery boy."

Silas could see his heart moving homeward.

He let him think a few seconds more and said, "I gotta go, Box. I'm going to leave you alone so you can thank Jesus for those shoes. And I'm going to thank Him for my new socks and my new friend. I'll see you later."

Box smiled and then did something that caught Silas by surprise: he hugged him. He didn't slap him on the back like a good old boy. He just hugged him, held him and squeezed hard for a few seconds. Silas hugged him back and then left him alone on the creek bank. Before Silas got out of sight of him, he looked back in Box's direction and saw him kneeling, his head bowed, a man making peace with his creator.

Walking back to the encampment, Silas's heart was lighter, and he was smiling.

He thought to himself, *I reckon it really is more blessed to give. It really is.*

And so now, in Cpl. Elder's squad at least, all God's children had shoes. And Pvt. Swann had his blessing.

This Great Sin

It was mid-morning when they broke camp and began the march to Seminary Ridge about a mile and a half to the east. In the few hours since sunrise, they had had a brotherhood breakfast, a small revival, and several baptisms. In addition to all this, Pvt. Box was now splendidly shod.

When asked about the shoes, Box would just smile and say, "Jesus give 'em to me."

It was clear to everyone that Swann was the only possible source. Many of the men, the preacher and Moses among them, smiled at him and gave him a pat on the back. It had been a good morning.

They arrived at Seminary Ridge around ten thirty. Pickets were quickly chosen to relieve the ones from other units who had been on duty since shortly after sunup. They were sent into the anticipated field of advance. On the right end of the Southern line, the pickets had pulled down fences and other obstacles to an orderly advance. However, in front of the Southern center and left, the fences were behind the Union picket lines. So the fences before Archer's Brigade still stood.

From Cpl. Elder's squad, Pvt. Box was assigned picket duty. He and the other pickets would take cover and exchange sporadic fire with the Yankee pickets. When the charge came, they would join in as the advancing line overtook their position.

As Box marched off in his new shoes with his fellow pickets, he turned back to his friends one last time, smiled, and said, "Remember, y'all, Jesus give 'em to me."

He, too, was different.

By eleven o'clock, preparations were largely complete. They were sheltered somewhat by the trees. Although they heard the sounds of a distant battle, they had not yet come under fire.

Some of the men had lunch. Others preferred not to eat so soon before combat. A few napped. An occasional artillery piece would fire for ranging purposes, and there had been a couple of brief artillery exchanges. With these exceptions, it was fairly quiet from eleven o'clock until about one on Seminary Ridge. By now, even the distant firing on Culp's Hill had subsided.

Silas thought it strange that silence had fallen so noticeably on them. For a while, the loudest noise he heard was that of one of his brothers snoring peacefully in the shade of a nearby tree. He could almost close his eyes and imagine himself at home on a Sunday afternoon, listening to his father napping on the couch in their parlor. He felt a welcome peace come over him. He still had a terrible ordeal before him, but at least and at last, he felt as if he were among friends. But he still had no best friend, no Sonny.

This peaceful interlude lasted until a little after one o'clock when first one and then the other 149 Confederate guns began their bombardment of the Yankee lines at the top of Cemetery Ridge. It sounded very impressive to everyone, and it did some damage to the Yankee defenses at the summit. Yet, as the Confederates would later learn, many of their shots were high, and they were using defective fuses, which caused their shells to explode late, beyond the intended targets. While they did considerable damage in the Union rear, they left the emplacements at the summit essentially intact.

At about a quarter past one, a few Union guns began to reply with intermittent fire. An occasional shell would burst in the treetops above the Southerners. They took some casualties. The men of the Fifth heard that the worst of it was to the south, to their right, where Kemper's Brigade was being pounded by enemy artillery. But for most of the hunkered-down assault force, the worst part of the shelling was that it gave them a foretaste of what they would endure as they crossed almost three quarters of a mile of open ground between them and the enemy.

The Union guns kept firing for about an hour and a half. Their bombardment was sporadic and never as intense as that of the Confederates. Finally, at about a quarter of three, their fire petered out. The men were ready for it to stop, and they were ready to get on with the thing. When they heard the order, they eagerly stood up and took their positions amongst the trees. But their own batteries were still firing. Then, a seemingly endless ten minutes later, the Southern guns fell silent.

To his right and left, through the trees, Silas saw units being addressed by their commanders. He spotted other units in prayer. Maj. Van De Graaff appeared before them and spoke.

"Men, our day has arrived. Friday, July the third, 1863 is the day for which the Fifth Alabama Infantry Battalion and the Army of Northern Virginia will be forever remembered by a grateful nation. We are not here in this foreign land because we wish to be. We are not here to conquer and subjugate. We are here in hopes of avoiding being conquered and subjugated.

We are here because our home has been invaded and our family threatened. The only way to prevail in this struggle is to take the fight to the enemy on his own soil. We are righteous in our cause. Not only do we have the right to protect our families and homes, but we are obligated to do so, just as any honorable man would be. Today, we shall win our independence. On this day, we shall show those who would oppress us that it is not worth their cost. Today, we will convince them to leave us in peace so we can all eventually go home.

"Men, the sacrifices we make today are not just for our country, but for our mothers and fathers, our wives and children, and for each other. Our objective is that little stand of trees you see at the crest of the ridge. Before those trees stands a low, stone wall that stretches the width of the field. You will find your foe behind that wall. The wall makes two right angles in that area. That angle and the stand of trees is where we will camp tonight."

He paused and then said, "It seems it has all come down to this. Spend your blood well, men. Let's get it done." Then, sounding like a worried father, he said, "Be brave, boys... be brave. Show mercy where you can. May God bless us all. Now I am going to ask Brother Elder to lead us in a brief prayer."

The men smiled at the way the major had emphasized the word brief when asking the preacher to pray. They were all familiar with the preacher's affinity for lengthy prayers. But the preacher, being the devout man of God that he was, was not about to let such an opportunity pass without at least the tiniest of sermons.

He said, "Men, I'll make this quick."

A slight smile crept across the major's face.

The preacher continued. "In the fourteenth chapter of John, Jesus said 'Let not your hearts be troubled.' In Luke, chapter 23, he said, 'Today shalt thou be with Me in paradise.' And Revelation 21:4 says, 'And God shall wipe away all tears from their eyes: And there shall be no more death, neither sorrow nor crying.'

"Let us bow for prayer."

Every hat was removed, every head bowed as the preacher began.

"Dear heavenly Father, as we stand here on Jordan's stormy banks, we humbly ask You to give us the courage to face the task before us. Forgive us our sins, Lord, especially this great sin called war, for we are soldiers, Lord, and death-guilty. In this battle, Lord, whether we prevail or whether we are vanquished, let us acquit ourselves honorably. And, Lord, please keep our souls safe in the cleft of Your rock until that day when You shall wipe away all the tears from our eyes and take us home with You to Canaan's fair and happy land. Hear our prayers, oh Lord, for it is in Jesus's precious name we pray."

And they all said, "Amen."

All Set to Go

After the prayer, they reformed their lines. The Fifth would be in the front and center, on the cutting edge of the charge.

Moses saw the preacher making his way back to his position and pulled him aside, saying quietly, "Preacher, ain't there something we can do to get Swann and Box out of this? Especially Swann. Surely one helpless little boy, more or less, ain't gonna make any difference in something this big."

"I'm sorry, Jack," the preacher said. "This is a maximum effort. Everybody goes. And who knows but what Swann might make a difference up there. And Box is already on the picket line. We can't do anything about him now."

"I don't think Swann has even fired his weapon yet. How can he make a difference like that?" Moses asked.

"Only the Lord knows, Jack."

"Maybe he could help the cooks today," Moses persisted.

"The cooks are all going up with us, Jack. There's nothing we can do."

"Maybe he could pull picket duty in the rear," Moses said. "He's just a yard kid."

"No," the preacher said. "Those pickets are already on duty, and they were chosen from the outfits that saw action yesterday. And besides, this army is full of yard kids."

The preacher paused and then said, "Jack, Silas has to go up with the rest of us. There's nothing any of us can do about it. Besides, I don't think he wants any special favors."

Moses did not respond, but the preacher could see that the big man was not yet ready to concede defeat in the matter.

Finally, the preacher said, "Jack, we all have to go up the hill. If it's the Lord's plan that all of us live, we'll all live. If it's His plan that only one survives, then that man will survive. All life belongs to Him. It's out of our hands, son. I'm not a betting man, but if I was I'd put my money on you as the man with the best chance of getting through this thing."

"Me? Why me?"

"Because you've got Rose praying for you right this minute. She's a special child. Her faith is strong, and that makes her prayers strong."

"You don't really believe that's going to make any difference today, do you?"

"Don't you believe she's going to keep her word and pray for you?"

"Sure, but—"

"Well, don't you believe in the power of prayer?" the preacher asked.

After a few more seconds of silence, the preacher smiled.

Finally, Moses answered, "Preacher, prayer is a sweet thing, and there is no doubt in my mind that my little Rose is praying for me right now. But there ain't no way prayer is going to stop a minié ball or a piece of grapeshot."

Moses stared defiantly into the good man's eyes. Cpl. Elder couldn't keep from smiling just a little more.

"You don't think so?" he said.

"No."

Still smiling, the preacher said, "Jack, someday—"

"Now, don't tell me He's gonna settle my hash," Moses said laughing.

"No," the preacher said with a chuckle. "He did that last night. But someday you'll know a lot more about the power of God's love than you do today. But let me give you your first Sunday school lesson right now. Here it is."

Looking back into Moses's eyes, he could see some doubt and maybe a little confusion, but absolutely no fear. And he saw no hate. That was gone forever. In its place, he saw only goodness and hope.

He put a fatherly hand on the man's powerful shoulder and said, "In God's love, all things are possible."

Moses smiled and said, "I hate to tell you this, Preacher, but I done heard that one."

A look of mild astonishment on his face the preacher asked, "Who, Rose?"

"Her daddy."

The preacher laughed and said, "So the Lord sent you the same message twice in two days. He's trying to tell you something, son."

"Let me ask you something, Preacher. Did Jesus really say 'Let not your heart be troubled. Today you will be with Me in paradise'? Did He say that?"

"They weren't together like that, but He said them. And He meant them."

With that, the preacher patted Jack gently on the arm and said, "I need to get in place," and strode to his position.

As Moses watched him walk away, he quietly said, "My heart ain't troubled 'cause I aim to be with Jesus today in paradise. I'm all set to go."

But the preacher didn't hear him.

Sturdy and True

Moses was positioned in the front rank. There were men to each side of him but no one before him except the flag bearers. He wanted it that way.

Presently, Silas appeared at his side and said, "I figured I'd go up with you if that's okay."

"Fine with me," Moses said with a smile, "if you don't mind being on the front."

"Actually, I'm just trying to get as close to Rose's prayers as possible," Silas said a little sheepishly.

"She is something, ain't she?" Jack said.

"That she is."

A little more time passed and Silas quietly said, "Some of the men think I'm a coward. Sometimes I think they might be right."

"Ain't no cowards here," Moses gently responded. "Not now. There's a lot of worried men, but no cowards, and that includes you."

Then Moses grinned and said, "We saw the way you scrapped Box's ass the other night. If any of the men thought you were a coward, they don't now. There's nothing wrong with you, Silas."

Silas smiled, saying, "Well, I sure hope you're right. But I know one thing for certain. Like you said, I am truly one worried man."

"With what we're facing, only the fools aren't worried," Moses said.

Then he added, "Listen to me, Silas. When we start up that hill, it won't be so bad at first. We'll just have to dodge a cannon ball here and there. Just a walk in the sun," he said with a wink. "But when we get within range of their muskets and canister, it'll get mighty hot mighty fast. When that happens, Silas, you'll be able to look behind you and you'll see a lot of good men, brave men, just turn around and walk back down the hill. They ain't cowards. It just ain't their day to die for their country. They'll live to fight and maybe die for her another day. You remember all those Yankees we fought the other day? We killed some brave men, but a lot more just turned around and walked away. Those could be some of the men we'll face today. You can bet they're worried right now, but there ain't a coward in the bunch.

"Silas," he said a little more quietly, "when we start closing with them and it heats up, I want you to know that you can turn around and walk back down the hill, and nobody will say anything to you. You'll have lots of company. I won't think any less of you. I've been there myself. And you'll live to fight another day."

Silas said, "I don't think I can do that, Jack. I don't think I can walk away. As much as I would like to, I just couldn't. I couldn't dishonor my father. I can't do that to him."

"Your father? Don't you think he would rather have you back home in one piece, even with y'all's honor beat up a little, than to never see you again?"

Silas had no answer. Jack could see that the boy was simply incapable of knowingly dishonoring his family, or his country, or his God. It just was not in him, no matter how great his fear. As Jack studied the boy, he began to understand the difference between fearlessness and courage. He came to know that his own lack of fear had never really amounted to courage. Looking at his frightened friend, he knew he was gazing into the face of a stronger man, a braver man than himself.

Finally, Silas said, "Sometimes it seems that all I can think about is going home. But now I feel like I'm so far away I just can't get there from here."

Jack's heart ached for his little friend.

He said, "I reckon we'll all be home someday."

"Jack, all I know to do is to walk up the hill until we've won or I'm dead. If I make it to the top, I probably won't be any good to anybody, but I've got to try," Silas said.

Finally, Jack relented.

"Okay, Silas. Listen. Stay close behind me, and stay low. If somehow we manage to get to the top and some Yank gets the drop on you, don't hesitate to surrender. Maybe you'll get swapped back to us in one of those exchanges. But, Silas, you're a soldier, and you'll do what a soldier has to do. Whether it's kill a man, or die, or walk away to fight another day, you'll get it done. And for the first time ever, I'm going into one of these things with a friend beside me. Finally, I'm not alone."

It was then Silas realized that Moses was his best friend, his Sonny. For a little while that morning, he thought it might be Box. But it was Wiley Jackson Moses. Of all the men in the Army of Northern Virginia, he was the last one Silas expected the Lord to send. But there he stood, sturdy and true. The old adage about God working in mysterious ways came to mind. He could not help but smile just a little at the sweet irony of it all.

They turned toward the enemy. No more words would pass between them until they reached the summit. Silas, though still frightened, now felt as though he could face his fate, for he too had a friend beside him. No longer conspicuous or alone, he was an American soldier in the Army of the South. He would do his duty and accept his lot. Like the others, his uniform was fading to brown.

A Field of Faces

As a splendid army in rags quietly stood together awaiting the order to advance, they looked up the rise toward the distant foe, each man in his own thoughts. But for the sound of their bonny flags flapping in the breeze, there was silence.

In the quiet before the storm, Moses listened wistfully as a blue jay bravely resumed its call from the battered trees behind him. As it called him home, he was reminded of autumn and his little cabin hidden deep in the cool, lushly forested hills of Calhoun County. Then he heard it no more. Positive he would never hear it again, he wondered if heaven would be anything like autumn in Alabama, the closest thing to paradise he had ever known.

His mind went to his mother as he recalled a sweet memory of her. He remembered her rocking him to sleep when he was very small. He felt a soft kiss on his forehead and heard her singing to the rhythm of her rocking.

>There's a nest for Robin Redbreast,
>
>There's a hive for Busy Bee,
>
>There's a hole for Jackie Rabbit,
>
>and a bed for me.

He thought of how young his mother must have been when she died, probably in her early or mid twenties. Grieving for her, he prayed that somehow during her pathetic life she had found Jesus.

The thought of her kiss took him to the night before as he remembered Rose's little arms tight around his neck and her kiss soft on his cheek. He knew that he had never been more of a man than a few hours earlier when, for a short while, he was a little girl's hero, her champion, her deliverer. He owed her so much. But all he could do was pray for her. And so he did. He silently prayed for her safety and happiness. And he ended it the same way he would end his daily prayers for the rest of his life.

"And, Lord, please let Rose be a nurse, a good nurse. For it is in Jesus's name I pray. Amen."

Rose had led him into a world he had always scorned, a world of noble compassion and of fellowship and reconciliation with a loving God. Even though he expected to die within the hour, he was, as usual, without doubt or fear.

When they started up the hill, his first step would be the beginning of a long journey in the company of an ever-forgiving God, from whom he would never stray. His spirit had never known such calm. In the midst of war, he was at peace.

In a field of faces grim with dread and resolve, his alone shone with a faint smile as he faced the high ground and serenely gazed at death.

1. Eleventh Corps
2. NY 126th
3. NY 108
4. NY 111th
5. NJ 12th
6. DE 1st
7. CT 14th
8. WV 7th
9. Sherrill & Smyth
10. PA 71st
11. PA 72nd
12. NY 10th Bat.
13. PA 106th
14. PA 99th
15. NY 42nd
16. PA 114th
17. MA 19th
18. ME 3rd
19. PA 121st
20. PA 2nd Cav.
21. NJ 1st: A
22. ME 4th
23. NY 1st: K
24. First Corps
25. VT 16th
26. VT 13th
27. PA 71st
28. PA 69th
29. NY 1st IB
30. US 4th: A
31. Hall
32. NY 1st: B
33. Harrow
34. First Corps
35. NY 13th
36. Elevnth Corps Skirmishers
37. 8th OH
38. MA SS 1st
39. MS 11th, 2nd, 42nd, NC 55th
40. VA 55th, 47th, 40th, 22nd
41. NC 33rd, 18th, 28th, 37th, 7th
42. NC 11th, 26th, 47th, 52nd
43. AL 5th Bat., TN 7th, 14th, 1st, AL 13th
44. NC 38th, 13th, 34th, 22nd, 16th
45. VA 38th, 57th, 53rd, 9th, 14th
46. VA 56th, 28th, 19th, 18th
47. VA 3rd, 7th
48. VA 8th

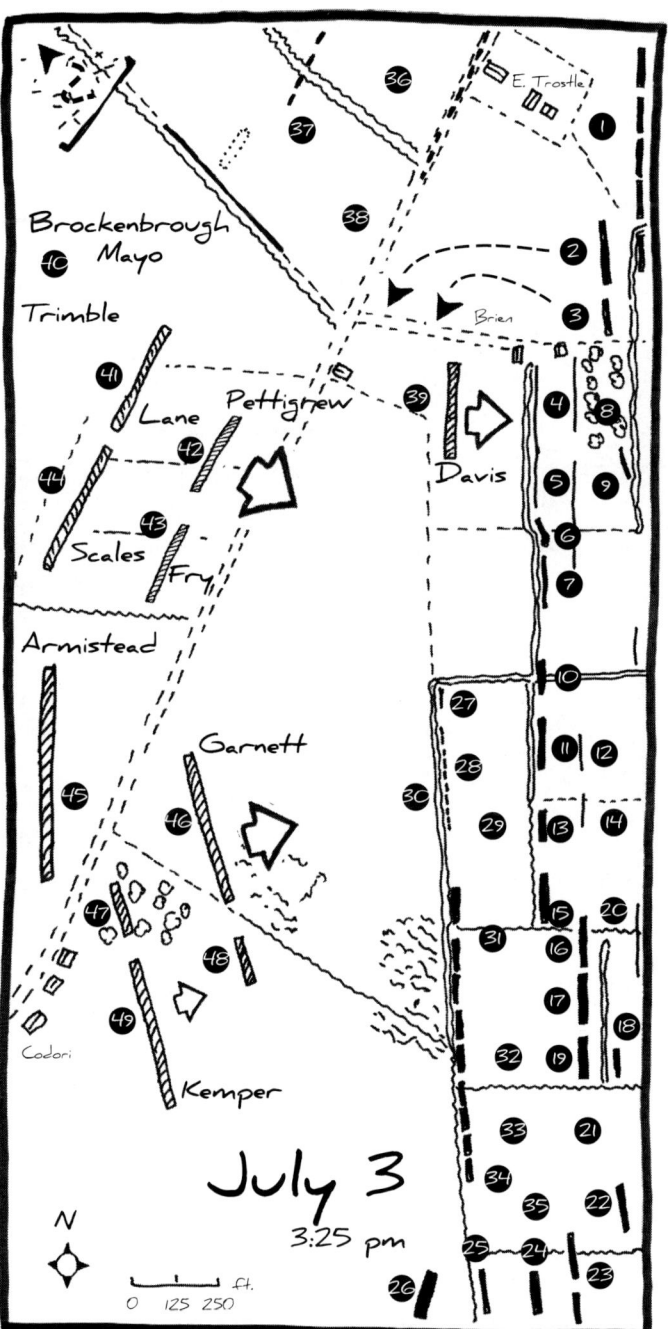

Eyes on the Prize

They heard the orders being bellowed up and down the line, and thirteen thousand men stepped off. Silas and Jack briefly put an arm around one another—one final brotherly gesture—as, together, they began their march into the maw.

Almost as soon as they started, they began taking cannon fire. Silas concentrated on staying close to Jack and hunkering down as he marched. It was as if he were bracing himself against a violent rainsquall like those that came in off the gulf in Mobile. Moses, however, never took his eyes off the prize. He marched erect, taking fearless strides toward death as if he had been living for this moment all his life. Only the doomed flag bearers marched in advance of him.

Silas couldn't see anyone but Moses before him and only a few others to each side. He didn't see the swaths of men taken out by cannon fire, but he could hear the rounds hissing through the air and bodies being ripped apart. More than once, he heard a man violently expel his final breath as a cannonball crushed it out of his chest. But the boy stayed near Moses, never looking up while the ground passed beneath him.

They reached the road, which gave them a little cover until they got across. Soon, they overtook their pickets, who fell into line. Not long after that, they came to a rail fence. Most went over it. Since Silas and Jack were in the lead, they didn't have to climb over any bodies, living or dead, to clear the fence. Moses easily went over it, but his scrawny little friend slipped between the rails and hurried to catch up, bullets whistling by all the while. Many of those following would die there. The cohesiveness of their formations, so essential to success, was destroyed at the fence, and they were never able to restore it.

By now, it sounded to Silas as if the men behind them were catching more grief than him and the others in the front. The Yankee artillery was firing over them as they got closer, hitting those in the rear.

As things momentarily seemed to cool off just a little, Silas worked up enough courage to glance around and behind him. What he saw filled him with pride in his Southern brothers and simultaneously broke his heart. No longer were there thousands of men, but mere hundreds of gallant survivors marching beside and behind the Fifth Alabama and the rest of Archer's Brigade. It appeared that the sides of the advancing force had been herded inward, toward the middle, toward the Fifth. But they kept their eyes on the little stand of trees as if paradise awaited them in its shade.

Silas looked around only for a few seconds, for things began to heat up anew. He put his head down again, his gaze fixed on the back of Jack's boots, following them up the hill.

When they were within a hundred or so yards of the summit, Silas saw the two men directly to his right hit the ground to take cover. These were men he didn't know, they having filled in the gaps left by the fallen. When they went down, he almost followed their lead, thinking everyone was doing it. But then he saw the men behind them stepping over their motionless bodies and realized the two were dead.

They had gone down so naturally, he thought, so uneventfully, so bereft of drama and fanfare. Both seemed to have broken their fall with their rifle butts, just as they had been trained, but were probably dead before they hit the ground. He couldn't help but lament at what a little thing, an expendable thing a man is in war. There is no time to grieve or say words. Just step over him and go on.

All this, from the time they had gone down until he had realized they were dead, had taken perhaps five seconds. He thought about how uselessly they had died, before they were able to contribute anything to the effort.

He found himself praying as he advanced.

"Please, Jesus, if I am to die today, let me do something worthwhile before I go. Let me make a difference."

Through all this, he had remained slightly behind and to the right of his friend. He asked God to forgive him for not being as bold as Jack and for marching behind rather than beside him. But then, everyone was behind the big man now. Silas could no longer see a flag bearer, so he followed Moses up the mountain.

As they neared the stone wall, the Southerners instinctively began to run, almost as if by command, toward the Union line, bellowing mightily as they went. The big guns, which had been firing over them moments earlier, were now firing loads of grapeshot directly into them like monstrous shotguns, leaving deep, wide gaps in their lines, gaps which were quickly filled by the next to die. Silas could hear rifle fire, Americans shooting at Americans through the smoke. He could see the Yankees desperately trying to reload. But now the Southerners were so close to the wall they didn't bother. After their arduous journey up the hill, it was almost with relief and joyous fury that they closed with the enemy. Eagerly, they rushed forward.

1. Eleventh Corps
2. NY 126th
3. NY108
4. NY 111th
5. NJ 12th
6. DE 1st
7. CT 14th
8. WV 7th
9. NC 11th, 26th, 47th, 55nd
10. PA 71st
11. PA 72nd
12. NY 10th Bat.
13. PA 106th
14. PA 99th
15. NY 42nd
16. PA 114th
17. MA 19th
18. ME 3rd
19. PA 121st
20. PA 2nd Cav.
21. NJ 1st: A
22. ME 4th
23. NY 1st: K
24. First Corps
25. VT 16th
26. VT 13th
27. AL 5th BTN, AL 13th, TN 7th, 14th, 1st,
28. PA 69th
29. NY 1st IB
30. VA 38th, 57th, 53rd, 9th, 14th
31. Hall
32. VA 56th, 28th, 19th, 18th
33. Harrow
34. First Corps
35. NC 33rd, 18th, 28th, 37th, 7th
36. NC 38th, 13th, 34th, 22nd, 16th
37. 8th OH
38. MA SS 1st
39. NY 126th (elements)
40. NY 108th (elements)
41. US 1st: I
42. VA 8th
43. VA 24th
44. VA 11th
45. Eleventh Corps Skirmishers

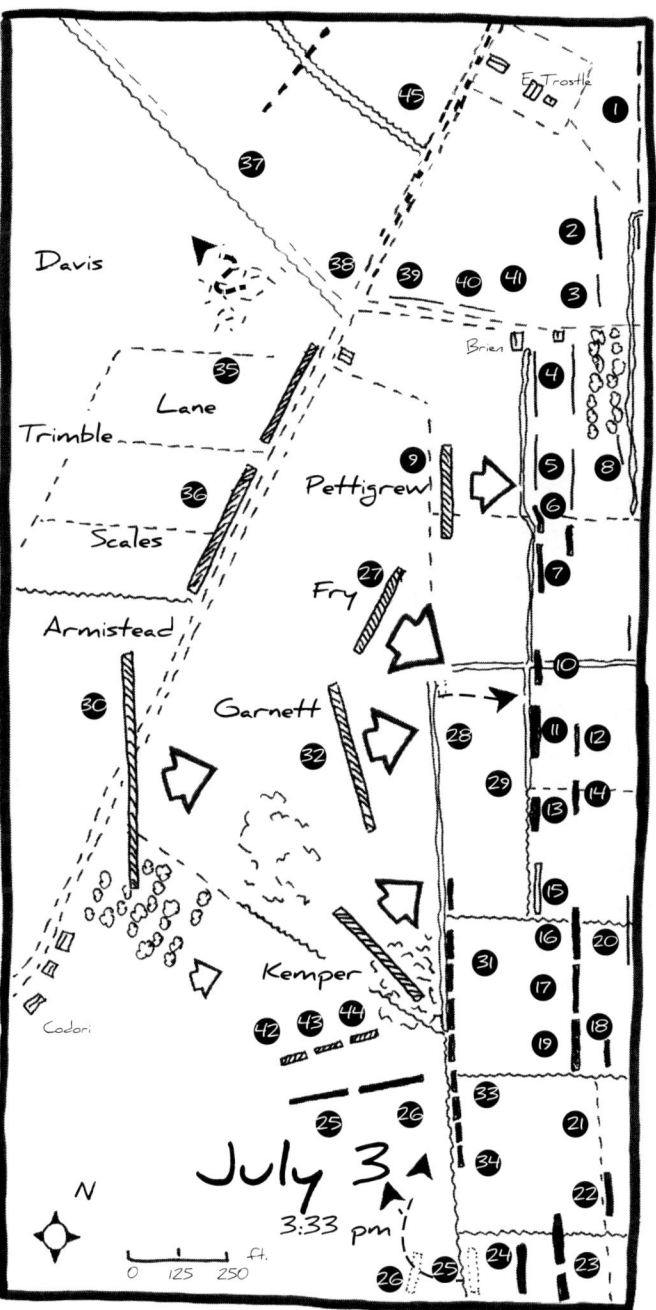

1. Eleventh Corps
2. NY 126th
3. NY 108
4. NY 111th
5. NJ 12th
6. DE 1st
7. CT 14th
8. WV 7th
9. US 3rd: F&K
10. PA 71st
11. PA 72nd
12. NY 10th Bat.
13. PA 106th
14. PA 99th
15. NY 42nd
16. PA 114th
17. MA 19th
18. ME 3rd
19. PA 121st
20. PA 2nd Cav.
21. NJ 1st: A
22. ME 4th
23. NY 1st: K
24. First Corps
25. VT 16th
26. VT 13th
27. VA 8th
28. VA 24th
29. NY 1st 1B
30. VA 11th
31. VA 38th, 57th, 53rd, 9th, 14th
32. NC 33rd, 18th, 28th, 37th, 7th
33. PA 69th
34. OH 8th
35. MA SS 1st
36. NY 126th
37. NY 108th
38. US 1st: I
39. Eleventh Corps Skirmishers
40. AL 5th Bat., AL 13th, TN 1st, 7th, 14th
41. NC 16th

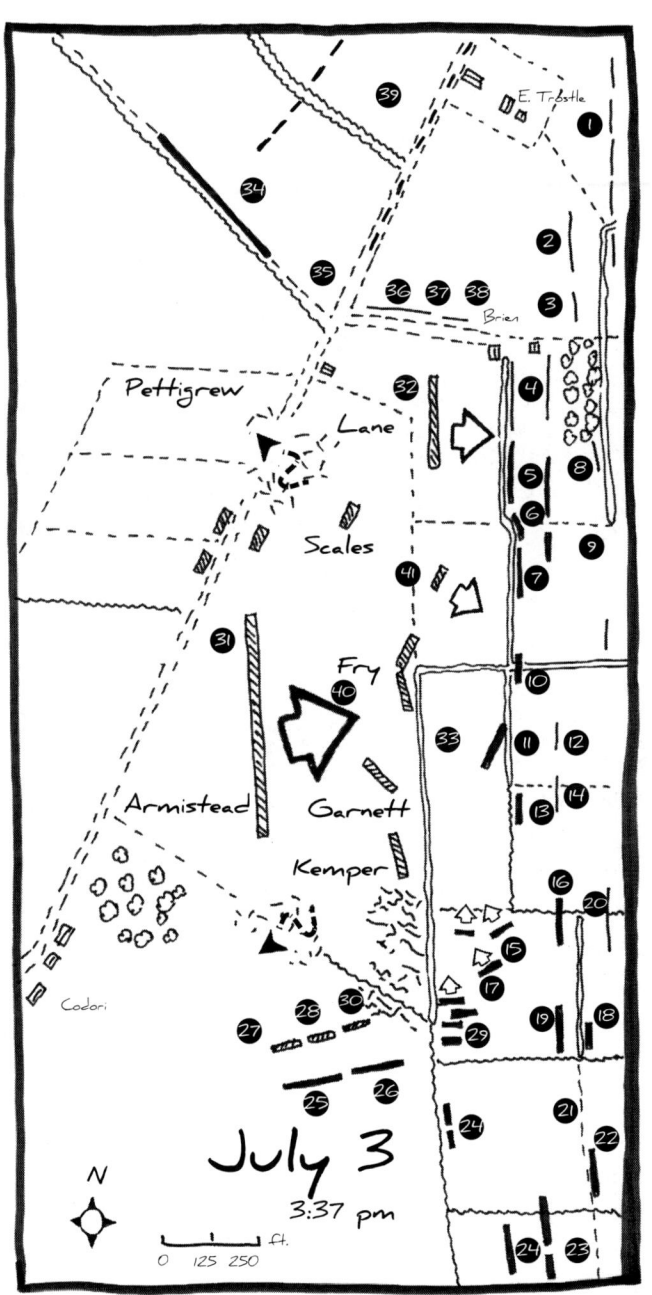

A legion of Banshees

Silas heard hundreds of savage Rebel yells as men of Tennessee, Virginia, and Alabama swarmed over the wall and smashed into the panic-stricken enemy with bayonets and rifle butts.

He looked up in time to see Moses's rifle get shot out of his hands. The man simply proceeded over the wall without it, fighting his way through the enemy with his fists. Silas clambered over after him and watched, mesmerized, as his best friend cleared a bare-knuckled path through some terrified Yankees.

Most of the Union guns in that area had been overrun and silenced, their crews dead or routed. But the sounds of mortal hand-to-hand combat were everywhere as the Rebels continued to pour into the angle, screaming in patriotic madness.

Strangely ignored by all around him, Silas stood alone and unchallenged in the eye of a lethal storm. In the din, he could hear the roar of the killers and the shrieks of the dying as men quivered on bayonets and skulls were crushed by rifle butts. On the crest of the ridge, in the angle of the stone wall, in the shade of the little stand of trees, death howled like a legion of banshees.

Silas, still near Moses and a little behind him, had done nothing up to that point but walk up the hill. He was unscratched and had yet to fire his weapon.

The enemy seemed to be getting fewer and fewer when a little blue belly about the size of Silas made a bayonet charge toward Jack. Unarmed, Moses calmly parried it away with his left arm and put his right fist into the middle of the little boy's face. The Yank went down on his back, his nose a bloody mass. Jack took the Yank's rifle and plunged the bayonet straight into the ground next to the boy, leaving the weapon sticking up like a tombstone. Then he bent down over him as if to say something in his ear.

With all the noise, Silas could not make out the words. While Jack was still down over the Yankee, Silas saw another man in blue rushing with fixed bayonet toward his unsuspecting friend. Jack stood erect in time to see the blade coming at his heart but not in time to avoid it. But there, by his side, stood his friend, Pvt. Silas Swann, probably the only man within a hundred feet in any direction who still held a loaded weapon. He had kept his powder dry and his load tamped down like his corporal had told him. When he saw the Union man rushing at Jack, he instantly pulled the hammer back on his musket. With the blade within inches of Jack's chest, Silas's weapon finally spoke. A .577 caliber lead slug tore through the running man's chest, sending him and his weapon backward to the ground.

Moses stood unfazed. He watched Silas drop his weapon as he went to the dying man to comfort him.

Though the fighting still roared mightily up and down the line, it had momentarily quieted around Jack and Silas as the South, for one of history's briefest moments, owned the angle.

Silas arrived at the man's side and knelt to calm the thrashing arms that sought to remove an unseen shaft from his chest. The gasping man could not speak, but Silas cradled him in his arms and stroked his face to calm him. As Silas wept for the man, their eyes met and, though no words were uttered, there appeared in the dying man's face a look of peace and forgiveness. The flailing hand calmed enough to touch Silas's face in reconciliation. Then the man's arm relaxed and fell as his eyes went blank and closed. As he wept, Silas bowed his head in grief and shame. He had taken a life and saved one. He had made a difference. He was a soldier.

The South had reached her sad zenith. Her tide of butternut and gray would soon recede as the North reclaimed the angle.

Silas felt Jack's gentle touch on his shoulder and heard him say, "Come on, son. He's with the Lord now. There's a bunch of his friends coming this way, and we gotta go."

Where All Is Peace

Silas looked up and saw what appeared to be the entire Army of the Potomac coming on the run. He quickly glanced around and saw only a few hundred of his countrymen still standing in the angle. Unarmed, he and Jack jumped the wall and took off running along with the others, back down the rise. It was death to tarry.

Silas could tell when the Yanks arrived at the wall behind them. He heard rifle fire and saw some men around him fall. But he and Jack kept running, flying like the wind down the slope. They were heading to their right, toward a narrow but dense line of trees that hid a shallow, rocky stream.

Most of the others ran back to where the charge had begun, but that was more than half a mile. This gave the enemy too much time to draw beads on backs. Silas stayed with Moses as they ran together toward the trees, leaping over the bodies of their comrades who had fallen on the way up, and they were many.

Silas could run like a yearling buck. Light on his feet, going downhill and unencumbered by a weapon, he felt as if he could almost fly. He was faster than Moses, who, though fast for such a big man, was inhibited somewhat by his bulk. Once Silas realized where Jack was taking them, he easily left him behind. He leaped another body, and it cried out.

"Silas!"

He slid to a halt, staying low. He looked back to see who had called. Moses came leaping over the body, and it shouted again.

"Jack, I'm hit! Y'all, help me!"

It was Box, his right leg shattered and bloody.

"Please don't leave me here, y'all. Take me with you. Drag me over to those trees. I got hit on the way up. I think I got the bleeding stopped but I can't walk."

Before he finished his last sentence, Silas and Jack had him under each arm, running as fast as they could toward the trees, still about a hundred yards distant. Box was trying his best to help with his one good leg and not to drag his bad one, but it was a slow and painful process.

They still heard shots behind them, and they saw men running down the slope to their left.

They were probably within fifty feet of the trees, and Jack said, "Come on, boys. We're almost home."

Then Silas realized he was on the ground, trying in vain to regain his feet. He looked for the others and saw Box facedown and motionless, his head broken open like a pumpkin.

He felt great pain in his lower back, and nausea came over him. He looked for Jack and saw him a few feet beyond Box, on his knees, feeling frantically of his side but appearing to be unhurt.

"Jack, I've been hit. I think it's bad."

Moses was instantly at his side.

"Come on," he said. "Let's get to them trees. Box don't need us now. He died with his boots on."

Jack simply picked his friend up like a child, and a few powerful strides later, they were in the shelter of the trees, tearing through the underbrush. Keeping him above the thorns, Jack carried him down to the stream, which the trees concealed, and began wading down the middle. The water was shallow and the bottom pebbly and firm. He figured he could make it back to their lines quicker that way than fighting the underbrush on the banks.

After a short distance, Silas pleaded with him, "Jack, please put me down. I can't take it anymore. Please. Let me rest against that rock."

Next to the stream, Silas had spotted a large boulder with a gently sloping, smooth face on the side nearest the stream. With the tenderness of a mother, Jack placed the boy on the ground with his back on the mild incline of the rock.

"Oh Jack, I'm sorry. I wet my pants."

Jack looked at the boy's blood-soaked trousers and said, "Lots of fellas wet their pants today, son. Lots of fellas."

"Jack, it hurts so bad. I feel sick. I don't think I can go on."

"Sure you can. We'll rest here a minute, and then I'll carry you real easy-like back to our lines, and they'll fix you up."

"No, Jack. I can't make it. They wouldn't be able to help me anyway. I'm bleeding too bad. I'm dying."

"No, you ain't. Come on. I'll just scoop you up real easy and—"

"No. No. Please," Silas begged as Jack attempted to get his arms under him.

"Please, Jack. Just leave me be. I'm done."

Jack looked at his ashen, anguished face and his blood flowing into the stream.

"Well," Jack quietly said, "I reckon we'll just rest here together for a spell."

"Jack, you need to go now. There's nothing wrong with you, nothing to keep you here. You're a soldier, remember? It's your duty to live and to fight for your country another day, like you told me."

"I'm not leaving you, Silas. And I'm not fighting or killing no more."

"Jack, you gotta go. Those Yanks might be coming down here looking for us any time now. I'll be all right. I'm not alone. I have Jesus. Remember?"

Jack watched as his friend gave himself up for dead. He realized the boy had become a man just in time to die.

"Remember, Silas, Jesus said, 'Let not your heart be troubled for today you will be with Me in paradise.'"

Even in his misery, Silas had to smile a little at his friend's first attempt to quote scripture.

"That's right, Jack. Like the thief on the cross, I'll be with Jesus today in paradise." Then he began to cry. "I killed a man, Jack. I took a life."

"And in taking that life, you saved mine." Accepting, at last, that his young friend was doomed, Jack, too, began weeping.

"Dammit, Silas," he said through his tears, "it was supposed to be me, not you. I had my heart set on being in paradise today. I tried every way to get killed I could think of without just letting them kill me, without just committing suicide. Hell, just following orders today should have been suicide enough. But instead of going to Jesus, here I am, stuck on Jordan's stormy banks, like the preacher called it. And I'm about to lose my friend. Silas, I don't want you to die, son. Can't we just try to get you back to the field surgeons?"

"No, Jack. I'd be dead before you could get me there. And even if you could get me there alive, I'd have to wait my turn. They're probably pretty busy right now. Don't worry about me. I'll be okay. It doesn't hurt so bad now."

Jack sat down beside him in resignation and said, "Back there, where you and Box got hit, I thought I got hit too. Something knocked me down. When I checked myself, I found this hole in my shirt."

He showed Silas a bullet hole through both the front and back of his shirt, about halfway between the middle and his right side.

"I know I've lost some weight, and this shirt's a little baggy now, and it was untucked and hanging loose. But, Silas, there just ain't no way in hell that bullet could of missed me. But I ain't got a scratch on me."

"You're right about that, Jack," Silas said. "There's no way in hell, but there is a way in heaven."

"It ain't fair, Silas. It ain't right. It's supposed to be me dying, not you. You wanna stay, and I wanna go. God just fouled up, that's all. He just fouled up."

Silas managed to smile again, "Don't you see, Jack? It's the little girl's prayers. Rose's prayers have delivered you."

As Jack stared at him, the realization set in.

Then he quietly said, with disappointment in his voice, "And I was so looking forward to it."

"Don't fret about, it Jack. You'll be there someday. It'll wait for you. You've got to understand that the Lord saved your soul because He loves you. But He saved your life because He has a plan for you. You've got work to do. You're going to live a long, happy life in God's sweet service. And when that work is done and you're an old man, Jesus will wrap His arms around you, just like He's wrapping them around me right now, and He'll bring you on home. I'll be there waiting for you. And maybe we'll go fishing together."

By now, each man was resigned to and at peace with his fate.

"Stay close to the Lord," Silas said.

"I will. I ain't never going back."

They heard more shots, closer now, and voices.

"They don't sound like Southern boys. Now you git, young fella," Silas said with a weak smile, trying to sound like a father, "before it's too late. And Jack," he said as he grasped his hand, "if you see my folks, tell them I love them. And tell them I'm sorry about how things turned out. And tell my mother I gave my shoes to a poor boy who had none. And, tell 'em... tell 'em I died like a man. And, Jack, tell my daddy, tell him... tell him I made it to the top."

As they wept, Jack managed to say, "I'll tell 'em, son. I'll tell 'em."

He lovingly brushed Silas's hair back and gently kissed him on the forehead, just like his own mama kissed him when he was little.

Each man knew what he had to do, what was expected of him. One life was ending. One was beginning.

There were more voices, closer now.

"Please go now, Jack. This is something I gotta do alone, just me and Jesus. Don't make me spend my last few minutes worrying about you and whether you got away. Don't worry about me. Dying's not so bad. Just go on now, while you can."

"Silas, I love you, son," Jack said. "And we'll see each other again someday."

"I know. When we're both in Canaan's fair and happy land, where all is peace."

They shook hands, a requisite among Southern men when parting. Moses then stood and took a few steps backward into the water, all the while looking into Silas's eyes. Then he turned and ran down the stream toward the Southern lines. Heartbroken, but no longer angry, no longer confused, he knew what lay before him. He knew what he had to do. He had a life to live, a life for Jesus, thanks to a loving God who saved his soul and a scrawny little boy who saved his life. He was again without doubt or fear.

Silas watched as Jack ran down the stream, escaping into life. As he rested against the rock, he saw his blood following his friend in the water and knew he would soon escape into death. With his mind faltering, he attempted to compose his final prayer. He would apologize to God for allowing himself to become entangled in this great sin, for not holding his life as dearly as he should, for losing it in a cause of man. But his time was nearer than he thought.

He looked toward heaven for hope and saw a perfect white dove alight in the branches above. Admiring it, he grew weaker.

Finally, his strength gone, his life over, he could only whisper, "Jesus, forgive me."

In times of war, many a life is lost unlived. A mother loses her baby, a father his son. Untold grandchildren remain ever nameless. A line is ended. And so it was with Silas Swann, a frightened little boy, the cherished son of an adoring family, a steadfast soldier of the South. Dreams die young, and plans go unfulfilled, but life somehow, somewhere, goes ever on. And where there is life, there lives hope.

As the dove took wing, the man closed his eyes, and his soul, forever safe in the loving arms of a mighty Savior, soared on wings of eagles from Jordan's stormy banks across the river to that fair and happy land on the distant, peaceful shore—the promised land.

The Road Home

It was finished. The Stars and Stripes fluttered again over the high ground. A brave Southern army lay broken beneath it. Yet its soldiers fought on for almost two more years in grim defense of their forlorn homeland before tenderly furling their bonny flags for the final time and walking the long road home, vanishing into history.

THE REUNION

July 1913

BOB LANKFORD

I am bound for the promised land,
I am bound for the promised land,
O who will come and go with me?
I am bound for the promised land.
      American folk hymn

TUESDAY, JULY 1ST

First Sight

It was a soft summer morning in Gettysburg. It was too early to be hot. The sun was still low and the shadows long as a tall young man waited in the shade. He watched as the morning train out of the South coasted to a gentle stop. He was not waiting for anyone in particular, just any of the old veterans who might be needing transportation to the reunion site. The reunion had begun a few days earlier. There were still a few stragglers arriving each day, though fewer with each train.

As he watched passengers disembark, he decided there would be no veterans arriving today. The few people who got off were met by family or friends.

Turning to leave, he caught sight of a tall, elderly gentleman standing on the platform in the midst of his luggage. He was not wearing a new uniform like the other veterans. Instead, he was in a white linen suit and a wide-brimmed, white hat. The suit was a little rumpled from the trip, but otherwise he looked quite the prosperous Southern gentleman—dapper, but not dandy.

The young man approached and said, "Good morning, sir.

My name is Michael Camardo. I live here in Gettysburg. Might I be of assistance?"

The old man smiled. "I hope so, son. I could sure use some assistance right now."

As they shook hands, the old man said, "Mr. Camardo, my name is Moses—Jack Moses. I'm looking for the Battle House Hotel."

"Why, it's right there," he said, pointing to a large building near the depot. "Let me help you with your bags."

They were both tall, big men. The two of them easily carried Jack's luggage to the lobby of the hotel, where he checked in.

As Michael and the bellboy carried the luggage to Jack's second-floor room, Michael said, "I guess you'll be needing transportation to the reunion site. You are here for the reunion, aren't you?"

"Yes, I am. But I'll be needing more than that. I have some business to attend to which will require the services of a horse and buggy. I need to visit several places around town."

"How about a truck? Would a truck do?" Michael asked.

"I don't much care to drive a truck," Jack said. "I prefer a horse and buggy."

"I have a truck. I can place it and myself at your service at a very reasonable rate. I can do the driving, and I can be your guide."

"Sounds fair enough to me," Jack said as they shook hands again. Thus began a friendship that would change Michael Camardo's life forever.

"Are you and your machine available now, this morning?" Jack asked.

"Yes, sir!"

"Good. Give me a little while to freshen up, and I'll meet you in the lobby, say, in twenty minutes?"

"Yes, sir, Mr. Moses," came the delighted reply. "I'll be there."

Jack tipped the bellboy and entered his room. Michael and the bellboy walked together to the lobby. Michael went on from there to the adjoining restaurant, which was owned and operated by his uncle.

"Uncle Nick," he said, "I found somebody. He said he has some business to handle, and he wants me to drive him around. Is it still okay?"

"Yes," said his uncle. "You know the rules. I'll need you and the truck from time to time. You know when to be back here."

"Yes, sir. I know. I'm sure I can work it out with Mr. Moses."

"Good," said Nick. "I'll see you a little before lunch."

The Rock

After Jack had freshened up, he asked Michael to drive him south of town, toward the battlefield. They traveled through the village and perhaps another mile at about fifteen miles per hour, which Jack thought was too fast and bumpy. When they came to a small stream, Jack instructed him to stop. They pulled off to the right side of the road. They were alone.

Puzzled, Michael said, "The reunion site is on up ahead."

"I know, son. But this is where the business I was telling you about starts."

Michael killed the engine, jumped down, and walked around the truck to help Jack down, but the old trooper was already on the ground when he arrived.

"What kind of horseless carriage is this?" Jack asked.

"A 1912 Harvester International," Michael said proudly. "It belongs to my uncle. He's letting me use it during the reunion so I can earn some money toward medical school."

"Well, that's mighty nice of him," Jack said almost absent-mindedly as he looked around, trying to get his bearings.

Then he looked back at the truck. It was tall, masculine, and shiny black—a handsome thing with red, wooden-spoked wheels; hard, rubber tires; red sides; and a high roof that ran almost the length of the vehicle. With two bench seats, the rear one could be removed to make more room for cargo.

Michael, being an American male, could not have been much more smitten with it if it had been a beautiful, big-eyed girl. Jack was a perceptive old man. He could see the boy's passion, and he remembered a little of his own passionate, albeit dark, youth.

Jack said, "I don't have one of these things. My carriage still has a horse in front of it, a sweet little mare named Rocket who knows all the places I like to go. I figure at my age I need somebody with me who knows the way home. But my children each have a horseless carriage. They like them. But they admit that mine is a lot easier to start."

After a few more seconds of admiring the truck, Jack said, "So you want to be a doctor."

"Yes, sir. More than anything. I've been praying for God to make it possible," Michael said.

He watched as Jack peered upstream, to the left of the road. Both were silent for a while.

Then Jack said, "I was here fifty years ago."

The stream was so small that the road did not need a true bridge to span it. It flowed under the road through a large pipe.

Jack stood next to the stream and quietly repeated, "Fifty years."

Michael said, "What outfit were you with, sir?"

"Fifth Alabama Infantry Battalion, Company B, the Calhoun Sharpshooters. I was in Corporal Elder's squad. Good men. Place sure seems different now."

Then Jack looked at the humble pipe and, glancing toward Michael with a twinkle in his eye, said, "Lot of water under the bridge since then."

Michael had to laugh a little.

"Will your vehicle be all right unattended here for a while?" Jack asked.

"Yes, sir. No one will bother it."

"Good," he said. "Now, this business of me calling you Mr. Camardo and you calling me sir is getting mighty old mighty fast. Why don't you just call me Jack, and I'll call you Michael."

"That's fine with me, sir. I mean, Jack."

They laughed again and shook hands for the third time, as if they were just meeting.

Jack said, "I need to walk upstream here a ways. I'm looking for something."

"What are you looking for?"

"A rock."

"You planning to hit somebody with it?" Michael asked, grinning.

"Yeah," Jack said with a smile. "I'm gonna knock me a smart-alecky young whippersnapper upside the head with it."

Michael laughed again, and they began following the pebbly bank upstream. Michael was young and athletic. He negotiated the sometimes-rough terrain easily. He was surprised at how well Jack handled it. The old man was pretty spry, but occasionally Michael would help him over a rough spot. Already, respect and affection between them was growing.

They had walked a fair piece when Jack stopped. Michael could see him staring at something ahead of them. Before them, next to the stream, lay a large boulder gently sloped on one side, about the size of a grand piano. Jack walked closer to it, and Michael followed.

As they approached the rock, Jack removed his hat.

He stooped down and caressed the sloped side gently and quietly said, "I'm so sorry, brother. I'm so sorry. Please forgive a penitent old man."

Michael knelt beside him, "Are you all right?"

Jack took out his handkerchief and dried his eyes.

"Yes, son. I'm okay. Here. Help me up."

They stood together and then settled nearby on another large rock more suited for sitting.

"Why don't we just rest here for a while, Jack?"

"Let's do. You talked me into it," Jack replied. "You know, Michael," he continued, "all the bad dreams I've had over the last few years, the nightmares, all the feelings of guilt, regret, and shame—I thought it might help if I visited this place again. But I'm not so sure now."

"Were you in Pickett's Charge?"

Jack nodded. "Corporal Elder's squad, like I said. Twelve brave men and me. Would have been fourteen total, but we lost a man two days earlier on the first day of battle. Normally a squad wouldn't have fourteen men. But our outfit had a squad lose about half its men and its corporal a month earlier at Chancellorsville. So they gave the survivors of that squad to our corporal. As far as I know, only two of us made it to the top. We were on the front row. Me and my little friend Silas there," he said motioning toward the sloped rock. "We made it all the way up. Stayed there and held it for a little while with two or three hundred other Rebs from various outfits. Young Silas saved my life while we were up there. Shot a Yank that was about to kill me. That's the only man he ever killed, and it near 'bout broke his heart, the grief of it all. Then we saw several thousand Yanks counterattacking, so we all got out of there in a great big hurry. All the other Rebs took off the same way they went up. Silas and I saw this little line of trees over here and thought we could make it here quicker than back to the starting line. There had been a small Union outfit here when we started up, but they were gone when we arrived.

"On the way down the hill, we came across one of our wounded squad mates. We each grabbed him under an arm and tried to help him to the trees. Some Yanks at the top of the hill fired on us. The fellow we were carrying was killed outright. Silas was hit bad, in the kidneys. I thought I was hit too. But when I checked myself, I couldn't find any wounds. I was all right. I could tell Silas was hurt, but I didn't know how bad it was. I was a big man then, so I just picked the little fellow up and ran toward the trees. When we got here, to the rock, he begged me to put him down so he could rest. I didn't know how bad his wounds were till I laid him down on that rock. His trousers were all soaked with blood. Poor little fellow thought he had peed in his pants. He apologized to me, he felt so bad about it."

Jack began to sob softly. He had not talked to anyone about his war experiences in a long time. His children had never heard all the things he was telling Michael. He figured it was safe to talk to him, someone who lived about a thousand miles from his home and whom he would never see again after Saturday. But the main reason he was talking so freely was because he just felt comfortable in Michael's presence. Though he had only known the boy a little over an hour, he already liked him and trusted him.

Jack went on. "Silas was just a young fellow, about your age, only seventeen. I was much older, one of the oldest men in the outfit. I had just turned thirty-three when we made the charge. I was ready to die. I felt like my life up to that point had been a total waste. I figured a suicidal charge was as good a way as any to end it. So when I was standing here on this creek bank fifty years ago, virtually unscratched and looking down at my mortally wounded friend, I was pretty confused.

"We talked a while," Jack said. "He told me he was dying, bleeding to death, and he asked me to go on back to our lines and leave him here. I told him I wanted to carry him back with me. But he begged me not to; he was hurting so bad. We heard some Yankees coming, and he told me to go on. So, I left him on that rock. Of all the things I've done, that's the one thing I can never quite seem to get over. It haunts me still."

"But you just did what he asked you to do," Michael said. "If you had stayed, you might have died too. What good would that have done?"

"That's what my wife always told me. You see, Silas was her little brother."

"So you and Silas knew each other before the war?"

"No. I was from Calhoun County, up in the northeastern part of the state. He was from Mobile, down on the coast. But when he was dying, I promised to tell his parents that he loved them and that he had died honorably. When the war ended in April of sixty-five, almost two years after Silas's death, we all just walked home. When we got to Calhoun County, most of the fellows I knew said their good-byes because they knew I would be going on to Mobile. It was only about another two hundred and fifty miles."

"That sounds like a pretty long walk."

"Well, I had a good pair of Yankee boots. They gave out

about the time I got to Mobile. So I retired them. I still have those boots at home, what's left of them."

He stopped talking briefly, gazing into the past again. Michael was fascinated by the old Rebel's story.

Then Jack snapped back into the present. "Well, anyway, we had a few Mobile men in the outfit who let me accompany them as they walked. When we got to Mobile, they told me how to find his parents' home, a big, beautiful house in a fine neighborhood. I have lived right there at that address since that day.

"I knocked on the door and the creature who opened it was the most beautiful thing I have ever seen. I had not known that my little friend had a sister, an older sister. Her name," and he paused, almost as if to savor the sound, "was Sally, Sally Swann. To me, those words will always be poetry."

Jack looked at Michael sheepishly and said, "I tell you, son, I had had lady friends before. After all, I was thirty-five years old. But I had never been in love up till then. Didn't know what it was. Didn't know what to expect. But whatever it was, it got a hold of me on that front porch that Sunday afternoon in 1865 in Mobile, Alabama, and it has never let go. I still love that lady just like I did a lifetime ago. We had been married over forty years when she passed on. We had four children. She made my life the closest thing to heaven a man could hope for on this earth."

He paused again. "She was just the sweetest angel on the planet. I was rough and crude, and she was refined and gentle. She took me just as I was—never belittled me or talked down to me. I didn't deserve her.

"Sounds funny, doesn't it, son," he continued, "to hear such an old man speak so passionately about his love of a woman. But someday, five, six, or seven decades from now, if you're fortunate enough to have had a long, happy marriage to a sweet lady, you'll understand. But I had to knock on that door and tell those four kind people that I had abandoned their Silas in his time of greatest need. I broke down and cried in their parlor.

Even though they had known for almost two years that he was dead, they cried too. I told them he loved them and that he had fought and died nobly, like a man, and that he had made it to the top."

"Four people?" Michael asked.

"Yes. You see, they had an elderly colored lady living with them. She wasn't a slave. She had been freed years earlier. She had helped rear Silas and Sally, and she was a part of the family. I feel like she helped rear me too."

"So," Michael said, "after you told them everything, what did they do?"

"They invited me to supper," Jack said smiling. "Can you see me sitting there? The four of them, freshly bathed, clothes clean and pressed, everyone smelling like soap late on a Sunday afternoon. And then there I was. I had been at war for four years, had not seen the inside of a house in all that time, had not had more than a few actual baths with soap, and I had just walked in from Virginia. I imagine I looked and smelled like a man made of horse manure sprinkled with dust."

Michael was laughing now.

"And the food," Jack went on, "the food was beyond my power to describe. After two or three months of living off squirrels, possums, berries, and whatever else we could catch or pick, I'm sure I made a fool of myself, gulping and slurping. But I was beyond caring. I was so hungry I just took enough time to wash my hands up to my elbows and then Mr. Swann said a quick prayer so I could dig in. The four people who were at that table with me that evening are all gone now, but when they were living, they used to have a lot of fun at my expense recounting the events of my first meal with them."

"It's a wonder you didn't hurt yourself the way you must have been shoveling it in," Michael joked.

"Yeah. Well, that's one of the things they would bring up each year at Christmas dinner," Jack said. "But they had a little cottage in their backyard, and they let me move into it. Mrs.

Swann ran a dry goods store, and she gave me some good work clothes, and Mr. Swann gave me a job in his lumberyard. I had some experience in lumber, so it worked out pretty good. In fact, about a year after he hired me, I was running that lumberyard for him. And not long after that, I married his beautiful daughter. The fellow she had been engaged to died at Pittsburg Landing. She sent her brother and her sweetheart off to war, but the only thing that came home to her was me."

Jack paused again and said, "I'm sorry, son, I know I'm boring you with all this."

"No, sir, you're not. Please go on."

"Later, man, later. I've got stuff to do. Do you know who owns this land?" Jack asked.

"I suppose the man who owns it is the same one that owns those cornfields we saw next to the road. I think his name is Robinson. He lives in the last house we passed on the left."

"I want you to take me to him. What's the best way to get there?" Jack asked.

Michael said, "I guess his house is just up that path. We might catch him at home or nearby if we go now."

"Okay," Jack said as he stood. "Let's get it done."

Farmer Robinson

They followed the path up from the stream and out of the trees to a little wagon trail that went between two cornfields. Soon, they approached a farmhouse from behind and went around to the front porch. Michael knocked on the door. A man answered it, accompanied by three small children. He came out on the porch, but the children stayed inside, staring at the strangers. It was obvious they had interrupted his lunch. He was still chewing.

"Mr. Robinson?" Michael said.

"Yes, I'm Robinson."

"Mr. Robinson, my name is Michael Camardo. You might know my uncle."

"Yes, you're Nick Camardo's nephew. My family and I eat at his restaurant from time to time. I've seen you there before."

"Yes, sir," Michael said. "I want you to meet a friend of mine, Mr. Jack Moses from Alabama."

Having removed his hat when he stepped onto the porch, Jack moved forward and shook hands with the man.

"Nice to meet you, Mr. Moses."

"Likewise, Mr. Robinson."

"I hope you aren't selling anything, because, whatever it is, I can't afford it," Robinson said.

"No, sir." Michael laughed nervously. "We aren't selling anything. Are we, Jack?"

"No, Michael, we're not selling anything," Jack said. Then, looking at the farmer, he said, "Mr. Robinson, it is plain to see that I have interrupted your lunch."

"That's all right, Mr. Moses. I don't usually eat lunch quite this early, but that's just the way it worked out today. What can I do for you?"

"Well, sir," Jack continued, "I hope you don't mind, but young Michael here took me down to your creek bank a few minutes ago. I'm one of the veterans who participated in the pleasantries here fifty years back."

"Say you're from Alabama?"

"Yes, sir, but the thing I want to talk to you about is that big, sloped boulder on your creek bank at the end of this path down here. You see, Mr. Robinson, fifty years ago my closest friend died on that boulder. He was only seventeen."

"You don't mean to drag that thing back to Alabama, do you?" Robinson asked.

"No, sir," Jack said, laughing a little. "No, sir, I don't covet your rock. I hope it stays right where it is forever. What I want to do, with your permission, is to have an inscription carved on the face of that rock in memory of my friend. They never identified his body. He's probably buried in one of those mass graves out there."

"An inscription, huh?"

"Yes, sir. Here it is, right here," Jack said, handing him a paper.

The farmer looked at it and said, "That's a lot of words. That'll cost you a pretty penny."

"Yes, sir. I know," Jack said. "I'm willing to pay you a fair price."

"Oh no, sir. I'm not talking about me, Mr. Moses," Robinson said. "I'm not going to charge you anything. I'm talking about the stone carver, the monument man. He'll probably have to charge you a good bit because that's a long inscription."

"Well," Jack said, "it's a big rock."

"Well, you go ahead and have it done. You have my permission," the farmer said.

Taking the man's hand again and smiling, Jack said, "Thank you, sir. It's a kind man who will indulge an old Rebel in his grief. Now we'll let you get back to your lunch. And I'll have a man out here as soon as possible to start on it. I hope to have it finished by Saturday morning."

"Good luck on that," Robinson said. "They don't usually work that fast."

"Well, I have to try," Jack said.

They all shook hands again. Jack and Michael began the walk down the road to the truck.

As they were walking, Jack smiled. "He was a right nice fellow for a Yank."

Michael laughed and said, "Yep, and right now he's probably telling his wife, 'He was a right nice fellow for a Reb.'"

"You know, there for a minute, when he asked me about being from Alabama, I thought he was going to tell me to clear out."

"Nah. All that happened long before he was born. He

wouldn't have done that. But we do have a few people who would have."

"There's some folks back home," Jack said, "who were born long after the war but who can remember it like it was yesterday."

Jack told Michael he was referring to what he called the "forget hell, folks," those people who dwell on the war and Reconstruction and nurture their hatred for anyone unlike themselves, especially coloreds and Yankees.

"But," he added, "those people think they are justified in their rancor due to the way the South was treated during Reconstruction. Son, you would not believe the crimes committed against the poor, defenseless people of the South—white and black—in the name of Reconstruction. We called it re-destruction down there. That's the very reason the Ku Klux Klan was founded, to offer some measure of protection. Unfortunately, it has grown into something quite different. There was a time early on when I actually considered joining up myself to try to protect innocent people from some pretty sorry Yankees. But I never did, and now I'm glad I didn't. I figured there were better ways. I just don't enjoy my anger like I used to. I try to avoid it with God's help. But some folks down South cultivate their hatred of the Yankees like it's a cash crop, and the Yankees seem determined to give them a never-ending list of reasons to justify that hate."

When they arrived at the truck, Michael made some adjustments on the dashboard, then walked to the front to crank it.

Jack, who had complained about the rough ride out, said, "As soon as you get your remorseless carriage started, I want you to take me to the nearest monument company. Y'all probably have several around here."

"We do," Michael said. "I'll take you to Johnson's. It's closest."

Esau Johnson

They traveled back toward Gettysburg but stopped on a little side street before they reached the town proper. The place was obviously a monument business, with stones and markers around the yard. They walked into the shop, where a small group of colored men were working on various stones.

One of the men, a short, powerful-looking man, said, "Can I help you gentlemen?"

Jack said, "Yes, sir. I need to speak to the proprietor."

"That would be me," the man said.

Jack, trying not to look surprised at finding a colored man in charge, stuck his hand out and said, "Jack Moses here."

The man smiled and shook Jack's hand saying, "I'm Esau Johnson. I own the place."

"Nice to meet you, Mr. Johnson. I have a job for you. I hope you can help me."

"I hope I can too, mister, did you say Moses?"

"That's right. Jack Moses."

"Okay, Mr. Moses. What do you have for me?"

"Well, sir, I have an inscription I want carved on a stone. But I can't bring the stone to you. I'll have to take you to the stone. It's not far from here."

"What's the inscription?" Mr. Johnson asked.

"Here it is," Jack said, handing him the paper.

The man looked at it for a while and said, "That's a fairly long inscription. How big is this stone?"

Jack said, "I think it would be best if you just let my friend and me show it to you. It's not far. Do you have a half hour? We'll have to do a little walking."

Johnson turned to his men and gave them some instructions. Then he climbed up on the truck behind Jack and Michael, and they started for the Robinson place.

As they pulled away from the shop, Jack looked back over his shoulder at Johnson in the backseat and said, "Let me warn you about this young fellow. He doesn't dodge any bumps. He manages, somehow, to hit them all."

Johnson smiled bravely.

They reached the rock on foot, and Johnson said, "Yep. It's big enough, and it's granite, like most of the stuff around here."

He ran his hand gently over the sloped side, much like Jack had done earlier.

"I can do this, Mr. Moses. Now, you have to understand that with me having to work out here instead of in my shop, and with that inscription being as long as it is, it'll cost extra. But I could save some time, and you could save some money if you would let me abbreviate some of these words."

"I would rather not change anything unless it's necessary."

"Okay then. In that case, it'll take a while."

"Well, about that. I need it finished no later than Saturday morning."

"Saturday morning? I don't like to work that fast. I do quality work, Mr. Moses, and I simply refuse to give any customer anything less than my best effort."

"Yes, sir. I understand and appreciate your concern with quality. I wouldn't want it any other way. But I'm leaving on the Saturday afternoon train. I surely do want to see it completed before I go home. Mr. Johnson, at my age, I'll never be able to come up here again."

Johnson said, "You were in the Fifth Alabama with this man in the inscription?"

"Yes, sir. He was my closest friend. Mr. Johnson, I want you to make it as easy on yourself as possible. Use the simplest lettering you have, nothing fancy. Don't bother to polish the stone or anything. Just put the words on the rock in such a way that they can be easily read. If you can do that by Saturday morning, I will happily pay extra. This means a lot to me."

"You do have the owner's permission, don't you?" Johnson asked.

"Yes, sir," Jack said. "That's been taken care of."

Johnson took a scratch pad out of his pocket and began figuring.

Soon, he handed Jack the paper and said, "That's what it will cost you, that figure circled down at the bottom."

Jack looked at it and said, "Fair enough. If it's okay with you, I'll pay you half now, with a check drawn on one of your local banks, and half Saturday morning."

"That's fine," Johnson said.

They shook hands on the deal, and Jack said, "When do you plan to get started?"

"Right now. As soon as you can get me back to the shop, I'll get back out here with my stuff and start working."

"Excellent!" Jack said, patting him on the back as they began walking back to the truck. "Get it done, Johnny—Err, I mean, get it done, Mr. Johnson."

Little Henry

After dropping Mr. Johnson off at his shop, Michael and Jack headed back toward the hotel.

"This has been a productive morning, Michael, thanks largely to you. Let me treat you to lunch, son," Jack said.

"That's mighty nice of you, but my uncle lets me eat free as long as I just order the cheapest meals. He won't let me get a steak unless I pay for it myself. And besides, I have to go with him to the reunion site in a little less than an hour to take some food out there."

"Well, I tell you what. I'll treat you to that steak as soon as we get to the restaurant. I think you'll have time to eat it."

"Yes, sir. You're the boss," Michael replied.

Jack laughed and said, "And don't you forget it, you young whippersnapper. Hey! You missed one," he added as they passed a large pothole.

Michael had only known the crusty old trooper a few hours, but already he felt drawn to him.

There were several eating establishments in town. The nicest, and the best, was the Battle House Restaurant in the Battle House Hotel. Michael's Uncle Nick owned and managed the restaurant and rented the space on the first floor of the hotel just off the lobby. He ran a tight ship. Nick Camardo was not a frivolous man. The man believed in work, and lots of it, as his employees liked to say, for himself and for them. Though a good man, he was not easily pleased, nor was he demonstratively affectionate toward his nephew or anyone else. He did not seem to have a nurturing spirit. His wife had died young, and he had never remarried. With no children of his own, his life was the restaurant. In spite of his Spartan character, he loved his younger brother's orphaned son, and he tried to do right by the boy.

Nick could not afford to send Michael to medical school and did not think the boy had much chance of earning enough to attend. But he indulged him and allowed him the use of the truck to at least give it a try. He continued the boy's modest salary at the restaurant with the understanding that both Michael and the truck would be available at lunch to run plates of hot food out to the reunion site to be sold on the spot.

Nick had also hired a young colored boy to fill Michael's position in the restaurant for as long as he would be absent. The boy's name was Henry Dewberry. He was a scrawny fifteen-year-old in rags. Everyone called him Little Henry. He had a quick smile and a cheerful disposition, both of which were apparently wasted on his boss. Michael, though, appreciated the boy's qualities. The Camardo household, consisting of just Michael and his uncle, was a fairly joyless one. But the restaurant, in spite of his uncle's grim managerial style, was a place of happiness for Michael, thanks to the employees and customers. And now Little Henry's smiling face was there too.

Michael and Henry had known each other for some time

because Henry's grandmother was the head cook—or as she liked to say, the kitchen manager. Even before he began working there, Henry would come to the restaurant after school and do his lessons because his grandmother did not want him going home to an empty house. Henry's mother had run away with a man a few years back and had not been heard from since. His grandmother's name was Precious Dewberry, but she was known by all as Big Mama. When her daughter left, Big Mama took on her grandson to rear. She was a stern disciplinarian, but she was not as joyless as her employer. She had a sense of humor, and she enjoyed Little Henry's presence in her life. She loved the child very much. But then Henry was easy to love.

Big Mama, unlike Little Henry, was of large build. But her formidable personality and sharp tongue, as much as her size, were the reasons for her nickname. Thanks to her, the kitchen at the Battle House Restaurant was a model of efficiency and cleanliness. Even Nick stayed out of her way. He had no need to correct her. They saw things pretty much eye-to-eye. They were a good team.

It was a little early for lunch, so Jack and Michael had no trouble finding a table. Jack began looking over the menu. Michael knew it by heart. He already knew what he wanted, and he wanted it rare.

Henry was cleaning a table nearby and Michael, seeing him, said, "Hey, Henry, I want you to meet a friend of mine."

Jack looked up from the menu and saw Henry's beaming smile.

"This is Jack Moses from Alabama," Michael said. "Jack, this is Henry Dewberry. Everyone just calls him Little Henry."

"Nice to meet you, Mr. Moses," Henry said.

"Nice to meet you too, Henry," Jack replied with a smile. "What's your job around here? Do you run the place?"

The boys laughed.

"Oh, no sir. I don't run anything but this cleaning rag and sometimes a mop and a broom. I just work here."

Jack, always one to look deep into a person, sensed the humility of Henry's character. But at the same time, he could hear the pride in the boy's voice at being even the humblest employee at the Battle House Restaurant. He liked Little Henry immediately.

They shook hands, and Jack said, "You probably have the most important job in the place. I'd better let you get back to your duties. I'll be here a few more days, so I'll be seeing you again. Nice talking to you."

"Nice talking to you too, Mr. Moses. I'll see you later," Henry said as he returned to his work.

As he and Michael ate, Jack watched Henry work his way around the room, cleaning tables and wiping off chairs as people vacated them and doing whatever else needed to be done.

After watching for a while, Jack said, "Michael, why is Little Henry dressed as he is? Is he that poor?"

"Yes, sir," Michael said. "I guess he is. I never really thought much about it. He has looked like that for as long as I've known him. He doesn't have any parents. I guess that's one of the reasons he and I are as close as we are. My parents are gone too. I live with my uncle. Henry lives with his grandmother. She runs the kitchen here for my uncle."

Watching Henry, Jack said, "He and his clothes seem to be clean, but his pants are too short, and his shirt is too big. The knees are almost out of his pants, and there's a small hole in the back of his shirt. And he's not wearing an undershirt. His shoes are almost gone. I know what it's like to be shoeless and in rags. Back home, when we see a child like that, our church or some church gets together to rectify the situation. It doesn't matter what color the child is. We sure have our share of faults down south, and the world is always eager to point them out to us, but as Christians we feel compelled to show compassion toward the poor, black or white."

"Well, sir, I guess we all just expect Henry to look like that," Michael said. "He never complains. I think Big Mama—that's what we call his grandmother—I think she must have some financial obligations we don't know about. My uncle pays her pretty well, but I think she has some sorry children in Pittsburgh who leech off her a good bit. Her real name is Precious Dewberry."

"Do you think she would allow me to help the boy?" Jack asked.

"I don't know, Jack. She's a good lady, and she's good to Henry, but she's pretty proud, if you know what I mean."

"I know what you mean," Jack said. "Didn't I see a clothing store just a couple of doors down?"

"Yes, sir. That's Mr. Joseph's place. It's called the Coat of Many Colors."

"Is Joseph his first name?"

"His last."

They finished eating, and Jack left money for the bill and tip and said, "Michael, I want to meet Big Mama right now. Can you arrange it?"

"Yeah, but Jack, she can be pretty touchy at times. She has a sharp tongue."

"That's okay. I'll try not to cry."

Big Mama

Michael escorted Jack back to the kitchen, where they found Big Mama scolding a large, but apparently defenseless, young white man about the quality of some produce he had just delivered.

Michael waited until she was finished with him. "Big Mama, I want you to meet a friend of mine. This is Mr. Jack Moses."

Jack stuck his hand out, but she just eyed him up and down for a few seconds, finally offering her rather limp hand.

"Nice to meet you, ma'am," Jack said as humbly as he could, without actually groveling.

"Michael," she said, "you know I don't allow any unauthorized people back here."

"I know, Big Mama, but he just wants to ask you something. It'll just take a minute."

"Yes, ma'am," Jack said. "I just want to compliment on your country fried steak. Surely anyone who can prepare country fried steak like that is from the South."

"Mississippi," she said coolly. "But I had the good sense to leave. I reckon you're from the South too, aren't you?"

"Yes, ma'am," Jack said as humbly as he could.

"Mississippi?" she demanded.

"Oh no, ma'am." Very quietly, he added, "Alabama."

"Hmph!" she said in open disgust. "Alabama and Mississippi: two raggedy little states standing back to back against the world."

"Well, they're home for some of us," Jack said, much less humbly than before.

Then she turned and said, "Michael, I don't allow nobody back here who smokes, drinks, or cusses, and I've never known one of these old Southern boys yet who didn't do all three, and lots of it."

"Ma'am," Jack said, "I don't smoke, and I don't drink." With his hat already in both hands, he pulled it up to his chest and with a high, strained, comedic voice said, "And I just cuss a little bit."

Against her will, she sputtered out laughing as Michael giggled nervously. Jack sighed in relief but was careful to maintain his comedic facial expression and the humble demeanor.

"Now I know," she said, still smiling, "that you didn't come back here just to brag on my country fried steak. You're sure to have lots of people in Alabama who can do it just as good."

"It was truly mighty fine," Jack said. "But I want to talk to you about Little Henry."

Her demeanor immediately changed back to one of suspicion.

"What about Henry?" she demanded.

"He's a working man now, Mrs. Dewberry, and I just want to buy him some serviceable work clothes."

"He don't need no charity. I take good care of Henry," she said.

"Yes, ma'am, you do. But the boy needs some clothes. If you'd just let Michael and me take him down to Mr. Joseph's place, we'd fix him right up. It wouldn't take more than an hour or so."

"I don't think he'd take your charity. He wasn't raised that way," she said.

"So are you saying that if Henry consents, I can do it?"

"I don't want him accepting charity from you or anyone."

Jack was tiring of this. If he had not been so concerned for Henry's well-being, he would have backed off at this point. But he pressed on.

"Mrs. Dewberry, charity is a good thing. It's a godly thing that benefits the giver as much as the recipient. Fifty years ago, about two miles from this very spot, a little colored girl extended her own sweet charity and kindness to me and led me to Jesus. She helped me turn my life around. Since that time, the Lord has blessed me spiritually and materially, and I have tried to give back what the Lord has given me by helping folks less fortunate. Sometimes a young person just needs a little help getting a jump on life, a little help getting started. I've helped white children and black children. But no matter who or how many I help, I have never missed what little money I spent on them because the Lord always gives it back to me, and more, in some way or another. I have never been able to out-give Him. I always get a blessing far greater than the value of any shirt or pair of shoes.

"Ma'am," he continued, "I am respectfully asking you. Please don't deny that precious child this little opportunity to get some decent clothes. He deserves them. And please don't deny me my blessing. At my age, helping a young fellow get started means a lot."

She was softening. He could see it.

"What all you gonna buy him?" she asked.

"Everything he needs," he said, "from socks and underwear to a hat and coat for this winter, if Mr. Joseph still has them in stock this time of year."

"Well, okay," she relented. "But no money. Don't give him any money."

"Not even a little?"

"Well, maybe a little, but no more."

"Excellent!" Jack said. "Now, do you think we can get him out of here for an hour or two without getting him fired?"

"You said an hour or so," she retorted.

"An hour or so and hour or two—let's not split hairs. We'll have him back this evening," Jack said.

"The lunch rush is about to start," she said, "but I'll arrange for someone to cover for him. Just get him back as quick as you can. And, Michael, don't you forget that you have to take Nick out to the reunion site in about ten minutes."

"Yes, ma'am. I remembered. I'll be back in time."

"I'll get Henry back as soon as I can," Jack assured her as he and Michael headed for the kitchen door, looking for Henry.

As they were walking through the door, Big Mama said, "He needs underwear, and lots of it."

"Consider it done," Jack said over his shoulder.

The Coat of Many Colors

They found Henry sweeping out from under a table and literally snatched the unsuspecting boy up by his arms as they walked toward the door of the restaurant. They quickly explained to him what was happening as they took the short walk to Mr. Joseph's place.

"You sure Big Mama don't mind?" Henry asked in disbelief.

"Not only does she not mind," Jack said, "but she told me to buy lots of it."

Michael laughed, and Henry just stared slack-jawed at Jack as they walked.

"Jack," Michael said, "I'm going to have to leave as soon as we explain everything to Mr. Joseph. I won't be gone more than an hour. I'll probably be back before you're finished."

"That's okay," Jack said. "We can handle things."

They got to the Coat of Many Colors and quickly explained the situation to Mr. Joseph, who leapt into action. As Michael left, Mr. Joseph was already measuring Henry. He was soon dragging out pants, shoes, shirts, socks, and underwear. He had some coats and winter hats left over from last year and was happy to sell them in July at a nice discount. So Jack bought two coats and two hats—one for everyday use, and one for Sunday go to meeting. He had discovered that Henry and Big Mama were active in their Methodist church.

At one point during the trying-on of clothes, Henry came out of the dressing room wearing a Sunday suit and tie and new shoes. He walked up to Jack and said, "Well, how do I look?"

Jack, pretending not to recognize him, looked all around as he said, "You look very nice, sir. Has anyone seen Little Henry? Where'd that boy get off to?"

By the time all the damages were tallied, as Jack liked to say, Little Henry had seven changes of work clothes, two Sunday suits (one navy and one brown), two dress shirts, four ties to match the suits, one dozen handkerchiefs, two pair of dress shoes to match the suits, two pair of everyday shoes, more than a dozen pair of socks, a nice Sunday overcoat and a heavy everyday coat that came down far enough, as Jack said, to keep his scrawny butt from freezing in those Yankee winters. He also had a light jacket, a pair of gloves, underwear and lots of it, and a $50 bill.

All of this took about two hours to accomplish, and Michael was back long before they were finished.

As they left the store, all three loaded down with what Jack called plunder, Jack turned to Mr. Joseph and said, "Thank you, sir, for a most pleasant visit."

Mr. Joseph said, "Thank you, Mr. Moses, for your business, and thank you for helping Little Henry. He's a good boy."

Jack said, "Mr. Joseph, the pleasure was mine. It's been a while since I've had this much fun in one afternoon. Good day, sir, and may God bless you."

They made their way back to the restaurant. Jack was somewhat worried about the reception they would get in the kitchen. But when Little Henry, who was leading the procession, pushed through the kitchen door, Jack heard squeals of delight from Big Mama as she gazed upon her young working man in his new clothes and with his arms full of more. Michael and Jack followed closely, and all three of them piled their plunder on a table. Big Mama's hands were over her mouth in gleeful wonder. As soon as Henry had put his packages on the table, she gave him a big kiss on the cheek, and Jack thought he saw the child blush a little.

Big Mama looked over at Michael, who was a pretty sharp dresser in his snazzy, khaki driving cap, and slapped him on the arm saying, "He'll be right up there with you before long."

So all was well with Big Mama, but what about Uncle Nick? Would he be upset with Henry having been gone over two hours? That had Jack worried until he spied him on the other side of the kitchen. He was pretending to be preoccupied with some little chore, but Jack could tell he was watching the proceedings closely. He was wearing a small smile, which was, according to Michael, the equivalent of a large smile on anyone else. Jack relaxed.

Thank you, Lord, he prayed silently, *for this sweet little blessing.*

Then he saw Big Mama look at him and secretly mouth the words, *Thank you.*

Jack nodded almost imperceptibly.

After a few more minutes of Big Mama oohing and aahing over the new clothes, Michael said he would give them a ride home when they got off so they wouldn't have to carry all those packages by hand.

Jack quietly pulled Michael off to the side and told him he wouldn't be needing him anymore that day. It was already after three o'clock, and it had been a long day for an old man—a good day, but long.

Michael, Henry, Nick, and Big Mama still had the suppertime crowd facing them in just a couple of hours. It was Jack's intent to be in that crowd. He was already looking forward to another of Big Mama's dishes. Tomorrow, he would have Michael take him to the reunion site to begin the second phase of his quest: the search for Rose.

He made his way up to his room. Almost two years earlier, when he had reserved the room and paid for half of it in advance by wire, he made sure he would be no higher than the second floor. His once-powerful legs did not like climbing more than one flight of steps. But he felt light on his feet as he ascended the stairs.

A happy heart will do that for you, he thought to himself.

He unpacked, not having taken time to do it that morning. Removing his shoes and jacket, he stretched out on the bed for a most welcome nap.

Jack had frequently complimented his grandchildren on being good girls or good boys, or on being good helpers or good eaters or whatever compliment was necessary to encourage them in the right direction. After watching the old man napping in the parlor one Sunday afternoon, his youngest one complimented him on being a good sleeper. And so he was.

Levi Brookner

He awoke a little after five o'clock, greatly refreshed. He put on his shoes and jacket, straightened himself up, and walked down to the restaurant only to find it full.

After all, he thought, *this is the best place in town.*

He looked around for an empty table but found none. Then Uncle Nick approached him and told him of a gentleman dining alone who would welcome some company. Nick led him to a small table near the kitchen door. At the table sat a small man in blue. He appeared to be in his late sixties or early seventies, and he looked prosperous, as did Jack. He was wearing the uniform of a Union private. But this uniform was obviously custom-made and resplendent. Jack was not wearing a uniform, and he had no desire to.

Nick was about to introduce them, but before he could speak the man rose and said, "I'm Dr. Levi Brookner of the Seventy-first Pennsylvania."

Jack shook his hand and said, "Jack Moses, Fifth Alabama. Thank you, sir, for having me at your table."

"You're most welcome. You aren't wearing a uniform, sir," the doctor said.

"No, sir. I don't have one anymore. I barely had one when I was in the army. All that's left of it is a threadbare shirt with a couple of bullet holes in it and a pair of Yankee boots, uppers only."

Looking at the doctor's splendid suit, he added with a smile, "I knew you Northern boys had good stuff, but obviously I did not realize just how truly fine it was. You must have been the highest-ranking private in the whole Yankee army."

"I was," he admitted with a wry smile.

Jack chuckled a little at the man's dry wit.

Then the doctor added, "Actually, Mr. Moses, I was probably the most insignificant potato peeler they ever had. I was little, soft, and scared. I just did the best I could. I'm very fortunate to be here today."

Jack decided to like this man.

"We're all fortunate to be here," he said. "Did you participate in the pleasantries here at Gettysburg?"

"Oh, yes. I'm afraid I wasn't much help, but I was here," he replied.

"Me too," said Jack.

"You Southern boys may not have had much of a wardrobe, but you certainly managed to frighten the mortal hell out of me and a lot of my friends when you came up Cemetery Ridge at us that day," Brookner said.

"You were at Cemetery Ridge?" Jack asked.

"Yes, sir."

"Well, so was I. But I only got to stay at the top a little while because y'all ran us off," Jack said, smiling.

There was a pause in the conversation. Then Jack said, "Dr. Brookner, can you believe that you and I did all that stuff all those years ago and survived to live long lives when so many around us weren't so fortunate? Do you have any idea how blessed we are to be sitting here together tonight, fifty years later?"

"My sentiments exactly, my friend," the doctor said. Then he picked up his water glass and said, "May I propose a toast to the two of us, members in good standing of what a famous bard once called the 'happy few.'"

Jack lifted his glass. They drank a toast to themselves and to their long lives. And thus, a friendship was born.

"Mr. Moses, please call me Levi."

"Levi, just call me Jack."

The two old soldiers had a pleasant meal together, swapping humorous stories of their military experiences. Their mutual respect and affection grew as they talked.

Jack learned that Dr. Brookner was from Philadelphia and

that he owned a small, but excellent, hospital and clinic there, in addition to an elite medical school.

The good doctor's dinner companion was duly impressed.

"Not bad for an insignificant potato peeler," Jack said.

A Good Man

Jack was a little ashamed of his own seemingly mercenary accomplishments. But he shared his story with the doctor anyway. Jack had made his living in lumber, hardware, dry goods, and especially in banking. Though not a banker himself, he owned banks in Mobile, Montgomery, Tuscaloosa, and Birmingham. A very prosperous businessman, he made his story sound as modest as possible without actually lying about it. He knew he owed it all to God and to Rose's prayers.

Jack, over the last few decades at least, had been very generous with his wealth. He never hesitated to help someone genuinely in need. Skin color, religious preference, ethnic background—none of these things mattered to him. To Jack, they were all God's children. Whenever possible, he performed these acts of kindness anonymously, usually through the Southern Baptist Church of which he was a member. Sometimes, he used a discreet third party such as a pastor from another church or a teacher who had a needy child in his or her class. In the case of Little Henry, no suitable third party was readily available, so he joyfully handled the job himself.

Mr. Jack, as he was affectionately known, could be counted on to quietly solve problems and ease suffering. He was loved by all the good citizens of Mobile, both black and white. He was welcome in any home.

Jack had learned his philanthropic habit from his wife and her parents. Mr. and Mrs. Swann and Miss Sally had all been deeply involved in charitable works. Where the Swanns were Episcopalian (most of Mobile's leading citizens were either

Episcopalian or Roman Catholic), Jack was drawn to the less ornate, more direct and expressive faith of the Southern Baptists. He blamed his affinity for that denomination on what he laughingly called his hard-shell, heathen background. He joined the Southern Baptists in spite of their past practice of supporting slavery because they believed in something very dear to him: the eternal security of the believer. Most people just called it "once saved, always saved."

    Jack truly believed that his Savior, Jesus Christ, is God the Creator, and therefore the most powerful and merciful being in existence. He believed if a person truly accepted Jesus that person is permanently saved. He did not think Satan, or any other force in the universe, was strong enough to pry a soul out of Jesus's all-powerful, loving hands. And even though that person might backslide from time to time, that is not tantamount to becoming lost again. He did not argue with people of other faiths about it. He just lived it. Knowing he did not deserve it, he was nonetheless secure in his salvation. He knew it was not something he, or anyone, could earn through works or buy with money. It is a gift from a loving God, a gift that is never forced on anyone, but, when earnestly requested by a repentant sinner, is lovingly and eagerly granted and never revoked. As in Jack's case, the works would follow.

    Jack also knew that, sadly, many people just walk down the aisle of a church and join up without ever finding Jesus. He sometimes thought he could tell who they were. But he couldn't, not always.

    At first, Jack did good works in an attempt to atone for his prior life. Gradually, however, he came to the full realization that Jesus had already atoned for his sins. From that point on, he truly enjoyed his faith. He found himself taking deep pleasure in anonymously helping people. With each occurrence, he felt more and more humble in the realization that God was using him to bless his precious children.

    It seemed that all Jack touched turned to gold. He had

started out as a humble employee in Mr. Swann's lumberyard and was soon running it. Then, as Mr. Swann gradually retired, Jack, who by then was Mr. Swann's beloved and trusted son-in-law, slowly took over the operation of the hardware business as well. His wife, Miss Sally, looked after the dry goods business. Jack handled everything else.

The businesses grew with the rebuilding South. Before long, he saw the need to diversify. He bought a foundering bank in Mobile and turned it around. A few years later, he bought two other banks: one in Montgomery and one in Tuscaloosa. Later, he acquired another in booming Birmingham.

Mr. and Mrs. Moses established charitable agencies in all four cities. God was blessing him so abundantly he literally could not give the money away fast enough. He became very wealthy.

All that money naturally attracted the attention of a lot of politicians. Jack, however, avoided friendships with most of them, viewing them as a generally disingenuous lot who seldom did anything for anyone without the promise of something much more concrete than a mere blessing of the spirit in return. But he had a very small group of trusted friends who were career politicians and who, as Jack would say, were no more corrupt than their profession required them to be.

These men knew they could rely on Jack to address the legitimate needs of any worthy cause. They also knew never to involve him in any of their political schemes. Jack, in return, never looked too deeply into their activities, lest they be embarrassed. They were, after all, as he would remind Miss Sally, just politicians. One cannot expect a tomcat, even a likable one, to be anything but a tomcat.

Before Mr. and Mrs. Swann passed away, they, along with Miss Sally and Mr. Jack, pooled some money and set up what they called the Silas Swann Scholarship Fund. In and around Mobile, a deserving young scholar of any race or religion who lacked the resources to provide for an education could be sure the Silas Swann Scholarship Fund would provide significant assistance.

This fund was originally administered by Mr. and Mrs. Swann and Mr. and Mrs. Moses. Of those four people, only Jack remained. So now the fund was administered by Jack and his three surviving children: Paul Swann Moses, Silas Swann Moses, and Rose Swann Moses Elmore. Jack and Sally had lost their youngest child in his early twenties. His name was Wiley Jackson Moses, Jr.

The four of them handled the scholarship fund with great generosity and joy. All of Jack's children had big hearts full of Christian love, much like their parents.

Wiley Jackson Moses, over the span of a half century, had grown into a delightful old Southern gentleman whose heart was full of Jesus and whose soul was at peace with its Maker. God had transformed him into the exact opposite of his former self. He had had his share of trials and tribulations, but it would have been difficult to find a happier soul in this world. Even though he had never thought of himself as such, he was, by the measure of men at least, a good man. Rose's prayers had served him well.

That night, as he dressed for bed, he looked back on the day. It had been a good one. He put a pillow on the floor to cushion his old knees, and he knelt by the bed to pray. He thanked God for the nice people he had met on the train and for the new friends he had already made in Gettysburg. He was especially grateful for Michael, who had been so helpful. He asked God to be with Michael and Little Henry and Big Mama. He also prayed for Esau Johnson, the Robinsons, Mr. Joseph, and Levi. He thanked God for Michael's Uncle Nick and asked the Lord to bless the man's spirit with a little more joy. He prayed for his children and grandchildren in Mobile. He also prayed for his church congregation back home as well as for the congregation of a little colored church he had been visiting one Sunday each month for many years. And last of all, he prayed for Rose, for her happiness and well-being and, of course, that God would let her be a nurse, a good nurse. He prayed, "Send her to me, Lord, like before."

All these things he prayed in the name of Jesus.

Even though he had slept soundly on the train the night before, he was very tired from his trip and the day's activities. He would rest well that night. Tomorrow would be a big day. He would begin his search for Rose fifty years to the day after he had both found her and lost her. Also, tomorrow, he would observe his eighty-third birthday. He fell asleep with a smile on his face. He was, after all, a good sleeper.

WEDNESDAY, JULY 2ND

Breakfast with Levi

Jack awoke as usual around 6:30 a.m. without the aid of a clock. He felt rested after a good night's sleep. Dr. Brookner and Jack had agreed to meet for breakfast at 7:30. From there, Michael would deliver them to the reunion site. Not knowing about Michael and the truck, Levi had been using the local taxi service. He had been there a couple of days, so he knew his way around the reunion.

Jack and the doctor had chosen to stay in the hotel rather than in the tent city because they could afford it. There were other reasons too.

Dr. Brookner, being a Jew and an introverted man, felt a little uncomfortable among so many swaggering Irishmen. Fifty years earlier, he had been uncomfortable as the only Jew in a mostly Irish outfit, and he saw no reason to repeat the experience. They had not been mean to him or mistreated him. He just had not fit in. He had spent the last two days in their midst, but at night, he preferred the peaceful solitude and the privacy of his hotel room.

Jack, on the other hand, was only mildly interested in the

official reunion. A different reunion was on his mind. His dearest army friends had died in the charge. In the roughly twenty-one months from Gettysburg until the end of the war, Jack had only made a few friends. He had not allowed himself to get really close to anyone for fear of losing them as he had Silas. He remained a loner throughout the balance of his army days. The gregarious nature that had endeared him so to the people of Mobile did not even begin to show itself until he met Miss Sally. He did not really expect to find any army acquaintances at the reunion. Jack was searching for just one person. By and large, his hope of finding her lay in numerous prayers over many years.

When Jack and Rose had last seen each other, she had assured him they would meet again. Jack had expressed skepticism, but Rose's faith was strong, and she had insisted that it would come to pass. In the ensuing lifetime, his faith in prayer had grown to match hers. He, too, believed they would see each other again in this life. He also knew that if it was going to happen it would most likely be at this reunion. All she knew of him was that his name was Jack Moses and that he was from Alabama. All he knew of her was that her name was Rose Blount—he, of course, had no idea what her married name, if any, might be—that she was sixty-one years old, and that she was almost surely a nurse, and a good one.

Jack's logical, rational mind saw very little chance for the reunion he so dearly wanted. But his faith in prayer and in a generous, loving God kept his hope alive. Those things were also keeping Jack, himself, alive. After Miss Sally's death a few years earlier, his health had begun to fail. He had a bad heart and had almost died twice. His children had nearly forbidden him to go to Pennsylvania for fear he would not survive the trip. They finally relented because they knew how much he wanted to find Rose, and because they knew they really could not stop him. Jack had asked God to let him live long enough to attend the reunion in hopes that Rose would also see this as their last opportunity to find each other and would come looking for him. He knew it was a long shot, but like two good men had told him a half century earlier, in God's love, all things are possible.

Jack and Dr. Brookner met at the same table they had shared the night before. They enjoyed each other's company. Dr. Brookner felt comfortable around Jack, and Jack, who felt comfortable around almost anyone, respected the doctor's reserved nature.

Little Henry was buzzing around the restaurant wearing his new work clothes and an even larger than usual smile. He worked his way around near Jack's table.

"Good morning, Mr. Moses."

"Good morning, Master Henry. How is our young working man doing today?"

"Fine, sir! Just fine," Henry said.

"Henry, I want you to meet a friend of mine. This is Doctor Levi Brookner from Philadelphia. Doctor Brookner, this is Henry Dewberry, a working man, and as such, the better of us."

Levi smiled and extended his hand. "I'm honored to make your acquaintance, Mr. Dewberry."

"Likewise, Doctor Brookner. I've seen you here before," Henry said as they shook hands.

"Yes. I've been here a couple of days. And what do you plan to do when your career here in the restaurant is over? Are you still in school?" Levi asked, making conversation.

"Yes, sir," Henry replied. "I still have three more years to go."

"And then what?" asked the doctor.

"I want to be a teacher, but that requires college. I don't know how I'll be able to afford it, but I'm going to do my best."

That was the first time Jack had heard anything about Henry's hopes and aspirations. He immediately began to worry about the child's long-term happiness and well-being. Clothes are a temporary thing, but an education is something no man can take away. And to be a teacher, that would be an honorable profession for a man of Henry's qualities. To Jack, Henry seemed to have the makings of a fine educator.

The Ride Out

Michael appeared, cheerful as usual. He sat down at their table and began talking with Jack, who introduced him to the doctor. They shook hands and exchanged greetings, but nothing else passed between them. To Jack, Michael seemed a little subdued in Levi's presence. Jack told him that the doctor would be riding with them out to the reunion site.

On the way, Levi and Jack sat together on the rear seat. Levi began filling Jack in on the details of the reunion. About fifty thousand honorably discharged Union and Confederate veterans had come from as far away as California. They were from all theaters of the war, not just Gettysburg. The tent city, or the Great Camp as it was called, was situated in the field adjacent to the site of Pickett's Charge. The Great Camp was divided into separate areas for the Union men and the Confederates.

"I reckon the organizers, in their wisdom, did not wish to press their luck," Jack commented with a grin.

"I think it was a wise move," Levi said, smiling.

The doctor went on to say that the U.S. Army Corps of Engineers had erected over six thousand tents to house the veterans, each tent sheltering eight men. The camp covered 280 acres and included 47 1/2 miles of streets. It was illuminated by five hundred electric arc lights and included thirty-two ice water fountains. There were 173 field kitchens manned by over two thousand army cooks and bakers who provided three hot meals a day for the veterans and camp personnel. They also served ice cream throughout the day.

Soldiers of the Fifth U.S. Infantry and the Fifteenth U.S. Cavalry guarded the camp and its supplies and provided security. The Pennsylvania State Police and National Guard were also present, as well as several hundred members of the Boy Scouts of America, who served as escorts, messengers, and aides.

Medical care was provided by the army and the American Red Cross. The state of Pennsylvania also provided medical staff. By now, several hundred patients had already been treated for everything from stomach disorders to heat exhaustion.

Dr. Brookner said, "I'm afraid a few men have passed away here since the reunion began."

"That's not nearly as bad as it was the last time we were here," Jack said. "It's going to be hot today. I can tell. We might lose some more."

"Tell me, Levi," Jack asked, "do they let the Rebs and Yanks mix during the day?"

"Oh, yes. And for the most part we've gotten along pretty well—only a few pathetic fistfights so far."

"Ha!" Jack had to laugh. "I can just imagine. I reckon 'pathetic' is an apt description of a fight between two fellows who do good just to climb out of bed each morning."

They bounced into the reunion site, and Michael slowed to walking speed. Jack noticed the spiffy new suits—both blue and gray—many veterans were wearing.

"Just look at those uniforms," he said. "We never had anything nearly that nice. Some of those outfits are almost as nice as yours, Levi."

"Many of the Southerners' uniforms were provided by the United Daughters of the Confederacy," the doctor said.

"Well, that's mighty nice of them," Jack said. "By the end of the war, we Rebs didn't really have much left in the way of a uniform. We just wore whatever we could scrounge up. I wore a pair of Yankee boots the last two years of the war."

"Yes," Levi said. "I remember seeing Southern prisoners in rags, some with no shoes, and wondering where the Confederacy found so many men who fought so valiantly under such deprived conditions."

"They didn't have much choice, Levi. When someone invades your home, you fight. Even if you are ragged and shoeless, you fight," Jack said. "But we always admired the material wealth of the Union Army. And before the war ended, we came to respect the valor of its men. After all, y'all are Americans, like us. I reckon the valor should not have been too much of a surprise."

Michael drove to what was known as the Great Tent, which had been erected in the field of Pickett's Charge. It was the site of daily programs, with speeches by dignitaries and the governors of several states. But most of the time, between the official speeches and programs, the old soldiers were allowed to take the podium and relate their war experiences to the few hundred men sitting around in chairs. To some, the Great Tent became known as the "Tall Tale Tent." Many of the stories were of a humorous nature and had undoubtedly been much embellished over the decades. Other stories were more somber. But memory sweetens with time, and few of the stories contained any bitterness.

The Young Trooper

Jack and Levi found seats near the podium. They were glad to get off the remorseless carriage and even happier to be in the shade. Just as they sat down, some army people showed up with a tub of ice cream. The two of them and Michael happily indulged, and when the treat was finished, Jack released Michael to assist his uncle.

"I'll see you at lunch," Jack said. "You know what to bring me."

"You know what I want too, don't you, Michael?" asked the doctor.

"Yes, sir, I know what you both want. Uncle Nick and Henry and I will deliver it right here around noon," Michael said.

"Excellent!" said Jack. "Run along now, and we'll see you at lunch."

They watched Michael crank the truck and drive toward town.

"Fine boy, that Michael," Jack said.

"Yes. Certainly seems to be," said Levi.

"Wants to be a doctor."

"Takes good marks and hard work," Levi said, "and lots of money. And to be what I consider a good doctor, it also takes selflessness, a willingness to sacrifice, and a desire to serve."

They were silent for a while.

Then Jack said, "Levi, my family has been granting scholarships to folks for a long time, mostly to children in south Alabama and a few in southeast Mississippi and the Florida panhandle. We usually send them to the University of Alabama or Alabama Polytechnic. We send the colored children to one of several good little colored colleges we have down there. So I know about what it takes to put a child through college down south. But when it comes to a highfalutin Philadelphia medical school, I'm pretty much in the dark. Michael is trying to earn enough for school by using his uncle's truck to ride people like us around. I intend to be generous with him at the end of the week, but I fear he will never be able to earn enough to enroll this fall. I think we are his only customers at the moment."

"I can tell you for a fact, my friend," Levi said, "that unless he has some resources we don't know about, it is out of his reach, even for a relatively inexpensive public college."

"He doesn't," Jack said. "You said it takes good marks, hard work, and money, among other things. What do you say we locate the local schoolmaster after supper tonight and inquire as to Brother Michael's marks, work ethic, and concern for his fellow man? If Michael will provide those commodities, I will provide the money. Do you think there would be a place for him at your school this fall?"

"Oh, yes. I'm very close to the man who owns the place," Levi said, smiling. "If our young friend meets the requirements, we will have a place for him. Even though we only admit a handful of students each year, we have not yet reached our limit for this fall. I think we can even find a little part-time job for him in the hospital or clinic so he can earn a little pocket money and gain some firsthand experience, get a little blood on his hands, so to speak. And as a reward for your generosity, we can probably talk the old tightwad who owns the place into giving you a modest discount on the tuition."

"Excellent! Wonderful! Outstanding!" Jack exclaimed. "We'll look into it tonight."

About that time, a young soldier approached them with a tray of ice water. As they each took a glass, Jack said, "What outfit are you with, son?"

"Fifth Infantry, sir."

"Fifth Infantry! Hey, that's my old outfit," Jack said, winking at the amused doctor.

"Really sir?" asked the young man. "You were in the Fifth?"

"Yes, siree! Served right here at Gettysburg," Jack said.

"I never knew the Fifth was at Gettysburg," the boy said.

"Why, sure, son, the Fifth Alabama. We walked right up that hill there and evicted a bunch of you Yankees," Jack said, nudging the trooper on the arm.

By now, Jack and Levi were having a good laugh, and the young soldier smiled and said, "Well, sir, I'm from South Carolina myself. I'm not a Yankee."

Jack, with comic indignation, said, "A South Carolinian in the Yankee Army! Why, you danged traitor!"

"Yes, sir. I'm proud to be here. I hope to make a career of it," the soldier said.

Jack, realizing how seriously the young man was taking his ice water duties, said, "I'm sure you're a fine soldier, son. The South Carolinians I knew when I was serving were a tough, committed bunch. Good luck in your career. I hope you don't mind a fellow like me having a little fun with you."

"Oh no, sir, I don't mind. Someday I hope to be an old codger myself."

The doctor laughed a little harder than before, and without so much as a smile, the soldier went back to dispensing ice water.

Jack gave Levi a few seconds to get his mirth under control and then, with a faraway look in his eye and a dreamy tone in his voice, he said, "Yes, sir. I was beginning to think that boy was totally bereft of all humor. But I reckon he showed me."

Levi began laughing again, and he shook in silence for some time, in spite of his efforts not to. Jack just smiled as he watched his friend struggle.

Jack's Story

Jack and Levi listened to a series of war stories as told by various veterans from each side. After a man from New York finished his story, Jack waited about a minute, and when no one else rose to speak, he stepped up to the lectern. The few hundred men very politely grew quiet, and Jack began to talk.

"Gentlemen, my name is Jack Moses. I was in the Fifth Alabama Infantry Battalion. I participated in Pickett's Charge right here on this field. I have thoroughly enjoyed all your stories. But back home in Alabama, we have a saying that when it comes to fish stories and other tall tales, the first liar doesn't stand a chance."

They laughed.

"That's why I've waited this long to speak. But I didn't climb up here to tell you any war stories. My war stories are about lives lost before they were lived. I have no desire to recount those events. No, my friends, I stepped up here to tell you that today I am celebrating my eighty-third birthday."

There was scattered applause and laughter. One old fellow got a big laugh out of the crowd and Jack when he shouted, "You don't look a day over ninety-eight!"

Jack waited for the laughter to subside. "Thank you, brother, for those kind words."

Actually, Jack looked younger than his years, but his looks belied the true condition of his health.

He continued. "To tell you the truth, my friends, I'm not sure exactly when I was born. I know with a fair degree of certainty that it was either late spring or early summer of 1830. My mother passed away when I was five, and my father never came around, so I never knew my exact date of birth. Now you are probably asking yourself how I arrived at the second of July as my birth date. Well, I am about to tell you.

"You see, brothers, I was lost. I was a lost sinner when this day dawned fifty years ago. But before I went to sleep that night, the night before that terrible day, a little, eleven-year-old slave girl led me to Jesus. May God bless her brave heart."

There was more applause and a few amens.

"So I decided," he continued, "to make this day, July second, my birthday. I honestly did not expect to have any more. If it had not been for the fervent prayers of that little girl, and for Jesus's sweet mercy, I would have died in the charge," he said, pointing up the rise.

"You see, my squad, twelve brave men all died that day, all save me. I went to no special efforts to preserve my life. I was ready to die. A friend and I even made it to the top—the only ones from our squad to do so. The Union men counterattacked, and we had to retreat. He died on the way down. By all rights, I should have died too. But Jesus saved my soul one day and my life the next. Over the last fifty years, I have tried to live my life as He would have me live it, for it belongs to Him. I live because of Jesus, so I live for Jesus. For the last twenty-one months of the war, Jesus allowed me to fulfill my military obligations without taking another human life. I can barely remember my life before Him. I have no desire to. I owe Him everything."

At this point, Jack reached inside his jacket and pulled out what appeared to be a brown rag. He unfolded it and held up his old uniform shirt for the men to see.

"What you see in my hand is the shirt I wore that day. As you can see, it has a hole in the back, and another in the front, near the right side, where a Yankee bullet struck me from behind as I fled from the top of the ridge. That same volley killed two other men, and I felt something knock me to the ground. I got to my knees and felt for my wounds, but I could find none. All I found were these two holes in my shirt. You are free to draw your own conclusions as to how that bullet missed me while piercing my shirt back to front. It is true that I had lost some weight on the march north, and the shirt was a bit baggy and probably untucked and flying free. But I can come up with only one explanation, and I think you know what it is.

"So now you understand why I celebrate my birth on this day. Before this day, I had no life, but because of this day, I have lived a long, fruitful life close to the Lord. And if my Creator sees fit to take me home today, I will not have been shortchanged. Many thousands of men lost their lives here at Gettysburg. But it was here, fifty years ago, that I found mine.

"Thank you for listening, my friends. May God bless you all."

Jack stepped down, and the hundreds of old troopers stood and applauded him to a man. His friend, the doctor, shook his hand, and they sat down to listen to the next man.

Levi's Story

For a while, no one stood to speak, and the crowd descended once again into general conversation.

Then Dr. Brookner turned to Jack and said, "Well, I guess it's my time."

A much smaller man than Jack, he decided to stand next to the lectern rather than behind it. He had never let his small stature inhibit him before, and he did not now. Standing there with one hand on the lectern and the other behind him, he began to speak. Everyone immediately knew he was not the average old trooper. The crowd quickly grew quiet.

"Gentlemen, I'm Doctor Levi Brookner of the Seventy-first

Pennsylvania. Of course, I was not a doctor then, in 1863. I was just a skinny, scared, little private, and I remained one for the duration. My unit was largely Irish in its makeup. There were only a few non-Irish in the outfit, me being one of them.

"As we waited up there behind that stone wall on that Friday afternoon in July, 1863, I watched the Confederates form up at the foot of the rise. My Irish comrades were full of fight and confidence. But I, never having won a fight in my life, was terrified. As the Southerners started up after us, our artillery opened up, but they came on. When they got into range, we fired on them with our rifles. We would reload as quickly as possible and fire into them again, but they came on. A lot of our men were shouting 'Fredericksburg, Fredericksburg,' over and over. We could barely see them for the smoke of our guns. But when the smoke would clear a little from time to time, they would still be there, fewer, but closer.

"My friends grew less cocky as the Rebels began to close with us. Suddenly, out of the smoke of their weapons and ours, they were on us by the hundreds, screaming like savages. I couldn't believe it. How any man could have walked up that hill through all that fire was beyond my comprehension. But there they were, and mad as hell. I was convinced they were all after me. I looked around for my comrades, but most of them were either dead, wounded, or just gone, if you know what I mean."

There was scattered laughter among the men as they looked at each other knowingly.

"By this time," Levi continued, "there were almost as many Rebels behind me as in front of me. The angle was full of them, so I decided to charge."

There was more laughter and a few whoops of encouragement.

"I quickly picked out the largest Rebel I could see nearby and rushed him with my bayonet. As I neared him, screaming as strongly as I could in hopes of scaring him away, I suppose, I realized to my shame that my prospective victim was unarmed. He had no weapon. I was having second thoughts, but I was beyond the point of no return. I would simply have to live with the shame of having killed an unarmed man.

"As I rushed him, he appeared to be unconcerned. He made no effort to evade my blade except that just as it approached his chest he calmly pushed it aside with his left forearm and broke my nose with his huge right fist."

The men were laughing in empathy now, all save one.

The doctor continued, "I landed on my back with this large Rebel, whom I had just tried to murder, standing over me. But where he had previously been unarmed, he now held my rifle firmly in both hands. 'Dead at nineteen,' I thought to myself."

There was more laughter from the crowd. The doctor could tell a pretty good story in his dry, understated style. But Jack was not laughing.

Levi went on. "I was dazed and I could tell that, in the angle at least, the Rebels were prevailing. My big Rebel looked down at me. He raised my rifle up to thrust the blade through my heart. In my dazed condition, I could not evade it, and I gave myself up for dead. The point came down with all the force that mighty man could deliver. It struck the ground under my left armpit, missing me completely. I looked up into the man's eyes as he looked down at me. What I saw in him was not anger, or hate, or a desire for blood. What I saw was sadness and grief—grief for all the men who were dead and dying. I don't think he had the heart to kill me or anyone. Why someone like that was attempting to make war is a mystery to me. God, in His mercy, had pitted poor little me against the biggest, the toughest, the kindest, and the most heartbroken man in the Army of Northern Virginia. The man simply was not a killer. He left me there with my broken nose and with my rifle sticking up out of the ground next to me. I just stayed there on the ground until our men counterattacked. There weren't enough Rebels left to repel them, so they retreated, and I was once again among my Irish friends.

"From that day forward, my friends looked at me with great

respect because I had not run away as some of them had. They even had me declared an honorary Irishman. Little did they know that I would have run if the Southerners had not surrounded me so quickly. They all thought I had somehow fought off all those ferocious Rebels until reinforcements arrived. I never told them the truth, that I was alive only because a big, softhearted Southerner chose to let me live. They all thought I was a hero. Now you men know the truth. After a half century, I have finally gotten it off my chest.

"Thank you for listening to my story, my friends. And thank you for letting me be just a scared little private again."

Levi stepped down to a loud ovation, handshakes, and slaps on the back by veterans in both blue and gray. When he got to Jack, he expected a handshake, but the tall man, with tears in his eyes, refused his hand. Instead, he gently wrapped his arms around his friend and hugged him like a brother. After sitting down, a perplexed Levi looked over toward Jack. But Jack was looking away, wiping his eyes.

Levi did not speak and pretended not to notice his tears. Jack soon regained his composure. By then, another veteran had taken the stage. Rather than stand behind the lectern, he put a chair on the stage and sat while he addressed the group. He wore gray.

The Arkansas Man

The crowd grew quiet, and he said, "Gentlemen, my name is Payne. I was in an Arkansas outfit. I saw action in the western theater. My most notable battle was Pittsburg Landing, or what you Northern boys called Shiloh. But I am not up here to speak of my war experiences. I, like Brother Moses there," he said as he smiled and nodded toward Jack, "do not especially enjoy recalling them. I would rather talk about my life since the war.

"As you can see," he continued, "I am a homely man. My

homeliness is not something I acquired in my old age. It has always been with me. I was an ugly child. Later, I was an ugly young man. And now, I am an even uglier old man. I guess it's true that some things never change. I survived the war without a scratch. My army friends told me it was because my face scared all the bullets away."

There was laughter. But they were careful not to laugh too heartily, for he truly was a homely man.

"I never had a lady friend all the time I was in the army. My friends told me not to worry, that some day I would find a nice, blind girl."

The laughter was a little bolder now.

"Truth is," he said, "I had been out of the army almost five years before I had so much as held a lady's hand. I was thirty-two years old. She was a beauty, just the prettiest thing I had ever seen, and the sweetest. And I was not the only one who thought so. She was hotly pursued by all the beaus in town. I got to know her at church. She was four years younger than me. She was a widow, her husband having died at Chattanooga. They had no children.

"I had learned by then not to let my heart get set on anyone because I knew there was no hope for me to win a lady's heart, especially one so beautiful. So I didn't pay her any special attention. I would see her at church, and she would come into my hardware store from time to time, needing this or that. I was always polite, but I was careful not to let myself look too long into those luminous blue eyes, lest I should fall. But it was a difficult task. I found myself thinking about her too much. My heart began to ache hopelessly."

He paused and said, "I hope you men realize how difficult it is for me to talk about this. This is something I could never discuss back home. I can tell you about it because I don't know any of you and because I'm a thousand miles from home. But I want to share this with you. Please hear me out. Be patient with me."

"Go on, brother. We're listening," someone said.

"Thank you. Well, I was trying so hard to protect my foolish heart from being broken that I guess she noticed me avoiding her at church one Sunday. She came into my store late the next day. She was a teacher and school turned out about three o'clock. She showed up a little after three. When I saw her walk through the door, my heart both leapt for joy and broke all at once, as it always did when I saw her. She was such a natural beauty, with a sweet, unpretentious smile."

"I said, 'Good afternoon, Miss Anna. What can I do for you?'

"She asked me if we were alone. She wanted to talk to me about something. I told her we were alone. She asked me why I was avoiding her. At first, I denied it, but then I confessed and told her why I was acting in such an unfriendly way. I told her that I was just an old crow and she was a beautiful creature of paradise and there was no sense in me letting myself get all lathered up over something that would never happen. So I figured the best way to avoid the heartache was to see as little of her as possible. I had even considered moving my membership to a different church. I couldn't believe the words that were coming out of my mouth.

"She listened to me and watched me grovel. I apologized to her for my behavior and told her I would resolve to do better. I asked her to forgive me.

"She told me I needed no forgiveness from her, for I had done her no wrong. Then she called me by my first name and said that good looks don't make the man. She said she had married her husband foolishly because of his good looks and realized her mistake too late. She said that sometimes the best man is not the best-looking one. She said that I was many times the man any of those young bucks were.

"I was about to faint. I couldn't believe what I was hearing. I had to hold on to the counter to keep from falling down. Would you believe that only about six weeks later, I worked up enough courage to ask her out?"

The crowd erupted in laughter. As the laughter subsided, the old man, still laughing a little at himself, went on with his story.

"Gentlemen, just three months after I asked her out, we got married. My life went from one of loneliness and deprivation to one of joy and fulfillment. She told me I was the world's greatest husband. I came home after work. I didn't drink or smoke. I went to church with her. I made her laugh. She said life with me was heaven. Can you believe that? I asked her once, in jest, if she wouldn't rather have a handsome man. She said that if she had wanted a handsome man, she would have married one. She told me she had tried it once and would rather have me and that it wasn't even close.

"My friends, I'm a Christian. I was saved as a child. But I never knew God's kindness would be bestowed on me so abundantly in this world. Our life together was heaven right there in Arkansas.

"We had each other, but we had no children. We were childless for about eight years and had just about given up on having any when God, in His mercy, blessed us with a little boy. And, thank the Lord, he looked like his mama and not like me."

"Amen!" someone said loudly, and they all had another good laugh along with the man on the stage.

He continued with his story. "He was a beautiful baby, a handsome little boy and a tall, handsome, well-built young man. I was so proud to be his daddy. He and I were the best of friends.

"Mr. Moses there said that today is his birthday. Well, today is our son's thirty-fifth birthday. He was born on the second of July in 1878. When he was eighteen, he joined the army. I advised against it, but he wanted to do it, and I couldn't stop him. That was 1896. Two years later, we were in Cuba, and he was there.

"When I was at Pittsburg Landing, I got to meet General Joe Wheeler. Just before my son left for Cuba, he wrote to tell me, among other things, that he had gotten to meet General Wheeler. I'm sure many of you know that General Wheeler served in the Confederate Army and later in the US Army and in Cuba. I heard that when he was in the heat of battle in Cuba, he once shouted, 'Come on, boys. We've got the damn Yankees on the run! Dammit! I mean the Spaniards.'"

There was a good fifteen seconds of uproarious laughter with an abundance of knee slapping and backslapping. The men were beginning to see one of the qualities that had endeared him so to his wife: the ability to make one laugh.

"Anyway," he said after things had settled down a little, "my son thought it interesting that we each got to serve with Joe Wheeler thirty-five years apart in two different wars, under two different flags.

"That was the last letter we ever got from our son. Under General Shafter, they attacked a little fortified village called El Caney on July the first, 1898. They took some casualties: eighty-one dead—a small number compared to what all of us are accustomed to. But our son, the center of our universe, was among them. He had just made corporal. He was so proud of those stripes. He loved the army. And he loved his country, the United States of America."

All the smiles were gone now, replaced by looks of concern and grief for their friend on the stage. The old man, weeping now, pulled a small American flag from his pocket.

"My son sent me this before he left for Cuba, and he loved it. The very thing I had fought so hard against, he died for."

He broke down momentarily and then regained his composure. The crowd was silent in their sympathy for him.

"I still have my precious wife. She is waiting for me in Arkansas. She is still the prettiest and the sweetest thing I have ever seen, and she still thinks I am the world's greatest husband. Whenever I start feeling sorry for myself, she gently reminds me that God also gave His only Son so that whosoever believes in Him should not perish but have life everlasting."

He paused, and then with great difficulty he said, "But we lost our little boy. God let us have him for twenty years. He died serving his country on July the first, 1898. His twentieth birthday would have been the next day. He would be thirty-five today, had he lived. But he didn't. Our lives go on without him."

The old man struggled with his grief and then resolutely continued.

"I served proudly in the Army of the Confederacy, and I fought hard for our worthy cause. I refuse to be ashamed of our noble struggle for independence. I will never apologize for our efforts to defend ourselves. We suffered much in the war and reconstruction. But this was his flag," he said as he held the little banner high. "This is my flag. Thank God slavery is dead and the Union was restored. I'm an old Confederate who is proud to be a citizen of the United States of America. Praise the Lord—we lost. May He always bless our precious country."

As he stepped down, he was surrounded and comforted by his friends, North and South. Jack and Levi were the first to console him.

Reconciliation

Lunchtime arrived, and the men began moving toward the 173 mess tents the army had set up for them. At the same time, Jack and Levi saw Michael's truck approaching. He was driving more slowly now that his uncle and a cargo of food were on board. On the backseat sat Henry. They were delivering hot meals that old men could eat: tender country fried steak or Swiss steak (take your pick), mashed potatoes, butter beans, soft rolls, and lemon pie. The Yankee Army, as Jack called it, was furnishing food for the roughly fifty thousand old troopers. But some of them preferred civilian chow. Jack and Levi were among them.

When they stopped, they were surrounded by those who had chosen Big Mama's cooking over the army's. Michael handed specially marked, covered plates to Jack and Levi, along with a glass of tea for each. The two made their way to the nearest picnic table, where they enjoyed a leisurely meal in good company.

Michael and Nick quickly sold the other prepared plates they had on the truck. Henry sold tall glasses of sweet iced tea and Big Mama's famously tart, thirst-slaying lemonade. Nick, on Jack's suggestion, had had Big Mama make up a batch of those two summertime beverages to cater especially to the Southern veterans' taste. They were almost as popular with the Northern men as with the Southerners. Henry soon sold out. They were so well received that Nick had decided to let Michael make what they called a lemonade and tea run to the reunion that afternoon and each morning and each afternoon for the next two days.

After about thirty minutes, the three men from the Battle House Restaurant collected their glassware and utensils and began loading the truck for the trip back to town.

Michael waved at Jack and Levi and said, "I'll see you this afternoon between three and four."

The two of them waved back in agreement. They watched and smiled as Michael drove very slowly and gently back toward town. The boy was very mindful of his uncle's presence.

"Perhaps he will be that gentle with us on the way back this afternoon," Levi said.

"Perhaps," Jack said as they chuckled a little.

Neither really believed it.

That afternoon, they listened politely to a dull speech by Pennsylvania's Governor Tener and then to several more tall tales from the stage.

As the sun got lower and things cooled off a little, they ventured out from under the Great Tent to creak around the field with the others.

As Jack and Levi looked up the slope, which had been the site of the charge, Jack said, "I walked up that hill fifty years ago. It sure looked different then. I don't mean that it has changed that much. The grass is still there, the wall, and some trees. But there's no smoke or noise, no dying. It just seems like a different place now."

"You probably looked very different then yourself," Levi said.

"I did, Levi. A half century will change a man, you know."

"You were a much bigger man then, weren't you?" Levi said.

"Yes. I was a little taller and a lot heavier."

Sensing the time was right, Levi said, "Jack, I noticed that you were especially moved by my story this morning."

Jack did not respond. He continued to gaze up the rise.

Levi spoke again. "Jack, I have never been one to make friends easily. I'm a loner. But in spite of the fact that we have only known each other for one day, I feel very close to you. To me, you are a trusted friend. If there is something you would like to tell me, please feel free. I am beginning to suspect what it is that's bothering you. Just go ahead and tell me about it."

Jack still did not speak, but he looked into Levi's eyes. The grief Levi saw there took him back to the battle. He knew Jack's secret, but he said nothing.

Finally, Jack said, "Levi, did that fellow say anything to you after he knocked you down?"

"Yes, Jack."

"He bent down, didn't he?"

"Yes," Levi said, "he bent down. There was so much noise he could never have been heard otherwise. He bent down to my ear and said—"

"Stay down, son," Jack said, finishing the sentence for him.

A few seconds passed before Levi said, "That's right, Jack. And I did as you said. You really were much bigger then."

Again, there was silence as they stood in the shade of a tree.

At last, Jack said, "You were wearing a red bandana above your left elbow. I'm almost sure."

Levi reached inside his coat and carefully retrieved a frazzled pink rag saying, "My sweetheart gave it to me for good luck. We have been married almost forty-seven years now. I keep it with me at all times."

After admiring his little treasure for a few seconds, Levi said, "Jack, I want to thank you for my life."

Smiling, Jack said, "Heck, Levi, it wasn't me. It was that red bandana."

After they had shared a little chuckle, Jack went on. "I'm not the one you need to thank. If we had met in battle just one day earlier, I would have pinned you to the earth without a second thought. You said I looked like a brokenhearted man that day. That was because the night before the charge, Jesus had broken my wicked heart and changed me from the most useless human in the world into one who no longer cared anything for his own life but who was determined to never again take the life of another person. I had already taken way too many. I hoped to die that day, but that hope went unfulfilled. But Jesus has allowed me to go from that day to this without killing anyone.

"Levi," he continued, "you don't owe your life to me. On the day after He saved my soul, Jesus delivered a precious little Jewish boy into a long, productive life. His love knows no bounds. He did the same thing for me that very day."

"But why did my story sadden you so?" Levi asked.

"I don't know. I guess when I came to the reunion I was hoping I might find at least one of my old army friends. I know they all died, but I thought that maybe someone had survived without my knowledge. But they're all gone. Deep down I've always known it. But when you started talking and I realized that the little boy whose nose I busted that day was the only person I encountered on either side who survived the battle, it just moved me to tears. I reckon you were the last person I expected to be reunited with."

The two men embraced, and Jack's sadness left him.

He said, "Like I said, I never expected to see you again, but since we're here, I feel compelled to ask your forgiveness for breaking your nose. I hit you pretty hard."

"You're forgiven, my friend. You're forgiven."

They continued to walk the field with some of the others. Jack was heartened by how well the former enemies were getting along. Just as his friendship with Levi was growing, so were others making lasting bonds with people from different parts of the country.

They had a pleasant afternoon, and about 3:30, Michael appeared with a truckload of iced tea and lemonade. He was alone. Nick and Henry were at the restaurant preparing for the evening meal, their busiest of the day.

Michael quickly sold the cold beverages and then made himself comfortable in one of the chairs next to Jack and Levi as he waited for his customers to finish their drinks.

"Well," Michael said, "have you boys had fun today? Are you about ready to go home?"

"If you mean the hotel, yes. I think we're ready," Levi answered.

They spent a little more time resting in the shade, and then they helped Michael collect his glassware. On the way back to town, much to their relief, Michael drove slowly and gently.

Jack looked at Levi and said, "It's the glassware."

"Precisely," Levi answered, smiling.

After resting and freshening up a little, Jack and Levi met in the restaurant for supper. With Henry buzzing about, Big Mama sticking her head through the kitchen door to receive high praise, and with Levi's good companionship, Jack had decided that this reunion business was just fine. He missed his family dearly, especially his little ones, the grandchildren. But he would be home with them soon enough, just a few more days.

Meanwhile, his hope of finding Rose was beginning to wane a little. He was hoping she would come looking for him. A colored lady among so many white men should be easy to find. But there were over fifty thousand people there, and the Great Camp was, well, great. He would pray about it, as usual, before he went to bed. But right now, he and Levi had other business to see after.

Mr. Campbell

They discovered that the headmaster of the local schools was a man named Campbell. Gettysburg was not very big. He lived within easy walking distance. They dropped in on him after supper. They were invited into a modest parlor and explained their business.

At the mention of Michael's name, Mr. Campbell laughed and said, "Ah, yes. Master Carmardo."

His reaction worried them a little.

Mr. Campbell went on. "Young Carmardo is full of—what shall I say?—life. Yes, let's call it life."

"Life is a good thing to be full of," Jack said, "that and hope. I've known some folks who were alive, but what they were full of was something else entirely."

"What are his marks like?" Levi asked. "Is he a good student?"

"Oh, yes," Campbell said. "He's one of our very best. He isn't our top student, but he's near the top. He's especially strong in science and math. I didn't mean to frighten you when I said he's full of life. He's a good boy, and he has been a hard worker for as long as I've known him. The teachers and students all love him. He told me he hopes to be a doctor. I remember telling my wife that he would be a good one because he is intelligent and perceptive. He has a good sense of humor. He would probably have a good bedside manner. And I think he would be especially good with children and old people. He has a kind heart. But…"

"But what?" Jack asked.

"Well, he cannot possibly afford medical school, especially one as exclusive as Doctor Brookner's."

"You let us worry about that," Jack said a little impatiently. "What we want from you, Mr. Campbell, is your objective opinion of Michael's ability to make it through medical school. Could he earn the required marks? Would he work hard enough to get through it? Would he stick with it, or would he lose interest when it gets tough? We don't want your opinion as his friend. We already know he's an affable young man. We want your professional opinion as an educator."

After a few seconds of indignant silence, Mr. Campbell said, "Mr. Moses, there is no doubt in my mind that Michael Camardo, given the opportunity to attend Doctor Brookner's school, would seize it with both hands and never let go. You don't have to worry about him not putting forth the effort or disappointing you. It won't happen."

"Well, Mr. Moses," Levi said, "have you heard enough?"

"I have, Doctor Brookner."

They thanked Mr. Campbell for his time and, after asking him to keep their visit a secret for now, they began the walk back to the hotel.

The Handshake

It was early summer, and the days were long. In spite of the lateness of the hour, there was still enough light to walk by.

As they walked, Levi said, "You said you are on a scholarship board. Will you be able to sell the other members on a scholarship for Michael?"

"It won't be a problem," Jack said. "I'm chairman of the board, and I am also the lone surviving founder of the fund. The other board members are my three children. I don't even need their approval to award a scholarship to Michael. Our bylaws allow me to award one scholarship per year without their concurrence if I so choose. I haven't done one yet, so I'll just make Michael's the one for this year. I'll go to the telegraph office and send my children a wire in the morning with all the necessary information. When do you think we need to tell Michael about this?"

"In the morning, before you send your wire. I think he needs to know about this before we go any further with it," Levi said.

"Yes, you're right," Jack said. "It certainly would be embarrassing if we awarded him a scholarship only to discover that he had decided to join a Wild West show."

"Jack, why don't you just wait till you get home to tell your children? Surely it will keep a few more days."

"Levi, at my age, and with my health being what it has been the last few years, I can't be all that confident of even getting back to Alabama. I don't want to take the chance of something happening to me before I get back and before they know about my intentions regarding Michael. They didn't even want me to come up here for fear I would have a spell with my heart. But I'm a grown man, and their daddy, and they couldn't stop me. I had to come. I couldn't pass up what is almost certainly the last opportunity I'll ever have to find Rose," Jack said.

"Rose?"

"Yes. The little girl who led me to Jesus. I owe her more than any other mortal," Jack said.

"Levi," he continued, "I know you're not a Christian, so you might have a little trouble understanding what I am about to say, but here it is. Before Rose helped me find Jesus, I was almost certainly among the vilest of souls on this planet. I was notorious in my home area in northeastern Alabama. I'm not going to go into detail because I was so wicked you probably wouldn't believe your ears, and because I'm too ashamed to tell you about it. But since I surrendered to Jesus, a sweet peace and calm has come over my life and replaced all that turmoil, hate, and anger. Thanks to Him, my last fifty years have been full of love and joy. After Jesus, I owe it all to a little girl named Rose Blount.

"I've been praying all these years," Jack said, "that the Lord would allow me to somehow find her in this life so I could thank her properly and publicly for what she did. I know there's only a small chance that I'll find her here, but my prayer is that she will come here looking for me and we will find each other. That is why I insisted on coming, in spite of my health and against the desires of my children."

"We can talk to Michael in the morning after breakfast," Levi said. "Then you can send your wire if it is still necessary."

They arrived back at the hotel and shook hands on their deal to make a doctor out of Michael Camardo. Then they retired to their rooms for the evening, for the hour was late, and they were old.

The window of Jack's room faced eastward, so he could not see the sunset. But he could see the shadows growing weak as night gently rolled in from the east. As darkness approached, he looked back on the day. He smiled as he recalled the stories he had heard. He grieved a little for the heartbroken Arkansas trooper. He marveled at his and Levi's miraculous reunion and at God's limitless kindness to an unworthy, old man.

Tonight, his prayers would be of praise and gratitude, and, as always, for the happiness and well-being of one little girl he had met many years before.

As his day neared its end, Jack, as usual, was without doubt or fear. His birthday had been a good one. But Rose had not been found.

THURSDAY, JULY 3RD

Two Heroes

Jack and Levi met for breakfast as agreed. Jack was truly enjoying the fellowship with the restaurant crew, Little Henry especially. He also enjoyed some good-natured banter with the sharp-tongued Big Mama. He was even beginning to see some of the soft side of Uncle Nick, what little there was of it. Michael was there too. He still worked in the restaurant as his driving duties permitted.

After Jack and Levi had finished eating, Michael approached their table and said, "Are you two heroes ready to go to the battlefield?"

"Anybody who rides on that truck with you is a hero," Jack said.

"Or a martyr," Levi added with a smile.

"Then I hope that makes us heroes," Jack said.

Jack and Levi had both grown very fond of Michael. He really was, as Mr. Campbell had said, full of life.

"Sit down, Jehu," Jack said. "The good doctor and I need to talk to you."

"Sit down who?" Michael asked.

"You mean to tell me," Jack said, "that a good Catholic boy like you doesn't know who Jehu was?"

Michael shook his head, "No, sir. I guess I'm just not that good a Catholic."

Levi said, "Jehu was a king in your Old Testament who had a reputation for driving his chariot like a mad man."

"Oh," Michael said as he glanced at a smiling Jack. Then he continued, "Well, before you two go any further with this, I need to tell you that I have decided to drive much more slowly when you are with me. I know the road is rough, and the truck rides like an old farm wagon, and it's hard on old people—I mean people who are older than I am. So I'm going to ease up on you. That is what you wanted to talk to me about, isn't it?"

Levi and Jack were smiling.

"You mean that's not what you wanted to talk to me about?"

Levi said, "Sit down, Michael. Surely you trust us enough to at least sit down with us."

The boy carefully took a chair as he warily eyed them.

"Your driving was not what we wanted to talk to you about," Levi said, "but we intend to hold you to that promise."

"Amen!" Jack said as he nodded in full agreement.

Levi began, "Michael, you are aware that I have a medical school in Philadelphia, aren't you?"

"Yes, sir. One of the best."

"Are you serious about becoming a doctor?" Levi asked.

"Yes, sir," came the quiet reply.

"Do you have any idea how much work becoming a doctor involves?" asked Levi. "And it doesn't stop there. Just being a doctor is very hard work. But the rewards are many. I wouldn't trade professions with anyone, except perhaps the idle rich, like our friend Jack here."

Jack just smiled, but Michael was not smiling.

"Well," Levi said, "Jack tells me you want to be a doctor. Is that true or isn't it? What do you say?"

"Yes, sir, it's true," Michael said almost indignantly. "I want very much to be a doctor. And, yes, I know about your school. But I doubt that I will ever be one of your students. Your school is much too expensive for me. I plan to work my way through a less exclusive institution."

"In some things, you get what you pay for," Levi said. "Take shoes, for instance. You can buy a cheap pair of shoes and what you end up with is a cheap pair of shoes. Or you can spend a little more and get a good pair, a pair that fits nicely and will last a long time and serve you well. Michael, schools are similar in that you can enter an ordinary school and exit a few years later as an ordinary doctor. Or you can attend an exclusive school, as you call it, and come out the other end as a skilled physician who is in the vanguard of modern medicine. You will be prepared to stay current on all the latest treatments and techniques. You will never have to worry about being left behind, not to mention the fact that people are just naturally more impressed by a sheepskin with our name on it than they are by some others."

"Doctor Brookner," Michael said, almost as if he were in pain, "I have known of your school almost all my life. There is no school I would rather attend than yours. I cannot tell you how much it would mean to me to be one of your students, an alumnus. But I will never be able to afford it. I'm just going to have to settle for the cheap pair of shoes and make them fit as best I can. And I'll be lucky even then. Right now, I can't afford any kind of school, medical or otherwise. When I found out who you were, I tried not to seem impressed because I knew your school was out of my reach. Doctor Brookner, I can't afford your school. It just costs too much."

The boy was close to tears. The hearts of two old men went out to him.

"Well," Levi said gently as he looked toward Jack, "that's where the idle rich come in."

"Michael," Jack said. Then giving the boy a little more time to settle down, he softly repeated, "Michael, many years ago, my wife and her parents and I set up a scholarship fund in memory her little brother who died out there on that boulder we visited the other day. It's called the Silas Swann Scholarship Fund. In the intervening years, we have sent so many children to so many different colleges and universities that I have quit trying to keep up with them. We have awarded scholarships to boys and girls, blacks and whites, Jews and Gentiles, Protestants and Catholics.

"Michael," Jack said, "I am offering you a full scholarship, plus a modest stipend, to attend Doctor Brookner's school. If you accept, you'll be our very first Yankee. He and I have discussed the costs, and it is expensive, but it's the best. We aren't that worried about the money. We sent a little girl to a fancy music school in New York not long ago, and it was just as expensive. And besides, Levi's going to give us a little discount—or what we call down South a preacher price—on the tuition. But, Michael, I need to know, with a fair degree of certainty, that you will see this thing through, that you will complete the course. Are you committed to this quest of yours to become a doctor?"

"Jack," Michael said, his voice shaking with emotion, "all my life, I have never considered any profession but medicine. I assure you I will stay the course. But what have I done to deserve this? I'm sure you know of some young people back in Alabama who are more deserving. I don't feel worthy of this."

Jack said, "Son, aren't you a good person? Haven't you always worked hard to earn good marks? Haven't you been a good friend to Little Henry when so many others ignored him, or worse? To us, those things indicate that you are smart, hardworking, and compassionate. Those are the qualities a doctor needs. Do you know of any specific reason you don't deserve this? If you do, you need to tell us now."

Michael stared silently at the floor, tears flowing.

"Michael," Jack quietly continued, "why do you think God, in His kind wisdom, sent Doctor Levi Brookner and Jack Moses to the Battle House Hotel, when virtually all the other veterans are staying in the tent city? Why do you think He saw to it that you were the first person I met when I got off the train? Why do you think He arranged for your Uncle Nick to introduce me to Levi? Do you think He went to all that trouble just so Levi and I could swap war stories and so I could impress you with my wit and wisdom?"

Still looking at the floor, Michael smiled faintly through his tears.

"I think not," Jack said. "He sent the two men who could make it possible for Michael Camardo to make a doctor of himself. You said you have been praying for this. Well, the answers to your prayers are literally staring you in the face, both of us. We've done the job God sent us here to do. Levi has offered you admission to his school this fall, and I have offered you a scholarship. The rest is up to you, son.

"We're your friends, Michael," Jack said. "We may be old, but we can remember what it's like to be young and unsure of the future. The three of us can settle your future right now. Old folks like us have a responsibility to help the younger folks get started in life. When you're a wealthy old sawbones like Levi, you'll probably have an opportunity to help some young smart-aleck make something of himself. But right now, it's our time to do the helping. Your time will come soon enough, sooner than you think. What do you say, son? Do you need some time to think about it?"

"No, sir," he instantly replied as he looked up. "No, Jack, I don't need any more time to think about it. I accept your scholarship. And if Doctor Brookner accepts me into his school, I promise to do my best to make you both proud."

"We're already proud of you, Michael," Levi said as Michael wiped his eyes with his handkerchief.

"I'll try not to get in your way, Doctor Brookner."

"You won't be in my way. I plan for us to spend a great deal of time together over the next few years. That's what it means to attend an exclusive school. We only admit a few students each year. You will be in an elite group. I will be personally involved in much of your instruction. You will be very close to all our instructors. I'm looking forward to our friendship growing in the coming years."

The three men stood, and Michael shook hands with Levi. Jack walked around the table to shake hands with him, but the boy hugged him instead. Michael could not speak for a while. He could only look at the floor and wipe his eyes. Finally, he shook Jack's hand.

"Can I tell my uncle?" he asked.

"You can tell the world, son," Jack said. "It's a done deal. We all shook on it."

Happy Clatter

As they smiled, Jack and Levi watched Michael quietly walk into the kitchen.

Jack said, "I'm going over to the telegraph office to send a quick wire, Levi. I'll be back presently."

Just as Jack reached the door, he heard Big Mama's delighted screams and Uncle Nick talking loudly in Italian. Jack turned to see a worried Levi following close behind.

"You're not leaving me here alone to fight off Big Mama's affections. I'm going with you," Levi said.

"But you've got to stay here to tell Michael where I am and that I'll be right back so he can take us to the reunion."

"Oh," Levi said as he looked over his shoulder in the direction of the dreaded onslaught.

Jack just chuckled and walked all the more briskly toward the telegraph office in the train depot nearby. He had prepared the message the night before with all the necessary information about Michael and about Levi's school. The telegrapher took Jack's paper and within minutes, it was done. He started back to the restaurant.

"Now," he said to himself, "Doctor Camardo's future is secure regardless of what mine may hold."

As he walked, he thanked God for putting this opportunity before him and for the blessing he was receiving. He also asked the Lord to bless Michael with a full and rewarding career as a doctor, and with a long, happy life.

"Make him a good doctor, a godly doctor," he prayed.

Already, this was a good day, a gift from God. Today, a fiftieth anniversary re-enactment of Pickett's Charge had been scheduled for the afternoon. It was really more of a revisitation than anything. A group of Southerners would walk up the hill to be greeted by a group of Northerners. Photographers would be present. Lofty words would be spoken. It was not the sort of thing a bunch of irreverent old codgers would necessarily cotton to. But this day, like the one a half century earlier, would be a memorable one for Wiley Jackson Moses.

Jack peeked in the restaurant door to be sure the action, as he called it, was over. With the breakfast rush finished, the room was almost empty. He saw Levi peacefully sipping coffee at their table.

Jack walked up and said, "Well, that must not have been so bad. You appear to have weathered the storm pretty well. I expected to find you dead, or at least wounded."

"No." Levi sighed. "She went easy on me. But she's laying low for you. She said all I did was let him in my school but that you paid his way. She said you'd get yours later—something about a great big kiss."

"Oh my," Jack said, visibly shaken as he glanced toward the kitchen door. "Levi, how about sticking your head in the door and quietly telling Michael we're ready to go. I'll be hiding—I mean, waiting—outside by the truck."

Jack hurried out while Levi, calm and smiling, slowly strolled toward the kitchen to beckon Michael.

As they were being gently driven to the battlefield, a now-subdued Jack sat in the backseat with Levi. Michael, excited and chatty, happily drove his handsome steel steed carefully toward the reunion site.

After listening to the driver's happy clatter and singing for a while, Jack loudly asked, "Levi, is it too late for us to undo that deal we did this morning?"

"I'm afraid so, my friend," Levi said just as loudly. "You told him he could tell the world, and that is precisely what he has been doing ever since. And don't forget Big Mama. We would have to deal with her, you know."

"Oh yeah. I reckon you're right," Jack said in resignation as he looked toward the smiling boy. "Well," he loudly added, "at least I'll be in Mobile, and he'll be in Philadelphia with you."

Michael, still celebrating, whooped in youthful delight, his two heroes smiling all the while.

They reached the Great Tent, and Jack and Levi climbed off the truck.

Jack asked, "Well, Doctor Camardo, do you think you can settle down long enough to tell your uncle what we want for lunch?"

"Yes, sir," he cheerfully answered. "You can rely on me. As soon as I get this lemonade and tea sold and the glasses collected, I'll head back to town, and then I'll see you two at lunchtime with Uncle Nick, Henry, and food."

A few minutes later, they watched Michael bouncing merrily toward town and then found seats in the Great Tent. There was no one speaking from the stage, only small groups of men scattered around in general conversation. Just by chance, Jack and Levi sat near a group listening to a Union veteran from Indiana.

The Indiana Man

The man was sitting among men in both blue and gray. He had their undivided attention.

At first, Jack and Levi were talking just to each other, mostly about Michael as he and the truck disappeared from view. As their conversation died, they began to hear more of what the man was saying. Jack turned in his direction so as to better hear the words and determine exactly who was speaking them.

The man was talking about race, and mostly about the people he referred to as "the coloreds." It was his opinion that it was good that the Union had been restored and that he had fought bravely to end the rebellion. But he lamented the fact that President Lincoln had seen fit to issue the Emancipation Proclamation.

"We could have ended the war much more quickly if we had simply told the Rebels they could re-enter the Union and keep their slaves," the man said. "The country would be united today, just as it is, except a few hundred thousand lives on both sides would have been spared. We wouldn't have the colored problem we have today. They would still be in their place, down south on the plantations doing honest work instead of running loose all over the country, stirring up trouble everywhere and multiplying like rabbits."

The man's words were fairly well received by some of the men in the group. Jack turned his chair so he could see and hear better.

Levi watched Jack's demeanor darkening and said, "Jack, don't let that man ruffle your feathers. You can find someone like him everywhere you go."

"Yes," Jack said, "but I didn't expect to find him, someone that outspoken, wearing blue."

"Yes," Levi said. "I'm afraid you Southerners haven't cornered the market on bigotry. It's doing quite well up North. During the war, we had some terrible riots in the North in which coloreds were singled out for mistreatment, to put it mildly. We Union boys have always liked to think that we are better than you people, but actually we're just as jaundiced in our views toward race as you. However, we're usually a bit more subtle about it. I've decided that the main difference in the Northerner and the Southerner, other than the accent, is that you Southern boys are more eccentric, perhaps just a trifle more interesting. Except for that, we are very similar."

"Levi, down South we've always known that you Yankees are just as racist as we are and that you are just more subtle about it, as you say. But you're the first I've ever known who would admit it. That's one of the reasons we fought so hard against you. We could see the hypocrisy. But that fellow is not subtle about it. Except for his accent, or lack of one, he could fit in back home with a group of rapscallions I know who love to hate anyone different from themselves. If this fellow here is anything like them, he probably doesn't think much of you either. And he probably thinks of himself as a great Christian too."

"Let's get some ice cream," Levi said. "I'm hot."

"You go ahead. I'm going to listen to this man a while. You can bring me a scoop or two if you don't mind."

"No, I guess I'll just stay here with you. Somebody has to be here to pull you off of him."

"Now, Levi, you know I'm too old for that kind of foolishness."

"Yes, I know. But do you?"

Jack did not hear the question. He had already raised his hand and his voice. With a smile on his face, he said, "My goodness, friend. I'm from Alabama, and I think I've heard those thoughts before. You sound like some acquaintances of mine who belong to a little club called the Ku Klux Klan. You ought to move south, my friend. You could become a grand wizard or some other kind of bigwig in the Klan. Your talent is wasted up north."

"Jack," Levi said.

"Oh no, sir," the Indiana man said, thinking he had found a kindred spirit. "There's no need for me to go south. We have a strong contingent of Klansmen in Indiana. You would be proud of us."

"Oh, you just can't imagine."

"Jack," Levi said.

"You should visit us in Indiana sometime," the man said, growing bolder in his words. "We have some programs and activities there which are intended to keep the coloreds under control and in their place, and which are working quite well, I might add. I think you would find them quite heartening."

"Well, friend," Jack said, "I might have a little trouble participating in some of those activities, since I am a Christian."

"Jack," Levi said.

"Oh, that shouldn't be a problem," the man said. "Many of us are Christians."

"Oh? What church do you attend?" Jack asked.

"I don't really attend church all that much, just a few times a year with my wife. She's there every time they open the door. She is always after me to go with her. But we in the Klan have our own services and speeches, or sermons, if you care to call them that," the man said.

"I don't care to call them that," Jack said.

"Jack."

More of the men were looking at Jack now. He stood.

"Jack."

"Mister," Jack said, "you aren't any more a Christian than my cat is. You're a Klansman. You can't be both. Your heart is full of hate. Jesus teaches love, or haven't you heard?"

The man was beginning to look uncomfortable.

"But since you're pining so much for the good old days of slavery," Jack said, "we'll bring them back just for you. Except this time, since you're so very fond of it, we'll let you be the slave."

Then, winking at Levi, he added, "And we'll let Big Mama be the master."

Levi's tension dissipated in his laughter.

"Sir, you're out of line," the man said as he stood.

"I'm in Jesus's line," Jack said. "Whose line are you in?"

The two stared at each other. Before the man answered,

someone announced that a church choir was about to present a program of hymns and patriotic songs.

Levi saw a great number of people taking the stage and excitedly said, "Come on, Jack. Let's get a good seat before they're gone."

He grabbed Jack by the arm and pulled him away from the glowering Klansman.

Dixie

The choir was very good. They sang many of Jack's favorite hymns, including "Jesus, Keep Me Near the Cross" and "On Jordan's Stormy Banks." They also sang "The Battle Hymn of the Republic," "Shenandoah," and "Dixie." The arrangement of "Dixie" was not the rousing march everyone expected, but rather a slow, almost hymn-like chorale that deeply moved the Southerners.

Jack liked "Dixie." The words, he thought, weren't hateful or belligerent. They seemed to him to be the words of a man yearning for home and sweet days gone by. When the choir sang it so slowly, in a melancholy way, Jack, too, was moved. He was thinking of home. With all her faults, he loved the South, and especially Alabama.

Southerners, he thought, weren't really as bad as many people seemed to think. They really weren't any worse or better than other folks. They were just different—like Levi said, a little more interesting. He thought that Southerners seemed to have a slightly greater tolerance for unusual people than their northern countrymen—perhaps, he thought, because the South itself was looked upon by the rest of the country, and probably the world, as unusual.

The relationships between blacks and whites were different in the South. Even though race relations were often strained, there were many close and cherished friendships between the races. The two were just closer in the South, both physically and spiritually.

The black Southerner was just as much a Southerner as the white one, and as such, just as inexplicable in his loves and his hates.

Some of Jack's dearest friends were black, both male and female. He attended a small, black Baptist church near his home one Sunday each month. The congregation in his own Southern Baptist church always knew where he was. On that one Sunday each month, his tithe would go to that little black church. Several times, over the decades, Jack had taken the pulpit to tell that precious little congregation the story of Rose and how she had led him to Jesus. They, along with his own church, were praying for him to find her. He expected their prayers to be answered in the affirmative. Still, he was beginning to worry.

He had not seen a colored female at the reunion proper. He had seen a few in town, but they were all too young to be Rose. And then there was Big Mama. He had asked her if she knew of anyone who might fit Rose's description, but she did not. He knew the chances of finding Rose living in Gettysburg were almost negligible, but he felt the need to eliminate that possibility.

He even considered that she might be on the medical staff at the reunion. There were a few colored ladies among the nurses. But again, they were too young to be Rose. Jack had even asked Levi if he knew of anyone in Philadelphia in the nursing profession who might be her. Levi could think of no one.

Jack had finally decided to quit worrying. He would just continue to pray about it and let his friends and family in Mobile pray about it and trust God to handle it in His own way. He wanted very much to find her, but he was at peace with whatever the Lord decided. He knew he would see her again someday. He just did not know whether it would be in this life or the next. However it turned out, he knew that God's will would be done, and that was more than good enough for him.

The concert lasted almost until lunchtime. The choir director then announced that they were about to sing their final song. He did not disclose its name, but when the pianist began playing the introduction, virtually every man, in groups and one by one, stood and removed his hat to sing. Jack stood with the others. With his spirit soaring and with a voice still clear for one so old, he joined with thousands of his countrymen as they began with his favorite verse of his favorite hymn, the one he had always thought was written just for him.

> Amazing grace! How sweet the sound
>
> that saved a wretch like me!
>
> I once was lost, but now am found,
>
> Was blind, but now I see.

His voice, though still a beautiful baritone, had been weakened by the years. But his heart was still in it. They sang every verse. Most knew them by heart. When it ended, there were "amens" and "hallelujahs" everywhere, followed by thunderous applause for the choir. It was a joyous time.

As he sat down next to Levi, who had not joined in the singing, Jack said, "Levi, my friend, I hope my joy does not offend you. I so hope to share it with you."

"You have just shared it with me, Jack. And I am not offended."

The choir made its way off the stage, and Jack saw the truck approaching. Perched on it were Michael and Uncle Nick and, almost unnoticeable between them, Little Henry.

BOB LANKFORD

A Clear Position

Jack smiled just thinking of Henry. But the smile left his face as he remembered the Indiana man. He tried to find his scowling face in the crowd. It didn't take long. The man was also watching the truck as it came to a stop near the tent. Jack observed the man watching Little Henry climb down. What Jack was feeling now was not Christian love. Without knowing it, he had allowed his anger toward the Klansman to turn into something akin to hate.

Hoping to protect Henry from the man's bigotry, Jack approached him and said, "That little fellow is a friend of mine. I would take it personally if he has an unpleasant experience here because of you."

"What are you trying to say, sir?" the man said.

"I'm telling you to leave the boy alone."

"And what makes you think I would do anything to harm him?" the man asked.

"I know your type," Jack said. "Let's just say I'm not willing to take any chances on what you may or may not do. Just leave him alone."

"And what if I want something to eat or drink?"

"Then buy from one of the others or go to one of the army's mess tents. I don't want the boy to have any contact with you. He already has enough problems," Jack said.

"I think I'll do as I please," the man said. "You have no right to instruct me. There are many men here who feel as I do. Some of them fought for the same cause you did."

The man was big, almost as big as Jack, and about ten years younger.

He added, "I'll be the one to determine my own conduct. You can do whatever you wish to do about it, if you think you're man enough."

"I wouldn't have to be much of a man to be more than you. That boy is more of a man than either of us," Jack said.

"That boy," the man said with disgust, "is a nigger. And you, sir, are a nigger-lover."

Jack had been called that before, several times. It had never bothered him before. But this time he felt a small twinge because he realized he was motivated by his hate for the man perhaps as much as by his love for the boy. But that did not deter him.

Henry was still too far away to hear what was being said. The conversation, in spite of its passion, was a quiet one. Only Levi was listening.

Jack said, "Mister, I try to love my fellow man, but sometimes, like right now, I fail miserably. You won't make me mad by telling me I love someone. You just stay away from that boy, and we won't have any trouble."

"I guess you think I might lynch him or something," the man said sarcastically.

"I don't know what you might do. I don't want to find out. Just avoid him. Leave him alone. If you feel the urge to lynch somebody, just lynch me," Jack said.

"You're talking like a fool," the man said. "You're not making any sense. Now I'm telling you to leave me alone. I'll conduct myself toward your little dark friend and anyone else however I see fit."

Once every fifteen or twenty years, Jack would come upon a situation that would send him back to his old, wrathful ways. He would always feel badly about it afterward and would beg God's forgiveness, which was always forthcoming. He would also vow never to let his anger catch him unawares again. But unfailingly, in time, it would.

As Levi began trying to discreetly pull him away, Jack said, "Allow me to clarify my position, sir. If you do or say anything untoward to that child, I will kick your sorry ass so far up your throat that those words of yours will smell like the horse manure they are for the remainder of your miserable existence."

Everyone was talking about lunch, and no one was aware of the exchange except the two men involved and Levi. The Klansman did not answer, but it was obvious that he was not intimidated. He was accustomed to confrontation. He also knew that he had a distinct age advantage on his would-be opponent.

Finally, he responded, "Those are the words of a Christian?"

The question cut Jack deeply. But instead of bringing him to his senses, it only heightened his anger. Levi managed to pull him away so they could get their food. Jack would not enjoy his lunch that day.

Damages

Jack and Levi received their specially prepared dishes of Big Mama's cooking and found a place at a picnic table. As Levi ate, he watched his friend picking at his food. Jack was just too worked up to do anything more than nibble.

"Jack," Levi said, "you need to relax, my friend. Try to forget about that man. He's not going to do anything to Henry."

"What worries me, Levi, is that he probably wouldn't have done anything if I had just left well enough alone. I'm afraid he might do something just to prove to me that he can. I don't think he'll hurt the boy. I'm just afraid he'll do something to ridicule or embarrass him. If he does, it will be my fault. I had to go and open my big mouth and make a fool of myself."

"Yes," Levi said. "Even the fool is thought wise when he remains silent, or something like that."

"Proverbs," Jack said, chuckling. "There's no danger of this fool ever being thought wise. How many times must the Master teach me the same lesson, Levi? When will I learn?"

"Try not to worry about it," Levi said. "We're both here to look out for Henry. I'm sure the boy is tougher than you think. Try to eat. You're going to have to climb that hill this afternoon, you know."

"Oh," Jack said, "you're talking about our little re-enactment of the charge."

"Certainly. Had you forgotten?"

"Yeah, I reckon I had, just for a minute," Jack said.

"You don't have to do it, you know, unlike the last time," Levi said, happy to have changed the subject.

"I know, but I sort of want to. Maybe it'll chase some ghosts away."

"Well then, young fella," Levi said, "you'd better eat your meat and potatoes."

"Yes, sir. You're the doctor," Jack said as he began to eagerly eat.

"Whoa, boy. Not too fast!" Levi said.

Lunch was proceeding without incident. The Indiana man was sitting a couple of tables over with some of what Jack called his bigot buddies. Little Henry had stopped at the table several times in the course of his duties, and nothing improper had happened. Jack was watching closely while he ate.

They were finished eating, and Jack heard Nick tell Henry to begin collecting the dishes and utensils in a large basket they had brought for that purpose. He also heard Nick admonish him to be careful not to break anything. Henry made his way around the tables. Most of the men were very helpful, carefully putting their dishes in the basket for him.

Laboring with a full load, Henry began the walk back to the truck. Jack could see his head above the seated veterans. Then, suddenly, he could see it no more. Instantly, he heard a loud sound of breaking dishes.

He saw a group of men rush to Henry's aid and heard a man say, "Mister, I saw you trip him. You did that a purpose."

Jack, Levi, Michael, and Nick all arrived at about the same time. Henry was already cleaning up the mess of broken dishes.

He said, "I'm sorry, Mr. Nick. I'll pay for everything. I promise."

"What happened?" Nick asked.

Before Henry could speak, one of the men pointed to the

smirking Indiana man and said, "That son of a bitch tripped him. I seen it all."

"So did I," said another.

"Yep. I seen it too," said a third man.

"I'm gonna knock your ass upside the head," Jack said as he started toward the Klansman.

Immediately, all four of his friends stepped in front of him and refused to allow him to pass. He was a little surprised at the quickness with which they had intervened.

Henry said, "You mustn't, Mr. Jack. You might get hurt. I'm not worth it."

Jack, looking down into the precious child's eyes, gently said, "Sure you are, son. You're worth it, all of it."

Nick, a formidable man himself, stepped up to the man who was now standing among his friends and said with his Italian accent, "Well, mister? Is it true what they say?"

After a few seconds of looking around a bit sheepishly, the man grinned and said, "Hell yes, it's true." Then he attempted to stare down the crowd and added, "I'll pay for your damages. Besides, he's right. He's not worth it. He's nothing but a damned little nigger boy."

There was more silence as the words sank into everyone. Jack could only see the back of Henry's head, but he could still see the hurt in the child.

Nick said, "There are some damages money can never fix, mister. I don't want your filthy money, and I would never take anything from Henry. I'll take the loss myself."

Jack's fury was quickly getting out of control. He stepped toward the man, and again his friends grabbed his arms.

He shook loose and, with a quiet, menacing voice that had not been heard in many years, he said, "You're about the most worthless pile of shit anybody ever stepped in. May God damn your wretched soul to hell."

Again, there was silence, absolute silence. No one spoke or moved. For a while, it seemed that no one even breathed. Then the victorious smirk returned to the Klansman's face. He had won, and Jack knew it.

"I'll see you there, you goddamned hypocrite," the man said.

Jack's gaze dropped to the ground, and he wilted like a flower, not because of anything the Klansman had said, but because of what he, himself, had said. Most of the men thought that Jack had taken God's name in vain. Yet it was that and more.

As if in a trance, almost oblivious to his surroundings, Jack slowly turned and made his way through the crowd. Once away from everyone, he found a place to sit. He needed to be alone. No one approached for a while.

Immediately, he put his head in his hands and began to pray. Weeping quietly, he asked God to forgive him, to remove the hate and anger from his heart and replace it with Christ's love. In Jesus's name, he fervently asked for consolation.

Henry, Nick, and Michael quietly began cleaning up the mess and collecting the remaining dishes. Still sitting alone, Jack finished his prayer. Raising his gaze toward the distant high ground, he wondered how many times over the last fifty years he had allowed his ferocious temper to sneak up on him. He also questioned if he would ever become mature enough as a Christian to control himself in all situations. Having all but given up on that, he was very disappointed in himself again.

Then Henry appeared before him. Smiling, he said, "Are you okay, Mr. Jack?"

Jack could not look on Henry's smiling face or even think about him without smiling a little himself. The sight of the child lifted his spirit, and he said a little prayer.

"Thank you, Jesus, for sending Henry Dewberry to my aid. I'm getting there, Henry," he said. "Thank you for asking. I have a little apology to make to that man from Indiana. When that's done, I'll be okay."

A Fine and Precious Thing

"About that man from Indiana," Henry said. "He was right about one thing."

A little surprised at Henry's statement, Jack asked, "And just exactly what was it he was right about?"

"Well, you know," Henry said quietly, "I am just a little nigger boy."

"Henry," Jack said, almost angrily. Then, after taking a deep breath, he gently said, "Henry, come here, son. Sit down right here next to me."

The boy took a chair and Jack said, "Son, that's a hurtful thing to say. You need to have more respect for yourself and for your people. You're a person of great worth. There's nothing wrong with being black. It isn't a crime or a sin. The Lord put just as much love and care into creating black folks as He did anyone. Jesus died for black sinners just as surely as He died for white ones. You know that."

"But, Mr. Jack," Henry argued, "my mama is not a nice lady, if you know what I mean." Then, staring at the ground, he paused and, with great shame and embarrassment in his voice, quietly added, "I don't even know who my daddy is. I don't think my mama even knows."

Hearing the pain in his voice, Jack said, "Henry, look at me."

He peered into the old Rebel's eyes.

"Son, you're looking at a man whose mother was not a nice lady, if you know what I mean. You're looking at a man who has no idea who his daddy was. You're looking at a man whose mother, in all probability, did not even know, herself, who fathered her little boy."

Then, putting his hand on Henry's shoulder he said, "Son, God doesn't hold you responsible for who your parents are. He only holds you responsible for who you are. And, Henry, you're a good man. From top to toe, inside and out, you are a complete and delightful specimen of American manhood. You are already more of a man than I ever was or ever will be. Henry, there's nothing wrong with you."

A few seconds passed, and Jack continued, "Listen, Henry, being black is just as wholesome, just as godly, as anything else. Black folks are just as noble, just as good, and, yes, just as bad, as the rest of us. We're all God's children in need of Jesus's sweet grace."

Jack gave the boy a few more seconds, then said, "I want you to always remember, son, that it's not the name that makes the man. It's the man that makes the name."

"That may be right, Mr. Jack," Henry said, "but I'm never going to be able to make any kind of name for myself because most people just treat me like I'm a little ol' black boy who'll never be anything or have anything. It hurts to get treated like I'm nothing. Sometimes I wonder why the Lord lets people act so ugly to me. If it weren't for Mr. Nick and Michael, I don't know what I would do."

"Son," Jack gently responded, "back home, we sing an old song. The last few lines go something like this."

A few seconds passed as Jack tried to recollect the words. Then he said,

> Tempted and tried we're oft made to wonder why it should be thus all the day long, while there are others living about us, never molested, though in the wrong. Farther along we'll understand why. Cheer up my brother. Live in the sunshine. We'll understand it all by and by.

A small smile slowly spread over Henry's face, and as Jack wiped the boy's tears away, two hate-filled eyes watched from across the way. They saw the genuine godly love between the two as a man who never knew his own father tried to be a father to a fatherless boy. Slowly, the hate was replaced by grief as a brittle old heart cracked and broke under the weight of shame accumulated over a lifetime of pointless malice.

Jack said, "The Bible says to be slow to anger and quick to forgive. The fool speaks without thinking. A wise man thinks without speaking. Even though I seem to be a little slow in learning those lessons, you need to remember them, son. The book of Romans says to try to do what is honorable in everyone's eyes and, if possible, on your part, to live at peace with everyone. Don't let yourself be conquered by evil, but conquer evil with good.

"Henry, never lose your God-given goodness. Don't forget the words of Jesus. 'Let not your heart be troubled.' He loves you so much, Henry. Be happy. Walk in the light. He has great plans for you. Would you give up on life and hope? Would you surrender to despair? You have a responsibility to live your life, for it is a precious thing, a great gift. Live bravely and with great hope and joy. Always look toward Jesus. He is the light. Walk in him. And Henry," he quietly added, gently squeezing the boy's hand, "you aren't just a credit to your race. You are a credit to the whole human race. And if you, my friend, are just a little nigger boy, and if you are absolutely nothing in this world but that, then a little nigger boy is a truly fine and precious thing. Remember son, it's the man that makes the name."

As Henry smiled through his tears, Jack could see his spirit strengthening. He could see his sense of purpose and self-worth growing. Henry dried his eyes with a brand-new cotton handkerchief.

As they stood, Henry hugged the man and said, "Thank you, Mr. Jack."

"And that's another thing, young fella," Jack said, "about this business of you calling me Mr. Jack. I've always just called you Henry. So from now on, I want you to just call me Jack. Just leave the mister off. After all, we're brothers in arms now."

"We are? What's brothers in arms?"

"Brothers in arms? Why, they're friends who fight together

against a common foe," Jack answered. "You and I fought together against that old bigot over there, that poor, lost soul."

"Oh," Henry said. "Kind of like soldiers in the army together."

"Something like that."

Wearing a mischievous grin, Henry backed up a few steps, saluted, and said, "Yes, sir, Jack."

Jack laughed and said, "Don't you salute me, you young whippersnapper! I was always a private and proud of it!"

Laughing as he trotted toward the truck, Henry whirled around and delivered another quick salute and shouted, "Yes, sir, General Jack!"

Thoroughly enjoying the banter, Jack shouted, "You better run." Then with his voice and fist shaking in mock rage, he screamed, "Ye danged Yankee!"

When Henry glanced back, he saw Jack with his hand over his mouth, looking worriedly over his shoulder toward his Northern acquaintances. Jack looked toward Henry to see him barely able to stand under the weight of his laughter. He figured one more good quip ought to finish the job.

"Why you," Jack shouted as he searched for just the right insult. "Why, you ain't nothin' but an old Methodist!" he screamed.

"That should do it," he said to himself.

He watched with great pleasure as Henry was helped onto the truck by Michael and Nick, who had been patiently waiting while Jack talked him. Michael was laughing almost as hard as Henry. Even the all-but-humorless Uncle Nick was smiling broadly.

As the three of them drove back to town, Henry's laughter subsided. But a smile remained as he pondered the things Jack had said.

That Jack, he thought. *That rascal Jack.*

Jack watched the truck disappear from sight and smiled,

thinking, *That Henry. That precious Henry. I reckon he always was easy to laugh.*

His thoughts soon turned to the unpleasant business at hand. His eyes searched through the crowd for the man from Indiana. This was not something he was looking forward to but had to be done.

A Poor, Lost Soul

Jack soon located the men who had been drawn to the Klansman. They were talking among themselves. But the man himself was not speaking; nor did he seem to be listening. Staring at the ground a few feet before him, he appeared to be in deep thought.

Jack slowly approached the group. Without Jack's knowledge, Levi, who had kept his distance since Jack's outburst, was following closely. As they neared the cluster of men, two of them rose.

"Easy, gentlemen," Jack said. "I'm not looking for trouble. I just need to speak to that man right there," he said, nodding toward the Klansman.

One of the men said, "You better not try anything, mister. We have you two outnumbered this time."

It was only then that Jack became aware of Levi approaching from behind. But he paid him little heed. His mind was on the Klansman.

Then the man added, "And you need to watch that smart mouth too."

Jack looked toward the Klansman, who had only barely acknowledged his presence by adjusting his gaze from the ground to Jack's feet.

Jack began, "Sir, I do not know your name; nor do I wish to. I do know that you are a child of God, and I am a Christian. That is all I need to know. What I am about to do is not something I want to do. But it is something that I, as a sinner forgiven by

Christ, am compelled to do. I am sorry I spoke to you so harshly. I do not want your soul, or any soul, to go to hell. I spoke in anger. I am no longer angry with you for anything you did or said. I am only disappointed in myself, and I apologize to you for the way I acted and I …" Jack paused at this point. "I ask your forgiveness."

There was silence, much as before when Jack had spoken in anger.

After a few seconds, Jack added, "You don't have to forgive me, sir. The Lord gives us that freedom. Just as we are free to accept His forgiveness or reject it, we are also free to forgive or not forgive. But if we accept His forgiveness, we are compelled to forgive others, as we were forgiven. It is expected of us. And if we offend someone, as I offended you, we are compelled to apologize and ask forgiveness."

The man remained silent, so Jack went on. "Just a few minutes ago, I asked for and received forgiveness from Jesus. He always forgives me my failures. And, alas, I keep him busy, for my failures are never-ending. But now I am humbly asking you for your forgiveness."

The men could hear the earnestness in Jack's voice. Almost as one, their gazes dropped, and their belligerent poses softened as they recalled their own transgressions and shortcomings. But the Klansman remained silent, staring beyond Jack into the distance.

Finally, Jack spoke again. "I reckon your silence is your answer. It sounds like a no to me, and that's okay. That's your right, and I really didn't expect anything else. I have done what I had to do. The Lord won't hold me responsible for your actions, but I am truly regretful of mine."

Never speaking, the Indiana man stood. Without looking at anyone, he walked out of the group, going toward one of the army's mess tents.

Someone commented, "I guess he wants some ice cream. That's all they're serving now."

As they watched the man walking across the field, Jack said, "No. It's not ice cream he's wanting. Hate comes easily to the spiritually weak and is eagerly embraced. Hate's easy. Forgiveness is hard. It requires strength of the spirit. That's what he wants. He probably won't find that in the mess tent. But who knows. With God, all things are possible."

The group slowly dissipated as the men, one at a time, simply wandered away, leaving only Jack and Levi looking at empty chairs.

Levi patted him on the back, saying, "Don't worry about it, Jack. You did what you were supposed to do."

"Oh," Jack said, "I'm not worried about that. I'm just worried about that poor, old, lost soul from Indiana. I could have been a better witness to him, but all I did was provoke him to anger. Jesus is mighty patient with me. I have failed him so many times."

Jack took a chair, and Levi sat next to him. They were alone.

The World's Only Sinner

Levi said, "You said you're worried about that lost man, but didn't he say he was a Christian? How can you know that he is lost?"

"Levi, a man as full of hate as he is cannot possibly be a Christian or a godly man. I, too, was once full of hate, and I was as lost as a man can be. That man probably walked down the aisle of a church and joined up one day a long time ago, but joining a church doesn't anymore make you a Christian than joining the army does. Becoming a Christian is something that happens in your heart. After that happens, then you join a church. When you accept Jesus into your heart and ask Him to forgive your sins, then you're a Christian, and it changes you. That old fellow has no room in his heart for Jesus. It's too full of hate. You know, Levi, you almost got to see one of those pathetic fistfights you were talking about. I sure am glad y'all stopped it before it went that far. That fellow would have probably killed me."

"Oh, I imagine you would have done all right," Levi said. "I seem to remember that you have a pretty mean right."

"Not anymore," Jack said. "That fellow is a lot younger. In all my life, I've only lost one fight. That would have been my second. Levi, there was a time in my life, before Jesus, when I thrived on conflict. I truly loved to fight. And when I fought, I fought for keeps, if you know what I mean. Then, on that night all those years ago, Rose led me to Jesus. Ever since then, I just haven't had the lust for violence I once had. Jesus turned me around 180 degrees. I know what He did in my heart and my life, and that's how I know that fellow from Indiana is lost. He just wouldn't do or say the things he does if he were saved. He would be a different person."

Some time passed, and no one spoke. Then Levi said, "Jack, you know I'm not a Christian. Do you think I'm a bad person?"

"No!" Jack said. "Surely you know I don't think that. You don't have to be a Christian to be a good person. Even now, I don't think of myself as a good person. The Bible says we all fall short of God's expectations, and even though I don't claim to be a better person than anyone, there is no doubt in my mind that I am a better person than the person I was without Jesus. I'm not a good person. I'm just a forgiven one. And I'm grateful for that forgiveness."

"You spoke of how you are compelled to forgive," Levi said. "Why is it that so many Christians refuse to forgive us Jews for putting Christ to death?"

"Why is it that so few Jews ask for it?"

"So you, like so many of your faith, hold us responsible for the death of your Savior?" Levi asked.

"He was your Savior too," Jack said. "Just because you refuse the sacrificial gift of his life doesn't mean He didn't suffer and die for you. He did. Tell me, Levi. Have you ever sinned?"

"Of course I have. I am a mortal man."

"Then you are responsible for the death of Christ just as much as I am and just as much as that man from Indiana is.

Like the Bible says, we all have fallen short of the mark. We Christians aren't better than other folks, although some of us seem to think so. We're just forgiven. And why have we been forgiven? Is it because we deserve it? No. We deserve hell. Is it because we earned it somehow with good works or by giving money to the church? No. We are forgiven for one reason and only one reason. We are forgiven because we asked to be forgiven. We got on our knees and swallowed our silly pride and begged Jesus to forgive us and help us do better. He joyously rushed into our hearts and lives and forgave us just as we were, sins and all."

Levi was silent, so Jack continued. "Levi, when I asked you why so few Jews have asked for forgiveness, I was not referring to the forgiveness of Christians. I was talking about the forgiveness of Christ. You don't have to worry about us forgiving you. We're just sinners ourselves, saved ones."

"So you don't hold any one person or group responsible?" Levi asked.

Jack said, "My friend, He was innocent, and yet He was punished for our sins, yours and mine. He bought those sins with His suffering and His life, and that gives Him the right and the power to forgive them, that and His own perfect divineness.

"But you asked if I hold anyone responsible," Jack said. "The answer is yes, I do. That would be only one man. The man who killed Jesus sits before you now. When the mob howled for His life, I howled the loudest. When they drove the nails through His hands and feet, I swung the hammer. No, Levi, I don't hold you responsible. It is I who killed Jesus of Nazareth. If I had been the world's only sinner, He would have still come to earth to die just for me. His love is that great. But if it makes you feel any better, Jesus Himself, in the tenth chapter of John, said that no one took His life but that He willingly gave it up. But I hold myself responsible because I made His death necessary."

"So you don't hate me and my Jewish brothers as so many of your brethren do?"

"How could I hate you? My precious Jesus commands that I love everyone, even my enemies—especially my enemies. So how could I hate you, my friend? And how could I hate the Jews? Jesus was a Jew, as were His disciples and the first Christians," Jack said.

"I haven't been without hate," Jack added. "Before I found Jesus, I hated all people, Jew and Gentile, and especially colored folks. But the one man I most despised was myself. Jesus taught me how to love my fellow man. He drained all that hate from my wretched heart and replaced it with His peaceful love. When He forgave me, I slowly began to forgive myself. It is taking a long time because I was a bad man."

The Only Way

Again, they were silent for a while.

Then Levi said, "You know, Jack. All those years ago, when I was in the army with all those Irish Catholics, they were nice to me even though they knew I was a Jew. It really was my fault that I didn't fit in any better than I did. But there were a couple of those fellows who told me I was going to hell because I had never accepted Jesus. They tried to convert me to Catholicism right then and there. They weren't ugly about it. They seemed like they were genuinely concerned for my well-being. In the years since then, I have had a few other encounters in which Christians—sometimes Catholic, sometimes Protestant—would tell me I was hell-bound. Sometimes they weren't very diplomatic about it. Other times they were just concerned, like my army friends. Why do people do things like that? Don't they realize that I am comfortable in my own faith?"

After some thought, Jack said, "Levi, that is a difficult question to answer. I reckon some Christians are just less tactful than others, just as some Jews are."

He paused again and said, "Surely you know how the Jews

looked down on the Gentiles back in biblical days. There are probably many Jews who still look down on us. I can only assume that you think your religion will get you close to God. And I reckon you plan on being in heaven with him some day. Yet, I have never had one of my Jewish friends—and I have several—sit down with me and say, 'Jack, I'm concerned for your soul. Let me tell you about my faith.' Are they being diplomatic to the point of letting me go to hell? Do they not love me enough to share their faith with a Gentile? Are they not concerned for me? Many Gentiles are concerned for the Jews. That's why they want to tell you about Jesus. All those years ago, most of the Jews rejected Jesus, their own Messiah. Yet the despised Gentiles listened to the words of Jesus, a Jew, and to the words of His disciples, all Jews, and put aside their own resentment and distrust of the Jewish people to follow a Jew. To this day, Levi, I don't think the Jewish people have more loyal friends on this planet than the Christians. Oh, there is always going to be an immature, angry faction in the Christian community that dislikes Jews. We are, after all, sinners. But I truly believe that most Christians love the Jews, partly because Jesus tells us to love all people, and also because I think most Christians think of the Jews as God's first love. We respect y'all for that. We cherish our Old Testament. How can we study it and not love our Jewish brothers? How can we tell all those wonderful Old Testament stories to our children and not love your people? I, myself, have great respect for your people and your faith.

"But you must remember, Levi, that Jesus, the Jew who suffered mightily for Jew and Gentile alike, told us that He is the only way to heaven. Even Jesus Himself asked the Father if there was another way to let this cup pass from Him. But the answer was that there was no other way. The cup did not pass from Him. The only way was for Him to die for us. And so He did. We cannot work our way into heaven. We cannot pay our way in. We cannot possibly be good enough to get in, for we all have sinned, and they don't allow any sin in heaven. Even the Pope needs Jesus's forgiveness, and you can be sure he knows it. I can't imagine Jesus going through all that agony and humiliation just to provide one more way of several ways to heaven. In the fourteenth chapter of John, Jesus said that the only way to the Father is through Him. The only way to heaven is to ask Jesus to forgive you and let the innocent blood that He shed wash your sins away. I'm not very eloquent, and I'm certainly no theologian. Yet I know I'm going to be in heaven someday because a long time ago, a Jew loved me enough to allow Himself to be punished for all the terrible things I have done so that I could escape that punishment myself. But I had to request that wonderful gift in order to receive it. Jesus doesn't force it on anyone. Nor does He withhold it from anyone who sincerely requests it.

"Jesus is God, Levi," Jack said. "He is God the Son, and no one but God could have changed me the way I was changed. He is real. No false God could have done what He did. I love Him with all my soul. His spirit is with me always. He comforts me in my pain and gently corrects me when I fail Him. He is my only hope and the only hope for this poor, old world."

There was another long pause, and Jack finally said, "Levi, my friend, how long have we known each other now? Is it three days yet?"

"Actually," Levi said, "we met fifty years ago today."

"Oh yeah," Jack said as they smiled. "I forgot. But Levi," he said, speaking earnestly again, "even though we haven't gotten to spend a lot of time together over the last half century, I feel almost as close to you as if we were brothers. I honestly believe God put us here together so we could put Michael through your school. And even if I don't find Rose, that in itself will have made this trip worthwhile. And, Levi, please be tolerant of us Christians. If we try to share our faith with you, it's because we love you like our precious Jewish Savior loves us all. We're concerned for your soul."

No more words were spoken for a while. They sat there together, gazing up the slope.

Eventually, Levi patted Jack on the hand and said, "Thank you, Jack, for those words. I guess I'm just too old and too much of a Jew to change now."

"No," said Jack. "As long as you have your wits about you, you're not too old. And you can never be too much of a Jew to accept your own Messiah. You think about it. Pray about it, and discuss it with your most trusted Christian friends back home. Don't close your heart to Jesus, Levi. This is too important."

Levi looked at Jack and, hearing the concern in his voice, he relented and said with a smile, "Very well, my friend. I'll think about it."

"And pray about it," Jack quickly reminded him.

"And I'll pray about it," Levi said. "I promise."

Jack smiled and said, "Thank you, sir."

The two former foes stood and embraced.

A Walk in the Sun

They were about to sit down again when Levi pointed to a group of Union men and said, "That looks like my Philadelphia Brigade Association forming up. It must be time for us to walk up to the wall so we can properly greet you Rebs."

"Yes," Jack said, pointing to a group of Confederate veterans, "that must be Pickett's Division Association. Well, Levi, I reckon we better report for duty to our outfits. Hopefully, we can finally put this thing to rest. And I certainly hope you Northern boys are a lot more hospitable this time around."

"Well," Levi said in feigned indignation, "I suppose the quality of our hospitality depends on whether my nose gets broken."

They parted, laughing, and went to their respective groups. It was close to three in the afternoon. Levi's group of a few hundred Northerners had completed their walk to the summit, with Levi and many others being in the angle of the stone wall as they had been before. There were men from other units up and down the length of the wall, awaiting the men in gray.

As Levi made the trek up to the wall, his comrades chatted on the way. But Levi, still the loner, the quiet misfit, kept to himself. He still was not comfortable in large groups. He much preferred the quiet companionship of his trusted friend, Jack Moses. As he climbed the gentle incline over hundreds of yards of open ground, he thought about Jack and what he and the other Southerners had endured as they made the same trip fifty years earlier. He could not help but respect them and pity them. But fifty years ago, he had mostly just feared them. They had been a fearsome army of fell fighters, indeed. But they were vanquished. Their country, which they had so bravely defended, was no more. Its flag, though still fiercely loved—and hated—owned no soil over which to fly. It was a flag without a land. Even though the old Rebels were now once again loyal to the stars and stripes, the stars and bars would forever fly in their hearts. One cannot make the sacrifices they had made under a flag without falling deeply in love with it.

Levi had seen the resolute respect the old Southerners had displayed toward the American flag. He had also seen the fierce fire in their eyes whenever someone produced even the tiniest Confederate battle flag. He truly believed that fire would soon die with the old men.

"One more generation," he surmised, "and that will be gone forever."

Meanwhile, Jack and his group of old Rebels were forming up near the Great Tent. He kept looking around for a familiar face. He hoped that perhaps one or two of his old squad mates had survived without his knowledge. After all, except for Box, he had not actually seen any of them die. He thought they may have been taken prisoner and somehow survived the balance of the war in one of those lethal Union prison camps. But then, few survived those camps. Deep down, he knew they were all gone. He alone had lived. He searched in vain.

As he thought back on that heartbreaking day, he remembered how he had made his way back to the Southern lines after leaving Silas by the brook. He remembered the Fifth mustering for a headcount that evening and discovering that Cpl. Elder's squad was gone. The preacher, Kirby, Box, Williams, Miller, White, the others—and Swann—all gone, except for Jack. Alone, he stood where the squad would have been, in their stead. In his mind's eye, he could still see the stares of other men in the company as they gazed upon the large gap in their ranks and him, its lone occupant. He remembered the guilt he had felt for standing there without the others, for surviving.

He lingered in the past and recalled that it had then been less than twenty-four hours since he was made aware of the great guilt he bore for the life he had lived. He had asked for and received forgiveness for those sins. He had understood his guilt completely. It was easy to for him to see why he had felt so shameful about so much. But he was puzzled by the pain he felt as he stood as his squad's sole survivor. Though his heart was still in agony over Silas, Jack knew he had conducted himself honorably throughout the charge and retreat. Yet he felt shame, shame, for once, that he did not understand. He would never understand it or resolve it. It would follow him throughout his long life and, for the most part, he would keep it to himself, sharing it only with his wife.

As he stood among the milling veterans, Jack gradually became aware of someone staring at him. He met the man's gaze.

The man smiled sheepishly and said, "Please excuse my rudeness, sir. You seem vaguely familiar. You aren't wearing a uniform, but I heard you talking earlier, and in spite of the fact that you were talking to a Northerner, you sounded Southern. And you are standing here amongst all us old Rebels. May I ask, sir, what outfit you were with?"

Jack studied the man briefly and decided he did not know him.

"Fifth Alabama," he said quietly.

"Regiment?" the man asked.

There was another pause and Jack softly said, "Battalion."

"Archer's Brigade," the man said as he smiled. "I was in the Thirteenth Alabama. I was Lieutenant Rowe back then. I'm just old man Rowe now."

Jack still could not place the man, but he was uneasy about renewing this old acquaintance.

Then the man said, "And might I ask your name, sir?"

"Moses, Jack Moses."

The man was clearly surprised, but he was smiling more broadly than before.

"Moses," he said as he laughed. "Well, I'll just be damned."

"I sure hope not," Jack said.

"You and I met at Fredericksburg," the man said. "I kept you from shooting a young Union trooper. You more or less threatened to kill me when the war was over."

Jack recalled the incident and started to feel a little uncomfortable.

Old man Rowe continued. "That didn't worry me too much at the time because I didn't really expect to survive the war anyway. And then, at Gettysburg, I heard that you had been saved. Colonel Fry said that was why we lost the battle. He said if you could have stayed lost another couple of years, we would have won Gettysburg and probably the war."

"Well," Jack said, "it sure changed me all right—getting saved, that is. But that isn't why we lost the war. We just got whipped by a much larger, stronger, wealthier foe. And if it hadn't been for Jesus, I would have died in the charge with all those other men. That would have been the end of me, and we still would have lost."

"Oh, I know," Rowe said. "I was just joking with you. And Colonel Fry was just joking too. You were much of a man back then, feared by all."

"No, I wasn't much of a man. I was a pathetic, despicable

little excuse of a man. I don't seem to remember instilling much fear in you that day. However, I still remember how the muzzle of your pistol felt on my temple," Jack said.

"I'm sorry about that, Mr. Moses. I just couldn't let you kill that boy."

"I know. You did the right thing. I'm glad you stopped me. I already had enough on my head without adding that boy's murder to it. I truly hope he has lived a long, happy life somewhere in Yankee land. He might even be somewhere around here today."

The man was clearly relieved to discover that Jack no longer coveted his life. He said, "I can't tell you how welcome those words are. I reckon you really were saved."

"Oh yes, I was definitely saved. The incident you mentioned was something that happened in my first life, before I found Jesus. There is nothing about that life that I am proud of. It was a total waste, a loss. So please forgive me if I don't seem all that eager to discuss it with you. I would much rather talk about my last fifty years with Jesus rather than my first thirty-three with Satan."

"I'm listening, Jack. I hope you don't mind me calling you Jack."

"Not at all; that's my name."

"Good. You can call me Homer."

"Well, Homer, just to make it short and to the point, I went to Mobile after the war and married the sweetest, finest Christian lady in the world. We had four wonderful children together. And even though I lost one of my boys and, later, my wife, I have had a wonderfully peaceful and full life. The Lord has been mighty good to me."

"I'm glad to hear that, Jack. He's been good to all of us. Otherwise, we wouldn't be here. We'd be with the others out there in one of those mass graves. But you were a mighty ferocious man when I saw you at Fredericksburg. Something tells me you are equally ferocious in your faith now. I'm a Christian too. But I doubt that I am as strong as you. It shames me to say that I am not as steadfast in my faith as I should be."

"I seem to remember that you had a fairly steady gaze back at Fredericksburg. I didn't see any weakness in you then, and I don't see any now. You're probably underestimating yourself," Jack said.

"You know, Homer," Jack continued, "you're the only man from Archer's Brigade I've seen since I've been here."

"That's because so many died here at Gettysburg," Homer said, "and a lot more since. But there's a roster you can sign in the headquarters tent. You can see who else from your unit is here. I looked at it when I signed up, and Archer's Brigade has a few fellows here, but I don't think anybody had signed the Fifth's roster. I got here kind of early, and it could be that someone has signed in since then. It was a small outfit. Best I remember, y'all only had a few men at the surrender. You might be the only one left."

"That might be," Jack said. "What few friends I had died in the charge. I didn't really make any new friends for the rest of the war, not close ones anyway. You're the closest thing to an old army acquaintance I met since I've been here."

"Jack," Homer said, "standing just over there is a group of Archer's men, about eleven or twelve of us. All three Tennessee units are represented, and, of course, the Thirteenth. But we don't have anyone from the Fifth. We'd be honored to have you walk up the hill with us. What do you say?"

"Sure, Homer," Jack said without hesitation. "Lead the way."

He followed the lieutenant just a few paces to a small collection of men who watched them as they approached.

"Gentlemen," Homer said, "I want y'all to meet Private Jack Moses of the Fifth Alabama Infantry Battalion. As far as I know, he is the only man from the Fifth who is here. Archer's Brigade is reunited at last. Once again, we are whole."

"Moses," one of the men said. "Are you the same Moses that—?"

"Yeah, I'm him."

Smiles slowly spread over their faces and quickly turned to laughter as they closed in around him to shake his hand.

"Welcome back to the outfit, Jack," one said. "I shook your hand on that creek bank a long time ago."

Another man simply said over and over, "Glory be." Then he said, "Son, I watched you get baptized. I'll never forget it. I'm honored to meet you at last."

Jack smiled and said, "It's been a long time since anybody called me son. I kind of like it. Makes me feel like a young whippersnapper again. And I remember that day too. It was fifty years ago today."

They all nodded.

"You remember? I got baptized that morning, and we charged up this hill that afternoon."

They nodded again.

"Jesus got me through the charge and the rest of the war," Jack said.

"Amen," somebody said. "He got us all through."

As his ancient brothers in arms chatted, Jack looked at them and the several hundred old men standing around him. Some were gaunt and bent, others pot-bellied and prosperous. He could not help thinking back on how they had looked the last time they stood together on that now hallowed ground. They had been grim and lean, tough as pine knots—and proud.

Pride, he thought. *What a fool I was.* Then he remembered himself and the Indiana man and their conduct a few hours earlier and thought, *What a fool I remain. But at least I'm a forgiven one.*

In a field of faces scarred by the years, his, like the others, was nonetheless tranquil in the knowledge that their victory over death so long ago was fleeting and that the reaper would soon harvest them all. Their lives had been lived and could no longer be lost. They were content with their fate. An old man does not fear death as a young one does. If he lives long enough, or if he lives too long, death approaches as a welcomed friend. This is especially true of men of faith. They had conquered life and befriended death. Even though they would forever be remembered as unrequited rebels, all, save a very few, were at peace.

It was a warm day for Pennsylvania, much like it had been fifty years earlier. But they were Southerners and accustomed to the heat. They had hats to protect their balding heads and were ready for their walk in the sun.

They were chatting like schoolboys when a cheerful army captain appeared before them.

He had a megaphone, and through it he shouted, "Gentlemen! Gentlemen! Let me have your attention, please."

The crowd grew quiet.

"Thank you," he said. "Gentlemen, we will soon begin our walk to the wall. There is no need to hurry. We will make this a leisurely stroll. I will accompany you up the rise, but I will let you set your own pace. As long as we get up there and back by dinner, or supper, as you call it, we'll be fine. Are there any questions?"

"Yes sir," one old-timer said. "Are they gonna be ugly to us like they were the last time?"

As the laughter subsided, the officer smiled and said, "They are under strict orders to behave as gentlemen."

"That's good," someone shouted, "because we're gonna kick their asses this time."

A chuckle was running through the crowd when someone else shouted, "Hell, we kicked their asses last time, but they had so many more asses than we did we couldn't kick 'em fast enough."

There was much hearty laughter, and the officer, still smiling, said, "And I hereby order you to conduct yourselves as gentlemen too."

"We don't take orders from no damned Yankee officers," someone quickly shouted.

"And we don't follow them up no damned hills either," a second man added.

"What kind of accent is that?" the first man demanded. "Where the hell are you from, boy?"

The laughter had stopped, and most of the men were beginning to look a little uncomfortable when the young captain bravely admitted, "Gentlemen, I'm from Massachusetts."

There was an uncomfortable pause, and another man shouted, "Another damned Yankee slaver looking down his nose at us and telling us what to do!"

There were a few seconds of mumbling among the men when one of the veterans stepped forward and approached the captain. The old man stood beside the young captain and put his only arm around the man's waist and, with a voice weakened by the years, he spoke, and every man listened.

"Men, I'm Lieutenant Parker of the Forty-second Mississippi. At the top of the rise, behind the wall, our countrymen await us with smiles and open arms. Standing before you are two American infantry officers. Together, we will lead you to the summit, and I have no doubt that, to a man, you will be as magnanimous on this day of reconciliation as you were courageous on that day of battle so long ago. Follow us, men. Let's get it done."

The happy chatter returned to the group as the two officers turned and led them up the rise toward the once hotly contested wall.

Jack's friends were an affable lot, and, being a gregarious man himself, he was soon having great fun hearing and telling what he called benign lies, stories so farfetched and comical that not even the most gullible soul could possibly mistake them for the truth. This was an art form that Southerners had long ago developed to great heights. Wiley Jackson Moses had a great appreciation for tall tales well told. He was more than a fair hand at telling them himself.

Merriment ran through the group as they walked. They were

like boys on a hike. It was so different from their last journey over that ground that it seemed to most, Jack included, like a wholly different place. It was a good stretch of the leg to the top, several hundred yards. As they neared the wall, they grew quieter as some tensions naturally arose. They approached the wall eye-to-eye with their Northern countrymen.

Jack was looking for Levi and noticed that things had grown still quieter as some of the old Southerners tried, with some difficulty, to climb over the wall.

Then he heard someone with a decidedly Northern brogue say, "Here, Reb. Let me help you."

Both groups immediately broke into laughter and joyous whoops with a smattering of Rebel yells as the Southerners swarmed over the wall with the help of their Northern friends.

In spite of the happiness of the occasion, the noise of the celebration took Jack back to the battle.

In an instant, he wheeled around and said, "Silas!"

But the boy was gone. Then someone took him by the arm and urged him toward the wall saying, "You're next, soldier."

He found himself being helped over the wall by men in gray behind him and men in blue before him. When he steadied himself on the other side, he looked up and realized one of his helpers was none other than his old friend, Dr. Levi Brookner of the Seventy-first Pennsylvania. When Jack saw Levi's smiling face and the faded red bandana just above his left elbow, he threw his head back in delighted laughter. They embraced and slapped each other on the back in their celebration.

As the others were helped over, the hearts of hundreds of old men soared with happiness and relief. Lifetimes of resentment, grudges, and hate suddenly evaporated in laughter, kindness, and brotherly love. Fifty years of malice was swept away and replaced by understanding and tolerance. Old foes ceased to be enemies and became countrymen once again.

They fell into boisterous, mixed groups of men praising each other's ferocity and valor. They had a brief ceremony in which they spoke noble words, traded ceremonial flags, and shook hands over the wall while photographers took pictures.

In the celebration, Jack and Levi drifted apart. Jack found some of his friends from the walk up the rise and spent a little time with them and their new Yankee buddies. It was not like this all along the wall, but in the angle, at least, the two groups had turned the re-enactment of Pickett's Charge into a huge party of handshaking, backslapping, and uproarious laughter.

After a while, Jack stepped back to watch in delighted awe as God, before his very eyes, was healing the land. While he watched, tears came to his eyes as he thought about Silas and how much he would have enjoyed this happy moment.

"He was such a good boy," Jack said to himself, "so brave for one so young and so small of stature. If only I could have somehow saved him."

Gradually, the men began climbing back over the wall. In small, talkative groups from both armies, they made their way back down the hill toward the Great Tent. Jack was not in a group. He was walking in the midst of other men, but he was alone in his thoughts. He was still thinking of Silas.

As he walked down the slope, he looked off to his right, toward the line of trees that had sheltered him and Silas in their flight from the wall. Almost without knowing it, he drifted in that direction. When he realized what he was doing, he stopped to ponder which path to follow. As he stood there, he saw the young Massachusetts captain and the old Mississippi lieutenant walking together to his left, down the slope. They were the last ones to return. No one was behind him. He was alone.

He was drawn to the trees almost as strongly as on that other day. He walked past the spot where he thought he and Silas had picked up Box. Then he reached the place where he believed Box had died and Silas had been wounded.

The closer he got to the trees, the further back in time he went. He entered the tree line almost as desperately as he had before. He tore through the underbrush, and the underbrush tore at him and his clothes until he reached the stream. As before, he went down the middle of the ankle-deep brook until he caught sight of the rock. He stopped short of it, as if he expected to find his young friend there. He cautiously approached the boulder, his old hands trembling from exhaustion, confusion, and panic.

"Silas!" he cried. "I'm here, boy. I came back for you. Where are you, son?"

When he reached the stone, he looked at the place where his friend had lain so long ago, and he saw the partially completed inscription on its face.

Still confused, he began to read, "At this spot on July 3, 1863, Private Silas P. Swann—"

Suddenly, his mind cleared, and he was painfully jerked back into the present. He placed his hand over his eyes and began to weep.

"Oh, my God. Help me. I must be losing my mind. What an old fool I am."

He dropped to his knees before the stone and cried out, "Silas. Oh, Silas. I'm so sorry. Please forgive me, son. Please forgive me."

He wept bitterly. He prayed and sought comfort for his breaking heart. But comfort would be a while in coming.

Finding His Friend

Levi arrived back at the Great Tent feeling good from the walk. His spirit was still cheerful from the joyous fellowship he had experienced at the wall. He looked for someone with whom to share the joy. He looked for Jack but could not find him among the crowd. Looking up the slope, he saw only the two infantry officers still talking and laughing as they approached the tent. There was no one behind them.

Levi approached them and asked, "Is there still anyone up there at the wall?"

"No, sir," the young man said. "We were the last to leave."

The old officer added, "We saw no one up there as we were leaving, sir. Are you missing someone?"

"I'm not sure," Levi said. "He's probably here in the crowd somewhere, but I haven't been able to find him yet."

"Is there something we can do?" the captain asked. "We can go back up to the wall and look for him if you think it's necessary."

"Let me look down here first. He's probably here somewhere," Levi said.

"We can send some troops to search for him if you don't find him down here," the captain said.

"Hopefully, he's here somewhere," Levi said. "If I don't find him soon, I'll let you know."

"Very well," the captain said. "Let me know if you need us. I'll be nearby."

"Thank you, sir. I will."

When Levi turned to the crowd again, looking for Jack, he saw Michael pull up on the truck. He was alone, as Nick had decided that Michael could handle the afternoon lemonade sales by himself so he and Henry could remain at the restaurant to prepare for the dinner rush.

Levi hurriedly made his way through the crowd to the truck and climbed up so as to better search the crowd for Jack's face.

As he climbed up near him, Michael said, "Now there's a thirsty fellow for you. Where's your partner?"

"I don't know, Michael," Levi said. "I saw him at the top of the hill, but I haven't seen him since. I can't find him down here, and the last two men off the hill said they didn't see him up there. I'm afraid he might have fallen or something. He could be lying on the ground and we wouldn't be able to see him from here. He has a bad heart, you know. I'm worried about him. Do you see him anywhere?"

Michael quickly scanned the faces. "I don't see him."

After their walk in the sun, the men were eager to slake

their thirst, and in mere minutes, Michael had sold the lemonade and tea. He was hurriedly collecting the glassware as Levi continued to look through the crowd. As Michael gathered the last of the glasses, he remembered the rock.

"I think I know where he is."

"Where?" Levi asked.

"Climb up while I crank the truck. I'll explain on the way."

Considering that he had an old man with him, and all those glasses, he drove too fast. It was a bumpy ride, but Levi did not complain. They were both very concerned for their friend.

As they approached Farmer Robinson's house, Michael had just finished telling Levi about the rock and the path leading to it.

The truck lurched to a stop and Levi said, "You run on as fast as you can. I'll get there as soon as possible."

Michael leapt off the truck and began running. He was big and powerful, and he ran as only a young man can. His stride was effortless and long. He would be there in less than a minute.

Levi carefully climbed off the truck, thinking to himself, *We don't need two injured old codgers on our hands.*

Once on the ground, he walked as quickly as his legs could carry him. Like many old men, his legs simply refused to run, especially after their arduous walk to the wall and back, not to mention the ride on the remorseless carriage. Levi was like Jack, who had explained to his rambunctious grandchildren on several occasions that he was too old to run and too proud to try.

Jack was sitting on the same stone he and Michael had occupied just two days earlier. He heard Michael's frantic footsteps approaching, and when he appeared, the look on Jack's face was one of apprehension.

"Jack!" Michael said as he rushed to him. "Are you okay? You look like you rolled all the way down the hill."

"Michael, son, you scared me. I didn't know who you were. But thank God you're here."

Soon, Levi appeared and, seeing that his friend was not

seriously injured, said, "My word, Jack. You look as if you just re-fought the whole battle and lost."

"What, again?" Jack said.

Michael said, "You said I scared you because you didn't know who I was. Why would you be fearful of anyone you might come across down here?"

"I was afraid y'all might be the Yankees."

As Jack realized what he had said, he laughed, and the two Yankees laughed with him. They each took a seat next to him on the sitting stone and talked for a while so Jack could settle down and clear his mind a little more.

"Well," Levi said, "it looks like you were right about us being Yankees."

"Yeah," Jack said. "I never thought I'd be so happy to see a pair of bluebellies."

"A Catholic and a Jew at that," Levi pointed out as they all chuckled.

"Ain't that the squirts," Jack said. Then he quietly added, "Two Yankees, a Catholic and Jew, and a man couldn't ask for finer friends."

After a short pause, he said, "If they find out about this back home, they'll throw my silly ass plum out of the Klan."

They resumed their laughter for a little while.

War Dreams

"Well, gentlemen, so much for mirth," Levi said. "Let's get down to business. Jack, are you hurt? Do you have any injuries that Doctor Camardo and I need to know about?"

"Nah. I don't think so. But I'm afraid I might have wiped out Brother Robinson's thorn crop."

"Seriously, Jack," Levi said, "what happened?"

"I'm not real sure, Levi. When we started back down the hill, I just sort of drifted over this way and decided to come down the same way I did the last time. This is the place where my little friend died back then."

"Did you have a war memory come back on you?" Levi asked. "I have treated several old troopers who have had that problem."

"Levi," Jack said, "for a long time, I had no such problems. But as I got older, I began having what I call war dreams. It got worse after my wife died. Sometimes I wake up confused in the middle of the night. Once in a while, I even get a little confused in the middle of the day, like today. It does make me feel a little better knowing some other fellows have the same problem. I mean, I'm not happy they have it. I'm just glad I'm not alone."

"I know what you mean, Jack," Levi said.

"Do you ever have dreams like that?" Jack asked.

"Not bad ones. Not yet anyway. Something tells me I didn't see as much action as you did," Levi said.

"And you're a good bit younger than I am," Jack said. "Maybe you'll be spared. Levi, I think I just started walking down here and got confused. There for a little while, I thought I was back in the war. I wouldn't tell that to anyone except my doctors and maybe my children. But this place was the worst part of the war for me. This is where my best friend died. This is where I left him to die."

"Now, Jack," Michael said, "you know that's not quite how it was. You told me he asked you to leave because the Yankees were coming and he didn't want you to be killed or captured."

"That's true, Michael," Jack said. "But he was my best friend, just a boy. He saved my life at the wall. I hope you never experience war, son, but if you do, you'll understand what I'm about to say. Combat changes men and groups of men. It creates a bond between them like nothing else can. Even fellows you don't like become important to you. But this man here," he said, pointing to the rock, "was special to me. I should never, under any circumstances, have abandoned him. He deserved to die with his friend at his side, regardless of the cost. But I cut and ran. And I thought I was tough. He was twice the man I was. He was brave, and he loved the Lord. He was just a kid, not quite as old as you. He was a little fellow, and he wasn't physically strong, but he would stand up to bigger fellows to protect the weak and helpless.

"Michael, I served with a bunch of the toughest, most courageous men you could ever find," Jack said as Levi nodded in agreement. "But, son, Silas Swann was the best of us. He was the youngest and the smallest. He had only been in the army a few months. He probably couldn't have whipped anybody in our outfit. But he was our finest man. And he died at seventeen, right there. He lost his life before he could live it. He never got to snuggle up to his sweet wife on a cold night. He never knew his children or his grandchildren. I don't think the boy had ever been kissed."

Jack had to pause briefly to wipe his tears.

Michael said, "You don't have to go on, Jack."

"No, no," Levi said quietly. "Let him talk, son. Let him talk."

Jack continued. "Michael, war is a great sin. Most wars are silly things, not worth one life. But sometimes a fight comes along that needs to be fought. There are times when war is the lesser of two evils, the greater evil being what would happen if you didn't fight. The trick is to know the difference. God is strong, and He can take care of Himself. But sometimes good needs a champion, a defender, a hero.

"Some people will tell you," Jack continued, "that we should never fight any war under any circumstances. Yet those folks don't hesitate to enjoy the freedoms given them by the sacrifices of those willing to fight and risk death. Other people seem always eager to go to war. These are usually people who have never seen it firsthand and who are in little danger of ever having to."

Jack went on. "We've been fortunate in that we've only had one real war since the War Between the States, the one with Spain. Even that one wasn't worth one life, American or Spanish. And then there were those heartbreaking campaigns against our own natives, the Indians. But I'm worried about Europe. Those people have a lust for war like no one else in the world. They love their weapons too much. They're always mad at one another, and their anger is never allayed. And they all speak different languages. Do you think all these old enemies who are here for this reunion could get along as well as they have if they didn't all speak the same language, more or less? I think not. There probably wouldn't even be a reunion if we didn't have a common language. The only common languages the Europeans have are music and war. And they're very fluent in both. I'm afraid that, before this decade ends, they will have a terrible war over there. I just hope we can stay out of it. But if we can't, it will be your generation that fights it. I pray it never comes to that.

"But the war Levi and I fought," Jack said, "was probably unavoidable. I think it turned out the way it needed to turn out, the way God willed it to turn out. Both armies were fighting for some of the right reasons and some of the wrong reasons. Most of the Yanks thought they were fighting to end slavery and restore the Union. But what they did was invade, burn, pillage, and rape their sister country, and it continued long after the war had ended. Most of the Rebs thought they were defending their homes. But in defending their homes, they were also defending slavery, the world's most despicable institution. As in most wars, there is enough guilt to go around. But since the South lost, she got saddled with all of it. The only way to resolve the slavery issue was to fight a total war to a bloody finish with a clear-cut winner and loser. And that's what we did. Politicians could never have resolved it. It had to be soldiers."

After a pause, Jack said, "Silas was my best friend. He gave me my life, and then he lost his. His mama and daddy lost their precious little boy. The least I could do was hold his hand while he died."

Jack could not go on. His friends let him weep. They did not speak again for a while.

When Jack's sobs subsided, Levi quietly said, "So, you're having an inscription put on that rock for him."

"That's right. Looks like that fellow has made some progress on it. Oh no! Because of me, that good man is going to have to work tomorrow, on Independence Day. I reckon I really am an old poot after all."

"A what?" Michael asked.

"An old poot. That's what my grandchildren call me behind my back. But they don't know I know it. It's a term of endearment. Really, it is," Jack said.

Levi laughed, but Michael shook his head and said, "Alabama!" Then Michael went on. "Jack, I'm sure Mr. Johnson knew about tomorrow being the fourth and figured it into his price."

"Well, I'll just have to give him a little extra."

"No, Jack, you don't have to give him any extra. He figured it in!" Michael said.

"Son," Jack said as he emphasized his words with his hands, "you'll find that in business, good will is worth much more than any few extra dollars you may pay someone for a job well done."

Michael, shaking his head again, muttered, "Yes, father."

They laughed a little more. Levi said, "Jack, we need to get you back to the hotel so you can clean up and we can treat those scratches. We'll have you ready for dinner tonight."

"Do you think we're through for the day out at the battlefield?" Jack asked.

"I think so," Levi said, nodding.

"I know so," said Michael.

They helped Jack up off the rock and walked slowly back to the truck. No one spoke, except Jack.

"It's been a rough day, boys."

Michael gently drove them back. They were quiet all the way.

Quite the Stoic

They escorted Jack to his room. After his bath, Levi could tell that he had some bad scratches on his legs, forearms, and hands. But there was nothing that would not heal on its own with a little help. Levi gave him a bottle of alcohol and told him to bathe his wounds twice a day, starting right then.

Jack said, "You must think I'm a lot braver than I really am. You know that stuff is really gonna light me up."

"I'm counting on it," Levi said. "That's what kills the germs."

"I don't have anything against germs," Jack said. "I believe in live and let live."

"Yes, but they don't share your beliefs. They aren't Christians," Levi said. "Now go ahead and do it."

As Michael watched Jack standing there in his baggy underwear with his pathetic old legs covered in scratches and bulging veins, and as he listened to the almost comic exchange between Jack and Levi, he felt the urge to both laugh and cry.

Finally he said, "Jack, if you don't do it I'll have to do it for you."

"My goodness, son," Jack said, "I wouldn't want to put you through that." Then Jack turned to Levi, and with a wink, he added, "Some bedside manner he has."

"Just get it done, Johnny Reb," Levi said.

Jack bravely took the bottle and poured some alcohol into the palm of his hand. As he prepared himself for the shock of alcohol on open wounds, he looked down at his legs and studied them briefly.

After a few seconds, he said, "I declare, looks like I swapped legs with a jaybird." He paused and added, "And threw my butt in for boot."

Levi laughed, but Michael had to turn away to hide his moist eyes. It was at that moment he realized he loved Jack like a man loves his father or grandfather. It had nothing to do with the scholarship. It would have happened anyway. He continued to look away as Jack bravely applied the alcohol. He would have done it for him had it been necessary. But since Jack was doing it himself, he preferred not to watch him in his discomfort.

Michael often heard that the parent eventually becomes the child and the child the parent. He and Jack were just in the third day of their friendship, but Michael was already deeply concerned for the old man.

As he looked back over the last three days, Michael realized that Jack had very quickly become his friend, perhaps his closest one. He concluded that somewhere along the way, Jack had become much like a father to him. He knew that Jack had remained his father until that evening at the rock, when he began his transition from father to son and Michael from son to father.

Michael slowly turned to watch Jack's torment. He knew that as a doctor he would have to view painful things, so he forced himself to look. In spite of the questions he had raised about his own bravery, Jack really was quite the stoic as he slathered on the alcohol.

When it was over, Michael handed Jack a clean pair of pants, patted him on the back, and said, "Got it done, Johnny Reb."

A Splendid Gift

After Jack had dressed, they started downstairs toward the restaurant. Levi asked Jack how he was feeling.

Jack said, "I feel fine. I'm a resilient old poot."

"Well, you got part of that right," Levi said.

"Yeah," said Michael, "the last part. Your grandchildren really are quite perceptive, you know."

Laughing, Jack said, "Y'all are just trying to make me feel at home. And to think I took the train all the way from Alabama for this."

They agreed to keep Jack's adventure to themselves. They all wanted it that way. They had a restful dinner, with Jack picking up the tab. As usual, Big Mama stuck her head through the door long enough to receive her well-deserved accolades. Little Henry was in and out of the dining room, smiling as always, and seeming none-the-worse for his encounter with the Klansman.

After dinner, Levi excused himself and returned to his room to read and rest, claiming the day's activities and excitement had fatigued him.

After Levi disappeared, Michael said, "How about you? Are you through with me for the day?"

Jack looked at his young friend and said, "Michael, I know I've been an awful lot of trouble today, and I want you to know how much I appreciate all you've done. I hope you understand that what I said up there about your bedside manner was just a joke."

"I know."

"But there's one more place I want to go today since we probably have a couple of hours of daylight left," Jack said.

Michael bowed and made an elaborate gesture toward the door and said, "Let's get it done, Johnny Reb. My remorseless carriage and I are at your disposal."

Reinvigorated by his bath and Big Mama's food, Jack spryly climbed onto the truck as Michael cranked it.

As he climbed up beside him, Michael said, "You know, Jack, you really are a resilient old poot."

Jack just smiled and said, "Yes, but I haven't always been, you know. Many years ago, I was a young one. But now I'm an old one. I am truly blessed. God is so generous."

"Well, where to?" asked Michael. "Back to the reunion site?"

"No," said Jack. "I want to visit a little spot to the west of town on the other side of Herr Ridge. When I was coming in on the train the other day, I saw what I think was a logging road or maybe a farm road running parallel to the ridge. It looked like it might lead to a little creek I know of down there. That's where I want to go."

So they headed west on the Chambersburg Pike, then

turned southward on a narrow road that ran next to Herr Ridge on their left.

Once they were on the little road, Jack said, "Just keep it 'tween the ditches till I tell you to stop."

Michael was driving slowly because the road was fairly rough. He had borrowed a cushion from the restaurant to provide Jack with a little more padding. They were going slowly enough for Jack to get a good look at the scenery passing by. The road stayed fairly close to the ridge on their left, but Jack was looking mostly to his right. Motioning Michael to stop, he stood up and looked around briefly.

"No, this isn't it," he said as he sat back down. "No stream. Drive on, Jehu."

They had driven very slowly just a few minutes more and were nearing the southern end of the ridge with a little stream on their right when Jack again motioned Michael to stop. He stood again and slowly perused the area.

"I think this is it," he said after a few seconds. "There's the stream."

Michael pulled off to the side of the road and helped Jack down. He could almost see Jack going back in time as they took the short walk toward the creek, which grew somewhat larger as they walked downstream.

"What is this place, Jack? I don't know the name of this stream, but I think it flows into Willoughby Run south of the Fairfield Road."

"This is where I was baptized, son, where my life changed directions. This is where Jesus turned a lost sinner into a found one. I've never been the same since, thanks to him."

When Jack talked, he did not look at Michael. He just looked at the creek and the trees and spoke as if he were leading a tour.

"Over there," he said, turning and pointing to some distant trees, "is where my precious little Rose led me to Jesus—held my hand while I got on my knees and prayed the sinner's prayer.

And right here" he said, turning back toward the creek, "is where Corporal Elder—the preacher, as we called him—baptized me. God bless them both. The preacher died that afternoon in the charge. You see, Rose led me to Jesus the night before the charge, and the preacher baptized me the next morning. After I was baptized, I stood here on the bank of this little stream and shook hands with a bunch of fellows who wanted to wish me well. That was a new experience for me.

"There was a little string band nearby, playing hymns and gospel tunes while we shook hands. I still remember some of the words to one of their songs. I've heard it many times since."

Jack paused a few seconds and then, as he continued to gaze across the stream into the trees, he began quietly singing the words.

> My latest sun is sinking fast
>
> My race is nearly run
>
> My strongest trials now are past
>
> My triumph has begun
>
> O, come angel band
>
> Come and around me stand
>
> O, bear me away on your snow-white wings
>
> To my immortal home.

Then he turned toward Michael and, looking into his friend's eyes, he continued.

> O, bear my loving heart to Him
>
> Who bled and died for me
>
> Whose blood cleanses from all sin

And gives me victory

O, come angel band

Come and around me stand

O, bear me away on your snow-white wings

To my immortal home."

Then he looked away from Michael and gazed at the water flowing past them. They watched a leaf float by and pass out of sight downstream.

"I was the only man from the preacher's squad to survive," Jack said. "I was the only one who wanted to die. I was truly hoping that a band of angels would bear me away to my immortal home that very day. But it was not to be, not that day at least. As Silas was dying, he told me that Rose's prayers had delivered me through the charge. The last time I saw her, the night before, she promised she would pray me safely through the battle and that we would meet again someday in this life. I didn't believe her. I was a new Christian, and, except for my own conversion, I had not yet seen the power of prayer at work. But I saw it the day of the charge, and I have seen it many times since then.

"The Fifth Alabama was sort of a conglomerate outfit with four companies that had been put together to form the battalion several months after the war began. At one time, early on, we were called the Eighth Infantry Battalion, and we had a Florida outfit with us and an artillery unit. Then they were assigned somewhere else. I don't know much about those other companies, but Company B, the company I was in, started out with about 154 men. We came to Gettysburg with maybe 135. When we surrendered, about twenty-one months later, we had forty-four men still standing, and some of those were replacements, not part of the original group. The whole battalion only had three companies and about 125 men at the surrender. And like I said, a fair number of them were replacements. Had it been asked of them, they and the others who were there that day would have defended their beloved South to the last man. And they very nearly did. Yet, to this day, some folks think they fought and died for slavery. But the Lord spared that handful of souls, what Shakespeare called the 'happy few.' And I was among them. Rose's prayers got me through the rest of the war virtually unscratched. Prayer is a mighty thing, Michael. Never underestimate it."

Then Jack turned his gaze from the land and looked into Michael's eyes again. "That is why I am so very hopeful of finding her before I go home. Rose and I have both been praying for our own reunion for fifty years. We have faith in prayer and in God's kindness. I am convinced that He will lead us to each other in the next two days."

"How do you know she's even alive?" Michael asked.

"She's alive," Jack said as if there were simply no question of it.

Michael could see the absolute, total faith in Jack's face, and he could hear it in his voice.

"You're a good Catholic boy," Jack said. "Don't you believe in the power of prayer?"

"Sure I do," came the weak reply.

Hearing Michael's lukewarm response, Jack said, "Didn't you tell me how you had been praying for God to somehow get you into medical school?"

"Yes."

"And wasn't that prayer abundantly answered this very day?"

"Yes."

"You need to be a little more aware of your surroundings, son. If you just open your eyes, you'll see answered prayer all around you."

"Yeah. I guess so," Michael said. "I have a long way to go, don't I, Jack?"

"Nah. Don't worry about it. The Bible says not to worry about anything but to pray about everything. Before you can see answered prayer, you first must pray. Besides, you're so far ahead of me when I was your age, well, there's just no comparison. You're a fine young scamp. We don't give scholarships to just any old Yankee. Like I said, you're the first," Jack said, patting him on the back.

"But, Michael, if you'll just pray every day, ask God to pull you closer in, to make you a better man, a stronger Christian, you will soon see a difference in your life. God answers the fervent prayers of a righteous man. The answer isn't always yes, but there will always be an answer if you are on the lookout for it."

Jack began looking out over the creek again.

He said, "It was right here that I took off my good Yankee boots and left them in the care of a friend. Then Silas and I waded out to the middle where the preacher was waiting. There must have been two or three hundred men watching from the banks. I was so notorious, so infamous, they showed up just to be sure it was really me."

"Aw, go on, Jack. I just can't believe that."

"What can't you believe? That there were that many men there?"

"No. I just can't believe that you were that bad," Michael said. "You talk as if you were the devil himself."

"I was that bad, son. Believe it. I wasn't the devil himself, but I was well-acquainted with him."

Michael laughed and said, "Does he have a tail and horns?"

"No, he doesn't," Jack said without smiling. "And he doesn't carry a pitchfork either."

"You talk like you've seen him."

"I have. He used to visit me in the middle of the night a long time ago, before I got saved. I haven't seen him in many years, but I remember him well. I used to have a little cabin in the woods back home in Calhoun County. Once, or maybe two or three times a year for a long time, I would wake up a few hours before dawn. Somehow, I would just know to look out my window. I still don't know whether I was dreaming or not. But either way, it was him. There he would be in a little clearing next to the cabin, standing in the moonlight. I can tell you this: he's the biggest fellow I've ever seen, and I've seen a couple of big-guns. He's naked, and he's bald except for a few scraggly little hairs on his head. And he's white."

"You mean he's a white man?"

"No. He's not a man at all. He's the beast. He just has the general form of a man, except a lot bigger, and muscled up like you wouldn't believe, but lean and rangy."

"Well, you said he was white."

"Yeah, but I don't mean Caucasian, like us. I mean he's white, sort of grayish white, like ashes. He's a dusty, ashen white, like gray powder. And he's got a big ol' head, but no eyes that I could see. His eyes were like a skull's eyes, empty and black, just sockets. I would look out the window, and he would be there in that clearing maybe seventy-five to a hundred feet away, just staring at me. It was like he had come to check on me and remind me of who I belonged to. The moon would always be at his back. His face would be in the shadow, but I could see that scruffy hair on his head and those hollow eyes. And he would just look at me for a while and then be gone. I would just blink my eyes, and he would be gone. Everything else would still be there the same as before—the moon, the meadow—everything but him. There was never any doubt in my mind as to who it was. It was him. It had to be.

"He hasn't visited me in over fifty years now. I don't miss him. Jesus put him on the run. I was a different person then. I led a low life. I was a little taller than I am now, and I weighed about 250 pounds. I used all that God-given strength in the service of Satan. That's why he paid me all those visits. I was a bad man, so bad that almost everybody in the Army of Northern Virginia had heard of me. I was a totally worthless specimen. My notoriety was such that when the preacher pulled me up out of the water, some fellow I didn't even know jumped in, boots and all. He shouted that if Jesus could save Wiley Jackson Moses, He could save anybody, and that included him. He wanted to be the next to be baptized. Then other men began jumping in, and they had a regular revival right there in the middle of this creek. Poor old Preacher was just about tuckered out from dipping all those men that morning. But he was a happy man, getting caught up in a spontaneous revival like that. My guess is that some of those men who got saved that morning went on to be with the Lord that afternoon. That's what I was hoping to do myself. I didn't expect to live, didn't want to. But Rose's prayers carried me through. And I here I stand today, on the bank of this stream again, fifty years later, having come full circle, a happy old man who has been allowed to live his life in spite of his efforts to throw it away. And all this because of the fervent prayers of a humble little girl. God bless her sweet soul."

They were silent for a while as Jack gazed at the creek and into the cherished past.

Then he said, "You know, I marched up that hill in front of everybody but the flag bearers. I just walked straight into the teeth of death and walked out unscathed, all because of Rose's prayers. I had hoped to die and was pretty disappointed to still be here and not in heaven with Jesus. But as he was dying at the rock, Silas told me that God had a plan for me, that I had a life to live and work to do. You pretty much know the rest of the story. I left him there to die just barely out of childhood and I, the world's greatest sinner, somehow survived to live a long, joyous life filled with God's trials and blessings. You never know how God's plan will unfold. You just try to stay close to Him and ride it out."

Michael could tell that Jack was in the mood to talk, so he remained silent, waiting for him to speak again. It was not long before he did.

"A man can't fully understand just what a wonderful gift life is until he can look back on his own and see it in its entirety. My life is all but over. But I can see the whole thing behind me now. I tell you, Michael, life is a splendid, priceless gift from a loving

God. The only significant drawback to life I've been able to find is that the longer a fellow lives, the older he gets. Occupying a worn-out, old body isn't always a lot of fun. But then that's just another of the Lord's trials for us to bravely endure on the road to paradise. Like they say, this too shall pass.

"Michael, I hope God blesses you with a long happy life so that you can someday look back in wonder at what you were given. Life is a fascinating journey, with surprises all through it. Just when you think you've turned your last corner, God lets you stroll down one more beautiful lane and shows you another golden day. When I left Alabama, coming north, I was looking for a cherished old friend. Even though God has yet to lead me to her, He has led me to three precious new ones: Levi, Henry, and you. Try as I may, I have never been able to out-give Him. And even though I once held my own life in low regard, I wouldn't take anything for my journey now."

Michael did not speak, but as he stood beside him, he slipped one arm around the old man and gently embraced him. After a short while, they sat on a log to rest. To the west, the sun was descending toward Knoxlyn Ridge, and dusk was setting in. He thought Jack was about to ask him to take him back to the hotel, but his friend was not quite through.

"You know," Jack said, "right before the preacher baptized me, he said, 'For ye were sometimes darkness, but now are ye light in the Lord. Walk as children of light.' I thought that was a mighty nice thing to say. I had no idea he was quoting from the Bible."

"Sure. That's in Ephesians," Michael said.

"That's right, young fellow," Jack said, "fifth chapter, eighth verse. So you have been listening in church after all."

Michael smiled proudly and said, "Well..."

"That's why the preacher used that Scripture when he baptized me," Jack said. "He knew me, and he knew just what a piece of horse dung I had been.

"Back home in Mobile, in the northern end of the Church

Street Cemetery," Jack said, "there is a large tombstone, and on that stone is just one word: Moses. Buried there are my sweet Sally and our youngest son, Wiley. They each have a footstone with their names and dates on them. There is a place for me next to my wife, and my footstone is already there. It has my name on it, Wiley Jackson Moses, and my date of birth, July 2, 1830, and it has a blank spot where my date of death will be inscribed. And below that are the words, 'For ye were once darkness, but are now light in the Lord.' I'm sure you noticed that it isn't the King James translation."

Jack produced a small New Testament from his coat pocket and said, "That is from my little 1901 American Standard translation. I chose it because it just seemed to describe me better than the King James. I like the use of the word *once* in place of *sometimes*. I wasn't sometimes darkness like it says in the King James. I was in darkness from the time I was born till I got saved. Since then, the world has been a place of light for me, and I have been a different man."

"Michael, my friend," Jack said. "You are my friend, aren't you?"

"We both know I am."

"Michael, I want you to do me a favor."

"Just name it."

"I want you to pray for me tonight before you go to bed. Ask the Lord to send Rose to me tomorrow. God hears the fervent prayers of a righteous man, you know. Or have I told you that already?"

Not waiting for an answer, he went on. "Pray fervently for Rose and me to find each other. I'm going to pray, and I have a bunch of folks back home praying for us. My faith is strong, and my hopes are high. I just know tomorrow will be the day."

"I'll pray for you, for both of you. You can rely on me," Michael said.

"Thank you, son. Let's head for the house."

They arrived back at the Battle House just as darkness was

closing in. Michael dropped Jack off and went on home. Two righteous men prayed fervently that night.

The day had started well and ended well but had been rough in the middle. Jack was tired, and at first he struggled to sleep. But peace soon covered him, and, as he was known to do back home, he slept well and had hope-filled dreams.

FRIDAY, JULY 4TH

Faith in Today

Jack awoke refreshed. He went through the alcohol bath routine, as Levi had instructed. Before dressing, he knelt and said his morning prayer, asking that his sins be forgiven and expressing his gratitude for a good night's sleep. He made his usual request on Rose's behalf and ended with a fervent request to find her. For all this, he prayed in the name of Jesus.

Jack had never been ashamed of his faith. Over the last fifty years, various people had complimented him on the strength of his faith and the boldness of his witness. His response was always essentially the same.

He would say, "After the sweet miracle Jesus performed in my life, how could I be any other way?"

Jack met Levi and Michael for breakfast. Michael's routine would be a little different that day. Instead of returning to the restaurant, he would stay with Jack and Levi most of the morning. He would return to the restaurant only briefly at mid-morning to pick up the tea and lemonade. But he would not return to the restaurant again until lunch to pick up Nick and Henry with the food.

Nick had approved this plan because he knew Michael

wanted to help Jack look for Rose through the morning and because President Wilson was scheduled to speak in the Great Tent that afternoon at 1:30. Michael wanted very much to see and hear the president. He would have enough time to deliver Nick and Henry back to the restaurant after lunch and return to the Great Tent in time for the speech. After the president's comments, he would return to the restaurant again to pick up the goods for the afternoon lemonade and tea run.

But right now, his mind, like Jack's, was on Rose. He, too, had prayed for their reunion. His faith was not yet as strong as Jack's, but today would provide a step in that direction.

As the three men rode together toward the reunion site, Levi could not help but notice Jack's happy mood.

He looked at his friend's smiling face and said, "Have you been drinking some of that stuff I gave you to put on your legs?"

The others laughed, and Jack said, "No, my good doctor. You know I don't drink."

"That's right, and you don't smoke either," Levi said. "And you just cuss a little bit."

"I reckon I'm just high on God's sweet mercy," Jack said. "You see, today is the day Rose and I will be reunited."

"Oh," Levi said, "is that all it is? So He told you it would be today?"

"Well, not in so many words," Jack said. "I'm going home tomorrow, so it has to be either today or tomorrow. Today would be better, so I have faith in today. However, if it's tomorrow, that will be just fine too."

"And if it's never?" Levi asked.

"Oh, it won't be never. It will happen someday, either in this life or the next. His will be done," Jack said, smiling. Then he added, "A lot of people are praying for this, Levi. If it doesn't happen in this life it'll be because God had a good reason. It won't be for lack of prayer or faith. Isn't that right, Jehu?" he said, looking toward Michael.

"Levi," Jack said, "it will happen eventually. Whether it will be now or later, I don't know. But it will happen."

Levi stared at his two companions and saw their faith. After a few seconds, he smiled, shook his head, and said, "Christians."

Jack chuckled and put one arm around his cherished friend, squeezed him gently and said, "Oh ye of little faith."

Old Crackers

They arrived at the Great Tent and after they had climbed down off the truck, Jack said, "Remember, men, keep your eyes peeled for a colored lady. She is sixty-one years old, but I haven't seen her since she was eleven, so I have no idea what she looks like now. About all I can tell you is that she was a skinny little thing back then. But she shouldn't be too hard to spot amongst all us old crackers."

They had about an hour and a half before Michael had to return to the restaurant for the lemonade and tea. So they found a place in the shade of the tent and arranged their chairs in such a way that they could see the comings and goings on the road below.

There was much activity, especially among the army personnel, due to the expected arrival of the president in a few hours. They observed this constant milling of people toward the road a few hundred feet away.

Their conversation had come to a halt. The three of them were sitting in the shade gazing over the field when someone hurriedly approached Levi.

"Hey, mister," the man said, "didn't I hear you say that you're a doctor the other day?"

"You did," Levi said.

"There's a feller right over yonder that needs your help."

They looked to where the man was pointing and saw men

gathering, looking toward the ground. The man led them through the crowd.

Someone said, "We've sent for the army doctors. They should be here pretty soon, but maybe you can help him."

They looked down to see an unconscious man struggling to breathe and turning blue in the face. Levi knelt beside him and began to do what little he could to comfort him.

"I don't have my kit, my bag. I don't think it would make any difference if I did," Levi said. "This doesn't look good."

As they watched Levi work, Jack quietly said to Michael, "You know, son, from a distance, a life seems an insignificant thing. There are so many," he said as he looked out over the masses. "We throw them away so casually in war. But yet, in this world at least, we are each given just the one. And so we cling tenaciously to it in our diligent efforts to stay on this side of the river, the stormy side, as long as possible. And all the while peace awaits us on the other shore. Sometimes I wonder why we fight so hard to stay here. But the Lord made us that way for a reason."

Two army doctors arrived, and Levi said, "I'm sorry, gentlemen. He's gone. There was nothing anyone could have done. It was quick. Like we used to say when we lost a friend in battle, for him, the war is over."

"Thank you, doctor," one of the officers said. "We'll handle it from here. We appreciate your efforts."

Levi nodded and returned to his chair with Jack and Michael following. They sat down and were silent for a while.

Then Jack said, "Are you all right, Levi?"

He didn't answer, but after a few seconds, he turned to Michael and said, "Michael, I wish I could say that the time will come when losing a patient will no longer bother you. But, son, the truth is if you're a good doctor, a truly good one, that day never arrives."

The three of them sat together in silence as they watched the milling crowd below, looking for Rose.

I Am He

No one spoke for about twenty minutes. Then Michael said, "Jack, what's happening over there?"

Below them and to their left on the road was an army officer with a megaphone. The crowd was thick, but he was slowly making his way through as he spoke into the megaphone. The distance was too great for them to hear what he was saying, but Michael's sharp young eyes soon saw something else.

"Jack!" he said. "Look a few feet behind him. There's someone with him."

"You know I can't see that far, son. Tell me what you see."

"A woman!" Levi said.

"Yes," Michael said. "A colored woman."

They were silent as they stood and stared down the slope.

"I think I see her," Jack said. "She's wearing white."

"She's wearing a white dress and a wide-brimmed white hat," Michael said.

His voice trembling with excitement, Jack quietly said, "Praise God, boys. It's her. Quick. Y'all help me get down there."

"You want me to drive you down there?" Michael asked.

"In this crowd?" Jack said. "We'd kill somebody. Let's just walk down there fast."

They all took off, and Jack immediately said, "But not too fast, Michael. I'm old and slow."

"Few things are more disgusting than a slow poot," Levi observed in dry, professorial tones.

"Especially an old one," Michael helpfully added as he slowed to Jack's pace.

They began making their way through the crowd, hoping to intercept the officer and his charge without losing them in the melee. They could tell they were getting closer as the officer's voice became louder.

They heard the words, "… searching for a Southern soldier named Moses."

"Almighty Jehovah!" Levi said. "It is her!"

She was walking slowly behind the officer, who had been so kind as to listen to her story and take a little time out of his busy morning to help her. All the old soldiers kindly made way for her and the officer, allowing them to pass through as he announced, "This lady is searching for a Southern soldier named Moses. He is from Alabama. If you know of such a man, please speak up."

As the crowd stepped back, making room for them, she suddenly became aware of three men standing before her. The officer stepped to one side so she could see all three men clearly.

Jack could see her now. She was tall, slim, and elegant, a lady of noble bearing. He took a few steps toward her. As they looked at each other, he recognized her.

Those eyes, he thought. *It's her.*

The crowd grew silent as Jack stepped forward, slowly removed his hat, and softly said, "I am he, Miss Rose. It is I you seek."

She covered her mouth with her hands as she began to cry. He went to her, and in each other's arms, they wept for joy. Michael smiled, as did Levi as he shook his head in wonder. The officer quietly returned to his duties, and hundreds of old men watched the joyous reunion in pleased silence.

A Complete Circle

As they had a nice cry together, Jack took two handkerchiefs from his coat pocket and gave her one. He had brought an extra one just for this occasion. Keeping the other one for himself, they began to laugh as they wiped their tears.

"My, my, Miss Rose. You're all grown up," he said.

"Don't you mean all grown old?" she asked.

"You'll always be young to me. And I will say this: you have grown into a lovely lady."

"I seem to remember a certain Confederate soldier telling me I was ugly," she said with a smile.

"Oh, Miss Rose, I'm so sorry about that. Don't you also remember that same soldier apologizing profusely? Can you ever forgive me?"

"Mr. Moses, you know I forgave you a long time ago. Besides, I was ugly."

"No, you weren't. You were just a gangly little girl going through an awkward stage," Jack said. "I was just being mean when I said that."

"Well," she said, "you are forgiven. How could I not forgive you with all you did for me? I owe you so much."

"You owe me?" Jack said, puzzled.

Before Jack could continue, Levi said, "Jack, aren't you going to introduce us?"

"Oh my goodness. Levi and Michael, I want you to meet the first mortal friend I ever had after my mother: Miss Rose Blount." Jack paused and said, "I'm afraid I don't know your married name or even if you married at all."

"I did," she answered, "and it's Taylor."

"Mrs. Rose Blount Taylor," Jack proudly said, "I want you to meet two of my dear friends, Doctor Levi Brookner of Philadelphia—whom I've known almost as long as I've known you—and Master Michael Camardo of Gettysburg."

The two men had already removed their hats. They shook her hand ever so gently, for they could tell she was a true lady.

Rose turned again to Levi and said, "Are you the same Doctor Brookner who has the hospital and medical school in Philadelphia?"

"I am," Levi said.

"I am truly honored to meet you, Doctor Brookner," she said. "I, too, am in the medical profession. I'm a nurse, and, like you, I work in Philadelphia."

Beaming with pride, Michael said, "I'm going to be one of Doctor Brookner's students this fall."

"Congratulations, Michael. I'm sure you know what a wonderful school Doctor Brookner has and how blessed you are to be one of his students," Rose said.

"Yes, ma'am, I know. It's answered prayer," Michael said.

Rose looked at him and said, "So you know about the power of prayer too."

"I'm learning, thanks to our friend Jack Moses," Michael said.

"And I learned it from a little girl named Rose who led me to Jesus a long time ago," Jack said. "The circle is complete."

"I remember how you doubted me when I told you that you would survive the battle and we would meet again someday," Rose said as she looked at Jack. "What do you think of prayer now?"

"The day after I last saw you," Jack said, "your prayers delivered me through the charge on this very piece of ground and into a long, happy life. From that day to this one, I have never again doubted the power of prayer."

Then Jack said, "Miss Rose, I'm so happy to find you that my face is beginning to hurt from all this grinning. Why don't we all walk up to that big tent so we can get out of the sun and sit down and rest a little."

And so the four of them began the slow walk up the gentle rise toward the Great Tent, talking and laughing along the way.

A True Lady

The three men soon knew they were in the company of a great lady. She had a keen mind and a rich sense of humor. She had Levi, and especially Michael, laughing on a regular basis with her gentle, self-deprecating wit.

Jack only smiled, his face still hurting. He remained in a mild state of pleasant shock from having found her.

"Prayer," he said to himself.

When they reached the tent, Michael and Levi scrambled to find her a chair. After she was seated, Michael found three more, and they all joined her in a little conversation circle. Michael and Levi were chatting with her as if they were the ones who had spent the last half century searching for her.

Jack looked on in amazement. Her beauty was not the kind that would instantly attract a man's attention. It was much deeper. After watching her for a while and listening to her talk, and after seeing Michael and Levi practically grovel at her humble feet, he realized she had a beauty of the spirit the likes of which he had seen in only two other people: his wife and her mother.

There was nothing pretentious about her—not her clothes, not the way she carried herself, not her smile, not anything. Her deportment was one of peace, calm, and kindness such as could only be attained through a lifetime spent in close proximity to God. She was a true lady.

Jack and Levi were men of considerable wealth and noble accomplishments. Someday, Michael would match them in his own way. But as they sat there with Rose, they all realized they were in the presence of one greater than themselves, one who humbled herself in the service of God and His children and in doing so had achieved immeasurable, immortal greatness.

The time fairly flew, and Michael said, "Well, folks, it's time for me to make my lemonade run. So if you'll excuse me, Miss Rose, I'll be on my way."

He stood and tipped his hat to the lady.

Jack said, "I'll walk you to the truck, son. I'll be right back, Miss Rose."

As they walked toward the truck, they could hear Levi explaining the lemonade run to Rose. When Jack and Michael arrived at the truck, Jack pulled out a piece of paper and a pencil and began to write.

After a few seconds, he handed the paper to Michael with some money and said, "Do me a favor, son. Take this to the telegraph office, and don't leave until he sends it. He'll know who to send it to. There's more than enough money there. You can keep the change for your trouble."

"You know it's no trouble, Jack."

"You keep it anyway. Now go on or you'll be late and your uncle will fuss at you."

When Michael arrived at the hotel, he trotted to the telegraph office, where he and the telegrapher read the message together to determine the cost.

It read, "I have found her. I have found her. Praise God, I have found her. But for the years, she is unchanged. If anything, she is even finer now than then. Spread the word. I have found her. Praise the sweet Lord."

The telegrapher said, "You know, Michael, I can cut out a lot of this repetitive stuff and save Mr. Moses some money."

"No, sir. Just send it like it is," Michael said,

"Okay. Just thought I'd try to save him a little money."

"Thanks, but I don't think he wants it changed."

"He's got a note here that says to send it to the same person," the telegrapher said.

"Yeah. He said you'd know," Michael said.

"Yep, I've still got the one he sent yesterday. I'll just send this one to the same person down in Mobile. Tell him I'll take care of it."

"He told me not to leave until you send it, and I'm in a little bit of a hurry."

"Oh, okay. I'll just do it now."

Michael watched the man send the telegram. He paid him and pocketed the change. Then he ran to the restaurant to pick up the lemonade and tea. Nick had everything ready for him to load onto the truck.

For the Good of the Child

As he was loading the truck, Michael told Nick about them finding Rose. Nick had heard the story about her from Michael, as had Henry.

Nick said, "I want you to take Henry with you on this run. I want him to meet this lady."

As Michael watched Nick walk back into the restaurant, he realized that he had probably underestimated the man. He knew Nick to be a good man. His uncle had always been good to him, but Nick Camardo had never been a warm person. He was not the type to nurture anyone, not even a child. Big Mama had been the first to say that Nick believed in work, and lots of it, and it was an accurate statement. But now he wanted Henry to go to the reunion site, not for the good of the restaurant, but for the good of the child.

Michael recalled how Nick had come to Henry's defense against the Klansman. He remembered how he had stood up to the man, making his statement about there being some damages money won't fix. At that moment, he had been so proud of his uncle, but he never told him so. They had never had that kind of relationship.

Michael found Henry and told him about Nick's instructions. The boy could not hide his disbelief.

"You think I'm lying to you?" Michael said.

"Just let me check with Mr. Nick," Henry said as he began to turn.

Michael laughed as he grabbed his friend and pulled him toward the truck, saying, "You're coming with me, you little poot, and that's an order from Mr. Nick himself. It was his idea. You don't think I like you that much, do you? Now come on. We're running late."

"Okay. I believe you," Henry said. "But why does he want me to tag along with you? He needs me here more than you need me there."

"Because," Michael said, "we found Jack's friend, Miss Rose, and Nick wants you to meet her."

Henry was incredulous. He did not know miracles could come in pairs. First, after fifty years, Jack had found Miss Rose. Then Mr. Nick had ordered him, Little Henry Dewberry, to take off from work, with pay, so he could meet her.

After a few seconds of thought, he grabbed a menu and said, "What's she like?"

"Henry, she's so nice. You'll like her. She's such a lady."

When they arrived at the Great Tent, Michael told Henry where to find them.

"Don't worry about the lemonade and tea, Henry. I'm used to handling it alone. You just go on and find them, and take this with you."

Michael handed him a basket containing four glasses and said, "I know Jack and Doctor Brookner want lemonade, but I don't know what Miss Rose wants. So I put three lemonades and a tea in there. Give Miss Rose whatever she wants, and you take whatever is left after Jack and Doctor Brookner take their lemonade. I'll be over there as soon as I'm through here."

"Okay," Henry said, just happy to be included. "I don't care what I get, lemonade or tea. Either one is fine with me."

Michael was already busy selling cold drinks to thirsty men as Henry happily carried the basket to his friends.

Lemonade or Tea

He found them where Michael said they would be, the three of them talking quietly.

Henry walked up and said, "Hey, folks. I brought your refreshments."

"Henry!" Jack said. "I wasn't expecting you. Come here, son. I want you to meet someone."

Henry took a couple of more steps forward, and Jack gently put his hands on the child's shoulders, pointing him toward

Rose, and said, "Henry, I want you to meet a very special person in my life. I want you to meet Mrs. Rose Blount Taylor. Miss Rose, this is Master Henry Dewberry."

Rose held out her hand, and Henry very sheepishly shook it and said, "Pleased to meet you, ma'am."

"I'm very pleased to meet you too, Henry," Rose said.

"Henry, this is the lady who led me to the Lord just a couple of miles over there," Jack said pointing westward. "It was a while back when she was just a little girl."

"Yes, sir," Henry said. "I heard about her. Michael told me. And he gave me these drinks to bring to you. I've got lemonade and tea, Miss Rose. Which do you want?"

"I'll have lemonade, Henry. And thank you so much for remembering us," Rose said.

"And what will it be for you two gentlemen?" Henry asked.

"I'll have lemonade," Levi said.

"Well," Jack said, "I told Michael I wanted lemonade, but I've had a craving for tea flung on me. You don't happen to have an extra glass of tea on you, do you, Henry?"

"I sure do. Here you go. And I'll have lemonade," Henry said.

"Oh, Henry, did you want the tea?" Jack asked. "Did I get your tea?"

"No, sir. Lemonade is just fine with me. Honest."

Rose was smiling as she noted the tenderness with which Jack dealt with the child.

"Well, if you want the tea, speak up, but you better do it quick 'cause I'm about to jump in," Jack said.

Henry grinned and took a big, noisy slurp of lemonade and said, "Too late now, Jack. I just jumped in."

They laughed and began enjoying their refreshments.

"Where's Michael?" Levi asked.

"He's over there selling drinks," Henry said.

"Why aren't you helping him?" Jack asked.

"Nick gave me a little time off so I could meet Miss Rose," Henry said.

After a pause, Jack looked at Levi and said, "Well! Nick Camardo did that?"

"Yes, sir. He told Michael he wanted me to meet her," Henry said.

Jack and Levi smiled at each other.

"Perhaps Mr. Nick's love of work, and lots of it, has been overstated," Jack said.

"Or perhaps," Levi said, "Mr. Nick has changed just a little over the last few days. People can change, you know."

"Yes. I've heard of such things," Jack said.

"You seem to have changed quite a bit yourself, Mr. Jack," Rose said. "The man I first saw fifty years ago bears very little resemblance to the one who sits before me now. I must say, I like the change."

"Well," Jack said, "if a man doesn't change in fifty years, it's probably because he's been dead all that time. I have changed from a young man to an old one. But thanks to a certain little girl's prayers, I was given the opportunity to change while so many around me were not so blessed."

"The kind of change I see in you only comes from living close to God," Rose said. "I'm probably the only person still living who saw you back then and who would be in a position to note the change."

"Well, there might be one more who came close to seeing me they way I was," he said, glancing toward Levi. "But I think you're probably right. I reckon you're the only one. I did meet a few men yesterday who remembered me from back then. But they didn't really know me, only my reputation. By your statement, I'm assuming your parents and your grandfather have all passed on."

She nodded in the affirmative.

"I'm so sorry, Miss Rose. They were fine people," Jack said.

"Thank you, Mr. Jack. But don't you worry about them. All of them were ready to go. You'll see them again someday," she said with a smile.

The four of them enjoyed a leisurely few minutes sipping their cool drinks in the shade. Like the others, Henry was completely at ease in the presence of Miss Rose. Now he knew what Michael was talking about when he said she was such a lady. She was truly different from anyone he had ever known. His own grandmother was a good woman. But Big Mama did not have the humble, yet almost regal bearing Miss Rose had. He found himself enjoying her company very much. He was sweetly smitten. She seemed to be very interested in Henry.

"Henry, what plans do you have for your life?" she asked. "Are you going to continue at the restaurant with your grandmother? I hope you understand just what a wonderful gift it is to be free to make plans, free to hope. You should appreciate that and take your life plans very seriously. The man who gave me that gift is sitting right beside you now."

"Who, Jack? I thought Mr. Lincoln did that."

Levi chuckled a little.

Rose smiled and said, "For many, perhaps. But for me and my family, that man was Private Jack Moses of the Confederate Army. He and a small group of his friends did it at great personal risk. You must take your life and your freedom very seriously, Henry. Many people sacrificed much to provide it for you. Enjoy it, but don't waste it. It is far too great a gift to trifle with."

Henry looked at Jack next to him, who seemed to be a little uncomfortable on being so publicly praised, and said, "Yes, ma'am. I take my future very seriously. I don't plan to stay at the restaurant any longer than necessary. I plan to be a doctor."

"A doctor?" Jack said, surprised. "I thought you wanted to be a teacher."

"I did, but I've been praying about it, and I think God wants me to be a doctor."

"Oh, dear," Jack said as he looked at Levi, "another one."

Levi smiled and quietly asked, "Henry, what are your marks like? Do you do well in school?"

"Yes, sir," he said. "I have good marks. I'm one of the best in my grade. I'll graduate in three years."

Then Henry looked back toward the truck and said, "I'd better go check on Michael. He might need a little help. Please excuse me, Miss Rose."

"Certainly, Henry," she said.

They watched him trot away; then Jack said, "That child means a lot to me, Levi. I'm afraid I won't be around in three years to see that he's taken care of when he graduates."

"Sure you will, Jack," Levi said. "Don't you remember? You're a resilient old poo—person."

"Yeah, but when you're my age and you have a bad ticker, you learn not to plan things too far out," Jack said. "But what about your end of it, Levi? Could he get into your school?"

"Only if his marks are as good as he says they are and he is strong in science and math. And, as you know, he needs good recommendations from his teachers about his character and his willingness to work."

"We both know what a hard worker he is, and I'll vouch for his character," Jack said.

"Jack, we've known the boy three days. I'll have to talk to his teachers."

"We've known him as long as we've known Michael."

"And we talked to Michael's schoolmaster," Levi said. "Jack, don't worry about it. I'll stay in touch with Henry through Michael. Henry still has a lot of growing up to do, but he has three years in which to do it. By then I'll know if he qualifies for admittance. If he qualifies, I'll save a spot for him. I promise. He'll be our first student of color. But by then, who knows, he may have decided to become a teacher again."

"Yeah, well, either way, I need to figure out how to provide him with a scholarship, even though I might not be around anymore," Jack said. "I've got a feeling his grades are as good as he says. Even if he decides to be a teacher, that will still require a scholarship. I'll write a letter to my children tonight."

"But you're going home tomorrow," Levi said. "You'll probably get home before the letter does."

"I know, but nevertheless, I'll write a letter tonight and just put it in my coat pocket. If anything happens before I get home, they'll give it to my children."

Levi could see that Jack was truly concerned about dying before he could arrange Henry's scholarship.

"Jack, nothing's going to happen," he said. "But go ahead and write your letter if it makes you feel any better. And don't forget that I'll be in touch with your children from time to time in regard to Michael. If necessary, I'll tell them about our conversation here today."

"Yes, that will help. But I'll write my letter anyway," Jack said. "And you're right, Levi. Henry has a lot of growing up to do. But everyone is entitled to a childhood. Henry is still in his, but I'm confident that he'll grow into a fine man in due time."

"Michael and I will keep an eye on him for you," Levi said. "I won't forget him, Jack. You can trust me."

Jack slowly smiled and patted Levi on the knee and said, "Of that, my friend, I have no doubt."

Rose observed in silence, smiling faintly as she watched two old men making provisions for a young man's future. As she watched, she realized that her prayers for Jack over the last half century had been answered many times over. She had never really doubted that they would be. But it was nonetheless heartening for her, knowing what he had been, to now see before her eyes a kindhearted, God-filled old gentleman more concerned about the wellbeing of a little colored boy than his own seemingly imminent passing.

Thinking back to that night so long ago when she was still just a little girl, Rose remembered her wise, kindly grandfather; her sweet mother; and her brave father. They were all gone now, passed on to their rewards. She thought of how blessed she was to have been a part of that sweet little family and how fortunate they had been when they lived in Virginia to have had such gentle, loving masters as the old man and his wife. And she remembered her old friend who was sitting before her now: Wiley Jackson Moses. What a beautiful young man he had been—tall, strong, and fearless. She remembered his handsome face when she had spoken to him about Jesus and how that formidable man had stooped to hug her and thank her for what she had done. And she recalled how he and two of his brave friends had led them to freedom. And yet now all he could talk about was what he owed her. Yes, her prayers had been answered. She found herself wiping a small tear with the handkerchief he had given her.

She heard him say, "Are you all right, Miss Rose?"

"Yes, Mr. Jack. I'm just fine," she answered as she looked into his face, no longer young, but still fearless and so kind. "Thank you for asking."

Michael and Henry soon appeared, their lemonade and tea duties fulfilled.

"What's next on your schedule, Michael?" Jack asked.

"Henry and I need to return to the restaurant to help Uncle Nick get ready for the lunch run. Now that we've found Miss Rose, I need to help him, so I guess we'll see you then. Do you two want your usual?"

"I do," said Jack.

"Me too," said Levi.

"How about you, Miss Rose?" Jack asked. "What do you want for lunch?"

"Here. I have a menu for you," Michael said as he handed it to her.

"How thoughtful of you, Michael," she said.

"Actually, it was Henry's idea," Michael admitted. "He's the thoughtful one."

They all smiled at Henry while he smiled at the ground.

"Thank you, Henry," she said.

"You're welcome, Miss Rose."

She placed her order, and the boys departed.

Army Sawbones

It was late morning, and President Wilson was not scheduled to speak until 1:30 p.m. They had some time to kill before lunch, so Jack and Levi escorted Rose to the main hospital tent. There were several nurses on duty there, and the army had set up sanitary facilities exclusively for them so a lady could powder her nose, as Jack put it.

As one of the nurses showed Rose to their facilities, Jack and Levi looked around.

"See anybody you know?" Jack asked. "Do you know any of these doctors?"

"No," Levi said. "These are all army doctors. I don't know any of them."

"Well," Jack said, "if I get sick again while I'm here, I want you to tend to me yourself. Please don't relinquish me to any of these military sawbones. I saw enough of them when I was in the army."

"That was a long time ago, Jack, and a different army, I might add. These men are pretty good from what I've seen," Levi said.

"Yeah, I reckon our doctors did the best they could under some mighty tough circumstances. I'm just grateful they never had to treat me for anything."

"If they never treated you, how did you come in contact with them?" Levi asked.

"Well," Jack said, "after Gettysburg, I was a chaplain's assistant for a while. His business took me to the field hospital frequently. I have to admit this place looks mighty nice compared to what we had. These doctors seem to be mighty relaxed and calm. Our fellows were so frantic and busy sawing off arms and legs that I made it a point not to get too close to them for fear I would get snatched up and quartered. I felt almost as sorry for the doctors as I did for their patients. It was a horrid mess, Levi. But I reckon you know all about that."

"Well, actually it has been my good fortune never to have

been placed in a situation like that, either as a patient or a physician, except, of course, for the time I was treated for a broken nose," Levi said. "I was a lucky soldier."

"It wasn't luck, Levi. You were blessed," Jack said. "We both were. We still are."

The Greatest Among Us

As the three of them walked back to the Great Tent, they talked, and Jack learned that Rose's husband had passed away about two years earlier. She had two children: a son and a daughter. They were both educators in the Philadelphia school system. She was a grandmother. He also learned that she had been a nurse all her adult life. She, like Levi, lived and worked in Philadelphia. But where Levi worked in his own hospital, clinic, and medical school with his relatively affluent clientele, Rose had, for decades, toiled in public hospitals, working shifts and tending to Philadelphia's poorest citizens.

Jack was so proud of her. There was no doubt in his mind that his prayers had been answered. She was a good nurse. She was a fine lady, as fine as any he had ever known. She fairly glowed with godliness. People were drawn to her. Yet she was humble and quiet.

Jack caught himself staring at her more than once. After fifty years of yearning to see her, he just couldn't look at her enough. He was proud to be seen with her, to be seen tending to her every need. He doted on her like a loving son dotes on his mother.

They sat in the shade of the tent and passed the time sharing stories of the last five decades of their lives. Some were happy, some funny, and some sad. As Jack had said many times, such is life.

The crowd was growing larger in anticipation of the president's visit in a couple of hours. There were still veterans telling their stories from the platform, the same platform from which President Wilson would speak after lunch.

After a man from Wisconsin finished his story, Jack watched him step down and take his seat. He was looking toward the man and away from Rose. He turned his head and noticed Levi holding her hand, helping her up the steps to the platform. A hush fell over the crowd as she walked to the lectern. She smiled as the last of the whispers died. From at least two thousand men, the only sound that could be heard was one poor soul's stomach growling loudly and long. Then she spoke with a surprisingly strong voice.

"Gentlemen, my name is Rose Taylor. I am a nurse. I live in Philadelphia. I, like many of you, was here fifty years ago. As you might suspect, I was not in anyone's army. I was too young."

There was some laughter as she continued. "I was only eleven years old, and as you may have guessed by now, I was a slave."

The crowd grew still quieter. She had the complete attention of every man there.

"I was born in Virginia. My parents and my grandfather and I all belonged to an elderly couple who had a little farm in northern Virginia. They were very kind to us. We were blessed in that way. They even taught us to read, which was against the law in many places. But after his wife died, the old man wanted us to leave. He told us we were free, and he gave us a wagon and a pair of mules and told us to head north to Pennsylvania. We would have gone east toward Maryland, but we thought Mr. Lee's army was between us and that state, so we did as Master told us. We headed for Pennsylvania, not knowing that General Lee would meet us here.

"We were captured by the Confederates just outside Gettysburg. We and our wagon and mules were handed over to a group of men from Alabama who were given the responsibility of delivering us to the provost to be returned to Virginia and slavery.

"I had been free for less than a month. Even though I missed my home in Virginia, I loved my freedom. It broke my heart to have it so close at hand but yet so far out of my reach. It saddened me still more to see my parents and grandfather quietly grieving over our lost liberty."

By now, some of the Southerners had dropped their gaze to the ground.

"But God, in His kind wisdom, placed us in the custody of godly men. There was a heated discussion, and even a fight, but they decided to disobey their orders and set us free. They all could have been shot for their actions, but they decided to do what Jesus would have them do. Three of them were chosen to lead us out of the Confederate lines to safety at great risk to them. We had to go through several guard posts. But after we passed the last one and had traveled perhaps another mile in the moonlight, we stopped. The soldiers told us we were on our own. We were free. Afterward, my grandfather said that when the Yankee president tells you you're free, that's nice, but it doesn't necessarily make you free. But when a Confederate soldier tells you you're free, you're truly free."

The old Southerners were no longer looking at the ground. They raised their gaze to look into her eyes. They saw God's love and forgiveness. They saw a godly lady. They saw a countryman.

She continued. "As our wagon pulled away and we left those three brave men standing in the night, I thanked God for them, for their love of Jesus and his teachings. I prayed for them, and for one in particular, for they faced a terrible battle the next day. I have learned today that those dozen or so Rebel soldiers who gave me and my family our freedom so long ago all perished the following afternoon in Pickett's Charge, all save one, the one for whom I prayed so fervently. Of the men who so bravely gave us our liberty, he alone survived and is here today.

"For half of one century I have prayed for this day, the day on which I would find this man to thank him for his courageous act of kindness toward me and my family. His name is Wiley

Jackson Moses, and I want him to join me on this platform so he can receive the recognition he so richly deserves."

Wiping his eyes, Jack stood and slowly mounted the platform next to Rose. They embraced to the vigorous applause and cheers of the men. After a few seconds, Jack raised his hand, and they became quiet.

"Friends," he said, "Miss Rose would have you believe that I am some sort of hero or maybe even a saint. Even though everything she said was true, she left out some rather pertinent points. She forgot to say that the fight she mentioned was between her father and me. I fully intended to kill the man. But just before I could deliver what I expected to be the deathblow, she bravely stepped between us. Some of you may have been here two days ago when I told my story of how an eleven-year-old slave girl led me to Jesus. Well, Miss Rose is that little girl.

"She stepped between me and her father just as I was about to murder him. Yes, I was a terrible, useless man, owned by Satan. Miss Rose stared me down. Right there and then, Jesus convicted me of my sins. I didn't know what was happening. I just knew that it was more than I could bear, because my sins were great.

"She stared at me till I could stand no more. Then I ran away into the night, the Lord thrashing my soul all the way. I don't know how long I was gone, but after I snuck back into camp, she found me and talked to me about Jesus when everybody else was afraid to even come near me. She helped me pray the sinner's prayer, and I got saved that very night. For me, nothing has been the same since. Except for Jesus himself, I owe her more than anyone who ever lived.

"I reckon what I'm trying to say is this: in spite of what she said while ago, she is the brave one, not I. She is the hero, not I. And if there is a saint here today, it is most certainly Miss Rose, not I. It is I who owes her everything. She owes me nothing."

Then, smiling at Rose, he said, "She got it all exactly backward. And it was her prayers the next day that saw me safely through the charge. Of the men in my squad, I alone survived into a long, happy life because of Mrs. Rose Blount Taylor and her saintly prayers. She is the greatest among us."

"And now, gentlemen," he added, "if you will excuse us, I'm going to escort Miss Rose over to the mess tent and treat her to some of that free army ice cream."

The men stood and delivered a strong, lengthy applause as Jack helped her down from the platform. He took her hand and led her through the parting sea of blue and gray, followed at a respectful distance by Levi. Old heads were bared by the hundreds as the crowd divided before them, the somewhat more courtly Southerners—hats in hands—nodding, almost bowing ever so slightly.

So often, the greatest among us are anonymous in this world. They lead lives of quiet, unacknowledged service to God and His children. They travel almost unnoticed through a world obsessed with self. Only those closest to them know of their greatness. But they speak not of it, for they know the acclamation of man only serves to embarrass them. Their humility is such that they deem themselves unworthy of even the faintest praise. They pass from this world as quietly as they pass through it. Their glory comes not in this life but the next. Rose was such a person.

Never in her life had she been publicly recognized for any of the countless selfless, godly acts she had performed. It had never occurred to her that any was due. She knew she had treasures awaiting her in heaven.

Yet God, in His kindness, allowed His humble child to experience this one fleeting moment of worldly glory, not because she wanted it, but because Jack had been praying for it for fifty years. It was an answer to his prayers, not hers.

As he led her through the crowd of admirers, he fairly beamed with pride at having her by his side, on his arm. She had a noble, yet humble grace that comes only through a lifetime of self-denial and service to God.

After they left the crowd behind them on the way to the mess tent, Levi caught up with them and said, "Jack, don't you know you shouldn't be eating ice cream so close before lunch?"

"I know, Levi," he said, "but I'm hot. It's been a long time since I've spoken to so large a crowd, and ice cream is the strongest thing they're serving right now. Besides, we'll just eat a little bit, won't we, Miss Rose?"

Rose smiled and nodded as she said, "Yes. Doctor Brookner, we'll be sure to take little bitty bites."

A Young Jewish Man

The three of them were still talking happily when they arrived at the mess tent and requested just one scoop each. Good to his word, Jack only ate a little, as did Rose. Levi, however, returned for a second scoop, only to be laughingly chided by Jack for eating so much just before lunch.

It was a pleasant little while. The three of them talked and acted a little silly as they ate their ice cream. Pretending to get a headache from his cold treat, Jack grabbed the bridge of his nose and crossed his eyes, thus eliciting girlish giggles from Miss Rose and solemn headshaking from a barely amused Levi.

Jack said, "That little routine usually gets big laughs out of my little ones. But as they grow older, I have to work a lot harder to get results. But not long ago, I observed one of them using it to pretty good effect on his friends."

"Oh my, what a sobering thought," Levi said. "Yet another Jack Moses is being reared in Alabama as we speak."

"I truly hope so," Rose said.

Jack said, "Levi, I thought you were about to tell me that my eyes could stick that way and how silly I would look riding the train cross-eyed all the way to Alabama."

"No, my friend," Levi said in feigned disgust. "I've given up on you. I've decided that your grandchildren are right. You really are just an old poot."

Jack laughed heartily, and much to Levi's relief, so did Rose.

"Is that what they call you?" she asked.

"Behind my back." He proudly nodded. "They don't know I know. I have always thought of it as a term of endearment. But the good doctor thinks it is an apt description of me."

"I'm sure," Rose said, "that it is a sweet term of endearment."

"Thank you, Miss Rose," Jack said, vindicated.

"As well as an apt description," she added.

"Thank you, Miss Rose," Levi said after they had stopped laughing.

The three of them enjoyed the ice cream and the company for a while in the mess tent as guests of the US Army.

Their lives forever linked by the battle, Jack and Rose had always known of their connection. But only recently had Jack and Levi become aware of theirs. Through Jack, Levi had also been made aware of his own debt to Rose, and he felt the need to say something.

"Jack," he said, "with your permission, I would like to tell Miss Rose our story. I think she has a right to know."

After a few seconds of thought, Jack said, "Permission granted. Go ahead."

Perplexed, Rose looked toward Levi.

Levi said, "Rose, Jack and I met here at the battle on the day of the charge. We only discovered this two days ago when we were telling our stories at the Great Tent. I was in the Seventy-first Pennsylvania, which was one of the units at the top of Cemetery Ridge during Pickett's Charge. Jack and I met up there. I charged him with my bayonet. He was unarmed, having lost his rifle on the way up. He brushed my charge aside with his left arm and smashed my nose with his right fist. Then he took my rifle, and, with all his might—and he was a mighty man then—"

"Yes, I remember," Rose said.

"He thrust it down, barely missing me. I expected him to

pull it out of the ground and try again. But instead he bent down and said, 'Stay down, son.'"

Rose was smiling knowingly by now. "I can assure you, Doctor Brookner, if you had had that encounter twenty-four hours earlier, you would not be here today."

"I know," Levi said. "That's why I brought it up. Jack has thanked you for what you did for him. I, too, wish to thank you for what you did, for in helping him, you almost certainly saved my life. I owe you almost as much as Jack does. Thank you!"

Rose smiled at Levi and gently touched his hand and said, "Doctor Brookner, you owe me nothing. Jack owes me nothing. We all, yourself included, owe everything to a young Jewish man named Jesus. It all began with His love, and that is what has delivered us, all three of us, to this day."

Levi smiled in silence. He knew he was looking at a God-filled lady. Nor did Jack speak. He, too, just gazed at her, a tranquil smile of loving respect on his face.

Day Turned to Evening

It was a nice summer day, and time fairly flew as the three of them talked and laughed.

Seemingly from nowhere, Little Henry appeared, saying, "Hey, everybody. It's time to eat. They told us where you were, and Michael sent me down here to get you. Your food is waiting for you in the big tent."

"Let's go, y'all," Jack said.

Michael had their meals ready for them. It was just him and Henry. Nick had stayed at the restaurant because he could not take the time to hear the president speak. He and Big Mama would have to work doubly hard through lunch, but they wanted the boys to see and hear the president. So instead of the usual practice of returning to the restaurant, Michael and Henry would stay for as long as it took President Wilson to finish his speech. They were both pretty excited about it.

After lunch, the five of them made their way toward the main stage, the one from which the president would address the crowd. Much to their delighted surprise, they discovered that some of the veterans had saved the three chairs they had occupied an hour or so earlier. Henry and Michael, both young and fit, found standing room nearby.

The president and his party soon appeared on the stage, accompanied by a brisk performance of "Hail to the Chief," performed by a large army band. After the usual gaudy introduction, he stood and strode to the podium to fairly enthusiastic applause. There were a good many people from the town in attendance. Many army personnel were there to hear the man speak. It was a big day for Gettysburg.

Jack thought highly of President Wilson, but his mind wandered a little during the speech. It was his opinion that an honest politician is one who is no more corrupt than his profession requires him to be. In this regard, Jack respected Wilson. But sometimes he yearned for what he termed a slightly scandalous butt kicker, someone like Teddy Roosevelt, who, though far from perfect, could get things done.

But, Jack thought to himself, *Wilson will do. We need an occasional scholar in that office.*

At one point, the president referred to the battle as a great and terrible day.

Levi leaned over toward Jack and whispered, "I can't recall the greatness, but I'll never forget the terror."

Jack replied with a slight nod.

The president did not drone on as long as some had feared. He even said one thing that got Jack's attention. When referring to the veterans he said, "Their day has turned to evening."

That's right, Jack thought. *My day has turned to evening.* Then, looking at Rose, he thought, *but that day was mighty fine.*

It was not long before the president sat down to great applause and shouting, presumably, in Jack's estimation, in gratitude for the brevity of his speech as much as for its content.

Jack could not help but ask himself, *How in the world did a boy who can't lay it on any thicker than that ever get elected to the highest office in the land?*

Thousands of old men stood and clapped long and hard for the leader of their country. Now they could all say they had seen and heard the president. Nobody could ever take that away from them. Most would be hard-pressed to tell anyone what the man had said, but that was not the point. They had seen the critter. That was all that mattered.

All His Little Gifts

After the speech, there were a few photographers taking pictures of the president with various dignitaries and Union war heroes. Mr. Wilson apparently had pressing business elsewhere. The picture-taking session did not last long.

Jack said, "Michael, do you know any of those photographers? Is there a local man among them?"

"Yes, sir," Michael said, pointing to a tall slim man. "Mr. Plemons there has a studio in town."

"Does he do good work?"

"I guess so. He takes all the school pictures."

Jack quickly gathered his friends and herded them in the man's direction.

"Mr. Plemons," he said, "before you put your equipment away, I wonder if I could commission you to photograph my friends and me?"

Within minutes, Jack and Rose were standing in the bright sunshine trying hard to smile without squinting. They stood there, hand in hand, offering proof positive to their loved ones back home that they had found the person of whom a family legend had been made. Jack had his picture made with each of his four friends individually. Then he had a group picture made of the five of them together, Rose standing between Jack and Levi, with Michael standing behind Levi and Henry standing in front of Jack with Jack's hand on his shoulder. Then the boys had their picture made together with Rose; and Rose, Jack, and Levi had theirs made with Rose in the middle.

"Well, Mr. Plemons, do you think these will turn out all right?" Jack asked.

"I don't see why not," he replied. "We had good light and handsome subjects. How many copies do you want?"

"I want five copies of each print."

"Five copies for you?"

"No. One copy of each print for each of the five of us. We will give you our addresses, and you can mail them to us, except for Michael and Henry. They can just pick theirs up at your studio," Jack said.

"Do you want five-by-sevens?"

"No. Let's go with eight by tens. My eyes aren't what they use to be. So total it up, and I'll write you a check for all of it. And don't forget to figure in the postage."

Levi had finally given up on paying for anything when Jack was around. The two boys were more than happy to let Jack cover it since they were both virtually penniless. Henry had fifty dollars, but he was saving that. Rose understood why Jack wanted to pay everyone's way. He was receiving a sweet blessing in his old age. At this point in his life, money meant very little to him. He felt that money was worthless unless it was used. It was a tool with which to do good. To Jack, a pile of idle money was not worth any more than a pile of rusty nails. Rose did not want to deny him his blessing. In her love for him, she just smiled graciously and accepted all his little gifts.

Smiling at Yesterday

Michael and Henry returned to the restaurant to prepare for the afternoon lemonade and tea run. The other three found a nice breeze in the shade of the tent and spent some time relaxing and talking about anything that came to mind. A young man wearing a kilt and carrying bagpipes mounted the stage and began playing some Scottish and Irish airs and a few hymns. Afterward, he stepped down, hot and sweating.

Levi offered him a chair, saying, "Here. Sit down and cool off a little."

Jack sternly added, "And remember what your mama told you about keeping your knees together. There's a lady present."

The man glanced toward the ever-demure Rose and then back toward Jack's grim countenance and slowly closed his knees.

This would be their last day at the reunion. Levi and Rose were leaving for Philadelphia the next day on the morning train. Jack was leaving a few hours later on the five o'clock train, or what he called the evening train. He had begun thinking of it in that manner when he heard Mr. Wilson say that his day had turned to evening.

Rose was becoming concerned about the sweet old man who was doting on her every wish. He seemed happy, but he also appeared to be convinced that his death was close at hand.

"Jack," she said, "are you looking forward to going home tomorrow?"

"Very much so," he said. "My little ones bring me so much joy. They keep me young and laughing. I even miss my old cat. She's useless, self-centered, and sweet. She talks too much, and she likes to spend lots of time in my lap. She's just the way I like them. But, Rose, I have to admit that I dread our parting tomorrow. I'm not sure how well I'll hold up."

"I know what you mean," she said. "I hate to lose you again. But, Jack, let's not be sad. Remember, the Bible says to be happy in all things. Just think of what we've been given. We found each other. Our prayers were answered. Soon, it will be time for us to part again, to go home to our loved ones. Let's make these last few hours happy ones. After all, we now have each other's address. We can correspond. I expect to hear from you often. Please don't be sad. You and I are singularly blessed. We share a unique blessing, and that blessing unites us for eternity. Nothing, not even death, can take that away from us. Someday, it will unite us again forever."

Jack was smiling again as he said, "You're right, Rose. I feel better already. Once again, you have come to my rescue. Dying doesn't frighten me. After all, it's only death. It's just a part of life, just as birth is. And now that I've found you, I am a satisfied man. Whenever the Lord takes me home, He will be taking a man at peace. Thanks to you, I can smile at yesterday and look forward to tomorrow when paradise will stretch out endlessly before me. I'm all set to go."

It seemed like just a short while until Michael reappeared with lemonade and tea. It would not be long before he would be on his way back to the restaurant with his three passengers. The evening was quickly passing away.

Jack and Levi had made a few friends at the reunion, and they would occasionally see one of them walk by and spend a few minutes with them, saying good-bye and wishing them well.

It was only about forty-five minutes after he had arrived with lemonade and tea that it was time to for Michael to take the three of them to town and away from the reunion forever. Michael helped Rose into the rear seat of the truck, and Jack climbed up next to her. Levi sat in front with Michael.

As they slowly began their trip back to town, Jack sat quietly as he gazed for the final time up the rise toward the stone wall. He turned and watched the battlefield recede in the distance. They crossed the little stream where he and Michael had stopped on his first day there. He watched the Robinson house go by and hoped to see the children playing in the yard, but they were not there.

They went by the little side street where Esau Johnson's shop was located. Jack could see it a little ways down the street. But there were no signs of life. The large doors were closed.

Well, he thought, *that's okay. Hopefully, I'll see them all tomorrow.*

Big Mama's Cake

They arrived at the hotel, and Michael directed Rose to the ladies' parlor so she could freshen up. She was staying at a colored lady's house, the friend of an acquaintance. But she would join Jack and the others at the restaurant for supper. Afterward, Michael and Jack would deliver her to the house where she was staying.

Jack and Levi each retired to their rooms for a few minutes to clean up for supper. Nick had reserved a large, round table for them. There would be five in all since Michael and Henry were joining them. Jack was picking up the tab, as usual. No one resisted. Nick had given Michael and Henry an hour off. Jack thought that was pretty decent of him considering it would probably be a busy hour.

Supper went well. Michael and Henry, it seemed, were a pretty good comedy team. They kept the old folks laughing through the meal.

It came time for dessert, and Rose, Jack, and Levi were trying to decide between apple cobbler and pecan pie. Michael and Henry merely smiled at each other and looked toward the kitchen door as Big Mama proudly marched out holding a large, white birthday cake with five candles on it, placing it on the table in front of Jack. Nick, Big Mama, and the two boys all burst into a raucous version of "For He's a Jolly Good Fellow." Rose and Levi applauded in delight, but Jack was quiet, truly surprised, and touched.

Big Mama said, "I know it's a couple of days late, Mr. Jack, but such as it is, happy birthday! And it has five candles on it. One for you, and one for each of your friends seated this table, and also because I couldn't find room for no eighty-three candles on that cake."

As they were smiling at Jack, he stood and said, "Thank you, Big Mama. You're too kind. But you're two candles short: one for you, and one for Nick."

He hugged her, and with one arm still around her, he said, "I reckon I'm supposed to say something, but I don't know what to say except thank you all. And if I had another earthly life to live, I think I would just move up here and spend it with you sweet, wonderful people. I never knew it was possible to grow so fond of so many people in so short a time. You each know how dearly I hold you, all six of you, in my heart. Here we are, this little band of friends, young and old, black and white, Jew and Gentile. I will never forget you. May the good Lord abundantly bless each of you."

Jack paused a few seconds, and then, as he gazed at the smiling faces of his friends and then at the cake, he said, "Now, I want a big piece with lots of icing."

The laughter returned, and they all had some cake with a glass of Big Mama's ice cold, tart lemonade.

After washing his cake down, Jack said, "Big Mama, your cooking is just unbearably delicious. I don't suppose you would consider a proposal of marriage, would you? Remember, I don't smoke or drink, and I just cuss a little bit."

"Law, Mr. Jack, you ain't serious!" she said, a little embarrassed.

"What's wrong? Is that little bit of cussing too much for you?" Jack said with a grin.

"Naw, it ain't that. You probably don't cuss no more than I do, 'cept I just keep mine to myself."

"Then I reckon you think I'm too old for you. Is that it?" Jack said, still smiling.

"I swan, Mr. Jack. I've done been there, and I don't care to go back. I've never understood why folks marry time after time. Why in the world would anyone who's been married want to be married?"

"Yes." Levi nodded. "It is my observation that marriage has a way of ending shallow relationships."

Jack smiled and quietly said, "I tell you this, Big Mama. If I could go back and do it all over again with my sweet Sally, I wouldn't hesitate one second. For me, marriage was wonderful."

"Then you were blessed, Mr. Jack," she said.

"That I was," he admitted as he smiled. "Love was good to me. Fortunate indeed, and rare, is he whose heart has never been torn by love. And so, blessed I remain. Your fine Southern cooking has been a real blessing for me. I can't tell you how nice it has been having all this good food way up here in Yankee land. It has sustained me in a far country."

"Well," Big Mama said, "us Southerners gotta stick together."

"Yes," Jack said direly. "We have to watch these Yankees like a blame hawk."

"Ain't that the truth," she said as she cut her eyes toward a grinning Nick.

Henry asked, "Can we have some more cake?"

"What y'all need with more cake? You'd just eat it," she said.

"Well..." Henry said, a little bewildered.

"Sure you can," she said, laughing. "But I'll cut it myself. I've seen how you and Michael cut a cake. How 'bout you, Jack? You want another piece of cake?"

"No, ma'am," he said. "I better not."

"Why not?" she asked. "There's plenty left."

"Why not? Because I'd just eat it. When it comes to cake, I'm just as bad as the boys."

"Well," she said smiling, "I'll cut you a big piece and keep it in the kitchen for you to pick up tomorrow afternoon before you leave. How's that?"

"That's fine," he said. "I'll have it on the train tomorrow evening after supper. A fellow always needs something to look forward to—a piece of cake, a sunrise. Just about any little old thing will do."

It was a pleasant evening for all of them, a time they would each hold dear for as long as they lived.

After the festivities, Jack and Michael delivered Rose to the place she was staying. Michael returned Jack to the hotel, and he retired to his room to prepare for bed. He said his prayer and ended it as always, with his special little prayer for Rose.

"Lord, be with her always. And let her always be a good nurse. And, Lord, thank You for sending her to me again and for letting a sinner such as I live to see this day."

He paused, and then added, "And, Lord, when my time comes, please let this poor, unworthy servant depart in peace. In Jesus's name, I pray. Amen."

He climbed into bed, but he was restless and had trouble falling asleep. He thought the problem might be that big piece of cake with lots of icing.

Finally, to settle his mind, he thought of one of his favorite hymns. As he recalled the words, his mind began to calm. As sleep approached, he softly sang to his Savior.

> Jesus keep me near the cross,
>
> There a precious fountain,
>
> Free to all, a healing stream,
>
> Flows from Calv'ry's mountain.
>
> In the cross, in the cross
>
> Be my glory ever,
>
> Till my raptur'd soul shall find
>
> Rest beyond the river.

SATURDAY, JULY 5TH

Good-bye, Miss Rose

It was early, and the cool of the night lingered as his last day began. The sun was low and the shadows long, much as his first morning in Gettysburg had been. Jack had awoken in time to watch darkness flee the dawn as the sun peeked through his open window. Long ago, a dear friend had admonished him to savor the sunrise, for each is a gift from God. And so he did.

The four of them—Rose, Levi, Michael, and Jack—met for breakfast at the restaurant, Michael having fetched Rose earlier. There was no longer any question of who would pay the tab. Michael happily acquiesced and ate like a field hand, as Jack put it. Levi felt compelled to protest at least a little, if only very quietly. Rose graciously accepted Jack's gesture with a quiet, "Thank you." She knew how much it meant to him to do something, even the smallest thing, for his friends, and especially for her.

Not much was said as they ate together. Little Henry passed by a time or two in the dispatch of his duties but had only enough time to smile and say hello and little else. Jack wanted very much to spend some time with him before he left town. But right now, Rose and Levi were on his mind. They were leaving together for Philadelphia on the morning train.

They all remained quiet as they waited at the depot. Michael was standing near the tracks, watching and listening for the first sign of the train. Levi, Jack, and Rose were sitting on a bench together, Rose between the two men. She and Jack were holding hands and looking almost like a married couple. Occasionally, someone would stare briefly or glance back for a second look. But many of the old veterans and most of the townspeople had heard their story by now and understood their relationship.

Rose spent most of the time smiling at her old friend and patting his hand in hopes of consoling him. Jack, however, could barely bring himself to look at her, so great was his grief at the thought of losing her again.

Finally, he turned to her and said, "Rose, there's nothing I can say to tell you how grateful I am for what you did for me all those years ago. I lack the words. I'm not even sure the words exist that convey the depth of my gratitude. What I owe you cannot be calculated in this life. Nothing I do can ever repay you. I don't want you to leave without knowing that."

Jack was fighting back the tears, but Rose did not even try. She smiled at him as she wept.

"Jack," she said, "don't forget what you did for me and my family. My parents and my grandfather spoke so lovingly about you until the end of their days. My children and grandchildren think of you as the equal of Moses in the Bible, leading the children out of bondage. You are legend to us. We all love you."

"Rose, you know I love you. I named my daughter after you. When I met you, my life began. Ever since that night, I have lived to find you. Now that I have done that, I feel like my life is over. God has let me live long enough to find you and tell you that your prayers for me were not wasted. They were beautifully answered. I have lived a full, happy life close to Jesus. I have no regrets. All my prayers for us have been answered. I am so looking forward to seeing my children and little ones again. But if God, in His wisdom, takes me home before then, I want you to know that I am ready. I have my heart full of Jesus and my eyes full of a precious lady, the one I have been seeking all my life. I have not been cheated. No matter what happens now, I am going home. And it all began with a brave little girl a long time ago."

She could not speak, nor could he. There was nothing more to say. They sat there together holding hands and quietly shedding bittersweet tears.

The train arrived, and Michael appeared, gathering her luggage. The four of them walked to the train. Michael took her things onto the last car and arranged for her and Levi to sit together. They would be in Philadelphia in time for a late lunch.

Michael returned to the group on the platform and shook hands with Levi, who said, "I'll see you in a few weeks. I'll be in touch with you before then."

"Yes, sir, Doctor Brookner. I'll be there. I can't tell you how excited I am."

"Oh, the excitement will wear off when you've been there a little while. I have every confidence in you. You'll do just fine," Levi said.

"Come on, Miss Rose," he added. "We had better climb onto the train before it starts moving. I'm too old to run it down."

They chuckled, all save Jack.

He stared into Rose's eyes and said, "These are the arms I want to feel around my neck once more before I die."

She put her arms around his neck and kissed him softly on the cheek. They clung to each other for what to Levi seemed an eternity.

Then the man shouted, "All aboard!"

Levi said, "We really must go now, Miss Rose."

They broke their embrace, and Levi hurriedly shook Jack's hand. But Jack was watching Rose as Michael helped her onto the train. Levi climbed on board, and the two of them remained standing on the platform of the car, holding to the railing. The train began to move slowly, with Jack walking along beside it. She was so near that he reached out to her, and she managed to grasp his hand. The train began gaining speed and soon became too fast for an old man to keep up. Her hand pulled out of his, but he continued to walk to the end of the platform.

She said, "Good-bye, Jack. I love you, and I'll never forget you. Good-bye."

As he looked into her eyes, he instinctively removed his hat and held it high in a final, victorious good-bye while she waved her handkerchief in reply. And thus, they bade farewell until she passed from view. Slowly, he lowered his hat and held it over his heart, looking down the tracks long after she was gone.

The platform was vacant again, except for the old man gazing wistfully into the distance with his young friend by his side. They would stand there for some time in silence as Jack looked back into his life—a life he knew would soon end—and as Michael looked forward into his own.

Still peering down the tracks, Jack finally said, "Life."

"What? What did you say?"

"Life, son. What else can I say? Life. She gets on a train; waves good-bye; and, just like that, she's gone. A wonderful gift from a loving God. My time is near, Michael. I know it is."

Then he turned to his friend and said, "But that's just fine, son, because I've lived my life, and it can't be lost. And even though my time is ending, my life goes ever on."

They walked to the hotel in silence.

The Dove

As they arrived in front of the hotel, Jack said, "I need to visit Farmer Robinson's place. Can you take me there?"

"You know I can."

He helped Jack onto the truck and, after cranking it, climbed up beside him and slowly started for the Robinson place.

When they arrived, Mr. Robinson was not in sight, but his children were playing in the yard. Mrs. Robinson appeared at the door, and Michael explained to her that they were going to walk down to the creek to look at the inscription. Meanwhile, Jack was talking to the little ones. The morning's good-byes had left him a little depressed. But after a moment of conversation with the smiling children, his mood improved markedly.

As the two of them began the walk to the rock, Michael could not help but notice that a smile had returned to his friend's face.

"Feeling better now?" he asked.

"Oh, yes," Jack said. "I think the Lord put those youngsters out in their yard just to cheer me up and to remind me of my little ones back home. And also," he said as he patted Michael on his strong young back, "to remind a morose old man that life really does go on. I'm fine now, Michael. Thank you for asking."

When they arrived at the rock, Jack approached it in a circle, walking around to the sloped side at a distance, almost as if he were fearful of what he would see. After he had looked at it for a few seconds, a smile of relief appeared on his face.

"Come on around here," he said. "I want you to see this."

Michael stood beside him as they admired the stone together. The letters were not ornate. The words were easy to read and spread out across the stone in perfect balance. Above the inscription was the figure of a dove of peace with an olive branch in its beak.

"Read it to me, son," Jack said.

Michael looked at it a few more seconds and began.

AT THIS SPOT ON JULY 3, 1863
PRIVATE SILAS P. SWANN
FIFTH ALABAMA INFANTRY BATTALLION, C.S.A.
A SOLDIER OF THE SOUTH
AT AGE 17, PASSED FROM JORDAN'S STORMY BANKS
OVER TO CANAAN'S FAIR AND HAPPY LAND
"LET NOT YOUR HEART BE TROUBLED"
"TODAY YOU SHALL BE WITH ME IN PARADISE"
HE MADE IT TO THE TOP

After reading it aloud, Michael said, "That's very nice. I think Silas would like it."

"You're right. He does like it. I know it. And he likes this too," Jack said as he ran his hand over the likeness of a dove. "I think Mr. Esau Johnson did a mighty fine job. Mighty fine."

Michael nodded in agreement and said, "Let's sit down and rest a minute."

He was not tired, but he thought Jack might be. They sat on the usual sitting stone nearby. They could admire Mr. Johnson's work just fine from there.

Michael said, "You didn't ask him to put that dove on there, did you?"

"No. He did that on his own. It's so kind of him," Jack said.

"He'll probably charge extra," Michael said.

"Oh, Michael, can't you see that I don't care about the money. It doesn't matter. The dove is what matters. The money is a little thing, a transient thing. The dove … the dove is forever."

Then he patted Michael on the knee and added with a smile, "Someday, son, you'll understand. When you're an old man, you'll know what I'm talking about. It's hard for a young fellow who has to scrape for everything to understand just how insignificant money is in the long term. And right now, you're probably thinking that the people who say money isn't important are the ones who have plenty of it, and there may be some truth to that. But one of these days, after you've been a financially secure physician for a number of years, you'll understand what old Jack was trying to tell you way back here in 1913. You'll find yourself looking fondly back on these penniless days of your youth, and you'll realize that even though money is nice, it cannot by itself deliver real happiness, permanent happiness, to anyone. Real happiness, everlasting happiness, comes from having Jesus within. The Bible says to be happy in all situations. I've tried to do that. Often, I succeed. But sometimes I fail. But my sadness is always fleeting, and my happiness will be eternal because I have Jesus in my heart.

"Michael, I know some people who are rich but pitifully miserable. I know others who can barely keep body and soul together. Yet they are happy and at peace because they look to Jesus for their needs. As long as the world continues to put its hope for happiness in the accumulation of material wealth, it will continue to be disappointed. I was a happy man before I became a wealthy one. My wealth has neither added to nor detracted from my happiness. My happiness began on the night of July 2, 1863. You know the story. I was penniless, more penniless than you. Even my life was worthless. I was sure to die the next day. But as we started up that hill into those guns, I had a serene happiness about me. Why? Because I had Jesus."

"You're a true Christian, Jack. I don't think I've known anyone quite like you. I'm not so sure I can ever be like you."

"Sure you can, son. You can be a lot more than I ever was. You're way ahead of me when I was your age. Just pray every day. Read your Bible, and stay close to the Lord. You'll see. You'll see," Jack said as he placed a fatherly arm around the boy's shoulder.

There was a pause, and after gazing toward the inscription for a while, Michael said, "Jack, why do you think God let Silas die so young?"

After some thought, Jack said, "Well, I don't know. He has a purpose for everything He does, and He owes us no explanations. But sometimes, in His love, and for His own good reasons, which we may never understand, He takes back what is His and gives it to someone else. Mr. and Mrs. Swann sent their son off to war and lost him. What they got back was me. I became their beloved son and heir. I fathered their grandchildren in his stead. Their line continued through me rather than him. He died a boy, but here I am, old and full of years. Life is strange—fascinating, but strange. Or have I told you that already?"

"If you have, that's okay," Michael said. "You tell me as often as you like."

They stood, and Jack removed his hat as he took his last look at the rock.

He quietly said, "Good-bye, brother. I'll see you soon."

Then they left.

When they arrived back at the Robinsons' house, the farmer and his family were sitting on the porch and steps waiting for them.

Mr. Robinson met them in the yard, saying, "Good morning, Mr. Moses," as they shook hands. "Are you pleased with Mr. Johnson's work?"

"Very much so," Jack said. "I think he went above and beyond, as they say."

"Me too," said Robinson. "I think he did a fine job. It's a beautiful memorial for your friend, and I want you to know that we're proud to have it on our place. It means a lot to us. In fact, my wife and children have decided to plant flowers around it. That is, if you don't mind."

"Mind?" Jack said, "I think it's wonderful. And I'm sure young Silas appreciates it too. He was just a child himself, a child who had to grow all the way up all at once. He loved beautiful things. And I want to thank you, Mr. Robinson, you and your sweet family, for being so gracious about this thing. Without your kindness, that inscription would have forever remained just an old man's prayer. But now, thanks to your Christian heart, this old man can go home at peace."

Jack stooped and hugged the three children and shook hands again with Mr. and Mrs. Robinson. As he and Michael rode away, Jack and the Robinson family waved at each other until they were out of sight.

Then Jack said, "To Johnson's, Jehu."

An Enduring Gift

As they arrived, they saw that the big shop doors were open, but the place appeared deserted.

Michael shouted, "Mr. Johnson!"

Soon, he appeared from the back of the shop.

"Michael," he said. "Mr. Moses. Good to see you," he added as he shook hands with them. "It's Saturday, so my help is off today. I often come down on Saturday morning to piddle around and tidy things up a little."

"Hey," Jack said, "I might could help you out a little there. Piddling is my specialty. I've been doing it for years, ever since I retired."

"I envy you, Mr. Moses," Johnson said. "I'm looking forward to the day when I can just piddle and fish all the time."

"Don't be in too big a hurry, my friend," Jack said. "Don't wish your life away. The day will arrive soon enough when you will look longingly back on the days when you were young, strong, healthy, and busy grappling with life's trials, large and small. Michael and I were just talking about that very thing."

"Yes, I suppose you're right. I have to admit that I like my work," he said. "My wife and I are blessed. We have two healthy, happy children, both grown and married. We even have one grandchild, and she is truly grand," he said with great joy in his voice.

"My goodness," Jack said, "you look too young to have grandchildren."

"I'm forty-one," Johnson said. "I got an early start on life."

"Well, I'm twice your age, young man," Jack said. "My life had barely begun when I was forty-one. But the main thing is that, even though I got a late start on it, I did at least get to live it."

"Unlike your young friend out there at the rock," Johnson said.

Jack nodded and said, "Yes, unlike he who... well, no need in going into that again. Well, anyway, I came here to settle up with you. I was going to skip out on you, but young Camardo here wouldn't let me. Said it would be the wrong thing to do. He shamed me into doing the right thing for a change, and here I am."

Michael rolled his eyes in disbelief, and Johnson chuckled as he pulled out his invoice.

"So what do I owe you, Mr. Johnson?" Jack asked.

"Just the balance of what we agreed on the other day. That's all," he said.

"What about having to work on Independence Day? Is there any extra for that?" Jack asked.

"Nah. I figured that in. I knew I'd have to work on the fourth in order to have it done by today," Johnson said.

"Told you, Jack," Michael said triumphantly.

"And what about that elegant little dove you put on there? Any extra for that?" Jack asked.

"No," he said. "That's just a little gift from me to Silas. I'm sure he was a fine boy."

Jack was a few seconds in speaking, and a look of concern came across Johnson's face as he said, "It is all right, isn't it? You don't mind, do you?"

His voice a little strained. Jack said, "No, Esau, we don't mind. Silas and I both think it's just fine, mighty nice of you. And we both thank you."

Jack wrote out a check for the balance of the bill and handed it to Johnson, who put it in his shirt pocket without looking at it.

They shook hands again, and Jack said, "I want to thank you again, my friend, for what you did for Silas and me. I'll always be grateful to you."

As they were shaking hands, Jack deftly slipped a bill, the denomination of which Michael could not make out, into Johnson's shirt pocket.

"That's not necessary, Mr. Moses," he said. "I didn't earn that."

"I know. It's a gift. True gifts are never earned. The gift you gave Silas will last as long as the earth itself. I'm afraid the gift I gave you isn't nearly as enduring. But you can at least take the good wife out to dinner with it. This life is short, son. Spend it," Jack said as they walked toward the truck.

Then he added, "You can't understand just how short it really is until you're approaching the end of it and realize that it has simply flown by. But you'll understand someday. Both of you will."

"Well, Michael," Johnson said, "I guess the missus and I will see you at the Battle House tonight."

"Looking forward to it, Mr. Johnson," Michael said.

Jack was quiet again as they drove toward town.

Finally, Michael heard him say, almost to himself, "So many nice people. The Robinsons. Esau Johnson. Precious people."

The Last Lunch

They were soon back at the hotel. It was almost noon, so Jack went into the restaurant and took a seat at the little table he and Levi had been using. The restaurant had almost become like another home to him, its staff almost like family. It seemed strange to be alone there at that table, without his old friend. He was feeling a little down.

There was always something that needed to be done in the restaurant, so Michael went directly to the kitchen and went to work. Jack soon caught sight of Henry doing his job. The lunch crowd was pouring in now, and Henry had no time to do anything but wave. Jack smiled and waved back. Just that little interaction with Henry made him feel somewhat better.

It was not long until Michael brought him his food. His appetite was good, and he enjoyed his meal in spite of not having anyone to talk to. It was then that he realized just how much companionship Levi had provided. He missed their quiet conversations. They had grown very close in just a few days. Looking back on the morning, he regretted not having spent more time with Levi, telling him good-bye. But his heart had been fixed on Rose, and rightly so.

From out of the kitchen, Big Mama appeared while Jack was eating.

She said, "Jack, I hate to interrupt your meal, but things are about to get real busy, so I decided to come on out here to talk to you for just a minute and bring your birthday cake to you."

"Thank you so much, Big Mama," Jack said as he stood and accepted the box she carefully presented to him. "Sit down," he added. "What's on your mind?"

"Well," she said as they sat, "I just want to thank you for what you did for Henry, and I ain't talking about the clothes. That boy is changed. He holds his head a little higher now. He's more driven, in a good way. He's making big plans for his life. He's still the same sweet, precious little boy he's always been, but now he's looking the world in the eye, face-to-face. He's convinced he's the equal of any man now."

"And he is," Jack said. "Equal to any, better than most. He's special. It didn't take me long to figure that out."

"Well," she said, as they stood, "I just wanted to thank you."

"And I want to thank you," Jack said. "I want to thank you, Precious Dewberry, for your friendship. I'll never forget you. You're in a select group. You are one of a few people in this world whose respect I truly covet."

"You'll always have it, Wiley Jackson Moses," she said as she kissed him gently on the cheek.

She quickly turned and walked toward the kitchen door, hiding her tears.

"Good-bye, Big Mama," he said as she walked away. "Good-bye."

When he had finished his meal, he found Nick to settle up with him for five days' worth of food, lemonade, and tea for himself and his friends.

As Jack was writing the check, Nick, who was a proud, self-reliant man said, "Mr. Moses, I want to thank you for what you are doing for my Michael. Without your help, I don't think he would ever be able to go to medical school. You're what Big Mama calls a blessing to us."

"Mr. Camardo," Jack said, "the scholarship is Michael's, but the blessing is mine. That young man has been a blessing to me ever since I stepped off the train. Someone has reared him well."

Smiling, Nick said, "I think he would have been a good boy regardless of who reared him. But no one forced you to give him that scholarship. You changed his life with that gift. We will always remember you with great affection."

Jack had not expected this from Nick Camardo. It was not like him to openly express his feelings to anyone, especially feelings of gratitude.

"Well," Jack said, "about that gift. It isn't really from me, you know. It's a gift from God. Michael knows that. He had been praying for it. I had the easy part. I just passed the Lord's blessing through me on to him. The burden now rests with Michael to do well in school and to be a good doctor. But I have no doubt whatsoever that he will do well. He will not fail us, my friend. And this business about remembering folks with great affection, let me assure you that I was more than just a little apprehensive about coming north. But Michael and Henry and Big Mama and you have each gone out of your way to make an old Rebel feel at home. I, too, shall remember each of you with great fondness for the rest of my life. Thank you, sir, for your kind hospitality and your friendship."

Nick said, "I owe you more than mere hospitality, Mr. Moses. I wish I could do something for you."

"Well," Jack said after a second or two of thought, "there is one thing you could do."

"Just name it, my friend."

"Be a friend to Little Henry. That's all I ask. If you will do that, I will be in your debt," Jack said.

"Henry's a fine boy. He and I are already friends," Nick said.

"Yes, I know you are. Stick with him. Don't abandon him."

"You can rely on me, Mr. Moses. I will always be Henry's friend."

"Thank you, sir," Jack said as they shook hands. "I'm going upstairs to take a little nap before I leave. For some reason, I'm just kind of tired. If you would tell Michael I'll see him in a couple of hours, I would appreciate it. Oh, and one more thing. I'm about to say something to you which you would probably rather not hear, but here it is anyway," Jack added as he looked into the steady gaze of his sturdy friend. "You're a good man, Nick Camardo. A bit grim at times," he said with a smile, "but a good man nonetheless. Good-bye my friend. May God bless you always."

"Thank you, Mr. Moses," Nick said. "I'll give Michael your message, and I hope you have a pleasant journey home." As he watched the old Rebel slowly ascend the stairs, he quietly added, "Good-bye."

Jack closed the door behind him and removed his shoes and jacket and lay down for a much-needed nap. Mostly, he felt good about things, about Nick and Michael and Big Mama, about Levi and Rose. But he was concerned for Henry. He wanted very much to talk to him just one more time. But he was unusually tired, and he quickly drifted off.

Mere Words

He slept hard but not very restfully. When he awoke, he did not feel as refreshed as usual. He had already packed his things before breakfast, so all he had to do was put on his shoes and coat and he would be ready to go.

Home, he thought. *It'll be so nice to get home amongst everyone again.*

He missed his family and his friends so much. He was looking forward to telling his friends in the little colored church near his house about how he and Rose had found each other. He even missed Ethel, his loquacious calico who thought she owned the place. They had a routine of him reading the paper every evening after supper with her in his lap. He could not help but wonder who she was bossing around in his absence and whose lap she was using.

He splashed some water in his face, and after he had dried it with a towel, he looked at the old man in the mirror and said, "Wiley Jack, you are ancient. Your life, boy, where do you reckon it got off to?"

He went downstairs to find Michael, fetch a bellboy, check out, and settle up with the hotel. Michael and the bellboy had to carry his luggage to the depot for him. Even though he and Michael had easily carried it to the hotel five days earlier, Jack was no longer able to lug it the two hundred feet or so to the platform. He felt bad about putting the bellboy to so much trouble, so he tipped him handsomely.

They found a bench in the afternoon shade and sat there in the midst of Jack's luggage while they waited for the train.

After they had been there a few minutes and he had caught his breath, Jack patted Michael on the knee in a grandfatherly way and said, "Michael, how are you feeling today, son? Do you have hope? Are you looking forward to your life?"

"Yes, thanks to you, Jack. I do, and I am."

"Hope. It's a wonderful thing, isn't it?"

Michael nodded.

"I have hope too, Michael," Jack said. "Even though I'm at the jumping off place, I have hope, eternal hope, because I have Jesus. For just the second time in my life, I can't see past today. Like I told Rose, I can smile at yesterday, but I yearn for the day when I can see paradise stretching out endlessly before me. But I cannot see my future here anymore. The Lord has answered all my prayers, kept all His promises. He owes me nothing, not that He ever did. But the only thing I can see now is getting on that train and going home. It's a mighty peaceful feeling. And somehow the thought of all this fills me with hope. It's a good thing, hope. We need it almost like we need air. It's hard to live without it."

"Jack," Michael said, "I want to thank you again."

"Let's not talk about that, son," Jack interrupted. "You can thank me by being a good doctor, not just a skillful one but a good one in the same way you're a good man. As a good doctor, you'll have to be a good businessman too, you know. Just remember that God's love and a reasonable profit make the world go 'round. If you remember that, you'll have so much money in a few years that you'll be looking for godly ways to use it and give it away. After you've lived a long life and when you know your time is near, you want to be able to look back and remember yourself as a good man, a noble man, God's man. You want to look back and see a man who helped young folks of any race, any religion get started in life. You want to look back and see a man who quietly helped poor old folks of any race, any religion get through their final days with dignity, in peace.

"And, Michael, I want very much for you to be a loyal friend to Henry. Don't forget him when you're somebody big and he's still just Little Henry. He needs you. Some people might tend to dismiss his importance in this world, but let me tell you, son, there's a lot to Henry Dewberry that most folks can't see. He's big in the eyes of the Lord. But he needs for you to be his friend. He needs hope too, just like us. A black child needs and deserves hope just as much as a white one. Be his friend, son. For as long as you live, be his friend."

"I will, Jack. I'll be Henry's loyal friend. I promise."

Jack smiled and relaxed a little as he patted Michael's knee in gratitude.

Then he said, "You know, Michael. I've been hoping to speak to Henry all day, but here it is almost five o'clock, and the opportunity just hasn't presented itself. I saw him at breakfast and lunch, but he was so busy we could only wave at each other. I really would like to talk to him, but I reckon it's just not going to happen. So I wonder if you could give him a little message for me?"

"Sure."

"I want you to tell him that no matter what happens, he and I will always be friends. Tell him to keep his school marks up, and someday there may be a scholarship available for him too."

"Are you going to give him one?"

"Well, that's a few years off, but if he qualifies, I sure hope to," Jack said as he pulled a small envelope out of his inside coat pocket. Written on it, Michael could see the words, "To my children, in the event of my death."

Looking at the envelope, Jack said, "I hope this letter to my children will assure Henry's scholarship."

Then he returned it to his pocket.

"Are your children goodhearted people like you?" Michael asked.

"Oh no. They're much better than me," Jack said earnestly. "They are truly fine people. They take after their mother."

Michael almost laughed, but he quickly realized that Jack was not joking.

"No, son," Jack said, "they're not like me. I'm just a vile sinner saved by the sweet grace of Jesus. My children, while they aren't perfect, are nonetheless noble, godly people, as was their mother. She outdid me in every way but one."

"And what way was that?"

Smiling, Jack said, "I married a whole lot better than she did."

Michael smiled and said, "Well, if you married better than she did, you must have married well indeed."

"That I did, son. That I did. I wish you could have known her. What a lady. What a lady," Jack said wistfully.

After a few seconds of letting Jack savor her memory, Michael said, "Jack, I have to say this. You're the finest man I've ever—"

"You don't have to say that, son," Jack interrupted.

"Yes, I do. You can't leave without letting me say this."

After a few seconds of silence, Michael quietly began again. "Jack, you're the finest man I've ever known. No matter how long I live, I will never forget you. You're a true gentleman. You're generous, almost to a fault. And yet, you're humble about it, always giving God the credit. My respect for and admiration of you will never end. I hope to be like you someday. I have come to think of you as my father." He paused briefly and quietly said, "I love you."

They stared at the tracks for a while, unable to speak.

Finally, Jack said, "Isn't it amazing, son, that we met right here just last Tuesday. It's been a wonderful five days, thanks to you."

Michael did not speak, but as they sat there together, he slipped his hand around Jack's weathered hand and held it ever so gently. Sometimes, mere words just are not enough.

After a while, Jack said, "There is one more thing I want you to tell Henry for me."

"What's that?"

"Tell him to always remember that it's the man that makes the name. He'll know what you're talking about."

"It's the man that makes the name," Michael repeated.

"That's right," Jack said. "Tell him that for me."

"I will."

As they sat there, it did not occur to them that the sight of two men holding hands might be just a little unusual in Gettysburg, Pennsylvania. But there they sat on that bench for the world to see. No one seemed to notice.

"Oh. I almost forgot about your fee," Jack said. "I talked to Mr. Drummonds at the bank when I went down there to close this account," he said as he produced his checkbook. "But I decided to leave it open and just let you have whatever is left in it for your fee after all the checks clear. I wrote one to your uncle and one to the hotel. And there's Mr. Johnson's check for the inscription. But even after those checks clear, there will still be a fair amount in there, more than enough for your fee, I think. Mr. Drummonds said you'll just need to sign some papers, and it's yours. I've already signed them."

Jack handed the checkbook to the astounded boy.

"It's not a fortune. Just a few hundred dollars. You'll need some money for train fare, clothes, books, and lots of other things. This will help you get started."

"Thank you," Michael said weakly.

"Be a good doctor, son," Jack said as he smiled and patted Michael on his knee again. "Be a good doctor."

"Yes, sir."

"You know, you'll soon go off to school and spend several years preparing for your career as a doctor, preparing for your life. You'll find a sweet wife, have a litter of little ones, and then you'll start trying to help them prepare for their lives. You'll find yourself immersed up to your eyeballs in life. You'll be so deep into it, so busy with it that you won't even notice when it starts receding around you. Then you'll wake up one day and find that your children are all grown and gone and having children of their own. You'll discover that you've quietly become an irrelevant old poot—loved and respected, but irrelevant nevertheless. And you'll learn to live with the fact that all those preparations you made a long time ago are now moot and that your life is essentially over. Prepared or not, we all end up in the same place. We are put in a cold, dark hole; we return to God's good earth; and this life is finished. And the next one begins. It's a cycle that will last as long as humanity. The only preparation that matters in the long run, the eternal run, is the preparation of your soul. When you have children, be sure you help them prepare their souls for eternity while you're still relevant, while they still listen to you. Life is uncertain. But death, my young friend, is a sure thing."

"Yes, sir."

"And about me being a gentleman," Jack said with a smile. "Let me say this. My mother-in-law was a wise lady, and she once told me that a gentleman is one who owns a jew's-harp but declines to play it in polite company. I've never even touched a jew's-harp, so there. And this business about me being humble—my lack of humility has always been one of my greatest shortcomings. I have tried many times to be meek and humble, but it has just never worked for me. The Lord has to forgive me daily for my boastful ways. But I can tell you this. If I could somehow manage to change my ways and be humble, I sure would be proud."

"And there's one more thing, Michael," Jack said. "This is important."

"Yes, sir. I'm listening."

"Son, when you get to school, choose your friends carefully. Surround yourself with people who take their faith and their profession seriously. And be sure you take them seriously yourself. Cultivate your friendship with Levi. He is a rare man, a fine man. That old Israelite knows his business. There is much you can learn from him that you'll never hear in a classroom. Learn everything you can from him."

"I will."

"And visit Rose regularly. She's one-of-a-kind."

"I will. I promise."

The Way Home

Michael carefully put the checkbook in his pocket. They were gazing toward the tracks in silence when someone appeared before them. A few seconds passed before they realized the man was staring at them. They looked up to see the Klansman from Indiana. Michael immediately stood and placed himself between the man and Jack.

"What do you want, mister?" Michael said in a not-so-friendly tone.

"I just want to talk to your friend there," He said, pointing to Jack. "I don't want any trouble. I just want to talk."

Jack could tell he was not a threat to anyone now.

"Let him pass, son," he said. "It'll be okay. Why don't you leave us alone for a few minutes?"

Michael slowly stepped aside and said, "I'll be right over there, Jack. I'll be watching."

"That's fine, son, but I won't need you. We're just going to talk."

Michael slowly walked away but continued to watch.

Jack said, "Have a seat, sir," as he patted the place on the bench where Michael had been.

"Thank you," the man said, sitting.

"You said you wanted to talk. Well, I'm listening," Jack said.

"Yes, well, it's about our little incident a couple of days ago."

"Yes?"

"I looked up your little friend today, the one everyone calls Little Henry. I found him working in the restaurant. I asked him if I could speak to him and about that time, the man who runs the place—"

"Nick Camardo."

"I think so," the Indiana man said. "Anyway, he started to throw me out, literally. But Little Henry stopped him and asked him to let me stay. Mr. Carmardo left us alone, and I told Henry how sorry I was about the way I acted the other day. I told him I was sorry about tripping him and especially about how I had spoken to him and of him. I told him I am just a sorry old man and that I would try to do better in the future. You know what he said?"

"I think so."

"He said, 'I forgive you.'"

"That's what I would expect from a man of Little Henry's caliber," Jack said. "He's a better man than either of us."

"He's certainly a better man than I am," the Indiana man quietly said with shame in his voice. "I would like to think that someday, before I die, I could be as big a man as Little Henry, that I could be strong enough to forgive the way he forgave me. Somehow, I just can't see myself ever rising to such heights."

Jack looked at the man and saw a difference in him.

He said, "What brought you to this point, my friend? Why did you feel the need to talk to Henry?"

"Well," he said, "it started the day all that stuff happened. After I tripped Henry, and after you almost knocked my ass upside the head…"

They both laughed a little, and Jack said, "I am truly sorry about that."

"Don't apologize. I deserve it," he said.

"We all deserve it, my friend. That's why Jesus came, so we could avoid what we deserve," Jack said.

The man studied him briefly and then quietly continued.

"Well, after I saw you and Henry talking, I began to realize that I have been in the wrong all my miserable life. Then you came back to apologize to me, and I was hurting so bad I just couldn't look you in the eye. I had to walk away. I couldn't stand it anymore. It has been killing me the last couple of days. My conscience has been like a barking dog. I didn't even know I had one. I just had to talk to Henry, to apologize to him. I can't explain the pain."

"You don't have explain it, friend. I've been there myself. I know about that pain firsthand. The Lord got hold of me and never let go. Pray He never lets you go either."

"I'm changed, sir. I don't think I'll ever be the same again. I hope I never go back to the way I was. I have wasted my life in hate. What an old fool I am," the man said, his voice strained with frustration.

"What a fool you were," Jack said. "The fear of God is the beginning of wisdom. The fool despises wisdom. You're not a fool anymore. Do you know what you need to do now?"

"Yes, sir. I need to clean my life up, to change my ways. And when I'm worthy, when I'm good enough, I'll ask Jesus to forgive me, to save me."

"Nope," Jack said. "You have it backward, son. If you wait till you're worthy, till you're good enough, you'll never get saved. You can never be good enough for salvation. You can never become worthy of it by yourself. It isn't something any of us can earn. It's a gift, my friend, a wonderful gift from a loving God. And like all true gifts, it is never earned and never forced on anyone. All you have to do is ask for it. He doesn't want you to wait. He wants you to come to Him right now, right this minute, just as you are, sins and all. Confess your sins to Him. He already knows about them anyway. And I can assure you, He's heard worse. Beg Him to forgive you. He will rush into your poor, old, aching heart, and He will clean you up and give you peace. You can't possibly do it alone. The good works and the worthiness come after you are saved, not before. He will make you worthy."

The man was quiet for a few seconds while he studied Jack and pondered his words. Then he said, "You mean I can be saved right now? I don't have to undo all the evil I've done? I just confess and ask Him for forgiveness, for salvation, and it's mine?"

"That's right, son. It's that simple. He never says no. How something that big can be that easy amazes me. Jesus did the hard part. He died an awful death so it would be easy for us. Why the whole world doesn't rush to His humble, nail-scarred feet will always be a mystery to me. Little Henry's forgiveness is a wonderful thing, but it won't get you into heaven. Only the forgiveness of the One who was punished for your sins can do that. And He's waiting to hear from you this very minute, ever eager to forgive. Surrender to Him, and He will give you eternal victory. Why people refuse His forgiveness will always baffle me. But there it is for the asking. People are always whining about God sending good folks to hell. But God doesn't want anyone to go to hell; that's why He sent His Son. But there are going to be a lot of good people there, people who are good by the measure of men. But if someone ends up in hell, it isn't because God sent them there, but because they, themselves, chose to go there. He gives us a choice. We can choose to accept the free sacrificial forgiveness of His only Son, or we can choose to reject that forgiveness. All the souls in hell are there because of their own choices, not because the Father wants them there. Some folks actually think they have a big set of scales up there by the pearly gates and they weigh your good deeds against your sins and if the good outweighs the bad, they let you in, unforgiven sins and all. Hogwash! There is no sin in heaven. Those who are still carrying it around with them are not admitted. The only way poor sinners like us can get in is to have our sins forgiven and washed away. And only Jesus Christ, the sinless Son of God, can do that."

"You know," the man said, "I have always hated God. I even denied His existence. It's a crime, the grief I've inflicted on my poor, sweet wife all these years. She is such a godly lady. And now, here I am having to admit that she was always in the right. And what is so strange is that I am so joyfully anticipating conceding defeat to her. But what do I say to God? How do I apologize to Him? How do I surrender?"

After studying the man briefly, Jack said, "Strange, isn't it, my friend. We spend our life loudly declaring our hatred for the One who gave us that life, while at the same time denying His very existence. We never think what fools we are to waste so much effort, indeed, our lives, hating something that does not exist. And then it is somehow revealed to us that not only does He exist, but that in spite of our hate for Him, He loves us. How does such a person apologize to the Creator of the universe? We do it the same way everyone else does. We get on our knees, and, in the name of Jesus, we beg. And forgiveness, love, and freedom are forthcoming. If we learn just that one thing in life, that will suffice for eternity. Life has been just one long lesson from the Master for me."

"What do I need to do? You think you could help me?"

"Let me take off my jacket, and we'll use it to cushion our

bony old knees," Jack said. "We can kneel right here at this bench, and I'll help you pray the sinner's prayer."

Michael was standing nearby, and he could hear most of the conversation. He saw Jack remove his coat and put it on the platform. The two men removed their hats and knelt with their knees on the jacket and their elbows on the bench. They ignored the sparse crowd milling around, and only a few people glanced toward them. Michael stood protectively nearby. He saw Jack put an arm around the man as they prayed.

Michael could not hear the words as well now—they were quieter. But he heard, "Forgive me, Jesus. Help me change. Give me strength. Give me peace." There were a few more words that he could not make out, and then he heard, "Amen."

The two arose, both smiling and in tears. They embraced gently.

Then the Indiana man said, "Thank you, mister. Say, what is your name anyway?"

"Not that it matters, but it's Moses."

"Moses," he said quietly. "Well, Moses, you certainly led me out of my wilderness. Henry told me I could find you here. I guess the Lord put you here just for me. I'll never forget you."

"Forget me, my friend. I'm just a sinner saved by Jesus, like you. Forget me and remember Jesus. Always remember Him. Stay close to Him. Jesus will make a man of you, a godly man. Read your Bible daily, and go to church with that good wife. You're blessed to still have her."

"I will. I'll go to church with her. She will be so pleasantly surprised. I'm looking forward to telling her what happened. I'm going to resign from the Klan. I suppose I'll have to find a whole new set of friends," he said.

"I had to do the same thing," Jack said. "Just pray about everything, and don't worry about anything. Stay close to the Lord. Go to church, and He will provide the friends."

"I will, Mr. Moses. I'm looking forward to going home. I'm looking forward to life like I never have before. I feel so different now. I'm so ashamed of what I was. But in spite of that, I can't explain it. I'm excited, but I feel so … so calm. All that turmoil is gone. I'm not angry anymore. It would be hard for anyone to pick a fight with me now. My wife needs to know about this. I don't want to wait till I get home to tell her. I think I'll send her a wire. The telegraph office is just over there. I know I'll never see you again, Mr. Moses, so I want to tell you again how much I appreciate you explaining everything to me and helping me. I don't know what I would have done if you hadn't—"

"Oh, we'll see each other again someday, on the other side," Jack said. "But you have work to do now. You have a life to live. And now Jesus expects you to help some other poor, lost soul find the way home like you did. That's your job now."

"Yes, I guess it is," he said. "That's a pretty good job to have. Maybe I can help some of my friends in the Klan. That would be something, wouldn't it?"

"Yes, that would be something."

"My wife will help me. She's experienced at that sort of thing. She'll teach me, and she and I are going to pray for you."

"Well, I appreciate your prayers. I learned a long time ago to never refuse anyone's prayers. And I want y'all to pray for Henry too."

"Yes, we'll pray for Henry. I owe that little fellow a lot," the man said.

They were silent for a little while, and Jack said, "Well, I reckon you need to send that wire now."

"Mr. Moses, I wish there was something I could do to express my gratitude."

"Just live a happy life close to Jesus. That's all you need to do for me."

"You're right," the man said. "I will. Good-bye, Mr. Moses, and thank you."

"Good-bye, my friend," Jack said as they shook hands.

Jack and Michael watched as the humbled, yet happy man walked toward the telegraph office.

"What happened?" Michael asked.

"He got saved. That's what happened."

"I wonder who showed him the light."

"Jesus, of course," Jack said, "with a little help from Henry. What rejoicing there must be in heaven right now."

A Prayer for Little Henry

Michael rejoined Jack on the bench. The train was running a little late, but they soon heard the whistle in the distance, and they both stood. Michael walked toward the tracks to watch the train pull into the station.

Jack turned toward the depot building. It was a little after five o'clock, and he knew that Nick and Henry would soon deliver supper to the depot crew. He still held a glimmer of hope of talking to his young friend.

The platform was moderately crowded, but through the milling people, Jack soon saw Nick appear from around the corner of the building, pushing a food cart. And then Henry appeared, struggling to keep up as he pushed another cart, heavy with food.

The train was entering the depot, and the activity on the platform became more frenetic. Jack shouted at Henry, but his old voice was too weak to be heard above the noise of the train. Henry followed Nick into the building without noticing him.

Over his shoulder, Jack saw the train coasting to a stop, and he caught sight of Michael coming his way. He said a silent prayer.

"Dear Lord, please don't let me go home without bidding Henry farewell."

A few more seconds passed, and Jack saw Nick come out of the building, closely followed by Henry pushing his empty cart.

Above all the noise, Henry thought he heard his name called. He stopped and turned toward the tracks and saw his old friend, a soldier of the South, slowly remove his hat with his left hand and raise his right hand to his brow in the most heartfelt salute he had ever rendered.

Henry and Jack had only known each other for a few days, but the love and respect between them was deep and everlasting. Even though Jack was almost seventy years Henry's senior, their kinship was that of equal men, brothers in arms.

Jack had liked Henry from the moment they had met because of his ready smile and sunny disposition. But as he had gotten to know him better, he realized that he loved the child. He loved him because he met anger with a smile, and he met hate with love and forgiveness. He refused to let white bigots make him into a black one. Henry Dewberry was above that. In Jack's estimation, Little Henry was a big man.

His arms ached to hug the boy. His heart hurt to tell him how proud he was of him. But Henry was a working man now, and duty called in the person of Nick Camardo. They knew they were seeing each other for the last time. Each would miss the other for the rest of his life. But while Jack's time was nigh, Henry would long and courageously sojourn on Jordan's stormy banks in the Lord's noble service.

Henry slowly came to attention and returned Jack's salute. Tears came to his eyes. He tried mightily, but he could hold them back no more. He heard Nick calling him. He lowered his hand and stared for a few final seconds into the eyes of the man who was the closest thing to a father he would ever know. He heard Nick call again. Turning from Jack, he wiped his tears on his sleeve and returned to his work.

The old soldier stood there watching as his friend disappeared around the side of the building. For some time after Henry had passed from view, Jack held his salute to his friend, one of the finest men he had ever known. Such was his regard for Little Henry.

Grief finally overtook him, and he lowered the once-powerful arm and whispered a prayer.

"Keep him close, Lord. Please, keep him close."

A Life to Live

"Your train is waiting for you, Jack," Michael said. "It's time for you to go."

Jack continued to look toward the building after Henry.

"Jack, did you hear me? It's time for you to go home."

Jack slowly turned in acknowledgement and said, "I know, son. I've known for some time."

"Here, Jack," Michael said as he somehow managed to pick up all the luggage except one small piece. "If you'll get that one, I've got the rest of it. We need to get your stuff onto the train."

"Sure, son. I can get this one."

Jack picked up his one small tote and followed Michael onto the train. He placed it in his seat to save his place. Michael delivered the rest of the luggage to his berth on the Pullman car. He returned to the passenger car expecting to find Jack in his seat and ready to go. Instead, he found the seat occupied only by Jack's little bag. He immediately caught sight of him through the window, standing on the platform by the train. He hurried off the car to his side.

"Jack, you need to get on the train."

"Not yet, son. Not yet," Jack said. "The man will yell when it's time. I don't want to get on till I have to. I sort of like it here. I like being with you."

"But, Jack, it's time for us to say good-bye."

"No. No more good-byes for me. I've had enough of them to last me forever."

Jack resolutely turned toward the train, grasped the handrail, and put one foot on the first step. There he hesitated. Michael could not believe he would leave without saying good-bye, but it appeared to be so. But with or without a good-bye, Michael Camardo would forever cherish his memories of the old man and their friendship.

After a few seconds, Jack released his grip on the handrail and took his foot off the step. He slowly turned toward the young man. The tears in his eyes told Michael all he needed to know. He instantly went to him and tenderly enfolded him in his young, powerful arms. Jack felt so frail to him. He held him ever so gently. Jack clung to him like a child to his daddy.

Finally, they broke their embrace, and Michael stood back at arm's length and straightened Jack's lapel like a proud father sending his son on a long journey. The tears flowed as God's sweet love passed between them. No words were spoken. None were necessary. None would suffice.

The man shouted "All aboard!" and a faint smile came to Jack's face. He turned to the train once again, and Michael helped him onto the steps and up to the platform of the passenger car.

There he stood, grasping the rail with both hands, as the train began to move. His eyes were fixed on Michael's and Michael's on his as the train pulled them apart. But just as nothing ever really separates father and son, nothing could ever come between Jack and Michael—not distance, not time, not death. Each would have the other in his heart always. But they knew they would never see each other again in this world, because Jack was going home.

In his kindness, God gave him one final rush of exuberant strength. A broad smile crossed Jack's face, and he removed his hat and powerfully waved it back and forth, high above his head, and strongly shouted to his friend.

"So long, Michael! I'll see you later, you young whippersnapper!"

Michael instantly leaped, whooping and waving his cap in joyous reply. The last thing they saw of each other was a smile. Michael watched the train gradually gain speed and disappear into the distance. He gazed down the empty tracks long after his friend was out of sight.

"Jack's gone… home," he said to himself. A trace of a smile still on his face, he thought, *Someday I'll go home too. I will see him again. But right now I have a life to live, thanks to a loving God and a funny old man.*

For Michael, the birds were singing their sweetest songs. The evening sun bathed his face in gold. Though he already missed Jack dearly, his heart was filled with hope. Having always been a good boy, he was now a good man. His goodness would stay with him always. For the rest of his long life, he would smile when looking back on these last few summer days of his youth and the old man with whom he had shared them. He was a better man now, and stronger, full of hope and promise. Though unchanged in many ways, he was not quite the same. He would never be the same again.

Rest Beyond the River

Jack stood on the back of the train and watched Michael and the depot become smaller and smaller in the distance.

I'm going to miss him, he thought. *I'm going to miss them all.*

After the depot had passed from view, he made his way to his seat and carefully placed his tote on the rack above him, as it contained his birthday cake. Smiling as he thought of Big Mama, he removed his hat and sat next to the window. The train was not very crowded, so he placed his hat in the seat next to him. It was doubtful anyone would need that seat. There were several empty ones.

He settled in and watched the village pass by his window. He was exhausted and spent, as was his life. But all he had to do now was watch the world pass by and rest all the way home. Still smiling, he thought back over his life and how blessed he was to have found Rose both times. He remembered how her arms had felt around his neck just that morning and so long ago and how her love had changed him.

The train headed west but would soon turn south toward Alabama and home. He watched the final remnants of Gettysburg pass. He went through the railroad cut where so many of his brave Mississippi brothers had died. The train crossed Willoughby Run, and he saw the Chambersburg Pike running parallel to the tracks. On the road and in the fields, he could almost make out the forms of valiant American soldiers marching eastward toward the village. He saw a grim army that had resolutely fought and died for the independence of a valorous nation, a nation that had died with its army and for a noble, yet tragically flawed cause.

As the train reached the western slope of Herr Ridge, he looked down the little road for the spot where he was saved and baptized. But he looked in vain, for the distance was great and the forest dense. Yet he could see one thing clearly now, something he had been unable to see when he had stood on that creek bank fifty years before. Behind him, he could see his life. And he was pleased. But his mind began to falter.

He slid down a little and rested his head on the back of his seat. Death would soon claim him, but he had lived his life close to Jesus, and it could not be lost. What was lost had been found. What once was darkness is now light. He had been forgiven by all, even himself. He was at peace.

Once again, he faced the high ground and smiled at death, for he was without doubt or fear. As his mind grew weaker, he breathed his final prayer.

"Jesus, thank you for my life. Thank you for my soul. And for hope. Thank you for hope and for everything. Thank you. And please, Lord, let little Rose be a nurse." His mind struggling, he weakly added, "A good nurse."

He was overtaken by the peace that passes all understanding, and a welcomed friend lovingly led him across that river to paradise on the distant shore.

Death is a door through which we all must pass. But for the redeemed, endless life more abundant lies beyond as death gives way to victory. And so passed Wiley Jackson Moses, the son of no man, a brother to all, a dearly redeemed child of God.

The journey which had begun so long ago was finished, and he was home, home at last. Home forever. Home.

Thus, it began. And thus, it goes ever on.

BIBLIOGRAPHY

Songs Used

"On Jordan's Stormy Banks" composed by Samuel Stennett and arranged by Rigdon McIntosh

"Amazing Grace" composed by John Newton, arranger unknown

"Jesus Keep Me Near The Cross" composed by Fanny J. Crosby, arranged by William H. Doane

"Farther Along" composer and arranger unknown

"Angel Band" composer unknown, arranged by Ralph Stanley

"There's a Nest for Robin Redbreast" composer and arranger unknown